The Club

RICHARD EYRE

PENGUIN BOOKS

PENGUIN BOOKS

Published by the Penguin Group
Penguin Books Ltd, 80 Strand, London WC2R ORL, England
Penguin Group (USA) Inc., 375 Hudson Street, New York, New York 10014, USA
Penguin Group (Canada), 10 Alcorn Avenue, Toronto, Ontario, Canada M4V 3B2
(a division of Pearson Penguin Canada Inc.)
Penguin Ireland, 25 St Stephen's Green, Dublin 2, Ireland
(a division of Penguin Books Ltd)
Penguin Group (Australia), 250 Camberwell Road,
Camberwell, Victoria 3124, Australia (a division of Pearson Australia Group Pty Ltd)
Penguin Books India Pvt Ltd, 11 Community Centre,
Panchsheel Park, New Delhi – 110 017, India
Penguin Group (NZ), cnr Airborne and Rosedale Roads, Albany,
Auckland 1310, New Zealand (a division of Pearson New Zealand Ltd)
Penguin Books (South Africa) (Pty) Ltd, 24 Sturdee Avenue,
Rosebank 2196, South Africa

Penguin Books Ltd, Registered Offices: 80 Strand, London WC2R ORL, England

www.penguin.com

Published in Penguin Books 2005

I

Copyright © Richard Eyre, 2005
All rights reserved

The moral right of the author has been asserted

Printed in England by Clays Ltd, St Ives plc

PENGUIN BOOKS

The Club

Richard Eyre has worked in the media business for thirty years. His various roles have included Chief Executive of Capital Radio plc, Chief Executive of the ITV Network, and Chairman and CEO of Pearson Television. However, on a plane one day, he had an epiphany and decided to turn his back on his corporate career to buy a cottage in Cornwall, where he renovated the garden shed and set about writing this novel.

He now holds a number of non-executive and advisory roles in a range of organizations, from the Eden Project and the Guardian Media Group to 19 Management. He is Chairman of RDF, a leading television production company, and of the Interactive Advertising Bureau.

Richard Eyre was educated at Oxford University and Harvard Business School and is a Fellow of the Royal Society of Arts.

He is married, with a son and daughter.

For my Father, who taught me to go for it

Acknowledgements

I decided to write this book on the BA flight into Luxembourg one Monday morning, when I was a television executive. Getting from there to here has involved the goodwill and encouragement of a great many people. My sincere thanks to them all.

Kate Parkin, whom I met at a Harvard Business School course ironically entitled 'Managing Change', helped me to upgrade this idea from daydream to opportunity. She also introduced me to Gillon Aitken, my splendid agent. Somehow Gillon saw something worthwhile in a very patchy first draft and, together with Kate Shaw, mentored my efforts to wrestle the book into publishable shape.

Originally I saw the book as a three-month sabbatical. Then I met Spencer Johnson, a best-selling author, who urged me to follow my heart, install myself in a place that 'nurtures my soul' and forget the three-month deadline. His advice was as invigorating as his margaritas.

My friends Nick Humby and Dr Chris Wilcock helped me in their specialist subjects, accounting and medicine, neither of which have ever been particularly strong suits of mine. Martin Lambie-Nairn designed the cover in a flash of inspiration. And twelve good friends waded through an early draft to give me invaluable counsel and inspiration. They are Steve and Jane Cox, Anthony Fry, David and Alison Mansfield, Simon and Nicky Marquis, Ollie Rice, Paul Smith, Jane Todd, and Tom and Hedy Whitney.

My editor at Penguin is Clare Ledingham. She has been fantastic – challenging and encouraging in equal measure. Surely no one has struck out so much verbiage with so much grace, or made a greater contribution to this book.

Finally, my wonderful wife, Sheelagh. When I first went home with the idea of walking out of my job in favour of a laptop in the garden shed, her encouragement was immediate, enthusiastic and unequivocal. With such support, this career change has required far less bravery than has been credited to me by friends and colleagues. She has tackled this latest scheme like all the others in our twenty-eight years together: jointly, passionately and with the conviction that I'm better than I really am.

Better one handful with tranquillity than two handfuls
with toil and chasing after the wind.

Ecclesiastes 4:6

The Cast

NON-EXECUTIVE DIRECTORS ON THE ACROBAT BOARD

Roger Collier	Founding shareholder
Celia Sharma	Managing Director of Equitus, Acrobat shareholder
Piers Carrick	Representative of Activa, Acrobat's largest shareholder
Arnaud de Vigny	Chairman of Activa, Acrobat's largest shareholder

ACROBAT ADVISERS

Dennis Weaver	Acrobat's investment banker
Hamish Perrin	Acrobat's stockbroker
Nik Kruger	Chief Executive, Channel 6
Sir Malcolm Ryan	Chairman, Channel 6
Ken Hathaway	Chairman, Charisma TV
Howell Snoddy	HM Minister for Broadcasting
Lord Markham	Chairman, Ofcom
Carrie McGann	Journalist, *The Times*
Gerry Duffy	Media Editor, BBC Radio 4
Hugh Ratledge	Editor, *Mail on Sunday*
Alastair Powell	Editor, *Daily Telegraph*

In the early hours of 31 March, a dark car nosed its way through London and out towards the south-west. Its progress, at first jostled by the stop-start of suburbia, gathered pace as it escaped the grip of the city. The driver's face, lit by the green glow of the dashboard and interrogated by the sweeping searchlights of oncoming traffic, appeared calm.

But the eyes betrayed a disquiet, a restless rehearsal of all that had happened over the last month; the events devised to even the score. But revenge is a hired hand – it will work for anyone but it is nobody's soulmate. It had provided no solace and had brokered no atonement.

The driver was not a stranger to success. This time, though, the achievement was the destruction of a company.

Monday, 1 March

Georgia Burrows sat at the kitchen table, one hand flat on the newspaper, the other clutching an outsize Starbucks mug to her dressing gown. The radio burbled and the room smelled breakfasty. Her hair was gathered haphazardly into a ponytail, her gentle features pinched by the severity of her reading glasses.

'Now there's a nice change,' said Charlie Burrows, running a hand along her shoulders on his way to the coffee pot. 'Normally have to make do with a fleeting glimpse of pinstriped bum at this time of day.'

She closed her eyes and lolled her head back theatrically. 'Oh, Charlie. Finally, finally, goodbye to all that. No more midnight phone calls from panicking clients, no more 6 a.m. wake-ups, no more partners' meetings . . .' The litany paused for a moment while she switched on a game-show voice. 'And no more partners means . . . ? No more politics.' She shook her head. 'Oh, thank you, God.'

Burrows considered his wife's intelligent face, her straight back, the sculpted sweep of her arm, beautiful where it lay on the table. 'Well, it's all right for some,' he said genially enough, picking up his jacket.

She slid the chair back. 'No, hang on, I've done you some breakfast: bacon sandwich.'

He attempted to sneak a look at his watch and they both saw it. 'Oh, right, brilliant, thanks.' Not that convincing. He replaced the jacket and sat down, at first trying to read her newspaper upside down. 'So then. What's the plan for day one of the rest of your life?'

'A gentle lead-in to all those things I've had on hold for the last twenty-three years,' she said over her shoulder. 'After cooking my husband a nice breakfast for the first time in living memory, I thought maybe we'd get the ball rolling with a soaky bath, a good book, maybe a little shopping, a gentle walk in the park perhaps. It's going to be one of those really gruelling kinds of a day I'm afraid.'

Burrows pulled a pantomime grin behind her back. As she turned he said, 'Well, you've earned it. Twenty-three years of lawyering has got to be enough for anyone.'

She put the plate down in front of him, and he weighed up his breakfast warily. 'And what about twenty-whatever-it-is years of media then, Burrows?' She stroked his hair hesitantly but thought better of it and, pulling her robe around her, returned to her chair. Absently he smoothed his hair back into position. 'Don't leave it too long, Charlie. Let's retire together while we still have our marbles.'

Charlie Burrows had done OK. Chief Executive of a major UK television company when he could still remember his fortieth birthday. And in the seven years since, he'd presided over the building of the largest youth channel in the country. For five years now, Acrobat's mix of programmes and sassy presentation style had made it the number one choice for under-thirty-year-old viewers, and highly profitable for its shareholders.

But one man's margin is another man's magnet. Having wooed those lucrative viewers from the mainstream channels as the upstart voice in British broadcasting, Acrobat's position was now itself under threat from the next round of trespassers: the new New. The ratings had begun to falter, and with them Acrobat's ability to charge the premium rates to advertisers which nourished its share price. It was a problem – not cataclysmic, but a problem nonetheless.

Burrows consoled himself with the creative abilities of Melvyn Davies, his Programme Director, and reassured himself that the predicament was shared with all the established broadcasters; but the ratings decline bothered him. The anxiety stalked him, catching him when he wasn't looking, needling him as he surfaced for each new morning, and playing as the incidental music to his day because, in the end, he had no solution to it. The on-air talent hated it, wanted to know what was going wrong, why couldn't he give them a better platform. The advertisers would use the decline as a lever to negotiate cheaper prices. The shareholders didn't get it, or pretended they didn't; the City analysts would drip drip about the loss of value. Meanwhile, the new guy at Channel 6, the most convincing of his rivals, made sure that certain credulous journalists were well briefed on each of Acrobat's troubles.

And he took it on his shoulders. Kept smiling. The captain, leading his troops through the blizzard by not letting them see he was cold. But it was new territory. The tricks that had worked in the past weren't doing it any more. Behind the inspiring smile was a profound chill.

He had tried to do it the civilized way. He claimed no sainthood, but he'd tried to make Acrobat a great place to work, to be one of the good guys. Wherever possible. He was trusted in the industry, respected for what he'd achieved, but now it bothered him that his reputation was balanced on the unsustainable.

He bit purposefully into his sandwich. A dob of butter dripped on to his shirt. He didn't see it. 'I'm too young for life on the golf links,' he bluffed, through a mouthful of bread. 'Things to do, companies to buy, ratings to win – hell, the BBC isn't begging for mercy yet.' He took a final gulp of coffee, this time making theatre of sweeping his watch into view. 'Oh hell. That was very nice, love, thanks. However, being now the sole breadwinner in this family . . .' He picked up his jacket and moved towards her. She fended him off, dabbing myopically at his shirt with a tissue. 'Excuse me, Mr Captain of Industry, you're about to go and beat the BBC into submission with half a pound of lard down your front.'

For an instant a mask of pure fury crossed his face, but he caught it and dealt with it, swallowing the expletive with a groan. 'Shhh.'

She laughed, trying to warm the moment. 'We'll get you out of there before long, Charlie Burrows.'

But nothing was further from Burrows's thoughts than getting out of there. By the time he hit the back seat of the car, the relentless agenda of life at Acrobat had once again embraced him in its symbiotic hug.

The double doors slapped the walls of the corridor in unison as the cart crashed through. Nurses, porters, visitors flattened themselves against paintwork scarred by previous arrivals at A&E. The cardiac team tried to tend the patient as they ran, their voices jolting with each step, a nurse holding the drip above his head, a doctor searching for a pulse as they banged the trolley from the ambulance to the trauma room – an impossible mass of wires, tubes and gauges.

Somewhere underneath it all was Henry Fleming FCA, Finance Director of Acrobat TV, who worried too much.

'You worry too much, Henry,' they said.

'It's my job to worry too much,' he replied. 'It's what I do.'

And now this. Fleming the control freak, totally not in control. Washing in and out of consciousness to ask what was happening to him, to try and wrench back responsibility; out again before he heard the answer.

In the emergency room the mess of tubes was unravelled and the hubbub resolved into clipped orders, instructions, responses. Maggie Fleming arrived at A&E reception and was shown to a plain room with plastic flowers and a coffee machine. A startled family looked up as she entered and they made eye contact, whispering a greeting of some sort, venturing a half-smile of fellowship.

'Slow yourself down, Henry,' she'd said, 'it's too much stress.'

'It goes with the turf,' he'd said. 'I'll be all right.'

She was right. He was wrong.

She sat for an eternity, flipping an old magazine. She read the front of the coffee machine and dropped some coins into the thing. The frightened family watched her, whispering admonishments to their wriggling child. She recoiled as she sipped the drink and nearly said something. Their expectation beseeched her to do so, but the weight of her own doubt and fear was immovable. She pulled out her phone; in unison, they watched every move. She put it away. She read and re-read the posters explaining the workings of the human respiratory system and how to become a friend of the hospital. She studied the minute hand of the clock, catching it moving, all the time listening to every slight noise from outside. Every clue, every door, every shriek of a shoe on the polished floor, every hubbub of a conversation, bleary like underwater.

For once he was so wrong. Reliable old Henry. Solid Henry Fleming, whom everybody leaned on. Who wouldn't be told. Would he ever know? For goodness' sake, how would she understand the finances, the investments, all that pension stuff? Come on, he'll be fine – it's amazing what they can do these days. They do this all the time.

When it was all over in the trauma room, a young doctor came to find her. Maggie was desperate to get away from the hopelessness of the waiting family, their eyes emptied by fear, searching hers for some reflection of their sudden, awful burden. 'Please don't tell me here,' she screamed, 'not in front of these.' But nothing came out, only, 'Hi.' The doctor sat down next to her and took her hand.

One of a thousand cars on one of a thousand London streets was the black Mercedes bearing Charlie Burrows towards the Acrobat offices and studios in Lancaster Gate. He nested in the back seat, his work papers cast around next to him, the newspaper badly refolded in the pocket in front. In the back section of his case, articles he'd kept, knowing they would be vital some time. When the case got too full, he'd throw away the lot with a sense of reprieve.

Despite a lifetime of contempt for fat cats reading the

FT in the back of limousines, he'd convinced himself that, for pragmatic and certainly not status reasons, he needed a chauffeur. In keeping with what he called his 'opportunity culture', and despite a slightly muddy former life, he'd accepted Mick Spring's application to move up from the delivery van to the job. Spring had repaid his faith with reliability, keeping the atmosphere relaxed and mostly getting it right about when to talk and when to shut up. He took personal responsibility for getting his boss to his appointments on time, despite the impossible targets created by Burrows's dependable deadline brinkmanship. Burrows repaid the effort by involving Spring in his life. After all, the guy listened in to all the phone calls in the car. Seemed the decent thing, to chat things over with him.

Outside the Acrobat office building, a road sweeper, wrapped in layers of dark clothing, attended to a little heap of dust he'd tamed into one place. The adagio of his movements set a stark counterpoint to the rush of wind and humanity around him. Mute and largely un-noticed, he executed the practised choreography he would repeat a thousand times today. Just doing his job. Behind him, a rush of wind dashed the pile he had carefully assembled and rocketed a supermarket bag up several floors to lodge, wriggling, in the naked branches of a tree.

As they pulled in to the pavement beyond him, Burrows raked together his papers, snapped his case shut and alighted from the car with new-day gusto. If he felt the stress of this week's challenges, he wasn't showing it.

'Thanks, Mick, see you later.'

*

Burrows was the first to arrive on the fifth floor. He turned on his computer and set off to see Acrobat's Programme Director, Melvyn Davies, aka 'Merlin' for the magic he produced down there in the Programme Department. The first floor, where the output was devised, researched and commissioned, was always a mess. The passion of the creative spirit, bold, restless and ingenious, is apparently not inspired by order. Burrows waved to the news staff, wondering, as always, how anyone could even think in such chaos, let alone sort the events of the world into an orderly flow of information from 6.30 a.m. to 11 p.m.

Melvyn Davies's office was typical. As Programme Director, he had more space than anyone else on the first floor, and his office had the prime location, overlooking the park and the Bayswater Road. But the additional space had merely accommodated more Pigpen indiscipline. His desk was invisible beneath stacks of papers, the daily ratings reviews, programme research reports and, on every flat surface, a small pile of VHS tapes. Paraphernalia that should have been moved through in its due time got stalled here – a junkshop chaos. The shelves that had been put up to display his collection of awards had long ago been filled, and now the trophies wore baseball caps and jostled for position with a lank pot plant, various tired executive toys and other useless supplies. Coffee cups took their place there for weeks at a time until redeemed by Monica, his tireless PA.

His hair mimicked the scramble of his life: short, fair and perpetually dishevelled by habitual sweeps of his hand. Around his eyes were the crackles of lines that hinted at laughter, intelligence, anxiety.

'All right, Melv?' said Burrows as he peered around the door.

'Morning,' said Davies, concentrating on unloading a pile of tapes and papers from a carrier bag into a small area at the edge of the desk. Somehow, nothing fell to the floor.

'Good weekend?'

'Yeah, good,' responded Davies. 'Bit too much of this for Kate's liking.' He nodded at the teetering pile. 'But at least I got to watch my son play football on Saturday. Won eleven–six. Usual swarm of seven-year-olds looping around a park, being shouted at by their dads.'

'Cherish those moments, Melv.' Burrows parked himself on the edge of a sideboard in the absence of any unencumbered seating. 'Anyway, before you get into the real business, any chance of a few words on the annual results presentation for next week?'

Davies made eye contact for the first time. 'Sure,' he said.

'Actually, let me give Henry a shout.'

Burrows called through the open door. 'Monica, will you see if Henry could join us for a couple of minutes? Ta.'

As Davies cleared a space on his sofa, a publicity photo of Solveig Nilsen slithered to the floor. Burrows settled in the space, careful not to topple the pile of tapes sitting next to him, stalling till his Finance Director arrived. 'So how's your new protégée coming along?'

Davies looked at the photo. 'Yes, Ms Nilsen. She's highly dangerous, loose cannon, massive risk, but I've not seen that much assurance in a young presenter for years,' he said. 'At her age most of them are so scared on camera they look like cardboard cut-outs. She's great. I think we may be home-growing the new Davina.'

'If you home grow them, doesn't that mean you haven't got to pay them a million quid a year?' said Burrows, watching Davies's expression carefully.

Davies snorted humourlessly. The previous week, the lead actor in Acrobat's soap opera had defected to ITV for a package trumpeted in the tabloids as a million a year. Davies wanted to match it, but Burrows had refused. The normally steady relationship between the two men had taken one of its occasional dives as each retreated behind opposing lines, their animosity fuelled by extreme, if predictable, positions. The Programme Director, anxious about the steady loss of ratings, denied the tools to defend; the Chief Executive, taking the big view, worried about increasing costs without increasing revenues; worried about the trickle-down effect of higher fees on all their other talent.

They'd get over it, but the anger of last week's dispute lingered at the edges of their conversation, not quite forgiven just yet. Davies fidgeted, uncomfortable that Burrows had brought it up. He pretended to reorganize something on his desk and didn't meet Burrows's eyes.

'I've given her a late-night political satire show. She'll either be brilliant or awful and we'll know after show one.'

'How late?' asked Burrows. 'After eleven, she can't do us much harm, even if she's terrible. What's the show?'

Davies looked up. 'It's called *Midnight Minus One* for the cunning reason that it is going out at eleven on the dot.' Davies's job demanded a constant stream of ideas in tune with – or preferably a little ahead of – the tastes and interests of younger, discerning viewers – the people with all the best possible reasons not to stay at home and watch the television.

'Sounds logical,' said Burrows, non-committal.

'The one cloud on my horizon is that she's asked for an urgent meeting this morning. Usually means one thing.'

'You can sort it, can't you, Melv?' asked Burrows, his mind moving on.

'We'll have the inevitable conversation about money, the next show and the future, but I wouldn't want to try and predict Solveig.'

Monica leaned into the office. 'No sign of Henry yet.' Burrows looked at his watch. 'Dorothy will call us when he gets here,' she added.

'Odd,' he said, shooshing forward on the sofa. His demeanour had shifted up a notch. Enough of the trifles. 'OK, Henry and I are putting the finishing flourishes to the analysts' presentation for the results announcement. Basically it's a decent story for last year – good revenues, good earnings growth, brilliant management team, blah blah. Henry'll do the numbers, but you know our friends in the City. They won't be interested in the history. I'll do something about future strategy, but the big issue right now will be audiences. Since, according to my phone list, that's what you do down here . . .' he looked up as if for confirmation. Davies smiled thinly. 'I thought you might do a bit on the programmes – fascinating insight into the world of a flawed genius and all that.'

Davies laughed quietly, meeting Burrows's eyes in tentative forgiveness. 'You know it's all luck. Want me to make something up?'

Burrows pressed on. 'Usual plan then, eh?' He

laughed deliberately to acknowledge Davies's efforts to relieve last week's confrontation. 'What they need is a glimpse of the Davies master plan to hang on to young audiences in the face of new competition. Which means you are the Chosen One on whom our entire future depends.' Burrows raised his eyebrows and pulled a cock-eyed grin.

'Oh good, so no pressure then.' Davies shrugged. 'I'll do a few charts and we can talk about them in a couple of days.'

'Good man, Melv,' said Burrows. 'This really needs to be good. The share price is a bit goofy. They've got the willies after the last six months.'

'So we're talking about how we defy gravity,' said Davies.

'Just a touch of the old Merlin magic.'

Their eyes met for a second. The vague plea from the man who wouldn't take his most earnest advice just one week ago. Burrows knew it too.

'Great,' he said, opening the door. 'Mon, where the hell is Henry?' he demanded.

'There's no response at Henry's home and his mobile's off,' she reported. 'Dorothy's left a message in both places.'

'Not like Henry.' At the door, he turned and clapped his hands together, rubbing them enthusiastically. 'So then, Melv.'

'Yes?' Davies looked up.

'Get the ratings up, will you?'

As normal life at Acrobat resumed for the new week, Henry Fleming lay in the coronary care unit, surrounded by bleeps and bulbs. From time to time he fought his way to the surface, his mind scrabbling for a grip on the world, before exhaustion grabbed him and hauled him back into its morphine depths. He felt so heavy. If only he could lift himself from the bonds of this prison, the chains that were plugged into his body. Dancing at the edge of his consciousness was an anxiety. He knew its presence but couldn't name it. All he knew was that if he advanced upon it, it backed into the mist and he lost it. Only by staying still could he make it out, but by staying still it was out of reach. He would begin to doubt it, but just as the disquiet was fading, it would press in on him, call his name. By the time his drug-deadened reactions spun around, it had danced back to taunt him from the edge of the fog.

Maggie Fleming sat at her husband's side, squeezing his hand, watching his eyes flicker, wondering what was happening behind them. This man, her safe place.

She looked up from her 'what-ifs' as the consultant and a couple of younger doctors entered the private room. She stood up, carefully settling his hand on the sheet, and shook hands with the doctors.

'Now then, Mrs Fleming, how's he doing?'

Her eyes jumped to his name badge and she decided in an instant not to attempt its pronunciation. She turned to the bed. 'Just the same, really.'

'Let's have a look, shall we?' The consultant turned his attention to his patient, looking over his glasses at the printouts as the doctors examined the bank of technology. He made unrevealing noises. 'Mmm, fifty years old . . . no prior incidence . . .' and turned his attention to Maggie Fleming.

'Mrs Fleming, was your husband under stress?'

'Well, yes.' She returned his gaze. 'But he's been stressed for as long as I've known him.'

'Right, right, right. Are you aware of any additional stress that he may have been under at the current time?'

She looked at him again. 'Not really. I think they've got the annual results presentation coming up, and he's been doing quite a lot of travelling but . . .'

'Where does he travel to?'

'Oh. America mostly. Occasionally Germany, but mainly Los Angeles.'

'Right, right. Now, the annual presentation – is that something we might expect him to be particularly stressed about?'

'I don't know. He's done it many times before.'

'Bad news to impart perhaps?'

'Not that I'm aware of. I think things are running pretty smoothly. Is he going to be all right?'

'Well, he's stable, he's in the right place, and we'll keep a very close eye on him. But at the very least he has had a major warning shot across his bows here.'

She sat down heavily again. 'Well, will *you* tell him that? I've been trying to get him to slow down for years but without much success . . . as you see.'

'Don't worry, Mrs Fleming. As and when he's back with us, I shall be giving him a very stern lecture.'

Charlie Burrows first met Martin Sumner when they were in their twenties, playing rugby together in Newcastle. It was a collision of ideas. They found an immediate fascination for the other's outlook on everything: sport, music, movies, women – and especially their jobs – each instinctively embracing the other's perspectives to adapt his own approach. Both men saw traits in the other that they coveted. They were both over six feet tall, both in their mid-forties. Neither was classically good-looking but the confidence they carried, and the easy repartee with which they dealt with the power they held, made them an attractive double act.

Sumner was sifting through his emails when Burrows returned to his office. 'All right, Charles?' he called.

Burrows went into his office, smiling at the familiar Geordie smack of his number two, which had the capacity to make him feel confident, supported. 'Good weekend, Mart?'

'You know, not bad, not bad.'

'Love interest?'

'Mmm . . . six out of ten.'

'Oh, so still no Mrs Sumner on the horizon then?'

'Not as such, but some potential accompanists.'

Sumner was still seeking his lifetime's partner, and no one could accuse him of not trying; the variety of his female companions – his 'accompanists' – was not a well-kept secret.

Burrows brooded as he sorted his papers from the weekend. 'Accompanists. You've got enough bloody accompanists for a symphony orchestra,' he grumbled.

'Strictly duets, me,' came the voice from next door. 'Charlie, you seen this email from Phyllis?'

'Not yet.'

'Looks like she's done some of her PR-type research that says you're not as famous as she'd like.'

Burrows appeared in his doorway. 'Here we go again. Time for a new whinge about my personal profile. Does she by any chance recommend a programme of inter-views with every paper in Fleet Street?'

Sumner was still reading. 'No, no medicine prescribed as yet. She just says your hot new rival at Channel 6 is turning City heads more than you are.'

'Hardly surprising,' said Burrows, moving to look over Sumner's shoulder. 'He's everywhere at the moment. How long's he been in charge now?'

'About six months?'

'Someone's decided to do a number on him, I guess.'

'Here we go,' said Sumner, reading from his screen. '"In our research we asked the following question: *Thinking about media companies, which do you think are the most dynamic in the sector?"*' Sumner affected a schoolma'am tone. '"Channel 6 has been nowhere since we started this survey, but in the last three months their performance on this measure has improved dramatically, together with the personal profile of Nik Kruger." And they think he's better-looking than you.'

'Bollocks,' smiled Burrows, moving to the door.

'Step forward Charles Burrows, Acrobat's hero,' announced Sumner.

'There's no point, Mart,' said Burrows. 'Those boys are in the story business and "ordinary bloke doing OK job" isn't a story. Huge success of celebrity CEO, followed by ghastly, embarrassing failure is their win-win. Two bites. Puff them up till they think they're something special, then bring them crashing back to earth. Bingo.'

'Well, you know what Phyllis is going to say. It's work-ing all right for Channel 6.'

'Only because wherever Kruger goes, he slags us off. Very clever. You think I should do that?'

'I think perhaps you should listen to your Communications Director. Might even get the share price up.'

'Of course I will.'

Sumner knew he wouldn't.

Solveig Nilsen got up from the table when Davies walked into the conference room. And kept going up. Six feet tall and close-cropped Norwegian blonde hair, she pursed her lips and stooped slightly to receive Davies's kiss. 'Sorry, Melvin. I know you are busy. I just wanted a few little minutes.' Her thick accent carried that unique Scandinavian blend of rural innocence and big-city carnality. 'Is it OK if I shut the door?' she said.

'Uh-oh, do I like the sound of this?' The door clunked behind her. She held his eyes as she slipped into her chair.

'Well, yes and no,' she said, slumping forward with her elbows on the table, her hands clasped in front of her. 'Yes, because you are not the only person in the world who thinks I'm brilliant. No, because Channel 6 have offered me a contract for a prime-time show if I can start immediately.'

This was not a new conversation for Davies. If you have great people, the competition will always try to poach them, so he'd had plenty of practice in these interchanges. Don't look flustered. Remember, they're always more worried than you. Maybe even Solveig.

'Well, first, obviously, congratulations.'

'Thanks,' she replied, surprised.

'What do you want to do?'

'Well, I would really value your advice, actually.'

Excellent: she was undecided. This was probably a discussion about pay or scheduling. It was odd how someone whose on-screen persona was so recklessly confident was just like everyone else when it came down to the big personal decisions.

'Look, your eleven o'clock slot on Acrobat will get you more viewers than peak time on Channel 6, and at this stage of your career, it's all about eyeballs – getting that face known . . .' He reached to cup her chin in his hands but thought better of it. '. . . by the largest possible number of people. If the audience like you, and they will, I already have a plan to move you up the card.'

'Yes, well that is the point really – Channel 6 are talking about making me the face of the station. So, as well as the show, I would be on all their ads, and popping up through the evening announcing stuff.'

Ouch. Was she bluffing? He couldn't possibly know, but if he was going to win her back he had to take everything she said at face value.

'Well, Solveig, I can't say I'm completely surprised, though I'm not sure where they're getting the money from. It's always been a bit of a shoestring outfit so far.'

'We talked about that. The new guy down there – Nik . . . something foreign . . .'

'Kruger.'

'Whatever. Anyway, he has apparently been out raising money to mount a big assault on Acrobat's audience.'

'Yeah, I know,' said Davies, affecting confidence, as if she were just confirming his intelligence. 'You're not the first one of my people they've come waving a cheque book at. Money good?'

'Money very good.' She bit her lip. 'Sorry, Melvyn, I think I can't say no.'

'Look, Solveig – this isn't about how much you pull in

over the next couple of years, this is about getting your career started properly. A fast buck isn't the point right now.'

'I know. It is just that I've got a horrible overdraft and a father who is trying to make me a doctor or a lawyer or something he can drink to at his golf club. Seeing his pretty little girl on posters all over London would show him I am serious – and give his horrid friends something to talk about.'

Davies could feel it slipping away. She'd thought this through after all. 'Solveig, we're committed to *Midnight Minus One*. We've press-released the show with your name on it, Ray has got an advertising sponsor lined up and we've sold airtime for all the youth advertisers in the breaks.'

'I know, Melvin and I'm really sorry. No one could have given me the start that you have, but I honestly feel I've got to grow up, maybe leave the nest, you know?'

Davies could tell she was embarrassed, which meant she wasn't negotiating with him. She'd decided. But if Channel 6 really had new funding to go after Acrobat's young viewers, Davies would have to give Ray Walker's sales team the ratings to keep the advertisers contented.

'Right, Solveig – I realize you've been made a great offer and I can see why it's tempting, but what if we took a little risk together?' Davies was thinking as he was speaking. 'What about if I decided that we move *Midnight Minus One* earlier in the evening . . . maybe to nine thirty, we change the title – obviously – and we advertise the show, which means you get plenty of personal publicity.'

'What are you saying?' She looked earnestly at him; she wanted to hear it again.

So with gathering optimism, Davies recounted plan B.

She grinned. 'OK – can you just do that?'

'You have my word on it. You get the publicity, you get a much larger audience than at eleven, all the profile, make Papa proud and . . .' he paused as if building to the grand crescendo, 'you get the privilege of continuing to work with me.'

She laughed. Good sign. 'And I can still do it live?'

'Still live, still raunchy – all the things we discussed.'

'And the advertising campaign? Will that be OK too?'

'Yup – we'll do some huge posters and make some promotional spots to run for a couple of weeks before the show launches. I'll talk to Phyllis and she'll do a PR number on you, get you in a few colour supplements.'

'And you would do all this?'

He paused, overacting. 'Hey. Not for just anyone. But for Solveig Nilsen . . .' He turned both palms up and pulled a magician's eureka face.

It was midday when Henry Fleming's secretary, Dorothy, arrived outside Burrows's office. Through the window, Burrows watched the silent movie as, wearing her distress like a veil, Dorothy talked to Paula, his PA. He watched Paula recoil at Dorothy's news, saw her move around the desk to place a caring hand on Dorothy's shoulder. Together they approached his office.

'Charlie, it's Henry. Can Dorothy pop in for a minute?'

'Sure,' he said, preparing himself to react properly.

'I've just spoken to Maggie,' gulped Dorothy. 'She's very sorry for not calling sooner, only she's been at the hospital.' She swallowed hard, composing herself.

'That's OK,' he said. Come on, woman.

'I'm afraid Henry had a massive heart attack yesterday.'

Instinctively Burrows's mind darted to the consequences of Fleming's absence, but he barged it back to the right responses. 'Oh God, is he all right?'

'No, he's not . . .' she bowed her head and tears ran down her cheeks. Paula placed an arm round her shoulder and nodded to Burrows, mouthing, 'He's alive.'

'Sorry.' Dorothy composed herself again and snuffled into a small tissue. 'He's in intensive care. They don't know what the prognosis is going to be.'

Burrows was rifling through what he knew of Henry Fleming's agenda, working through the damage, but he said, 'Pol, can you do flowers and call Maggie, tell her we're all thinking of them and if she needs anything at all, she's to let me know, right? Dorothy, you OK? Do you want to take some time out to get things together?'

'No, I'll be all right, I'm sure,' she sniffed. 'I'll go back to my desk.'

As they left his office, Burrows swore gently. 'Timing, Henry,' he muttered.

To lift the public profile of Channel 6, its Chief Executive Nik Kruger had taken to the circuit. He was out every night with the great and the good, cultivating relations with the press, opinion formers, regulators and MPs. It was a risk, since he was still learning a lot. But no one turns down the chance to meet a TV Chief Executive – especially the powerful, who never know when they might need a favour. Kruger had no trouble filling his diary with the right contacts, and so far his mix of South African bravado and sharpness of mind had impressed.

Today he would be having lunch with Hugh Ratledge

at The Ivy, for years the media industry's first choice for show-lunching. The food was good; but the point of being there was the reservations policy, which favoured the famous and powerful. So all eyes would sweep to the door to evaluate each new arrival. It suited Kruger well that his customers and competitors should notice his 'A-list' status and the quality of his Rolodex.

Ratledge, the irascible editor of *The Mail on Sunday*, didn't much care for television executives. He found their approach to the news merely sensational, and they fished in the same pond for the advertising money that enabled him to expand his paper. Yet Channel 6 was getting talked about, and Ratledge had a journalist's curiosity.

Nik Kruger arrived at the restaurant first. He was not good-looking but was always impeccably turned out. His suits were all Armani, his spectacles too. His hair close cropped in an effort to conceal the early thinning of his fringe. The New Year in St Bart's tan was only slightly fading.

Ratledge tucked his napkin into a maroon cardigan around which was stretched a suit, shiny with the light from the stained-glass windows. He set about his shepherd's pie with relish. Eventually he said, 'Well then, now tell me, how's business, Nik.'

Kruger gathered himself, his thoughts flicking to the piece of paper in his pocket headed 'Messages for Hugh Ratledge', and he dived into his story.

'It's going well for us at Channel 6,' he said, his clipped Johannesburg dialect a pointed contrast to Ratledge's Scottish burr. 'Everything's moving in the right direction, and I'm confident that we'll be in profit in the second half of next year at the latest.'

'I trust those aren't my profits you're after,' said Ratledge without looking up from the mess on his plate.

'No no, we're not after newspaper revenues; our strategy is to switch money out of other TV stations and into Channel 6.'

'*All* other TV stations?' grunted Ratledge, still apparently more interested in his food than the conversation.

'Well, one in particular,' smoothed Kruger.

'Acrobat?'

'Acrobat,' he confirmed, inadvertently mimicking Ratledge's intonation.

'I wish you well,' continued Ratledge. 'They've put a nasty dent in my revenues, I can tell you. That old laddy they've got there in charge of sales . . .'

'Ray Walker,' said Kruger.

'Yes, Walker. Man's an animal. Thinks that anything goes in the service of the good old firm. One of those.'

'He's not alone,' said Kruger. 'They're all a bit like that there. It's pure arrogance. They've got their spot at the top of the tree, and from high in the branches they think they can sneer down at the rest of us. Thing is, they think they're not vulnerable – so they are.'

Ratledge snorted, chasing peas around his plate.

'The scourge of success – complacency,' Kruger went on. 'The good ship Acrobat, nothing can go wrong. Well, maybe they could afford to think that way in the old days, when they didn't have any decent competition. But the market has changed and their assumptions haven't. So they *do* have an Achilles heel. Our job is to attack it.'

For the first time Ratledge made eye contact with Kruger. 'A refreshing point of view, Nik Kruger. Maybe you're on to something.'

'Off the record, Hugh, I'm not alone. I'm raising new money right now from some very blue chip investors who see the size of the opportunity.'

'Are you now?' Ratledge tilted his wine glass and appeared to be considering its colour in the light of the stained-glass window. 'Then maybe you and I could help each other.'

'I'm sure we could, Hugh,' said Kruger, leaning back from the table. 'Like a brandy with your coffee?'

'Love one,' said Ratledge, clasping his hands behind his head and smiling for the first time since they met.

When the email about Henry Fleming's heart attack went out in the afternoon, one person pondered it more carefully than the rest. Ray Walker was old school. For him, it was obvious that business success lay in relationships, not in bits of university paper with flowery writing on. He had been Sales Director at Acrobat from the very start. When advertisers had been reluctant to use television as anything but a mass medium, it had been Walker who had seduced them over their insecurities to use TV as a medium for reaching young people. Roger Collier, one of the founder shareholders, told everyone that, if it hadn't been for Ray, Acrobat would have been a big, expensive dream. But he'd done it. And having got his foot in the clients' doors, Walker was expert at squeezing himself further into the gap, until major advertisers abandoned the familiarity of other media altogether for the sexiness of TV. Once they were in, Walker would edge up the prices. Collier called it his crack-dealer approach.

Walker ran his domain as a dictatorship, his power absolute. He imbued his staff with an energetic sense of purpose by painting them as the saviours of the business from the dithering of the bureaucrats and the fecklessness of the creatives. And no one could doubt that the Sales Department was an enormously effective community. Its citizens knew the rules, success was rewarded with acceptance, bonus, and promotion; failure was punished by the ultimate rejection – 'not one of us'.

When Burrows joined the company, Ray Walker had survived his cull of the squabbling board, though the most vicious of the conflicts had raged between Walker and the Finance Director. The FD was fired, along with three other directors of the company. Having missed the Chief Executive's job himself, Walker offered himself as the natural choice as Burrows's deputy – 'Someone who knows where the bodies are buried.' Burrows reckoned if Walker knew that, it was because he'd knifed most of them personally. He deserved to go too. Culturally he was an outlaw, but there was no doubting the Sales Director's effectiveness.

Externally, Walker nurtured the fable that, while not actually on the throne himself, he was at least leaning over the back, the grand vizier prompting the king's best ideas. But his ultimate prize was the top job. At fifty-seven years of age this was not going to be in another company; but if a crisis should rock them, there would surely be the call for an experienced hand to take the Acrobat helm. The hospitalization of Henry Fleming was a useful step. But time was ticking. After the big six-oh, it would be too late. In the meantime, Charlie Burrows continued his boy-scout crusade to make Walker adopt his adversaries as teammates.

*

Kate Davies waited patiently while Monica located her husband. Eventually a distant, distracted voice came on the phone. 'Hello?'

'Melv, it's me.' Surely Monica had told him it was her.

The voice warmed a degree. 'Oh, hi, love. What's up?'

'Just thought I'd see how you were doing. See if you're hungry.'

'Oh, that's kind. Yes, I'm famished.'

'No glamorous showbiz lunch for you today, then?'

He laughed flatly. 'Can't remember one of those.'

'Well, perhaps we could make amends tonight.' Her tone remained persistently upbeat. 'Why don't I get a babysitter and we'll go somewhere nice.'

The line went quiet.

'Melv?'

'Sorry, just got an email . . .'

She wrestled her irritation into the background. 'Right.'

'Sorry, what was the question?'

'Melvyn, you're a bloody nightmare.'

'Sorry. I get a bit focused on it all when I'm here . . .' He tailed off disconsolately.

With an effort she said, 'I know you do, love. Look, do you fancy popping out for something tonight or I could cook or . . .'

'Oh no. Whatever you want to do.' She heard him sigh.

The wave of injustice rose in her. Why did he have to be like this? Why did he have to turn a perfectly nice offer into a problem? She wanted to hang up on him, but she knew that would only provoke a sulk. It was the extremes of his character which she had found so alluring ten years ago – and she still found the depth of his creative spirit swirling, unpredictable and fascinating. Yet his apparent mildness concealed a merciless temper when he was wounded. Not worth going there over a fish supper.

'Tell you what. Call me on the way home. We'll discuss it then.' And she was gone.

Sluggishly he put the phone down. He knew he'd hurt her, but as he returned to his emails he thought up reasons why it was her fault.

Following the Radio 4 News at 6.20 p.m., Gerry Duffy's Monday evening media business slot was a landmark for all the players in the media community. Duffy was good at picking up the gossip and skilled in separating the froth from the real beer. He had a track record of being first with the news of spats and spillages in London's media village. Thus he set the agenda for thousands of conversations in the bars and restaurants of Soho and Covent Garden.

'My guest this evening is Nik Kruger, who has been Chief Executive of upstart television station Channel 6 for the last six months. Nik, how's it going?'

'Good evening, Gerry. It's going like a train, thanks.'

'You spent ten years in management consultancy, one of the youngest-ever partners in your firm in South Africa, before moving to the UK and the television industry – why d'you do it? Presumably you had to swallow a big cut in your pay?'

'The consulting business was very good to me, but in the end I figured I'd probably made enough money for other people and it was time to turn my experience to a company that was mine to run. The trouble with being a consultant is that the moment you're out the door, they go their own cheerful way and you watch it all go up in flames.'

'So why television? Why Channel 6?'

'Sir Malcolm Ryan. . . .'

'Chairman of Channel 6.'

'That's right. I met Malcolm on a project. When he told me about Channel 6 and the prospect of new cash for the company, I immediately saw the potential waiting to be unlocked there. Time to put my MBA to work!'

'Was the company under-managed in the past?'

'All over the place. Nice enough people, but miles out of their depth if you ask me. But I don't want to comment on the past. I'm here to work on the future.'

'All right then, let's talk about the future. What's the secret?'

'Profile. Making a name for ourselves. Guerrilla marketing. I can't launch a challenge across every market segment, because everything I can afford to do, the opposition can do bigger and better.'

'The opposition. Who do you mean?'

'You know perfectly well who I mean,' said Kruger. 'Acrobat is our prime target.'

'That simple. Why Acrobat?'

'They've had it their own way for far too long. I'll pick up some audience along the way from the BBC and from other commercial companies, but in terms of the major stations, Acrobat is in the cross-hairs.'

'Tough target – they have a healthy start on you, an established audience, very strong advertiser relationships, and they can afford the kind of marketing campaigns to sustain that audience that Channel 6 can't possibly justify, even with your influx of cash. It's a very big adversary.'

'So were the dinosaurs. This is a market where big isn't best. Big means lumpy, slow, complacent, and these are not the keys to success in television today.'

'You're saying that Acrobat is lumpy and complacent?'

'I'm saying that Acrobat is not quite the athlete she used to be.'

'Solid management?'

'Solid management for twelve years ago. Who's having the new ideas there these days? It's not a criticism – you can't expect new tricks from old dogs.'

Duffy laughed out loud. 'Well, this is a contest we'll watch with interest. Let battle commence.'

'It has, Gerry.'

In his office, Charlie Burrows punched the remote control and the radio died. 'Right, that's it, you poisonous little bastard. Gloves off.'

Phyllis Grigson looked at him warily. 'What are you thinking?' she said.

The way she wobbled her head irritated him. Why did she have to know what he was thinking? Just once, why didn't she say what *she* was thinking? Because she didn't know? *Actually, that right now I am sitting face to face with one of the old dogs,* thought Burrows. But he said, 'I'll have him, that's all.'

Acrobat's closing share price   507p

Tuesday, 2 March

Arnaud de Vigny was very, very rich. From his château, a little way south of Paris, off the A-1, he ran a media investment empire that spanned Europe. It was a remarkable success story. Starting with a stake in a Dutch radio group, de Vigny had played his pieces with ruthlessness and dexterity to build TV and radio interests in each of the major countries of Europe. With the Frenchman's ear for the poetic, he called his group 'Activa'.

De Vigny's 29.9 per cent of Acrobat made him the company's largest shareholder. He longed to build on his stake, which was his most significant British investment. The Activa formula, proven in other countries, was to win control of one significant media company and use it as the platform for further acquisitions.

Piers Carrick arrived at the château for his weekly meeting after the short ride from Charles de Gaulle airport. Carrick was de Vigny's representative on the board of Acrobat, an ex-investment banker in his early fifties, the dashing English aristocrat from Central Casting. He had acted for de Vigny on the acquisition of the stake three years earlier and subsequently accepted the challenge to build the Activa empire in the UK. So far it had taken about two and three-quarter years longer than de Vigny wanted. The problem was Equitus, a highly aggressive fund led by Celia Sharma which had bought 20 per cent of the shares in Acrobat and secured a board seat just before Activa had bought in. Sharma had had a good run for her money and wanted out, but Arnaud de Vigny hadn't got where he was by paying the kind of price she wanted for her stake.

Carrick was shown into the elegant dining room, where a bow-tied butler poured him a spicy tomato juice. He sat in unnatural silence with the waiter, waiting for the arrival. The room was too large for a lunch for two people, but it provided a great expanse of wall for de Vigny to show off his latest art finds. Carrick involuntarily canted his head from side to side as he tried to get the measure of a large canvas which dominated the room. A large, badly drawn green square was suspended on a white background. As always, Carrick found himself wondering how much the old boy had paid for this one.

De Vigny arrived and shook Carrick's hand without eye contact. 'Piers,' he said, with charm but little affection.

'Hello, Arnaud, how are you?'

'Oh, fine. You know. Always some problems everywhere.' De Vigny, slight of build and with a tinny voice, had a reputation across Europe as a tyrant not to be tangled with. He was highly secretive and never spoke to the press, so the caricature of a mysterious business colossus had grown unchecked. Carrick attained instant respect in business circles by revealing his relationship with the Frenchman and couldn't resist overstating the degree of influence he was able to bring on his intransigent master. De Vigny accepted a glass of Meursault and waved Carrick to his place at the far end of the absurdly large table. The butler melted back through the double doors as de Vigny pressed a buzzer under the table to summon their lunch.

'I think you will guess what I'm going to ask you, Piers.'

Carrick laughed to indicate his equanimity, but de Vigny didn't respond. 'Acrobat, am I right?'

'Acrobat indeed. I am very bored with playing your waiting game. Perhaps Mrs Sharma has more mettle than you? *Non?*'

Talks on price between de Vigny and Sharma had broken down long ago, each believing the other to be pointlessly inflexible. Under the rules of the Stock Exchange, if de Vigny bought over 30 per cent, he would have to make an offer for the whole company at the same price, so if she coaxed a premium price out of him, he'd have to offer that price to all the remaining shareholders. Anathema to de Vigny's pride as much as to his purse. Meanwhile, Sharma believed it was obvious that the current market price was a fraction of the true worth of her controlling stake. Hence, stalemate. Such conversations as now took place between the shareholders were ritual affairs. No matter what arguments she pieced together with her team of bright young things, de Vigny was implacably opposed to any deal at a price greater than the market. And when de Vigny decided, that was it.

Carrick finished his glass and reached for the bottle. 'It's not that difficult to understand, Arnaud. Unless we pay her price, she's not going anywhere.'

De Vigny went from nought to sixty in a second. 'Why do you not understand this simple point? What is the point of paying you to sit on this board and just wait for her to a-c-t?' De Vigny pronounced every letter of the word. 'All over the media sector they are saying that Arnaud de Vigny cannot deal in the UK. Huh? I have Murdoch on the phone, Scardino, Redstone, Berlusconi.

Always the same question – "How about in the UK, Arnaud?" And your solution is what? To throw my cheque book at this problem. If I pay her price in UK, everyone in Europe will rub their hands together and think I have become Santa Claus. *Non?*'

Carrick heard him out and poured the wine. 'Oh come now, Arnaud. Seriously. It's a question of the strategic value of Acrobat for our future plans.'

De Vigny closed his eyes. 'No, no, and again no. You think calling it strategic means it's OK to overpay. Arnaud de Vigny does not overpay. Get it? It has gone on long enough.'

Carrick's public school composure was not visibly ruffled by the tirade. He maintained a half-grin. 'Arnaud, Arnaud, please.'

'No. No "Arnaud please",' rejoined de Vigny. 'Now it is the time to a-c-t. I will not be made a fool by this woman. She is a merchant; she will always want more. Well, enough, I say. We are long-term investors. If she does not accept market price for her shares, we make her look a fool. We drive down the price till she runs like a cock. *Non?*'

Carrick paused to cover his horror at de Vigny's proposal. 'There is the little matter of the rules of the Stock Exchange and, for good measure, the Takeover Code, Arnaud.'

'What do I care for these rules?' shrilled de Vigny. 'You get it done or I find someone else to manage my affairs in UK.'

'All right, Arnaud. I'm just saying that we must move with caution, or else your future position in the UK could be tarnished.'

'This is your job. You take care of it. Next week I will take a week for my holiday. When I come back, I want progress.'

Carrick tried to stir up some chat to keep them going through the cheese course and to prove his composure, but de Vigny finished his meal in near silence.

Ray Walker sauntered into his weekly sales meeting with the air of a man who knows he can do it. He only ever wore expensive clothes, though none of them really worked on him. Certainly his physique, earned over ten thousand business lunches, didn't help. Beyond a certain girth, designer shirts come untucked as easily as their cheap high street cousins. Walker's hair had thinned beyond the scope of most styling options, so outside the office he sported a baseball cap, a preposterous designer statement in a man of his carriage.

He bowled in, hooked a chair with his ankle and slopped a few drops of coffee from the garish pint mug that was usually attached to his fist. 'All right, ladies and gentlemen, let's hear it.'

One by one, the sales managers summarized their contacts over the previous week and outlined their plans for the coming month. Each understood the rule book. Full diaries. And full of real contacts that got converted into money for the station at the right price. Walker made sure that no one filled the order book by jobbing out the spots at anything below the rate which he set with his second-in-command, Sarah Golanski.

Walker always made budget. In lean times, he offered terrible numbers to the board, with the tip that if they didn't like them, they should take a look at how badly their competitors were doing. In the good times Walker would be prudent, offering numbers which no one could dispute, but which everyone suspected were probably too low. He taunted them with the risks of a demoralized sales force, so they always agreed his budget, which meant that Walker – and his sales people – always hit their bonuses.

'All right, people,' Walker announced as the final presentation ended, 'just a few things. First, I'm asking Sarah to put together a dossier on Channel 6. Nik Kruger obviously gave the game away with his emotional performance on the radio last night. Clearly they fancy their chances, so we're going to be ready for them, right? I want to know what they're saying, to whom and about what. By the end of today, if you please. Sarah will correct the spelling and add some comparison numbers and circulate it asap so that you're well briefed out there. I'm not prepared to have that cocky little snit pull the wool over our customers' eyes. Channel 6 is a pisspot little channel with a record of consistent failure. All right? I know they're getting some more money. But it takes more than money to build a track record. That's what we have and they do not. Got it? Right, let's make sure people understand that.'

Walker dealt with some more details which he announced as 'parish notices'. Then he paused and affected the tone of a ringmaster, employing sudden crescendos at points in his speech. 'And now, ladies and gentlemen, boys and girls, for today's big story . . .' He paused, relishing the silence, the whole room hanging on his next words. He delivered them grandly, gradually forsaking the fairground accent as he went. There is one person here who, joking apart, really makes the team tick, and I want to take this opportunity to say a big "Thank-you" to her, right? And also "Happy Birthday" because today, Sarah Golanski has reached the great age of thirty-five.'

Sarah Golanski was the only daughter of devoted parents whose legacy had been a few pounds sacrificially scrimped together in their will, some Polish family mementoes and an enduring confidence in herself. She had gathered a polytechnic degree and amassed a huge library of management books. Her magazines were *Hello!* and the *Harvard Business Review*; she read both avidly, consciously deploying the new language that arrived, shrink-wrapped, on her doormat every month from Cambridge, Massachusetts. The alchemy between Sarah Golanski and Ray Walker was inexplicable. Yet at some point she had been admitted to the very small group who enjoyed Walker's trust, a group that in his eyes could do no wrong. It was a place where she felt secure.

Walker watched her admiringly as she stood to acknowledge whoops and claps as if she'd just saved a penalty. 'She doesn't look a day over forty,' called one young man stupidly, to laughter all round. Walker surveyed the scene with a fatherly eye and a half-smile. Golanski had worked with Walker for ten years – an unusually long stretch in an area where high-fliers tended to get wooed away by competitors. He had ensured her longevity by lobbying strongly on her behalf at salary review times. As well as playing governess to their sometimes unruly charges, she was the acceptable face of the sales team, and other department heads would usually choose to consult Sarah when they should really have discussed difficult matters with the Sales Director himself.

The door swung open and Sylvia, Walker's devoted secretary of twenty-two years, tottered through with a trolley laden with precarious champagne bottles, jostling like commuters, and glasses chattering. She pouted triumphantly through too much pink lipstick as a cheer went up and several of the young men took up their positions, opening bottles, pouring them too quickly, and passing foaming and sticky glasses around the room. Though it was only just midday, a party began as Sarah opened her present – paid for out of the contents of the large brown envelope which had circulated the previous day.

They toasted her and demanded a speech. She swooped her shoulder-length black hair off her face, pulled a rueful face and raised a graceful hand until they were silent. She affected a most gentle, caring voice to say, 'Thank you, everybody, how sweet of you. I *do* feel loved.'

'Aaaah,' responded the crowd.

She continued, this time with a raucous sneer. 'Right, that's half an hour you owe me. Thirty perfectly good selling minutes when you should be on those phones, or out in those very nice, comfy cars we give you to *go out selling* in.' The team laughed and groaned and some shouted unfunny responses. 'However,' she continued, 'on this day of days, and since Ray is buying, I'll see you down the Mitre!'

More shouts and cheers as they emptied their glasses, one boy pouring the last inch of his drink on to the head of another, and the throng made their way to the end of the street and into Acrobat's local pub.

*

'Hey, Phil,' Paula Conley called out as Phyllis Grigson rounded the corner towards the Chief Executive's office. 'In you go – he's had a crap morning, Nik Kruger called him a dinosaur and Henry's in intensive care. So love up on him, won't you?'

'Oh great,' said Grigson, bowing her head with resolve as she entered Burrows's office.

The office was decorated with four or five ancient television sets. He kept a modest-sized desk and most of his meetings took place on the sofas. His pride and joy was an original Wurlitzer, which squatted in one corner.

'Hello Charlie,' she said pleasantly. 'You ready for me?'

'Sure,' he said. 'That little bastard has profoundly pissed me off, Phyllis. "Old dogs". Bastard.'

'Time to go to work. Profile, Charlie, profile. Did you read my email?'

'No, Phyllis, please, not the profile whinge again.'

'Charles, just listen and then decide. It's not cough mixture. Basically all the research is saying that Nasty Nik is, shall we say, turning heads a bit.'

'Oh, come on, Phyllis, so what? You know how this stuff works. Kruger has been working his butt off to get himself quoted all over the place, but he doesn't know what he's talking about half the time. All that your research is picking up is that people remember his name, that's all. Every time he opens his mouth, something stupid comes out. The man's a muppet.'

'Charlie, my dear, some – but not all – of that is true. However, if you'll take my advice, it does you no harm at all to pay attention to what the research is saying: you have a competitor who is being taken increasingly seriously. Your options are to bury your head in the sand or do something about it.'

Burrows folded his arms and leaned back in his chair. He considered the prim figure before him. Today's trademark two-piece was aubergine, set off with a gold brooch in the shape of a bow. Her hair was expensively styled, cut close to her head. As she talked, Burrows went to work on the thought that had occurred to him earlier. Phyllis Grigson was part of the daily scenery. The notion of moving her out gave him the frisson of excitement that change always provoked in him.

'All right, what ludicrous stunt have you dreamed up for me?'

She crimped her lips annoyingly. 'OK, good. It's just a simple package of measures to get you speaking at a couple of conferences . . .' (Burrows sighed) '. . . maybe a personal profile in the *FT* around the results?'

'Oh, for God's sake Phyllis. No personal profiles. You know I'm not doing that. I'll talk about the business, but I'm not having them crawling all over my life. I'm nothing more than a story to them.'

'It's their job, Charles.'

'Precisely Phyllis – and their agenda and my agenda couldn't be more different. You're a story when you're up, and they'll help you get there because it suits them. I'm not saying they're bad people – they can't help it. But, as night follows day, they'll want the follow-up. It'll happen to Nik Kruger. He's drunk from the cup – they'll have him.'

Grigson waited patiently for Burrows to finish. It was a theme she'd heard many times before. 'All I'm saying, Charlie, is that you would rightly criticize me if

I sat on this research. I'm sorry to be the bearer of difficult news and I know very well how wary you are of the fourth estate, but it need not be as great a risk as you think.'

'In your careful hands, etc.?'

'Absolutely, Charles. When have I let you down?'

He looked at her in silence.

'Will you think about it for me?' she said, nursery school eyebrows raised.

'I'll think about it.'

'Charlie, it's ten to,' called Paula from the doorway. 'I'm off to the Mitre for a birthday drink with Sarah. You coming down?'

Phyllis Grigson gathered her papers.

'Maybe later – I'm going to crunch through these piles of shite you keep dumping in my in-tray.'

'Mine is but to serve, my liege,' came the retort as she swung a coat around her shoulders.

'Say hi for me, will you?' he called. 'All right, Phyllis – we'll talk later.'

At two thirty Martin Sumner arrived back from lunch. 'Well, well, well, Charlie. Have I got news for you!'

Burrows leaped up from his desk and fell on to the sofa, waving to Sumner to do the same. 'Thank God for that,' he said. 'Anything would be better than this frigging paperwork. Whatyagot?'

'Well, it might make a change, but it's not much fun. I've just had lunch with a potential accompanist who just happens to work at the Broadcasting Ministry.'

Burrows shook his head. 'Don't you ever rest, man?'

Sumner looked innocent. 'Hey, I'm just a tragic

music-lover, all right? Anyway, mate, this is serious. It appears that they're investigating a complaint against us.'

'Oh, knock me down with a feather.'

'Well, actually this one is a little different from our usual whingers. This one is from a concerned viewer by the name of N. Kruger.'

Burrows came alive. 'You're kidding. He's made a formal complaint about us? Man, does he have a death wish!' He jumped to his feet and strode to his window. 'What's he said?'

'My source got a bit saintly at that point, but essentially Kruger's commissioned some research into the effects of Acrobat programmes on minors.'

'What? But the channel is for young adults. We're not targeting minors.'

'Exactly Charlie. He's playing to the government. Remember their manifesto slogan – what was it, "*Putting families first*"? Apparently the men from the ministry love it. They're creaming themselves that Kruger has broken ranks to direct the rest of us up to the moral high ground.'

'This is unbelievable.'

'Oh, just wait. It gets worse.' Sumner edged forward on Burrows's sofa. 'The ministry has decided to validate Kruger's research by secretly monitoring our peak time output. If they find enough sex and violence, they'll release the findings to the press to make an example of us.'

'What? We get dragged through some *Daily Mail* kangaroo court because someone says "bollocks" in a prison drama?'

'You got it.'

Burrows rested his head on the window with a bump,

surveying the traffic in Bayswater Road. 'Martin, we've got to stop this guy. This isn't putting families first. This is totally contrived to damage us.'

'Course it is. It's bloody clever, actually,' said Sumner. 'Kruger can't outspend us, but outrage is free. Those bland American imports he runs on Channel 6 are never going to upset anyone. But if we're going to keep it edgy for younger viewers, we have no choice but to lean on the boundaries.'

Burrows felt the crank of additional tension pull on him. 'We play it safe, we lose ratings.'

'More ratings,' Sumner corrected him.

Burrows drummed his fingers on the window sill. 'We've got to grab this, Martin. Before the government goes off building policies around these bloody MBA theories, maybe it needs an alternative perspective on Nik Kruger.' He pronounced the last words with lavish distaste. 'Unless you have a better plan, he's got to be systematically discredited.'

'Careful, Charles. He that lives by the sword, etc.'

'Exactly my point. Let's garrotte the little bastard.'

'I'm sensing this discussion is over.' Sumner smiled at his friend.

'It is indeed, Mart, and I thank you for your contribution to it.'

Summer flipped a look at his watch, catapulting to his feet. 'Right, look, I'm late. I'm seeing Rishi in finance to make sure he's coping while Henry's in hospital. Can I recommend you involve the Communications Director in whatever dastardly plan you're brewing there, Charles? I'll catch up with you later.'

Burrows stalked out of his office and rifled through

Paula's telephone book in search of the number for *The Times*. Moments later, he was connected to Carrie McGann, the newspaper's media editor.

'Carrie, hi!' he crooned, like an old media luvvy.

'Good grief, he lives! Charlie, to what do I owe this rare moment?'

'Long time no speak, on or off the record. Thought it was time to put in a call for old times' sake.'

'Great to hear from you, Charlie. What's happening that my readers should know about? How's Henry?'

'Henry's good – nothing to worry about, I think.'

'Good good . . . there but for the grace of God etc. . . . anyway, gimme the low-down – what's not fit to print?'

'All will be revealed at the results presentation next week, Carrie – we're in a close period till then, but my nearest and dearest are telling me I should get out more – or at least try and make it into your pages as much as your new best friend, Mr Kruger.'

'Ahh, I see – feeling a bit left out are we, Charlie?'

'No, not at all. But what's got into you lot? All of a sudden this moron is the font of all wisdom?'

'Oh, that's simple. He returns my phone calls, Charlie. It's quite amazing how it is possible to have rather a good relationship with sad old hacks like me, you know.'

'What are you saying – that because Nik Kruger gives you access to his private phone number, he's the one who gets the call for the learned comment?'

'Something like that – it's a two-way street. He makes it easier for me to do my job – I make it easier for him to do his job. Good deal, huh?'

'A very happy arrangement,' conceded Burrows.

'So you're phoning to see how you can make my job easier?' teased McGann.

Burrows laughed. 'Actually, I was phoning to say I might be up for a feature or something . . . if you wanted to do one, of course.'

'Charlie, I'd be delighted. In fact I've got a large hole on Thursday. I just had to pull a rather good profile for some legal gobbledegook reason. If you're up for it, I could very happily fill it with a large mugshot of your good self and a few well-chosen words. Got time now?'

'Blimey, that's a bit quick.'

'Time and tide, Charlie . . . all that old malarkey. We can do it now – otherwise it'll have to wait a few weeks.'

'Well, how about if I have a quick word with Phyllis Grigson and call you back?'

'The babysitter will cost you three weeks, Charlie. Copy deadlines for the media interview piece are upon us so, if it's all the same to you, I have my notebook at the ready. Mind if I tape the call, makes it a lot easier for me to make sure I get what you say right?'

'Get what I say right – this a new thing for *The Times*?'

'Ha ha, bloody ha. Come on then, are we doing this?'

'I suppose so,' responded Burrows, for some reason pulling out a clean piece of paper and pen himself.

'Right. Charlie Burrows, this is your life. Why are you in television? When did you start?'

'Oh, do we have to do the touchy feely stuff?'

'It's only a bit of context – don't worry about it, I don't want to know if you've ever smoked dope . . . you *haven't* ever smoked dope, have you?' Burrows laughed as Carrie McGann persisted. 'If I can't talk about the company because of your results announcement next week, I've got to talk about you a bit, haven't I.'

'OK, I started here seven years ago – about six and a half years before Mr child-genius Kruger.'

'My my, Charlie, you really have got it in for him, haven't you? What's he done?'

'Well, that's just the point, isn't it? He hasn't *done* anything. He just talks about it. And much of what he has to say is moronic. You're not going to quote me on that, are you?'

'Not if you tell me I can't, but it would be much better copy if I did.'

'No, I think that might be a bit pointed, coming from me.'

'Come on, Charlie – give me something to work with here.'

'OK,' he said. 'Why don't you say that sources in London's television community are already sick of Nik Kruger and his arrogant arrival on the scene.'

'Look, stop trying to write it for me, just tell me what you think.'

Burrows had some momentum now. 'I'll tell you what I think. I think the man is a muppet. He knows all the theory and none of the realities of this business. Television would be much better off without him . . . off the record.'

'Oh, come on, Charlie – that was vintage stuff.'

'I'm sure you'll find a way of synthesizing the essence of my meaning.'

'Really – you find nothing in Nik Kruger to recommend him? Sounds a lot like sour grapes, Charlie – most people seem to think he's very clever.'

'Look, no offence, Carrie, but anyone can take smug swipes and get quoted all over the place. The acid test is whether this guy can build a real business in one of the most competitive sectors in the world, perhaps by developing some of his own talent, as opposed to trying to hire all *my* best people.'

'Ooh, *good* gossip – names, ranks.'

'No, no one's going there, but it pisses me off that this guy arrives on the scene and spends half his life telling the world how rubbish we are, and the rest working his way down our internal phone list. Is it because he hasn't a clue how to build his own TV company? Or am I being unkind?'

'So you see Channel 6 as a major threat to Acrobat, am I right?'

'Now you're putting words in my mouth. No, you are not right. Acrobat has faced down competitors before. It's going to take a bit more than Mr Kruger and his crappy bought-in American shows to do us any lasting damage.'

'So, in one word, Nik Kruger is . . . ?'

'Dangerously incompetent.'

'That's two.'

'One was for free – that's the kind of guy I am.'

'All right, Charlie, now give me some more background and I'll craft us a little something special for Thursday morning.'

Burrows cradled the phone with his sense of justice restored and stabbed out an email to Phyllis Grigson.

Phyllis – you'll be pleased to know I have taken the bull by the horns and spoken to Carrie McGann at the

Times. I think it went fine – she had a gap on Thursday so there will be something on us. She tried to do a profile piece on me but I talked mainly about the market. She's not sure about the page layout at the moment but, if she can, there'll be a picture. Do you have any stock shots of my good side that we could send her? As instructed, I took a swipe at NM which seemed to go down well – I got the impression she was a bit fed up with him too. Is that it for another year now? CB

At 4.45 p.m., Henry Fleming FCA, who worried too much, opened his eyes. Maggie was at his side, a well-worn book in her lap. Her voice was gentle and mesmeric.

> The One remains, the many change and pass;
> Heaven's light forever shines, Earth's shadows fly.
> Life, like a dome of many coloured glass,
> Stains the white radiance of eternity.

Her eyes flicked to him and she immediately leaned forward and laid the book on the bed. She slid her hand into his and spoke very gently. 'Henry, hello, welcome back.'

Henry Fleming breathed out a grunt.

'I'll just tell the nurse you're awake.' She got up and pressed a red button by the bed.

Within seconds, the nurse was there, reading dials and paper from the machines, talking sweetly to Fleming as she went. 'Now, Mr Fleming, just because you're awake doesn't mean you're better, do you understand? I've seen people like you before, think you're some kind of superman. We're going to get you better very quick, but we're going to need your co-operation, all right?'

Fleming followed her bustling with his eyes. He was worried. He was so tired. He said nothing.

At 5 p.m. Melvyn Davies set off to see his mother. As he crossed the reception area, Ray Walker bundled through the revolving door, his Boss overcoat done up on the wrong buttons.

'Half-day, Melvyn?' roared Walker for all the world to hear.

Davies muttered a half-response but realized that Walker was expecting a proper answer. Immediately angry, he pushed past. 'I'm off to see someone,' he said.

'Someone with a few ideas, I hope,' retorted Walker humourlessly.

Davies heard his genial greeting to the security guard and stood, empty, on the pavement, choking for a rejoinder.

Forty minutes later, he was waiting on the doorstep of the tired little council house. Inside, he could hear the sound of someone pottering around, talking to herself. All the lights were on and the television burbling. He bent to the letter box and called, 'It's all right, Mum, it's me.'

The little woman had surely got smaller since he had visited her last, too long ago, his conscience told him. Since his father had died last Christmas, her need for her son's company had been acute, her ability to ask for it non-existent. She blinked at him through an open inch for a moment, before standing aside and receiving his kiss. She looked guilty, caught out by his arrival, roles reversed: son catches naughty mum. She led the way into the house, shuffling into the kitchen.

'I'm just having a little drink,' she said. 'Do you want to join me?'

Davies smiled a long-suffering smile and said, 'How little, Mum?'

'Oh, Melvyn,' she said. 'You haven't come here to scold your old mother.'

'It's not good for you, Mum.'

'Not good for me. What do I care what's good for me at my age? There's the bottle over there, help yourself.'

He had grown up in this house. Everything about it was familiar, normal. He opened the cupboard. On the window was a sticker he had put there as a boy. The window had a small crack across one corner, temporarily fixed with sellotape when he was still at school. It was yellow and curly now, but he didn't notice it. He pulled out a glass, crazed from many trips through the washing-up bowl, and picked up the wine bottle. Cautiously he sniffed at it, recoiling from the pungency of the bouquet.

'Cor, what the hell's this you're drinking?' he said.

'I don't know, what does it say?' She walked over to him, her slippers fussing on the linoleum floor. On the sink were the remains of dinner: two plates, one of them with the food untouched.

'You had company, Mum?' he called.

'No, love, just me.'

'Whose is this other dinner then?'

He saw a blush on her cheek. The bustling stopped. She wiped her hands on a tea-towel and glanced at him. 'It's your dad's,' she said.

He reached behind him and clutched the worktop as she picked up the plates, scooping the leftovers into the bin. He watched the routine, the old woman going about her business.

'Mum.'

'I know. You don't have to say anything.'

'But . . .'

'I miss him. I like cooking him his dinner.' She avoided his eye and pushed her way back through the glazed door into the sitting room. 'Are you going to come and sit down or not?'

Davies silently rolled his head back and picked up the bottle. He sat in his father's armchair. She took her accustomed place on the sofa in front of some TV soap opera, and they watched it together.

He took the opportunity of the commercial break. 'So then.' He swivelled in the chair to look at her. 'Are you really all right?'

She caught his eye for a moment, the babble of the commercials in the background, her head wobbling slightly.

'I'm a bit worried, Melvyn.'

He managed to keep his face calm. 'Right . . .' he said.

'I've had a letter.'

She pulled herself up with some difficulty and bumbled into the kitchen, opening drawers and talking quietly to herself. Davies looked around the room he knew so well, now seeing the deterioration, masked by the familiarity of his first look.

'Here it is. What do you think?'

Davies's heart leaped as he saw the bank's logo, the name of his father's company underlined in bold.

When Davies's father died, he left the furniture business he had founded in the hands of his wife. More than anything, Jack Davies had wanted his only son to inherit the firm. The boy had been given his first tool-kit at the age of seven. Night after night the old man would come home from his workshops and hold his son's small hands to the plane in the garden shed, cooing to him and marvelling at the smoothness of the wood, the uniqueness of each piece.

Though expert in his father's skills, Davies's ambition had never settled in the workshop with its heady scent of freshly planed ash and beeswax. Smells that could instantly catapult Davies back to his father's side as he conferred distinction upon the interchangeable planks that lay, banked in the store, until their day came. The sun slanting through the window, picking out deliberate lines through the dusty air, the hubbub of smoothing and turning, and the elderly conversation of his craftsmen. All through these years, young Melvyn's father had quietly promised him that one day all this would be his. There had been no debate.

But as the young man grew through college, he recognized that, alongside the love for his father and his undeniable desire to please him, there was a gathering sense that his creative ambition was not going to be fulfilled by sanding and shaping wood.

'Every single piece I've ever made has been unique,' Jack Davies would say. 'Every one of them is distinctive. Don't blend into the background, Melvyn. Be distinctive.' Yet this was the call that beckoned his son into television. Jack never took the television job seriously; for his son, however, the thrill of the studios, the lights and the countdowns steadily shunted the sleepy scraping of his father and his two old craftsmen away from his aspirations. Powerlessly and painfully, the old man watched it happen.

As the cancer closed its grip on him, his efforts to persuade Melvyn to accept the baton he had crafted became more desperate. In the end, they hashed out a compromise that didn't cost too many reckless promises. His wife would take over the running of the business, with Melvyn as 'Chairman', a part-time role which re-assured his father that the son would be at his wife's inexpert shoulder.

Davies knew it wouldn't work. But his father's assent to it had provided a shred of compromise which allowed him to depart in peace. As Davies knew it would, the nagging, grinding insistence of Acrobat devoured his time. His mother's efforts to run the company had been well-meaning, but her decisions were little more than stabs at guessing what Jack would have done. The customers had edged away, their departure slowed by the respect they had had for Jack Davies and their shared hope that his enterprise would live on.

'Mum, this letter says they've written before.' She was reading the page over his shoulder.

'Oh yes, I've got the others out here.' Again she went rooting in the kitchen, singing a little song under her breath. She returned with a supermarket bag which she laid at his feet, quietly returning to her seat.

'Mum, these are all sealed.'

'I know, love. I never really understood them, so there wasn't much point in opening them.'

Melvyn Davies felt hope draining out through his legs. 'Well, how come you opened this one?' He brandished the letter she had first shown him.

'Oh, that one came recorded delivery. I thought it might be some money.'

'No, it isn't, Mum.' He steadied his voice. 'It's the bank foreclosing on Dad's business. They're closing us down.'

She looked incredibly small, pathetic in the face of the incomprehensible forces that had done this. 'Oh dear,' she whispered.

He shifted to her sofa and put his arm around her tiny shoulders. 'Why didn't you call me?'

A tear flopped on to her cheek. 'Oh, Melvyn, you were too busy with your programmes.'

A scimitar could not have cut him deeper.

Acrobat's closing share price 505p

Wednesday, 3 March

Burrows's first meeting of the day was with Ray Walker. He set off early, opting to walk to the Sales Department via the intervening floor to do the 'leadership by walking around' thing. Of course he knew it was vital to see and be seen. But he winced at the small talk exchanged with people whose names he couldn't really remember, laughing at their hasty, unfunny observations to convince them they had a nice guy for a Chief Executive.

The sales department was certainly the most formal of the departments in the company; Walker insisted that his people wear business suits at all times. He demanded that his young salesmen wore ties and, though they would often be knotted an inch south of the collar, the uniform made the Walker team stand apart in the Acrobat dress-down culture. Burrows himself tried to look relaxed as often as possible, but he kept a suit hanging on the door in his office for those visitors who might confuse informal clothing for a casual approach.

Burrows waved at Sarah Golanski as he wove through the trading floor towards Walker's office in the corner. She was on the phone and raised her eyebrows, returning his grin. Thank God for Sarah, a real human being in this jungle.

Walker was also on the phone. Sylvia bustled around, in and out of Walker's office, to cover her embarrassment while Burrows waited for him to finish. He wondered why a woman of her age continued to wear so much loud make-up. What was going on in her head? She re-emerged with Walker's nasty pint mug and a look of relief.

'He's free now, Mr Burrows.'

'Sorry about that, just bringing in the revenue,' said Walker in response to the criticism that hadn't crossed Burrows's mind.

'No problem,' replied Burrows as he entered Walker's office. 'Always happy to catch you on the phone, making money. What's up, Ray?'

'Small thing really,' Walker began, his eyes on a note in front of him. 'Shouldn't have to bring it to you, but I know how you like to be involved.' Burrows nodded. 'I don't know if you know, but for once Melvyn gave me advance warning about one of his new shows – "Midnight Minus One" he calls it. "*MMOne*",' he added with heavy sarcasm.

'Yes, I know about it.'

'Good – so I have secured a deal with Southern Foods, who are going to sponsor it for a new decaff coffee, "Night and Day".' Walker spoke slowly and clearly for the sake of the non-specialist. 'I'm sure I don't need to remind you that Southern weren't advertising with us for the whole of last year, so this is actually a bit of a coup.'

'Congratulations.'

'Yeah, well – team effort. The problem is, no sooner have we got the deal signed and sealed than Melvyn gets it into his head to move the programme to nine thirty.'

'Oh yes, I think I know about this,' said Burrows.

'I'm delighted *you* do – it seems the only bugger in the place who doesn't is me, as usual.'

'Did Melvyn share with you why he's moved it forward?'

'Being held to ransom by the presenter, which is not acceptable. There's more to this than some little girl's ego. We're trying to run a business here. Someone's got to tell her to get back in her box. Am I supposed to go back to Southern and tell them I'm pulling a deal they've done in all good faith?'

'Won't they move with the show?'

'They might have, if they hadn't built the whole "Night and Day" campaign round a late-night show. The whole point is, you can drink this stuff at bedtime and still sleep. They've already shot the sponsorship trailers, so they're probably a hundred grand in the tank. What do you think they're going to say? "Oh never mind, we'll do some more."' Walker was hitting his stride now. Without any involvement from Burrows he seemed to be getting more and more annoyed. 'For God's sake, can't you get a grip round here – or do we accept that these people are running our business for us nowadays?'

'All right, Ray, let me talk to Melvyn. He has mentioned this to me, but I didn't know the position it would put you in.'

'Why would you?'

Burrows sighed. 'What does *that* mean?'

'Well, you're hardly a regular down here, are you?'

Burrows got up and moved to the door, just as Sylvia arrived with two mugs of grey-brown coffee and a flutter of her caked lashes.

'Well, now I know I'm so welcome, I'll be back,' he responded with a thin-lipped smile. 'Thanks, Sylvia – mind if I take this with me?' He lifted the coffee from her tray and paused in the Gents to pour it down the sink.

Waiting until Burrows had left the floor, Walker picked himself out of his chair and rolled into his deputy's office, closing the door with excessive secrecy. She looked up pleasantly.

'Look, Sarah, one for you, I think.' He fell untidily into a chair. 'Just bob down and tell Melvyn we've agreed to put *Midnight Minus One* back to eleven, will you? I've obviously spoken to Charlie and he's got the full picture now.'

'Oh, thanks a bunch, Ray. He's going to love that, isn't he.'

'Not really. Our glorious leader will no doubt grovel round there in due course to tell him, but it's important these people start to get their heads around the real commercial world. Charlie will sugar-coat it. We'll never get anything done round here if Melvyn doesn't understand that he can't hand over the reins to some little starlet and her ego.'

She watched the tirade, familiar with the moves, wondering how she could fulfil his commission while not destroying her relationship with the Programme Director.

Swearing under his breath, Burrows barged into the door frame as he made his way back into his office. Martin Sumner followed him in from his adjoining room.

'You all right?'

'Oh, nothing new – Ray's banging teddy on the cot because something changed in the tricky old world of modern television.'

'Anything you want me to do?'

'Fire him?' mused Burrows.

'Ooh, if only we had a buck for every time that thought's crossed our minds. Tell you what: let's give him till after the results presentation, then have a quiet word with him about succession management, perhaps retirement, a little golf, a little . . . hang gliding or something.'

Burrows threw his head back and laughed, reprieved by his friend's empathy. 'Perchance to dream. Do you think Sarah's ready to take over from him yet?'

Sumner pulled a sceptical face. 'Not really yet, but I hear rumblings that Channel 6 are looking to upgrade their Sales Department. She's the obvious choice for them.'

Burrows closed his eyes for a second, stifling a shudder. 'So here's your management starter for ten. Would you rather keep grumpy old has-been Ray if it means losing fragrant young Sarah? Are you actually prepared to sacrifice the exciting new face of Sales at Acrobat for the knackered old security blanket of the past?'

'Hmm, Charles – what do *you* think we should do?' They laughed and Sumner continued, 'Look, after the results, you and I will devise a plan of cosmic brilliance and sort all this out.'

'Sumner, where would I be without you?'

'You'd be a hopeless, miserable wreck, and we both know it.'

Sarah Golanski arrived at Melvyn Davies's office just as Solveig Nilsen emerged. Nilsen turned and gave Davies a high five, followed by a reckless kiss as he tried to look executive for Sarah's benefit.

She laughed and shook her head as Solveig whooped

her way out towards the lift. 'Successful session then, Melvyn,' she said.

Davies looked sheepish, but his eyes twinkled with triumph. 'We're there, Sarah, you're going to love the new show. We'll get a couple of stroppy letters from the Women's Institute, but we'll also get a ton of young viewers and, who knows, maybe even a gong or two.'

Golanski gripped him on the shoulder as she moved into his office. 'Can I have a couple of minutes?'

He looked up at a clock that had been stopped for the last two years at least. 'Yes, sure; thing is, Charlie wants me to pop up.'

'It's about the same thing. I can tell you, or Charlie can tell you.'

Davies swept a hand across his tousled hair. 'I'm not liking this. What?'

She cleared her throat purposefully. 'Basically, Charlie Burrows has decided that *Midnight Minus One* has to be shown at 11 p.m.'

Davies remained impassive, straightening a paper clip. 'And, let's see now. I'm wondering whether perhaps Ray may possibly have been involved in helping Charlie make that decision?'

'Right. Well, based on the original *MMOne* idea, we did a deal with Southern Foods which is linked to their campaign for this new coffee – "Night and Day". You can drink this stuff and still have a good night's sleep, it says here – but, put simply, it doesn't work if the show's not at eleven o'clock.'

Davies started to fidget, 'This is exactly the problem. He moans when I don't tell him about new shows, and when I do, *Whoosh*, they're gone. Abducted by their new dad in the Sales Department to throw to the geniuses with big chequebooks.'

She paused for a moment to indicate that she was not going to respond to his definition of the process. 'Yes, the trouble is that Southern have spent a hundred grand on the sponsor idents and so are . . .'

'Oh, come on, Sarah – of course they haven't spent a hundred grand on idents. That's just bullshit, so you people don't have to renegotiate a deal.'

'Melvyn, I hope you're not accusing the Sales Director of lying to the Chief Executive.'

'No, God, Sarah. Heaven forbid that anyone should ever accuse Ray of anything other than just doing a great job – and jolly pleasantly too.'

Golanski's niceness was buckling under this onslaught. 'Melvyn. I'm sorry. Right? The reason Charlie and Ray have taken this decision is because we have a difficult relationship with this client and they have an advertising budget of a quarter of a billion, which means that when they say what they want, they have our full attention. We got none of that last year, and this year we're in line for twenty-five million. In case you weren't thinking in those terms, that's an awful lot of programmes, right?'

Davies broke the paper clip in two. 'Let me tell you what will happen if we put this show back to eleven. First, I lose Solveig Nilsen – *we* lose Solveig Nilsen – who will go to Channel 6 to be the face of the station. That's two problems, Sarah: we need her playing for us and we don't need her playing against us. Second, that's our second major talent defection in a week. Not good when you lot expect me to go out there and persuade the best people that "Acrobat is a great place to work", or whatever the bollocks that Charlie parrots. Number three, and I'm sure this will not matter a toss to anyone in this fucking place, I've spent the last week working nights on this show to produce something we're all going to be proud of, including you jockeys in the Sales Department. And number four, I've given my word to Solveig that we're going to do this, and we're going to promote it heavily. But I guess that doesn't mean a thing here any more.'

'OK, I understand the position.'

'So you realize I've got rather a lot invested in this issue – and every now and then we should do what we believe in – not what some bloody ad-man tells us to.'

'It's a team game, Melvyn. We're supposed to be a team.'

'When is someone going to tell bloody Ray Walker that?' he shouted.

She stood up and marched to the door. 'Without Ray Walker you wouldn't have *any* programmes. So get used to it. I'm trying to do this nicely. I'm not going to stay here while you insult me and my boss. OK?'

He tried to come up with a rejoinder, but before he could she had gone, the door closing softly behind her.

'Well, Sarah Golanski,' he said, 'there I was, thinking you were friend. But you are enemy.' His eyes swept to his Bafta award, the highest acknowledgement of his creative achievement. He picked it up and turned it in his hand. Its weight reminded him of the night he was awarded it . . . the lights, the success, the back-slapping. He looked into its blank eyes. Meaningless. He dashed it to the floor, its emotionless golden face severed from its stand, turned away from the melodrama, into the corner.

*

Burrows opened an email entitled 'URGENT READ THIS BEFORE YOU GO HOME'. It was from Paula: 'Charlie you have to phone Phyllis Grigson back – she's going ballistic trying to get hold of you about your *Times* interview. Unhappy bunny. Pxx'

'Enough unhappy bunnies for one day, I think,' he said as he shoved the rest of his in-tray into the briefcase.

Nik Kruger concluded his dinner with Lord Markham, Chairman of Ofcom, the body which regulates all the broadcasters in the country. It had been an important meeting for him. The Chairman would not normally spend time one to one with the head of one of the minor channels, but he was intrigued by this newcomer who had made such an impression. He'd been impressed by Kruger's ability to come at the issues from a fresh perspective. Unlike many other licensees, Kruger appeared to be able to separate commercial self-interest from the touchy realities of public taste and decency with which Ofcom grappled daily. Theirs was a job that pleased no one; the public and the press accused them of toothlessness, while the broadcasters believed them to be interfering busybodies. But Kruger's outspoken commitment to the government's family criteria was impressive – and, frankly, enormously helpful. Finally, it changed the dynamics in the tiring battle lines between regulator and regulated. The fact that Kruger was bold enough not only to advocate the plan but to commit Channel 6 to it gave it an altogether different hue – and one that made Markham feel vindicated.

It was Kruger's sixth formal dinner on the trot and, having spent the weekend working on articles for publication and wooing prospective talent hirers, he was ready for bed. He declined the offer to join the Chairman in an Armagnac and cigar and was ready to leave when the bill arrived.

'Well, thank you, Nik,' said Markham. 'Delightful evening, and very stimulating conversation.'

'Thank *you*, Chairman,' responded Kruger. 'I've really enjoyed it.'

'Well, I think we should let you go home and get some sleep. If you don't mind my saying so, you look absolutely spent.'

Nik Kruger did not mind him noticing. In fact, he was quietly pleased that his exertions hadn't gone unremarked.

'How are you getting home?' continued the old boy. 'Is there a decent Channel 6 motor purring away outside for you?'

'There's a decent Channel 6 motor sitting round the corner, but I'm the chauffeur, unfortunately,' replied Kruger. 'Maybe when we've got a few years of profit under our belts I'll qualify for a seat in the back.'

'Well, thanks again, Nik, and all the best. We'll be watching your progress with interest.'

Kruger saw Markham into his Mercedes outside the restaurant and made for the side street where he had parked. In the sanctuary of the car, he sighed heavily, massaging his temples. What a life. He sat for a moment, his head boiling with schemes. It was crazy, trying to hold the whole game plan in your head when you were playing on so many fronts. In a few moments he concluded that he was too tired to make any sense of the waves of ideas, and gunned the engine into life. He knew they'd be back to assault him when his head hit the pillow, and he'd wake up in the morning with the feeling that he'd been in an all-night meeting. But he was wrong.

He sat at the traffic lights in Trafalgar Square and lolled back on the headrest. For a moment he gave in to the need to close his eyes, jolting awake at the horn of the cab behind. He waved his apology and set off down Northumberland Avenue to his death.

The best guess of the police at the scene was that he had not seen the lights change to red. The juggernaut was on its way out of Docklands with a full cargo of the morning's newspapers. The driver was in shock, but he said the lights his way had been green for some time. The handful of witnesses agreed that there was nothing he could have done to avoid the car.

The lorry batted Nik Kruger's car into the railway bridge and hit it again as it bounced back into the road, crushing the car beneath its full weight as it came to a shrieking sideways stop. A priest, out walking his dog along the embankment, administered the last rites and told the police that he thought it very unlikely that the driver would recover.

Acrobat's closing share price   505p

Thursday, 4 March

Charlie Burrows made his own coffee, wondering idly what had happened to his wife's new breakfast regime. At 8.15 he walked out into the crisp morning air, dragging his thoughts to the light of day. He dropped into the back seat of the car, to find Mick grinning at him triumphantly.

'I think you're gonna like this a lot.' He brandished the morning's *Times*, open at the media page. Rather than a picture of himself, a large picture of Nik Kruger faced him. The headline said simply: 'Dangerously incompetent?' In the body copy, one sentence had been repeated in large type: 'His contribution to the industry's dialogue with government has been at best lightweight, at worst gravely naïve.'

He read the story fast, his eye moving quickly across the page in a practised sweep in search of his own name. There was no mention of it.

'Ooh, Mick, I do believe you're right. She's done us proud.'

She'd got the lot; he picked out phrases and read them aloud. 'Senior television sources this week were querying just how effective Nik Kruger is . . . One senior source said Kruger should go back to management consulting where it's normal to be overpaid for incompetence.' Burrows laughed out loud. 'The TV business would be much better off without him . . . In particular, Kruger's position on family broadcasting penalties has attracted the anger of television professionals . . . Seems like everyone thinks he's a bit of an idiot.' 'Unless I'm much mistaken, all the quotes here are mine. I just went off the record – don't want it to look like a personal vendetta.'

'Do you think that'll shut him up?' Mick asked.

'I doubt it – but it might just make the rest of the world think twice before accepting that everything Mr Kruger has to say is pure undiluted genius. Especially the government, who should know better.'

'Mission accomplished then?'

'Mission very much accomplished, Mick,' he grinned, and read the piece again.

His cellphone rang. It was Phyllis Grigson. 'Quite a piece,' she said.

Burrows looked away from the paper for a moment. 'You haven't called to give me a wigging, have you, Phyllis?'

'No, of course not, Charlie. It is a little, shall we say, strong for my tastes, but I did manage to get hold of the journalist last night and tone down some of the more outrageous material.'

'I thought so,' said Burrows. 'You *are* telling me off. Look, I would have called you, but I had to do it then or wait weeks for the next possible slot.'

'That's fine, Charles, no harm done. When I spoke to Ms McGann, I did at least get assurance of your complete anonymity. But remember, it's a daily paper, and that's a lot of space to fill. Any time you want to be in there, just let me know. We won't have to wait for her to have a hole if we've got something to say.'

'Right you are,' said Burrows, enjoyment of his PR triumph now fully evaporated.

'Anyway the main thing is that you're happy with it.'

'Yeah, I thought it was fine,' he clipped.

Grigson stayed upbeat. 'And if this marks the first blush of a new-look media-savvy Chief Executive, then I shall be even more delighted to participate in the process.'

'Thanks, Phyllis.'

He put the phone down and returned to the piece. 'Can't believe it, Mick. Bloody woman called to tell me off.'

As they pulled up in Lancaster Gate, he looked in the mirror to relax his face, adopting the nothing-can-go-wrong smile they would expect.

When he arrived on the fifth floor, he found Martin Sumner hunched over a copy of the paper, with Paula leaning over his shoulder, reading the article.

'Bloody hell, Charlie, you really don't like this guy, do you?'

'You hear him on Duffy the other night? "Old dogs". Cheeky little bastard. Anyway, what makes you think it was me?' he said, his bravado ebbing a little.

'It's written all over your cherubic little face for one thing.'

'Really?' said Burrows, reorganizing his grin.

'Look, man, it's got your fingerprints all over it. Who are we supposed to think all these anonymous worthies are? A whole industry united in its loathing of Nik Kruger, and not one of them prepared to go on the record? If you ask me, this is a spectacularly lazy piece of journalism and every one of these quotes is from the same person. And who has the most to gain from Nik

Kruger being slowed down?' Sumner swept his arms around, indicating the offices they were in. 'Why, none other than Acrobat.'

Burrows walked around behind his deputy to read the piece again from this new perspective. 'Shit, is it that obvious?'

'Some of these phrases are classic Burrows.'

'Only to those who know you and love you so,' said Paula.

Burrows was distracted now. 'Thanks, Pol. Oh, that's not quite so bright then, is it?'

Phyllis Grigson arrived at 9.30. 'Charles, I'm afraid we have a problem.'

Burrows hadn't looked up, but the tone of Grigson's voice made him stop what he was reading. 'Let me guess – my *Times* piece again, Phyllis?'

Grigson swallowed and appeared to need a couple of tries before settling on the right words. 'Nik Kruger is dead.'

Burrows looked at her, his face begging for more.

'Yes, dead,' was all Grigson could manage.

Paula appeared in the doorway. 'Pol, not now,' he said; it felt as if waterfalls were cascading inside his legs as the belligerence of two days earlier returned to taunt him.

'Charlie, it's Carrie McGann – she says she's got to speak to you – something terrible has happened.' It was clear from her face that she knew.

'Oh no, no.' Burrows was numb. 'Put her on, Pol.'

He took the call.

'Yes, I know. I'm sorry . . . look, I'm here with Phyllis, can I put you on the speaker?'

The two of them gathered around the phone. McGann was crying.

By 10.30 a.m., Burrows had taken calls from most of the media and from the Chairman of Ofcom, who clearly had little doubt as to Acrobat's complicity in the 'disgraceful comments' about Nik Kruger. Some kind of aristocratic reserve prevented him from accusing Burrows. Instead, he seemed to gain comfort by rehearsing the dead man's strengths. Burrows agreed.

He had yet to return calls from the other newspapers, from Gerry Duffy, the presenter of the Radio 4 business news show, and indeed, from his own news room.

Hugo Trevethan, his Chairman, had called to say he thought the article had been very badly judged. 'Who the hell was responsible for it, Charlie?' he demanded.

Burrows's mind raced. This was too unpredictable and too sudden for him to risk confession so soon. 'It was a plan that originated in the PR department – I think it was the recommendation of our PR agency after they'd seen research that showed an upswing in Kruger's popularity.'

'What are you going to do? We've got to do something – I'd have thought it wouldn't lose us much to fire the PR advisers as a gesture?'

'If we start firing people, we just draw attention to ourselves. We should keep our head down. Right now, we are one of ten players who might have had it in for him.'

'But Gerry Duffy has already said on his radio bulletin that the signs are that the story came from Acrobat.'

'Where the hell did he get that idea?' stormed Burrows.

Phyllis Grigson was signalling to him in the doorway.

'Hugo, I'm going to have to go. I'll call you when things subside a bit.'

'All right, old man, good luck. I'll ring the non-execs – perhaps you could have Phyllis call me to give me the authorized version. And I'll put in a call to the Chairman of Ofcom.'

Burrows shuddered to think how Hugo would handle it, but the two chairmen were of an age and a background that seemed to simplify their communication. At least the old boy was ready to get his hands dirty. 'Phyllis is right here – I'll get her to call you when we're done.'

'All right, Charlie. Stay sane. Worse things happen in Russia.'

Still reeling from the banality of his Chairman's input, Burrows turned his attention to Phyllis Grigson.

'Charles, I think next on your call sheet should be Gerry Duffy. He's saying the comments came from here. He says it's a personal vendetta of yours.'

'We'll simply deny it then. He's just trying to cobble up a story.'

'No, we can't deny it, Charlie. I think you'll find he's done his homework,' she said apologetically. 'Um – he lives with Carrie McGann.'

'What? Oh fabulous. I don't believe this.'

'Apparently she's blurted the whole thing out to Gerry, and he's decided it's too big a story for him not to pursue.'

'I don't bel . . . Oh shit, Phyllis, why the hell did you get me into this?'

'Imprecise science, Charles – but let's spend our energies getting out of it, shall we? We'll do the post mortem later on. Oh, sorry.'

Paula's voice called from outside. 'Are you here for Gerry Duffy?'

Burrows and Grigson looked at each other.

'Yup. Stick him on,' called Burrows. 'Hello, Gerry, terrible news.'

'Terrible indeed,' clipped the journalist in his Cork accent. 'What can you tell me, Mr Burrows?'

'What can *you* tell *me*?' Burrows replied, more aggressively than he intended.

Duffy was nonplussed. 'I can tell you that Nik Kruger was killed last night on his way home. The police are working on the theory that he fell asleep at the wheel.'

'Oh, so you're not actually blaming me for his death, then.'

Duffy sniggered involuntarily. 'Why would I do that, Mr Burrows?

'Look, I don't think it's appropriate for me to say anything at this time.'

'Not asking you to, Mr Burrows. Off the record, were the views expressed in *The Times* a fair representation of your attitude to Nik Kruger?'

'Of course they weren't. The man's dead, Gerry. If you want a quote, we should be celebrating his achievements today.'

'Fine by me, Mr Burrows. I thought you wanted to stay off the record.'

'I do.'

'Only we know that the comments in the article yesterday came from Acrobat.'

'And how would you know a thing like that, Gerry?'

'Doing my job, talking to sources.'

'One source in particular, perhaps; one who ought to know better.'

Duffy spoke louder and more Irishly now, not so used to having to answer the questions. 'Look, if you're talking about Carrie, yes, we are seeing each other; yes, she is very cut up about what has happened; no, she has not told me her sources. However, I do know that she has been talking to people at Acrobat. I found that out via third parties.'

'All right,' said Burrows, writing on a pad as he spoke. *'He only knows the story came from Acrobat – not me.'*

'Maybe she knows the rules after all,' Grigson scribbled back.

'So, Mr Burrows, will you be hunting down the source of these regrettable statements?'

'Yes, of course. We shall take steps to ensure that our statements to the press are better co-ordinated in the future.'

'It's not so much a question of co-ordination though, is it? What we're talking about is the systematic bombardment of a competitor via the media. Do you think anything goes in your business, Mr Burrows?'

'I'll tell you what I think. I think your line of questioning is bloody close to the mark. The guy died in a car accident, not because he was *bombarded* by anything anyone said, in this company or anywhere else. It's a very competitive business – if you're going to be in it, you've got to be able to cope with criticism.'

'So you would condone the use of these tactics to damage a competitor?'

'Look, we're talking about a man with a wife and a

family. The consequences of this are much bigger than market competition.'

'He was a man with a wife and family yesterday too, wasn't he?'

Burrows slowed. 'Of course but . . . yesterday was just a day when we were all doing our jobs.'

'And that might include slagging off the competition.'

'Look, Mr Duffy, it's happened before in business.'

'All's fair in love and business.'

'No, actually I disagree with that strongly.'

'Ah, right. So would it be reasonable to assume that heads will be rolling, Mr Burrows?'

'You'll have to leave the conduct of this company to me, I'm afraid, but I give you my undertaking that this situation will now be properly managed.'

'Did you respect Nik Kruger, Mr Burrows?'

'Very much, yes.' Burrows was relieved to be able to say something big. 'The evidence was that he was making progress at Channel 6. He's put the channel on the map in a very short time.'

'Not surprising that he was rattling some people's cages then.'

'Probably not.'

'Sure.'

Burrows came off the phone. 'Well, thanks a lot for that, Phyllis. That was a truly terrific moment in my career.' He breathed deeply as he considered his next move.

Paula called from her desk, 'Charlie, Ray would like a word, says it's urgent.'

'When isn't it? Does he know what's happened?'

'Yes it's about that – he's been talking to the clients and wants to brief you on their reactions.'

'OK – send him up – and see if Mart's free at the same time, would you? I'm not sure I've got the strength for undiluted Ray Walker right now.'

Burrows could hear Walker making his way along the floor, his greetings to the PAs inappropriately light.

'Morning,' he said. 'All right if I join you?'

Martin Sumner slipped in behind him, aware of his brief.

Walker remained jovial. 'Well, that's one thing less to worry about, Charlie.'

Burrows looked aghast. 'Ray, the guy is dead.'

'Oh. I thought he was starting to get to you.'

Burrows laughed involuntarily, horrified by Walker's response.

'What makes you think that, Ray?'

'Stands to reason – new kid on the block, making a name for himself, painting the old guard into the corner. You're not used to that.' Walker paused to survey the damage. 'I'm not criticizing – no reason why you should be.'

'What's the view from the third floor then?' Martin Sumner re-directed the conversation.

'In short, the customers thought Nik Kruger was all right, but you know, life goes on. These guys are mainly interested in the price of their airtime. They liked where he was taking Channel 6, and no one thinks he's got a successor there, so they think the rise and rise of Channel 6 is now in question. In short, gentlemen, every cloud has a silver lining and I sense an opportunity here to get in behind the lines and pull back some of the money that's gone in to back his strategy.'

'Ray, man, you're a bloody nightmare.' Sumner rabbit-punched his shoulder.

'You can say that, Martin, but, come the year end, you're going to be wanting to know whether we took all the money out of this market that was there for us. Whatever nasty taste any of us has today will have gone when we see the revenue numbers in nine months' time. Unless anyone fancies telling the shareholders that we went soft as a mark of respect.'

'So, all is fine and dandy at the sharp end,' said Sumner.

'I'll let you know if anything comes up,' said Walker, as he bounced himself up off the sofa and departed.

'That guy,' said Burrows, looking at the floor and shaking his head.

'Is it just me, or was that "new kid on the block" bit just a little barbed?' said Sumner. '"You're not used to being the old guy painted into the corner . . ."? That's what he thinks you've done to him.'

'Ray really *is* one of the old dogs.'

Sumner snorted. 'That dogs business really got to you, didn't it.'

'I know it was just Kruger and his guerrilla marketing. But it's all calculated to undermine us. We're a young people's TV channel. It's incredibly damaging if people think Acrobat is run by a load of old duffers.'

'Kruger was playing to the gallery.'

'I know, but it sticks, that stuff. And you know what, Mart? We can't deny it.'

Sumner overacted his outrage. 'We're not that past it, are we?'

'Well, work it out. Two of our most senior executives are well on their way to sixty, and the average age of the board must be well over fifty. Frankly, Martin, even you and me are older than our target audience.'

'We're joost lads – don't worry aboot it, man,' said Sumner in his richest Geordie.

'I tell you, it bothers me more than Ray and all his bluster.'

'Yeah, well, don't you underestimate Ray Walker, Charlie. He never knows when he's beat. That's what makes him so good at his job. I tell you, Ray Walker goes to sleep at night plotting his comeback in Acrobat.'

'Well, there's only your job and my job for him to plot. I'll do you a deal. I'll make sure he doesn't get yours if you'll make sure he doesn't get mine.'

'Done,' said Sumner, shaking Burrows by the hand. He held his grip a little longer. 'Charlie, don't beat yourself up over this. It will pass, you know.'

Burrows let his hand fall to his side. 'I know. I'm just worried about what Duffy is going to say on the twelve o'clock news. That'll be the decider for how quickly it passes.'

Sumner nodded slowly. 'Yeah,' he said, thinking as he looked at the clock. 'I'll be back in ten.'

'And now the business news with Gerry Duffy.'
'Thank you, Kirsty. Tributes this morning have been pouring in for Nik Kruger, the Chief Executive of Channel 6, who was killed in a road accident last night. The police do not suspect foul play. Kruger, who was appointed to run Channel 6 six months ago, had created a name for himself very quickly in the highly competitive world of television. Sir Malcolm Ryan, Chairman of Channel 6, expressed the views of many people this morning.'

RYAN: *'We're all just stunned. Our thoughts and prayers are with Victoria and Joshua and little Amy this morning. Nik was doing a wonderful job for us and the whole company is in shock.'*

DUFFY: *'Hardly surprising then that competitors had launched a highly personal attack on Nik Kruger. Even this morning a national newspaper contained an unrestrained attack on Kruger, in which his professional competence was strongly challenged by anonymous rivals. Industry observers believe the source of these comments was Acrobat, Channel 6's arch rival. Earlier this morning, Charlie Burrows, the Chief Executive of Acrobat, assured me that he would personally conduct a full investigation into the circumstances of this very sorry affair and take all appropriate steps to deal with it.'*

'Did I say that?' Burrows bridled.

'This morning, questions are being asked about where the boundaries lie in acceptable competition. I spoke to Lord Markham, Chairman of Ofcom, who told me that on this occasion it had gone too far.'

MARKHAM: *'I think I speak for everyone in the industry in saying that the use of negative briefing to undermine competitors is not something we want to see. I would like to feel that Ofcom could play a constructive role in creating a more sensible level of rivalry.'*

DUFFY: *'Would you be prepared to reprimand stations you found to be involved in this episode?'*

MARKHAM: *'Well, I'm not entirely sure that we have a legal locus. But we are checking with our lawyers and we will take the steps we think are best designed to restore fair and effective competition.'*

DUFFY: *'Lord Markham, thank you very much. In other news today . . .'*

Burrows looked at his friend as he switched off the radio. 'Why, Mart? Why this? Why now? Haven't we got enough crap to deal with?'

'Not a vintage moment, for sure.'

Burrows spoke again with Hugo Trevethan, who reported that in his view the Chairman of Ofcom was in shock, horrified by Acrobat's role in 'this most tragic of dramas'. The fact that he had been the last person to see Kruger alive weighed heavily on him and appeared to be driving him to find a suitable way of expressing his distaste.

Trevethan's languid diction moved so much more slowly than Burrows's thoughts that he was able to fill in the spaces by coddling his anger at the stream of events which had put him in this position. One person was at the forefront of his irritation. And, what was more, this 'old dogs' thing needed managing. Not very bright to have a Communications Director pushing sixty in a company whose bread and butter depended on keeping it sassy for under-thirty-year-olds. Surely the person who represented Acrobat to this selective and opinionated target audience should share their instincts – at least be a member of their generation, for goodness sake. Fifty-whatever is a perfectly decent age to retire. The thought sat well with him: surprising, brave, opening new opportunities for younger people, change the dynamics among the senior team. Remove a Walker ally. It ticked some good boxes.

But seventeen years' service at Acrobat was a big deal.

There must be no hint that he had lost interest in the long-service employees. And this meant Phyllis, the duchess. Phyllis was without guile. It would be like hunting sheep. The plan was at best expedient, a long way adrift from the credo of corporate decency he had sold them all. He would talk to Martin but, despite the caveats, he knew he didn't want to be dissuaded.

He said goodbye to Hugo and, putting his feet on his desk, set out to explore his instincts. There was no doubt that the arguments he played to himself as to why she should stay were contrived, unimaginative. No one could criticize him for going that route: the conservative, status quo route. He hated that. His anger was much more compelling, spontaneous, authentic. Never react in anger. Yes, but this isn't a knee jerk, it's just the last straw. She's hung on so long that we never saw how off the pace she is.

The idea of a new hand felt good. It would be a nasty conversation, but that seemed to be his lot these days. Someone's got to do it. His distaste for his task was mitigated by the zeal of making rapid change, the sense that the City would applaud his resolve in the face of tough choices.

Kate Davies poured herself another cup of coffee. She hadn't imagined that life would be like this. She had worked at Acrobat in the mid-eighties when the company was founded. They'd been heady days, when all of them had lived and breathed and sweated the television station as it tottered into life.

For the people involved, it had been the time of their lives. When the day's work was done, they'd be together in the pub or they'd just open a bottle of wine around someone's desk. Outside relationships had given way to inside relationships and, like Kate and Melvyn, several long-term partnerships were founded. Back then, he was one of a gaggle of entry-level boys, a studio runner who decided to grow up for this sassy young woman. When he asked her to marry him, she laughed out loud, fixed him with her dancing eyes and, as he cast around for something else to say, she said, 'Of course I will.'

Kate had left to have their first son four years earlier, and she tried to stay in touch with the gradually dwindling band of friends who had been there at the start. As they all gradually, moved on to other lives, the sense that she was part of something unique dissipated. The birth of their second son drew her still further back into the home.

She knew enough still to discuss life at Acrobat with Melvyn, and she held strong, first-hand views on the main players. Yet he would madden her by saying, 'It's not like that any more.' She would try to stir the conversation but he'd protest that, since he spent all day and all night worrying about Acrobat, the last thing he wanted to do in their precious moments together was to keep going over it. She was sympathetic, but the deprivation had become a famine.

It was nothing new, she told herself; the plot of their life was just another dull old TV drama. She told herself it wasn't going wrong. He was fine . . . wasn't he? Same old Melvyn . . . wasn't he? Building a future for all of them . . . wasn't he?

Melvyn didn't seem to see it. Or maybe he did, but it wasn't urgent enough compared to the other things on his mind. Maybe he just didn't know what to do. Hide, and it will go away?

She absorbed herself in the kids and gnawed at the predicament that had progressively gripped her life. She knew she should say something, but the times they had to relax together were too precious to burden with something so leaden.

So she skirted it. If she talked about 'us', she did it gingerly so that he wouldn't be threatened. He wasn't, but he didn't pick up the hint either. It was as if he lived on the other side of a sheet of glass. They could exchange glances through it, but she couldn't touch him and he wasn't hearing what she was saying. And every failed attempt merely fogged the glass some more. So she stopped.

Phyllis Grigson had seen some trying days before, but as she gathered together her papers and a fresh cup of tea this was one whose end couldn't come soon enough. Charlie Burrows was on the phone when she arrived, and he waved her in.

'Celia, yes, I agree. But there's nothing I can do about that. We're into damage limitation now . . . yes, I'm just about to start a meeting with Phyllis now.' Picking up the mention of Celia Sharma's name, Grigson stood to attention and saluted, placing her dainty china cup of tea on his desk. Her antics annoyed him as he tried to ease his second largest shareholder off the phone without causing offence.

'Phyllis, sorry. Please.' He waved a hand at the chair by his desk. Burrows squared off some papers and cleared his throat. 'I have a proposition for you.'

'Oh really? What kind of proposition?' She wobbled her head.

'I don't want you to react to this immediately. Let me spell out the whole thing.'

'Fire away.'

He managed not to react to her choice of language. 'Phyllis, you and I see the role of PR very differently.'

She pouted. 'I suppose. That's normal with Chief Executives.'

'Yeah,' he said impatiently. 'Maybe hear me out, OK?'

'OK.'

'I have to communicate to you that the events of this morning are contenders for the award for "most embarrassing of my business life".' He looked at her for a reaction and she merely raised her eyebrows a fraction. Hearing him out. 'So the difference between us is that you like getting me into limelights I don't want to be in.' She said nothing. He started to feel stupid. Grigson clinked her ring on the china cup repeatedly. Burrows's frown went to the source of the irritation. 'Look, there's no point in padding it out. Call it strategic differences if you like, but basically this isn't working out any more.'

'What?' Now it was Burrows's turn to be silent. Grigson fidgeted distractedly. 'Was that what that cow Sharma was on the phone for? You're making me the scapegoat for this Nik Kruger thing?'

Burrows was expansive. 'No, Phyllis. This is not about Celia Sharma or Nik Kruger. This –'

'Really. Well, no one will believe that. This is about bad timing and bad briefing. No one could help the bad timing, but, unless I'm much mistaken . . .' she placed her index finger on her chin, feigning uncertainty '. . . the bad briefing was down to you.'

Her little act infuriated him. 'My point is, why was I put in that position in the first place? It was a flawed decision, Phyllis. It's always a flawed decision to go trying to cosy up with the bloody press.'

'No, Charlie. The press is there. You can engage with them or not engage with them, but they are still going to be writing about you, whether you love it or hate it. You remember that little old idea about free speech? That's why you need me: to make sure we talk to them on our terms.'

'Where were you when I needed you then?'

'I was . . .' Suddenly it dawned on her. She looked at him, pleading.

'You were in the pub.'

'No. Don't do this, Charlie. I realize how unpleasant this has been for you. Look, here's my advice. We keep our heads down and this will blow over. Never react on day one. It's always different in the morning. Tip from the old hand.'

'Phyllis, don't patronize me, please. This is not going to blow over. It is a question of trust. I'm sure you'd agree that the relationship between Chief Executive and Communications Director should be one of absolute trust.' She could see it coming. No way out. He squared up to her for his final line. 'I'm sorry to tell you that I feel that bond of trust has been lost.'

A tear made its way to the corner of her eye. He looked away, picking up a pen.

'I want to offer you a deal, Phyllis. No recriminations, but we set you up as Phyllis Grigson Inc., give you a guaranteed contract for a couple of years, and you get some flexibility and the chance to build up some equity for your retirement.'

She tried to place her papers gently on the table; they shook, grassing on her show of composure. Her chin trembled until she pressed her lips together. She drew herself up for her big speech.

'I've always tried to play this dreadful game with some degree of integrity. And up to this moment I've always thought of you as someone who would do the same. If I leave now, I leave with the blame for this appalling incident attached to me. I mean, I just wouldn't resign at a time like this. We have the annual results presentation next week, for goodness sake. Everyone will know I've been . . .' She swallowed the word, the awful F word. 'I, Charles, have spent thirty years in this trade, building a reputation as a professional, and I'm not about to trade you thirty years of impeccable reputation for two years of consulting.'

Burrows took out a handkerchief and tried to conceal the fact that he was wiping his brow as well as his nose. 'Look, we'll work on the terms together – we can make this work for you.'

'You can call it what you like, it will still add up to thirty pieces of silver.' The tear stood at the corner of Grigson's eye, like a sky diver, plucking up the courage to jump. 'No, I'm sorry, Charles, I'm not going to be party to your nasty little "get out of jail free card" ploy.'

Burrows laid down his pen with exaggerated care. This was it. 'Phyllis – I'm sorry. This is going to happen. The decision is made. We can discuss it for the rest of the night if you wish. You can be as rude to me as you like, but we're discussing how, not if.'

'And that's it, is it? That's your last word?'

'It is.'

Grigson held his gaze as she rose, then she raised her head and left the room.

Burrows followed her to the door, paused for a moment and turned right into Sumner's office.

'What was that about, man?'

Burrows slumped on to Sumner's sofa. 'That, mate, was the departure of Phyllis Grigson.'

'What?' Sumner threw himself back in his chair, linking his hands behind his head. 'You fired Phyllis? Bloody hell, Charlie.'

'I know.'

'For being old?'

Burrows looked sheepish. 'No, Martin. Not for being old. Irresolvable strategic differences.' Burrows recounted the story.

'So how have you left it?'

'I told her it's going to happen. It's all over, bar the shouting.'

'Phyllis won't shout. She's probably gone to cry.'

'Oh, thanks a lot, Mart.'

'Sorry.'

Burrows walked to the window. He sighed a long sigh. Quietly but resolutely he said, 'Sorry Phyllis.'

Within ten minutes Paula called out from outside Burrows's office, 'Charlie, you and Martin have an email from Ray.' Burrows and Sumner exchanged glances.

'That was quick,' said Sumner, turning to his computer screen. He skimmed the headlines, while Burrows looked out over the park. 'How lovely, Charlie. He's thoughtfully copied it to everyone on the board. Ray wishes to place on record his sense of disgust at what you've done to Phyllis Grigson. ". . . Loyal member of this company's staff and, as a matter of fact, she has been since long before you joined it yourself."' He read on, bobbing his head to suggest familiarity with the style, or great boredom with the content. "'Shafted her to get yourself off the hook with *The Times* . . . exhibiting more panic than leadership . . . Never seen such a brazen stunt and, believe me, I've seem a few in my time . . ."' Yes, Ray, I bet you have. I bet you have. Oh. And here we go, here's the punch line. "Reinstate Phyllis."'

'Or what?'

Sumner looked up. 'Or nothing, actually.'

'Oh. Not like Ray, is it? Normally he's got some devastating threat to ensure we take him seriously.'

Sumner walked across to join Burrows at the window. 'We have to assume Ray's a hostile witness. And God knows who he's talking to. I think I'd better go and have a word or two with our friend Mr Walker right now.'

'Yeah. Shut him up, will you, Mart.'

One hour later, Martin Sumner leaned into Burrows's office, his tie wrenched down and his collar unbuttoned.

'Good God, Mart, I said shut him up, not beat him up.'

'Just looking the part, Charlie – think it works? It's my "Don't jerk me around" look. Professional, with a twist of menace.'

'I personally am terrified,' said Paula from her desk outside.

'You personally can shut up,' laughed Sumner as he closed the door.

'How d'you get on?' Burrows slumped on to a sofa.

'Well, as we might have anticipated, Ray's high dudgeon is only partially to do with the injustice perpetrated against his bosom pal.' Sumner perched on the window sill.

'Really? What else does this have to do with him?'

'Oh, absolutely nothing, except the opportunity it presents for Ray to stride on up to the moral high ground.'

'The moral *high* ground. Ray Walker missed the turning for the moral high ground about forty years ago. What's he saying?'

'He's saying that the awful truth is known by just the three of us, plus Phyllis and the journalist.'

'And the journalist's bloody journalist boyfriend.'

'He's saying that it's for the three of us to rope ourselves together at a time like this as the three senior directors of the company.'

'What about Merlin? We do have a Programme Director. And a Finance Director, albeit one plugged into the mains in a hospital somewhere.'

'Yes, Ray has thought about this. He thinks Phyllis Grigson will be all right. And he has reckoned that this should be a moment which draws us three together as a management team.'

'And Merlin and Henry.'

'Or not. Ray thinks there's no reason to tell them. And, as Commercial Director, he would see no reason to share what he knows with anyone.'

Burrows swore under his breath. 'Commercial Director, what does that mean?'

'Apparently it's better than Sales Director.'

'Yes, but does a Commercial Director have any

enhanced purpose?' Burrows clunked his feet on to the coffee table.

'It's a Sales Director with a strong negotiating position, I suppose. He thinks that while Henry's recuperating, he ought to keep an eye on the film project.'

Burrows shrugged. 'Actually, not a bad idea. Ray fits right in with those bandits in Hollywood. What do you think?'

'Me? I'd tell him to stick it where he doesn't shave.'

'And what will he do then? We can't let him leave right now.'

Burrows noticed Sumner's raised eyebrows. 'Well, we'd *love* to let him leave right now, but we can't *afford* to let him leave right now.'

'What we'd also love is for Mr Walker to use his considerable influence to help Mrs Grigson make the right decision.'

Burrows snorted and placed a hand on each temple as he shook his head. 'Can we really not fire the bastard?'

'. . . he asked rhetorically,' said Sumner.

'I'll have 'im, Mart.'

'Tell him no. If you cave in to this, he's got you.'

'Yes, but if this would bring Ray on side . . . really on side, I'd do it in a heartbeat.'

'Leopards and spots, Charles. Ray is Ray. You can call him what you like . . . call him Master of the Universe, and he's still not going to change.'

Burrows got to his feet, joining Sumner by the window. 'If we made this conditional on a fundamental change to Ray's approach?'

'Doesn't work, does it? We cave in to Ray's demands to buy his team spirit?'

'Look, at this stage in the day, I don't think we've got a lot of options.'

'It's a knee jerk, Charles.'

'It's moving decisively to bring Ray inside, resolve Phyllis and avoid a press tomorrow morning that will wipe ten per cent off the share price, jeopardizing everything we're trying to do here. Come on, Mart, let's just get on with it.'

In the end it was going to be Burrows's call, and Burrows had made it. 'Right, so Mr Walker has a deal, does he?'

'I think he does, but with conditions attached.'

'I'll pass them on. Board approval?'

Burrows sighed 'Oh God, we haven't got time. By the time we've rounded them all up for a conference call, we'll have lost tomorrow morning. I'll sort it later. Just do it.'

Thirty minutes later, Sumner was back.

'Congratulations, Mr Chief Executive. You have a new Commercial Director who, as one of the three senior directors, sees the seriousness of the PR snafu we face and will use his considerable influence to help the former Communications Director make the right decision.'

'God, that's awful.'

'Save it for the memoirs, Charlie. Right now, it's working.'

At five o'clock, Paula tapped on the window and entered with an envelope addressed to Burrows written in brown fountain pen ink. She whispered, 'Thought you might want this straight away.'

It was handwritten on expensive personalized note-paper.

Dear Charles

I never thought I would have to write a letter like this. I should start by saying that since you joined the company I have very much enjoyed working with you, and hope that I have been able to give you good service.

I had hoped that such a relationship would have assured my continuance in post until my retirement in five years' time. I realize that the game belongs to the younger generation now, but I felt there was a place for experience, especially in a field like Public Relations, which is so fraught with minefields for the unwary.

It is because of one such minefield that I find myself in this position. You are right in saying that only two of us spoke to the journalist involved. I have to point out that my involvement was after the event. Had I not intervened, the article would have been clearly attributed to you. It is ironic to reflect that, had I been less professional, it would have been impossible for you to have made me the scapegoat for your own serious error of judgement. I shall have the dignity of knowing that I at least did behave properly to the end.

I wish to record that our conversation today was one of the most disappointing of my professional life. What should have been a dialogue between colleagues was a panic reaction from a frightened and inadequate leader. It was clear that nothing I said could affect the decision that had been taken in my absence and conferred upon me. Foolishly I thought I knew you better as a friend and colleague.

I realize the inevitability of my position, but I do not propose to creep away subserviently. I have taken legal advice and am of course aware of my rights. My case for unfair dismissal is beyond doubt. More importantly though, I am also aware of the damage I could cause to you and the company should I opt to take a more aggressive route. Your long-term reticence to deal with the media in any form would not work in your favour, should we find ourselves in conflict in the public domain.

The value to Acrobat of my silence is, I believe, quite high. I wonder if you would put the same figure on it as that agreed between myself and my advisers. My lawyer will call you at noon tomorrow. Unless we are satisfied with your offer, we will go public with the truth. Please don't imagine that this is in any way negotiable.

I will also want prior sight of the press announcement you will inevitably make, and a signed undertaking that neither you nor any of your employees will brief the media in a way that would change the tenor of the agreed release. This is not my favoured route, but please do not doubt my preparedness to take it. My reputation is worth a very great deal to me.

Despite the current circumstances I wish the company well. One cannot pour seventeen years into the success of an enterprise without hoping the best for it. As for you and me, I don't know whether we will find a way to put this behind us. Time may be a great healer, but right now I find your actions unforgivable.

Yours, Phyllis Grigson

Burrows passed the letter to Sumner. As he read it, Sumner said, 'Wonder if her old mate the Commercial Director helped her to arrive at the same figure as she dreamed up with her advisers. Want me to deal with this?'

'Actually, Mart, I can't think of anything I'd like more. Just make it nice and legal and we can get on with our lives.' Burrows swept a little sweat from his top lip and disappeared behind his hands. 'Just go and do us a classy deal, show me a press release, shut Ray up and everything I have is yours.' He emerged blearily. 'Well, I'll buy you a beer.'

Sumner strode to the door. 'On my way, boss.'

Forty minutes later, Charlie Burrows considered the deflated figure of Melvyn Davies slumped on his sofa. Despite the course of his day so far, he had chosen to ride out the flow of Davies's anger for the last half-hour.

'Look,' he suggested, 'what happens if we do the new Solveig show, exactly as you've planned it – just postpone it for a month or so, which will get us through this government review as well?'

'And what? Cobble something together from scratch for next week?'

'That's when Southern Foods want to launch their coffee. At eleven o'clock at night.'

Davies drew both hands down his face, pulling it into a mask.

'Cometh the hour, cometh the man, Melv.'

'I don't believe you're doing this to me. Again. All the bloody City presentations in the world aren't going to make the ratings any better if you don't back me, Charlie. Last week, all right, a million quid is a lot of money, but we said goodbye to a ratings winner, and you see what's happened? Everybody's head has dropped because we just sent them a message that Acrobat can't afford the best. And now, just in case they still believed in us, here we are again . . .' He slapped the table. 'It's a creative business, Charlie, for God's sake. It succeeds or fails on our ability to make great creative decisions around great creative people. But all that's just words words words as soon as the money men get involved.' Davies checked himself with a sigh. 'You make my job impossible, Charlie.'

Burrows sighed. 'I don't like any of our options, Melv.'

'But this is the one you're choosing, right?' He looked at Burrows intently. They both heard the defeat in Davies's tone. They both knew he'd lost.

'She's said "No" to Channel 6, hasn't she?'

'Sure. Based on a set of promises which I'm about to whip away from her so bloody Ray doesn't have to have a grown-up conversation with Southern Foods. There are other Southern Foodses out there – I promise you there are not many Solveig Nilsens.'

'I know, Melv. I'm really sorry. It's a horrible call, but right now I don't think we dare run the risk of turning off the Southern Foods money. I need good news for the results announcement, not . . .'

'Not doing the right thing.' Davies picked himself up out of the sofa, like a man with a second marathon to run, said, 'Fine,' and started his miserable walk to the door. 'Fine.' He turned towards the lifts and picked up his pace. 'Thank you, Sarah. Thank you, Ray,' he breathed in time with his strides.

On the way home in the car, Burrows talked about his day with Mick Spring. Georgia had phoned to say she wasn't cooking anything, so would he meet her at the Indian restaurant down the road from their house. Mick was a good listener. He held strong views on everything, especially Arsenal FC, national politics and life at Acrobat, enthusiastically passing on the meanderings of grass-roots opinions in exchange for a good debate on the activities of the day.

In the restaurant, Burrows had just sat down, idly noticing how far Georgia had got down a bottle of white wine, when his mobile phone rang, eliciting looks from around the restaurant, none more irritated than his wife's.

'Can't you ever turn that bloody thing off?' she breathed as Burrows frowned, holding up a placatory hand.

A conspiratorial voice with a thick Slavic accent said, 'The climate in Smolensk is outstanding at this time of year. No?'

'Mart, what you got?'

'I'm faxing a press release to you now, agreed with an ex-head of PR, with a three-year deal at fifty grand a year and a severance of another seventy grand.'

'How much is that?'

'Two hundred and twenty grand.'

'Excellent. What's the bad news?'

'The bad news is that I have had to let down a very pretty young lady in the worst possible way for this. But don't you start concerning yourself with my private life. Phyllis is all done and dealt.'

'Sumner, you're a gem. What would I do without you?'

'You'd be hopelessly stuffed, Charles. Just don't fiddle with the press release. We're absolutely on the deadlines. You've got about twenty-five seconds to read it.'

'All right. Look, Mart, I'm not at home. If you think the release is OK, just let it go.'

'Your wish, etc.,' said Sumner and hung up.

'Thanks, mate,' said Burrows to the empty line.

Georgia adjusted her head a fraction to indicate that she was waiting for his attention, that she was cross, that she wanted to know about the phonecall.

Burrows held both hands up in submission 'Sorry,' he said. Work over.'

'What did Martin want?'

'Oh you know, stuff . . . Anyway, tell me about your day. Learnt Spanish yet?' He looked up cheerily to a face that was far less certain than usual.

She returned his look with no confidence. 'What was Martin saying?'

Burrows looked into her eyes to see if he could escape this. There was something there he didn't recognize. 'I fired Phyllis today.' Put like that, even he found it shocking.

Again she moved her head to convey so much: shock, outrage, injustice, why hadn't he told her? She coughed and said only, 'I'm surprised you didn't say.'

Acrobat's closing share price   502p

Friday, 5 March

The sky was huge, blue, a hallelujah morning, as Burrows closed his front door on a sleeping Georgia and marched to his car. He barely said hello to Mick as he grabbed *The Times* and tore open the paper. In the companies section he found the headline he feared.

'Oh bugger,' he breathed.

Acrobat Off Balance

CARRIE MCGANN

Industry watchers yesterday expressed surprise at the timing of the sudden departure of Acrobat's veteran PR campaigner, Phyllis Grigson. The move comes just one week ahead of the company's full year results announcement, an event which would normally demand the full attention of the company's spin machine. All the more this year as analysts will be asking tough questions about declining audiences and revenues in the face of aggressive competition from Channel 6.

Acrobat management was involved in an embarrassing climb down just yesterday as a war of words ended suddenly with the death of Nik Kruger, Chief Executive of Channel 6. A spokeswoman for Acrobat said that Ms Grigson's departure was unrelated to these events.

One insider said, 'This is at best mis-management, at worst panic. There are enough questions surrounding

97

this company right now, without begging more.' Phyllis Grigson was unavailable for comment.

He arrived at his office at eight. His PA, Paula, was already in. 'Charlie, there was a voicemail from Sylvia when I got here. Ray seeks an urgent meeting at your earliest convenience.'

'I wonder whether it's OK with Ray if I take my coat off first.'

'You know Ray. They're always "urgent", even when they're not. Want me to fix something up?'

'No, not in the least, thanks. But since I am a professional, how about after lunch some time.'

He picked up the presentation drafted by Melvyn Davies for the analysts' meeting. He spent some time on it, making pencilled suggestions, but it was good. It hit the big questions and he could see Melvyn delivering it, swaggering back and forth across the stage. It would be a performance he could count on. He sketched out his own charts.

At two o'clock on the dot, he heard Ray Walker arrive at the end of the floor, his bonhomie overflowing with the ladies as he swayed towards the Chief Executive's office.

Paula stage-whispered from outside, 'Bandits two o'clock.'

'Hello, Paula, shall I go in?' said Walker as he arrived at Burrows's office.

'Charlie, Ray is here,' Paula called sweetly.

'Afternoon, Ray.'

'Seen the press today?'

'Yep. What do you think?'

'I think it was a difficult episode that has been resolved

as well as can be expected,' Walker blustered as if reading an announcement.

Burrows looked up at him and pulled off his glasses. 'Some damaging words in there, Ray.'

'Ignore 'em. They make most of them up.'

Simple. Done and ditched in the Walker way. Burrows almost admired the man's approach. Nothing too complex. 'So, we're back in the team, are we, Ray?'

Walker responded as if there had never been any doubt about it. 'I hope you're happy with my contribution to resolving the Phyllis Grigson situation. Can I say how much I'm looking forward to fulfilling my new role.'

'Sure, Ray, no problem. I hope Martin made it clear that this is a move that is designed to improve the team play in Acrobat. We are not going back to the games that used to distinguish this place seven years ago.'

'Well, thank God for that. As you know, I hate that political stuff. I just want to get on and do my job.'

Burrows missed the rhythm of his rejoinder, but opted not to say anything difficult. 'I'm delighted to hear it, Ray – me too.'

As she went down the stairs at the end of Friday, her mind satisfying itself that she had done everything necessary to take the weekend off, Sarah Golanski paused at the first floor. She turned and pushed through the double doors into the Programme Department. She leaned around the cabinets and pot plants, not surprised to see Melvyn Davies still at his desk. She made it to the doorway of his office before he spotted her.

'I just came to say "Thank you",' she said.

Davies looked up, unprepared. 'Thank me? What for?'

'For bailing us out on the Southern Foods front.'

'Oh that.' He pulled a face.

'I know Ray can be heavy-handed, but that account means a lot to us, and we had really gone in hard to get it. It would have been a nightmare to have had to tell them we couldn't deliver on our promise.' Davies stirred. She continued before he could speak. 'But I know the effect of it was that you had to go back on *your* promise.'

'Well, don't thank me. I was just obeying orders. If it had been my call, we'd be running the show at nine thirty next week. Presented by Solveig Nilsen.'

'I know, and I just want you to know that I appreciate it was a really tough call. Perhaps I could buy you a little drink on behalf of the Sales Department?'

Davies looked up, surprised, considering his response for too long.

Sarah Golanski's infectious laugh betrayed a trace of embarrassment. 'Not that hard a question, I hope. Just a friendly drink.'

Davies looked at her intently. The woman who had defined herself as his enemy hours earlier was here to shake his hand before he had put down his sword.

'Will Ray be there?'

'No no no, certainly not . . . unless you'd specially like him to be.'

He looked at her for the first time, and she smiled.

'What, now?' he said.

'Now.'

'Mitre?'

'Anywhere but,' she said.

*

Melvyn Davies had worked his way to the top over fifteen years at Acrobat and had been its Programme Director for the last seven. When he made it to PD, his wife Kate had granted him a short honeymoon, and then asked him to slow down. It wasn't as if she didn't understand. She had worked there. She knew the pressures in his life. But now she reasoned that working all hours, looking knackered and falling asleep at dinner parties was a package they'd endured in pursuit of the dream. She hoped she'd been supportive but, now that he'd made it, it was time for him to re-think the balance.

Davies agreed with the logic, and he aspired to the nobility of rewarding Kate's sacrifice with his own. At the same time, he wondered how the hell he was supposed to succeed as Programme Director of a major national TV channel while reducing his hours at work. But his hunger for the affirmation of his wife had made him agree that he would make a new start. Seven years on, the new start had been routinely pre-empted by crises, emergencies and celebrity tantrums that muscled his resolve out of the way.

Kate's admiration of her husband's achievements was gradually but inexorably subdued by the distance between his words and his choices. Beneath the still-friendly routine, an emotional fault-line was torn. Davies knew it, but he never acknowledged it and turned further into his work to make up the approval deficit. At the studios, his poise under pressure and his ability to make great judgement calls when the arguments were evenly stacked had earned him the title 'Merlin', which he pretended embarrassed him. No one really understood the alchemy that took place on the first floor, but from cash and talent

Melvyn Davies created their station. There, he was every-body's hero.

When the directors faced the twice-yearly interro-gation of analysts and journalists at the results presenta-tions, they would invariably be asked about the length of the contracts of the major stars and presenters, especially Dennis Milligan, news anchor and national celebrity. Charlie Burrows would think to himself, *Wrong question – you should be asking how long is Melvyn Davies's contract.*

Meanwhile, Kate busied herself with her boys and tried not to think about the earthquake that would surely come.

She was watching the late news when she heard the car door in the drive. There was a rustling and a slam as he shovelled his bags into the hall, and her husband appeared at the door.

'Hello, love,' he said.

She jumped to her feet, reaching up on tiptoe to put her arms around his neck. 'Hi, sweetie – yuk, Mr Smoky.'

'Oh, sorry, went to the pub for a quick one on the way home.'

Kate felt a pang of loss. Despite his distraction, she waited for him to come back each night. A little adult conversation.

'And how are they all in the Mitre?'

'Oh, you know – same as always – review of the week that was.'

'Well, it's the weekend – fancy a glass of wine?'

'No thanks, love; bit knackered. Got to go in on Sunday to rehearse the results presentation.'

Kate paused for a moment. They both heard it.

'Right.'

He dropped on to the sofa beside her, picked up the

newspaper and was immediately seduced by the television.

'Anything on you want to see?' she said.

'Not really.' He flipped the channel to Acrobat.

'Terrible about that Nik Kruger, isn't it?'

'Yes, awful.'

'Did he have kids?'

'Yes, I think so.'

'Oh, how terrible for his wife. Do they know what happened?'

'Um, sorry?' Davies had got involved in something on the TV.

'Come on, Melv – do they know what happened to Nik Kruger?'

'I think the police are saying that he fell asleep at the wheel of his car.'

'Not poisoned by Ray Walker for being too successful, then.'

Davies snorted mirthlessly. 'Ray Walker – what an arsehole.'

'He been a pain this week?' she asked.

'Ray can't help but be a pain. It's the only act he knows. He got Charlie to make me postpone Solveig Nilsen's show this week.'

'Postpone it? What did Solveig do?'

'She went ballistic – perfectly understandable, really.' He didn't take his eyes from the screen.

'What's Charlie playing at? I know you think I'm a scratched record, Melvyn, but he really does take you for granted.'

'I don't know. He's got me speaking at the analysts' meeting next week. It's good profile for me.'

'What do you need more profile for? Everyone knows who you are. He doesn't want to confront Ray Walker, that's all. Ray fights dirtier than the rest of you, so Charlie just goes further out of his way to keep the peace.'

'Charlie thinks Ray's a nightmare too. Won't do him any good in the long term.'

'Not done him any harm so far, has it?'

'Well, Ray is Ray, and I'm me.' There was a note of finality in his voice.

She paused.

'I'm doing all right,' he concluded.

'I know you are, sweetie. But you work too hard.'

'Tell me about it.' He folded the newspaper decisively. 'Well, those little monkeys will be up at about seven o'clock looking for Superdad, so why don't we get to bed?'

Again the pause was too long.

'Sure,' she said.

Acrobat's closing share price   492p

The Weekend, 6–7 March

For a couple of years or so, Henry Fleming had been bored with being a Finance Director. He was good – very good; everyone agreed that Burrows had done well to lure him from KPMG into Acrobat. Fleming had taken the challenge six years ago and had been a major part of the company's strategy since then, maintaining strong relations with the banks and running Investor Relations for Burrows.

At fifteen stone, he knew he was too heavy for five foot nine, so he was a regular subscriber to the succession of dietary discoveries. He bought the books, but they bored him and he would scrabble through them at weekends, before being distracted by the weekend newspapers or the bundle of work he had brought home from the office. He'd then attempt to put into practice whatever headlines he had picked up in his trawl through the latest book. However, for Henry Fleming, lifestyle tended to outweigh the heavy breathings of the health police.

Fleming had become increasingly bothered that the cost of movies to Acrobat was growing so fast. The new channels used movies as bait for the floating viewers and so the price of film packages from the Hollywood studios had been bid higher and higher.

Melvyn Davies reckoned that the schedule needed a major A-list movie at least once a month, with decent fillers for Sunday afternoons and late night. So, as the company grew, Fleming reasoned that Acrobat should be using its additional scale to buy its movies better. He argued that by investing in their production Acrobat could own a stake in some great movies, prevent other channels from gaining access to them, and make some money into the bargain.

Recognizing the restlessness of his Finance Director, Burrows suggested he set up a study into the proposition, to weigh up the risks and benefits of Acrobat entering film finance. Davies had been an early convert because of the success enjoyed by Channel Four in supporting *Four Weddings* . . . and other British successes. Despite his preference to disagree with everything Davies wanted, Ray Walker liked the signal that Acrobat was punching its weight against the big players. Though Martin Sumner was highly dubious, Burrows authorized the search for some investment opportunities, to be vetted by the board, like any acquisition investment.

Fleming was delighted and fixed his first trip to Los Angeles for the week before Christmas. Despite constant teasing from his colleagues about clandestine dinners with potential leading ladies, he reported a generous welcome from Hollywood and a large number of possibilities and invites to return. Thrilled as he was by his new friends, ever the cautious accountant, he hired George Salzman, a Santa Monica-based consultant with a gleaming list of film credits. In January he had brought the first project to the board; it was a movie based on the life of Marilyn Monroe.

Sumner had been highly disparaging, saying he'd seen a hundred movies about Marilyn Monroe and why the hell did Fleming think this would be any different.

Fleming recited the lines of his colleagues in LA, that Hollywood had never given Marilyn the full works. He regretted attempting a phrase which had sounded so good on the lips of one of the Americans, that Marilyn Monroe was 'culturally specific but thematically universal'. Sumner never let him forget it, guffawing for weeks after.

However, a new book about her life contained stunning revelations about her relationship with President Kennedy and her influence on American foreign policy at the time. Fleming's partners had snapped up the rights to the book and, having attracted one of Hollywood's leading screenwriters, Scarlett Johansson was now interested in the part. Fleming had parted with his share of the costs so far on an assumption that Acrobat would pick up all rights for the UK. Kinostar, a German specialist film financing company, had won the rights for Continental Europe, and Buena Vista had picked up the US and rest-of-world rights. Fleming's partners now needed a green light from Acrobat.

It all had to happen very quickly. If they were not going to lose their screenwriter, he needed a nod within twenty-four hours, since Disney was after him for a project of theirs. And, of course, Ms Johansson had a million and one films to choose from. To stand even a chance of recruiting her, the consortium had to look keen, decisive and confident.

Burrows reasoned that, if nothing else, this would be a good learning project. He could limit its downsides, and the upsides were the moon. And it would keep his trusted Finance Director from running off to a new job. It felt like one of those neat arrangements that tick lots of boxes at the same time and which don't come along too regularly.

The board hadn't much enjoyed the speed of the decision-making process but accepted the business logic and were seduced by the potential upside of a successful movie. The involvement of Buena Vista and Kinostar, whose bread and butter was in film financing, reassured them. They approved it.

Incarcerated in his hospital room, Fleming was finally on the phone to Hollywood. He had fidgeted through the day, fretfully waiting for his partners on the other side of the world to wake up. He had the staff wheel up the phone to his bed, though the nurse made a fuss about it. Finally he got through to George Salzman at five o'clock on Saturday afternoon.

'Henry, hi there!' chorused Salzman.

'George, thank God I got hold of you.'

'I heard you were in hospital – you in good shape?'

'Yes, fine – just a routine thing. Where are we on *Marilyn*?'

'Good news all round,' trilled Salzman. 'That was a great call you made to buy out the Germans.'

'Have you spoken about that to anyone?'

'No sir. Not outside our group. Last time we spoke, you were pretty clear you didn't want me to do that. Is there a problem?'

'No, no problem.' Fleming wiped his face with a handkerchief. 'I've got to do a bit of back-tracking to get the wires straight.'

'Whatever you say, Henry. Hope you're not getting cold feet here?'

'No, of course not. I would have liked some time to talk it over with my colleagues, that's all.'

'I keep tellin' ya, and you keep hatin' it, but this business is not like that, Henry. If you can't make the judgement calls, they don't want to know you. Matter of respect, you know. In LA society, it's not who you are, it's what you can authorize!'

'So you made perfectly clear.'

'Henry, it's a slam dunk. The Germans got problems at home with their share price. Fine. Tough shit for the Germans. Happy day for the Brits. Believe me, this one's going to fly. And our partners like the way you operate. This is the stuff of a great long-term relationship.'

'Well, let's get through this one first. I have to square this away with my board. Gotta go, George,' he added hastily, putting the phone down and quickly trying to push it away from the bed before . . .

Maggie Fleming strode in through the door to the ward, a fresh bouquet of flowers in her arms. Her eyes had alighted on her husband long before she was visible to him. She marched to his bed, dumped the flowers on his lap, her eyes ablaze. She yanked the phone cord from the wall and walked out. 'I don't believe you,' she said without looking back.

On Sunday morning, Martin Sumner shared a coffee with the latest in a long and delightful line of 'accompanists' and dissected the business sections of several newspapers. Sumner's love of his job was a love of winning. He fed it by reading incessantly about companies, devouring the accounts of what went wrong at Enron, Marconi or Worldcom with a forensic fascination, determined to decant the learning from them.

Out of the office, he competed. He kept up with the

rugby from time to time, and he played squash twice a week. Saturday was golf and on Sunday mornings he was to be found in the gym, setting himself stretch performance targets. Since his time today was foreshortened by the directors' meeting at Acrobat, he drove himself all the harder, peering over at the speed on the running machine next to his and setting his own faster. He moved around the machines, enjoying the fact that he had to increase the weight on each before he laid into it.

And inside the office he competed. 'Show me a finishing line and I have to get there first,' he said. 'Doesn't matter what the race is. Doesn't even matter if it's worth racing. Winning is winning. It is its own reward.'

He was still sweating and his hair was wet when he arrived at the office for the meeting. Burrows, Davies and Walker were already there. The strangeness of the empty offices was heightened by seeing each other in polo shirts and golf pullovers in the boardroom. Paula was on hand to make the changes and keep the coffee coming, and a woman from the PR agency had been drafted in to monitor the messages in place of Phyllis Grigson.

They re-worked the charts and rehearsed Davies on his presentation; then they came to the Q&A sheet prepared by the agency.

'Who the hell is going to ask *these* questions?' said Walker with a forced laugh. The armpits of his designer polo shirt were soaked. Dandruff sat on his shoulders. It occurred to Burrows that Georgio Armani would be horrified at the fate of this garment.

The PR woman fanned the twelve-page list of questions. 'The point is not to guess the questions accurately, it's to get you ready for anything that may come up on Tuesday.'

'Or tomorrow, for that matter,' said Sumner, ripping the top from an innocent bottle of water. 'Not sure which is worse, the London analyst community on Tuesday or our own bloody board tomorrow.'

'Then why don't we make an attempt to generate the kinds of questions that actually *will* come up,' persisted Walker. 'Look at this . . .' He affected a haughty, educated voice. '"There are signs of an advertising slowdown in Europe. What is Acrobat's strategy in the event that it affects the UK?" Know my answer to that?' He pushed his head forward, making the most of each separate word. '"Mind your own fuckin' business," excuse my French.' He smirked, clearly enjoying everything his statement had said about him.

'They're not interested in your sales policy, Ray,' Burrows intercepted. 'They want to hear reassuring noises from the Sales Director about how confident he is about the revenue.'

'Commercial Director.'

Burrows pressed on. 'Southern Foods back on the client list – it's an invitation to talk in general about how things are going.'

'Commercial Director,' repeated Walker.

'Commercial Director,' confirmed Burrows.

'Thank you – don't want to get demoted quite so soon.'

'What's this?' said Davies.

Burrows caught a glance from Sumner.

'Shit, Melv, I meant to get to you about this on Friday. We've changed Ray's title to Commercial Director.'

Davies did not look at Walker. 'Congratulations, Ray.'

'Thanks, Melv.'

'Why?'

Walker sat a fraction forward in his chair. He looked at Burrows. The silence was minutely too long.

'I'm sorry I didn't get a moment to catch you on this, Melv. Ray's done seventeen years as Sales Director. He's clearly made a huge contribution to the company and I wanted to express that in a form of promotion for him.'

'Great,' said Davies. 'So what does it mean – in practice?'

'Right. It means that I'll engage Ray in some broader management issues from time to time.'

'Like what?'

'Well, while Henry's out, he's going to keep an eye on the *Marilyn* project.'

'Didn't anyone think I might have an interest in that?'

Walker chimed in. 'Obviously I won't be making a move without conferring with you.'

'Not like you, Ray . . . with respect.' He continued to address Burrows. 'So what does this mean for me?'

'Business as usual,' he responded. 'You're the man who makes the audiences turn up.'

Walker tried again. 'You don't want to be wasting your time on the colour of the filing cabinets and how many paper clips we need.'

'Neither do you, Ray – do you?' The tension gathered like humidity in the room, causing them all to breathe more deeply.

Summer tried his hand. 'Melv, the point here is that as Acrobat gets bigger it needs to spread the burden of general management responsibilities so that Charlie has time to think strategically and not get swamped with all the day-to-day crap. I think it makes sense to get Ray doing some of that, and no sense at all to take your attention off whatever it is you do down there.'

'And that's it?'

'That's it,' Burrows confirmed to nods all round.

'And when are we going to bring in the rest of the world on this?'

'I thought I'd add it to the presentation on Tuesday,' said Burrows.

'Well, that's great news then, isn't it.'

'Melv, I apologized.'

'All right we haven't got time to worry about this any more,' said Davies. 'Try and remember to keep me posted on what colour paper clips you choose.'

The laughter was appreciative and, as they relieved the moment with unfunny comments about filing cabinets, Burrows mouthed, 'Sorry,' to Davies. Davies didn't meet his eyes as he mouthed back, 'No problem.'

Monday, 8 March

The atmosphere at the start of Acrobat board meetings was always odd. The various agendas of the different shareholders and the management were held together like a bundle of sticks by a thin string of politesse, and the nervy chairmanship of Hugo Trevethan.

Trevethan was mannered, articulate and ineffective. He had been brought in before Acrobat went on air, but since the serious money had arrived he'd survived solely because of the inability of the major shareholders to agree on an alternative. Trevethan just wanted to be loved, but the company had grown up faster than his abilities to chair it.

Trevethan had no solutions for the stalemate between his two largest shareholders. Celia Sharma and Arnaud de Vigny matched each other blow for blow with intransigence. Sharma, a strong believer that nothing of merit is ever achieved by reasonable people, continued to insist that the shares were undervalued, despite the fact that Equitus's investment in Acrobat had grown in value by 50 per cent in the last two years. Her fund was enormously successful and each deal built Sharma's reputation, so the stage was set for a highly principled stand-off between the two largest shareholders, both of whom found the other frustratingly closed to reasonable discussion. The independent directors tried to help Trevethan, but they also recognized that this was a head-to-head at which they were merely spectators.

Trevethan hated it. 'I don't know, she just seems so unreasonable. Is it really necessary to be quite so obnoxious at board events?'

'Oldest trick in the book, old love,' Piers Carrick replied. 'Make yourself so bloody frightful that we all think it's worth a premium to get rid of the old hag.'

'It's so unnecessary,' whined Trevethan. 'I remember when this was a civilized board.'

'Well, she may spoil our fun a bit, but I don't see de Vigny losing a lot of sleep about that.'

'She'll be gone soon, I expect; I mean, she's made a decent return on her money and . . .' Trevethan dropped his voice as Celia Sharma bustled into the boardroom.

'Good morning gentlemen,' she said, placing a slender briefcase by her usual seat. Trevethan and Carrick came to attention, chorusing platitudes about nice to see you, the market, the weather. Sharma fended them off with practised diffidence and took her place for the start of the meeting. Burrows, Sumner and Walker arrived together and made their way around, shaking hands and exchanging greetings. Just as the meeting started, Melvyn Davies shambled into the room, whispering, 'Sorry,' as he tipped a bundle of papers and a laptop on to the table.

They worked through the normal business of the board, and as tea was brought in Davies connected the laptop to run through his presentation for the following morning. He elicited mainly nods, and a hubbub of approval when he finished. Sharma was ready to move on. She pulled up a page of printed notes.

'May I ask some questions on the announcement now, Mr Chairman?'

'Yes, I think we're just into that part now, Celia, go ahead.'

'Right. Firstly, the Chairman's statement is far too downbeat. After delivering a fifteen per cent increase in revenues and a twenty per cent growth in profit, there's a real momentum behind the company. I can see no logic in using words like "satisfactory" about future revenue growth, especially if you're hoping to keep the share price up for future acquisitions.'

'Ray?' Hugo Trevethan cued him in.

'I don't see anything wrong with it. We had some one-off benefits like the mobile phone wars last year, which we can't necessarily count on going forward. So let's not over-promise, eh?'

'Even so, the whole cut of this statement is drab and downbeat. Can't we inject a bit of life into it?'

Carrick interjected, 'Through the chair, Activa is satisfied with the statement, which we think achieves the right level of prudence at the current time.'

All eyes turned back to Trevethan, who smiled pleadingly at Sharma. 'Celia, your move?'

'I've made my point, Hugo. I recognize the particular agenda of Monsieur de Vigny, but I hope no one thinks that depressing the share price is in the interests of all the shareholders.'

Carrick slammed his pen down on the table. 'That, madam, is a disgraceful allegation. Chairman, I insist it be withdrawn before this meeting proceeds.'

Trevethan looked bereft. 'Er, right, yes. Well, Celia, that *was* a bit strong.'

'Then I withdraw it,' smiled Sharma. 'Seemed to touch a nerve, though.'

Carrick began a further objection but Roger Collier intervened hastily. 'Chairman, on the subject of the revenues, I do believe the statement could be lifted a little in tone without being a hostage to fortune.' He returned to pore over his liberally highlighted board papers.

'How about "firm"? Forward bookings are "firm" instead of "satisfactory",' Sumner suggested.

'Excellent suggestion.' Trevethan grabbed at the lifeline. 'Celia? Piers?'

'What does "firm" mean?' grumbled Walker.

'It means "solid", but less than "good". Think horse-racing,' suggested Sumner.

'Think turds,' said Carrick. 'Firm is good for me.' He glared at Celia Sharma. 'May we continue?'

And so they moved on, negotiating words, inserting phrases, removing others, until they reached the end. Hugo Trevethan attempted to stumble his way through his highly annotated sheet to give them all a flavour of what they had agreed.

Carrick spoke for everyone, 'Well, that's a pretty terrible piece of committee drafting. Hugo, can't we leave this mess with the management to beautify?'

'Er yes, fine by me,' said Trevethan, looking at Sharma.

'Right – can we see it tonight?' she said.

'Sure,' said Burrows. 'I'll work on it with the advisers and get it to you later.'

'I think we're giving the executives quite a lot to do in a short time,' said Trevethan. 'So, unless there's anything else on the results . . . Good. Thank you. See you in the morning.'

Acrobat's closing share price   449p

Tuesday, 9 March

Hugo Trevethan smiled apprehensively at the throng of analysts and tried to raise his voice above the babble. At the table with him, looking scrubbed but underslept, were Charlie Burrows, Martin Sumner, Ray Walker and Melvyn Davies. Burrows and Sumner had been recasting the statement and the press release till gone 2 a.m. Burrows had got to bed at 3 a.m. and been back in the office four hours later to start the press calls.

Trevethan tried again, tapping his glass with an expensive fountain pen. 'Er, ladies and gentlemen, it is now after 9.30 so, if possible, could we get started, please?'

The analysts resolved themselves into rows and Trevethan began.

'Before I read the Chairman's statement, I'd like to introduce the four members of the executive team up here with me, who are going to answer all the difficult questions.' Trevethan stopped and caught Burrows's eyes. 'At least, let's hope they are.' He laughed nervously at the silent audience. 'You will notice one absentee. Henry Fleming is temporarily preoccupied at St Thomas's Hospital but is making good progress, we understand, and will be back with us soon.'

He introduced the executives, each behind his name card, each acknowledging his name with a nod.

'So, without any further ado, I will now read the Chairman's statement.'

Trevethan embarked on the piece of prose on which so much time, energy and confrontation had been expended the day and night before. He then handed the meeting to Burrows, who presented the numbers and the strategy. Then Melvyn Davies stood up for his maiden appearance in front of this audience.

He was superb. He swaggered in front of the suits, speaking with authority and humour on culture, television, entertainment, the shows that turn out to touch a nerve or that are rejected by audiences. He showed carefully chosen clips, including parts of Solveig Nilsen's test tape, to laughter and even a ripple of applause from the analysts. Burrows watched him with a fatherly glint.

'I hope I can take it, then, that you'll all be watching Solveig's new show,' suggested Davies, now at ease with his audience.

'When does it start?' an analyst called out.

'It's a secret weapon,' replied Davies. 'I'm not going to give away its location till we're ready to nuke the enemy!' More laughter and, as Davies took his place at the top table, the applause of one analyst was picked up and made a sporadic journey around the room.

Burrows leaned over, making eye contact, and patted his shoulder. 'Bloody brilliant, Melv,' he said under the spontaneous chatter provoked by Davies's presentation.

Hugo Trevethan cheerfully organized his deck of charts, more confidently now, raising his voice above the hubbub. 'Right, well, ladies and gentlemen. That concludes the formal part of the meeting. We would be pleased to answer your questions.'

Marcus Newman was Head Boy in the analyst pack; he and his team usually walked away with the annual award for best media analysts. By dint of longevity, reputation and rumours of a gargantuan salary, Newman had the respect of his peers as well as of the Chief Executives of the media world in which he specialized. So, unless some usurper tried to challenge his status, he almost always got to ask the first question. He stood to his feet, attracting Trevethan's eye.

'A question for Mr Walker, please, Chairman. Ray, how do you react to signs of softness in the European markets? Is this a trend you'll be watching carefully?'

Walker spoke more formally than usual, upgrading his diction for this crowd. 'Of course, but I won't be losing any sleep over what's happening on the continent. There's no evidence that whatever is going on over there is happening over here and, as I say, we are satisfied with the shape of the market.'

Newman was not so easily fobbed off. 'I'm guessing that there was a certain amount of debate over a word like "firm". Not as good a word as "strong"? "Healthy" perhaps?'

Walker looked uneasy. 'I suppose not,' he said.

'You suppose not. So what does "firm" mean if you had to translate it to a spreadsheet?'

Just as he was starting to speak, Trevethan cued him in, 'Ray.'

He started again. '"Firm" means what it says. You know how difficult it is to predict future order books until we reach the advance booking deadline, but the signs are that, despite the loss of some dotcom income and other one-offs like the mobile phone wars, we will be in good shape this year.' His upgraded accent was slipping a little. 'You will have seen from the Chairman's statement that Southern Foods are back on – good news. They start again this week, as it happens – as sponsors of one of Melvyn Davies's new shows, which we're particularly excited about.'

Davies caught Burrows's eye for the briefest second, a silent reminder of the impossible task he had been set. Burrows pressed his lips together, raising his eyebrows and looking away.

'All right, Ray,' shrugged Newman, pulling a sceptical face but conceding the floor with a nod.

A young woman stood. 'Melvyn Davies's comments about "the enemy" are reminiscent of the remarks attributed to Phyllis Grigson last week. Is Acrobat feeling under siege?'

Trevethan laughed knowingly, if unconvincingly, but, rather than dealing with it, he passed the question to Burrows.

'We're not complacent about the level of competition for our audiences and revenues these days. And yes, it *is* a battle for ratings – I think all of our rivals would agree with me on that. But I think we are well positioned to perform highly competitively here.'

A young man wearing a boggling combination of striped shirt and spotted tie caught Trevethan's eye. He pointed to him. 'Yes please.'

'Mr Trevethan, would you like to comment on the rumours of changes to the ownership rules. What can you tell us about the company's perspective on acquisitions?'

Burrows launched in as Trevethan said, 'Charlie.'

'Yes, this is an important issue for us. The current rules have been in place for ten years and the government is making the right kind of noises about raising the limits.

Ofcom is in favour of relaxation, and the industry is united in the need to allow further consolidation if the UK is to be a significant player abroad. So I'm confident that we'll get the decision we need.'

'So this is on the government's agenda right now?'

'Absolutely, yes. We believe that the change to the legislation will be announced within weeks and, when it is, we'll be ready to take advantage of the new rules immediately.'

'Though with the level of debt you are carrying from your earlier expansion, you'll be hoping to finance any significant transaction with equity, surely?'

If the share price stays up, thought Burrows. But he said, 'We would have no qualms about using our shares.'

'Mr Burrows, can we hear from you on the film project you announced earlier in the year? What reassurance can you give us that this isn't going to be another black hole in Hollywood for shareholders' funds?'

Burrows laughed unconvincingly. 'As you know, Henry Fleming is handling this for us. We're all averse to black holes, but particularly Henry. In his temporary absence, Ray Walker will keep a watching brief for us.'

'Care to put a number on your maximum exposure?'

'We're just dealing with a single film at the moment – playing ourselves in with some care – and our exposure will not exceed twelve million dollars.'

'And in the context of the last question about debt, you have the cash for that?'

'Yes, we do.'

And so the questions wove on, many of them much the same from year to year, as the analysts pieced together the components of their spreadsheets to forecast Acrobat's earnings in the year to come.

Finally, Trevethan said, 'Good, I think we've got time for one more question . . . yes the young gentleman here . . .'

'Is the overreaction to the Nik Kruger thing last week evidence of a management under extreme stress? I believe there have been a lot of rows recently.'

The executive team looked at one another and laughed unnaturally.

Burrows picked up the question. 'I believe in hiring the very best people and then listening to their points of view,' he said. 'Yes, that certainly creates more opportunity for impassioned debate than if I told everyone what to think; but I happen to believe we make better decisions that way. If the fact that we have strong discussions among strong managers is behind your question, then yes, I guess we are guilty as charged.' He looked at the questioner defiantly.

'I don't think any of us have a problem with that, Mr Burrows. What I am talking about is the overnight eviction of a woman who has been in post for seventeen years. Doesn't look very poised to me, and I understand there is a growing level of squabbling among your department heads.'

'You're going to have to be more specific. I don't recognize the behaviour you describe. This management team is stable, secure and effective.'

The young man persisted. 'And very big. At a time when Acrobat is under heavy pressure from competitors, can it afford such a top-heavy management structure?'

Some of the analysts turned around to look at the aggressor.

'I mean, the companies who are after your revenues are very much leaner than you. Too many chiefs. I see you've now got a Commercial Director, whatever that means, and a COO. Why do you need a COO as well as the rest of this lot? He hasn't taken any questions today.'

Burrows didn't wait to be asked to reply. In an instant he connected with the anger aroused by the prodding of the questions, the implied criticism of his abilities. All the frustration of yesterday's board, Celia Sharma, Ray Walker. And now this little witling, who would have gone from school to university to this bank and never had to make any of the decisions he judged himself so well qualified to critique. 'Unless you know very much more than me about running a television company, you're going to have to trust me on that, aren't you. In fact, one of the competitive advantages that comes with some scale is strength in depth in the management team. For the record, Martin Sumner is an invaluable member of this management team, without whom you would expect this group to add considerably less value for shareholders . . .' Hugo Trevethan was nodding encouragingly '. . . as far as I understand it, my job is to take the decisions that add value for shareholders, not count the executives.'

Almost inaudibly the young man said, 'Ooh, touchy.'

A crab apple flush had emerged from Burrows's collar. He caught Sumner's eye.

'I think that really is it, ladies and gentlemen,' announced Trevethan. 'Of course the team will be here for any further questions you may have. If you have any detailed financial questions, Henry Fleming's deputy, Rishi Kapur, is here – be nice to him . . .'

The rest of Trevethan's words were lost as the analysts and journalists poured forward to cluster around individuals, as if gathering autographs from celebrities.

Charlie Burrows was exhausted. After the analysts' meeting he had spent the day visiting their largest shareholders and on the phone to journalists, lunch with the *FT*, a radio interview with Gerry Duffy, all of them digging away at his defences, applying the heat to his account of Acrobat's performance in the hope that impurities would float to the surface.

Burrows had developed an ability to show composure when all inside was ragged. But in the relative privacy of his office, the stresses and the sleeplessness that he had packed away into their individual compartments all coalesced into a cohesive, remorseless weight, like one strong hand pushing down on his chest.

Paula Conley watched him through the window. In the end she opened the door. 'May I make a humble suggestion?' she said.

'Go home?' said Burrows, without looking up.

'Well, you have had a bit of a big day. And not much sleep last night.'

'I'll go down to the studios, remind myself we're not in widget manufacturing,' he told her.

The phone on her desk rang.

'Want to escape before I get that?' He shook his head. 'It's our Mr Perrin from the company's stockbrokers.'

He sat on her desk. 'Hamish, how are you?'

'Share price is off twelve, Charlie.'

'Twelve p?'

'Twelve per cent.'

'Bloody hell, we weren't that bad, were we?'

'Concerns about long-term revenue vitality mainly.'

'Well, they brought that assumption with them when they walked through the door. Didn't we kill it?' Burrows got to his feet and tried to pace to the extent of the phone cable's tether.

'Apparently not. They've gone away with the view that you'll be hard hit if the Euro mini-recession crosses the Channel.'

'Morons. We dealt with that.'

'Yes, well, second there's the competition point. There remains a sense that, as the leading youth channel, everybody's after your audience and revenues.'

'Everyone's *always* been after us, Hamish. For God's sake, for as long as you've known us we've had some bugger chiselling away at our audience or our best people.'

'I know.'

'But here we are still – comfortably ahead of the pack in all our key markets.'

'They were asking questions about the management, too. Ray Walker nearing retirement, no successor for Melvyn Davies and no real news on the FD. Whatever that boy said about senior management conflict. The question about Martin's role got some of them thinking too.'

'Well, for fuck's sake, Hamish, they don't think very far, do they? How can we get whacked for no successor to Melvyn and for having a successor to me?'

'Logical question, Charles. It's more of a feel, I think. They've been a bit worried that the management hasn't looked quite as poised as usual. You heard the question this morning. They don't like Henry not being there – he's a very reassuring figure for them.' Burrows was silent, so Perrin pressed on. 'But I don't think it's a clearly defined thing – sometimes the market doesn't think entirely logically.'

'You can say that again.'

A moment's pause, then: 'Sometimes the market doesn't think entirely logically.'

Burrows burst out laughing. 'Why do I do this, Hamish? I bust my arse, day in day out, to build value for a bunch of gutless lemmings who just lap up the gossip of the day and mark the shares down . . . Was there much trading?'

'No, not really; we'll see what happens tomorrow. I'll call you end of day tomorrow when the market's had time to think about things a bit. We'll make a few calls and see how they feel with the benefit of a good night's sleep.'

'All right, Hamish, thanks a lot.'

Mooching back into his office, Burrows dropped on to his sofa, his mind kicking over his future strategy in light of the day's developments. Over the last seven years they had steadily built the audience share of Acrobat, borrowing hard to buy expensive programme packages of sport and films, but establishing a strong franchise with the younger viewers so cherished by advertisers.

But continued growth of this sort would get tougher as new channels established themselves. The new channels had bid the price of film and football rights so high that they were no longer the saviours of the schedule. There were no quick fixes for audiences any more. The top talent would continue to get more expensive at the same time as it would become increasingly difficult, even for Ray Walker, to command the kind of price premium that would satisfy the City.

Acrobat would need to find new sources of revenues and new ways to reduce its operating costs. The classic argument for acquisition. Hitherto, the government's media ownership rules had prevented them from buying another TV broadcaster, but the noises emerging from the government and from Ofcom signalled that a relaxation, allowing Acrobat to acquire some of its rivals, was coming soon.

Burrows and Sumner had worked hard with Henry Fleming on their options. They knew that when the regulations were lifted there would be a feeding frenzy as rival broadcasters raced to buy up the best stations. The principal target of Acrobat's affections was Charisma TV, a small TV broadcaster whose strength lay in its particular appeal to the more well-heeled viewer. Like young people, the well-off are a harder audience to attract and so command a cost premium with advertisers. Alongside Acrobat's youth appeal, upmarket little Charisma TV would be an excellent fit.

But here was the catch. Buying Charisma – or making any other acquisition – would demand a healthy share price and the confidence of investors. The timing was critical. Once the ownership rules were relaxed, a deterioration of Acrobat's share price would make it more likely that Acrobat would be prey and not hunter.

It was 8.15 p.m. In Studio 1, Acrobat's weekly news analysis programme was half way through. As the commercials rolled into the break, Dennis Milligan leaned back in his leather chair, joking with members of the crew as a woman headed for him with make-up brush poised. Here, beneath the brilliance of the lights, was the only activity in the building. With one exception. In the PR Department, seated at Phyllis Grigson's old desk, a solitary figure finished an email and clicked 'Send'.

Acrobat's closing share price   395p

Wednesday, 10 March

Phyllis Grigson pulled her feet up on the sofa with a cappuccino and the morning pile of newspapers. The ritual had been transferred from her office to her home. But where the overnight machinations of London's journalist population had previously set the agenda for her day, if anything they now emphasized its emptiness.

The calls to her mobile had begun at 8.30 last night. 'Just checking, Phyllis. Are you in Acrobat at the moment?' 'Interesting email Phyllis – is this the vendetta beginning?' She flatly denied them all. But this morning she knew what she was looking for. Her practised eye moved quickly down the pages of the business sections. The Acrobat pieces were not hard to find. Most had dredged up the usual forced headlines about Acrobat on the high wire, Acrobat juggling, playing with fire, she'd seen them all before. She made for the *Guardian*. It was the lead story in the Media section. *ACROBAT TUMBLES*. She breathed in a whistle.

Shares in Acrobat, the UK's largest specialist television company, fell 12 per cent yesterday after a turbulent meeting in which Charlie Burrows, Chief Executive, was pressed to defend accusations of management conflict at the company. Under pressure from analysts, a beleaguered Mr Burrows was forced to defend his management team against suggestions that pressure on revenues was creating an atmosphere of panic at the top. Defending the role of Mr Martin Sumner, COO, Mr Burrows described him as 'an invaluable member of the management team, without whom the group would add less value for shareholders'. An internal source, who declined to be named, described the management of the company as 'dysfunctional' and 'drawing up internal battle lines'.

Acrobat was reporting profits up 20 per cent on revenue growth of 15 per cent, but analysts do not believe that this level of income growth can be sustained if the European slowdown spreads to the UK.

It was the same story in the others. The journalists had all relegated the financial results to the second half of their articles in favour of Burrows's loss of cool under questioning and the stories of management dissent. Phyllis sipped her coffee, imagining the overdrive at the office. She surveyed the scene of newspapers around her feet, harbouring a wash of satisfaction at their workmanship.

Burrows took the call from Hamish Perrin at the stockbroker's at four thirty.

'They're a bit spooked, I'm afraid.'

'How bad?' said Burrows. 'I've been in shareholder meetings all day, so they've all told me we've been slipping. Where did we finish?'

'Three eighty-one.'

'Shit.'

'I know. Not so bad today, but it's 15 per cent over the two days.'

Burrows breathed heavily, the anxiety clawing at his insides. 'Where's this coming from, Hamish? Just because somebody blabbed something to a hack doesn't mean the company's on its knees.'

'No, well, it didn't help. Not much new to report, really. Tricky analysts' meeting. Nasty press would have hit the smaller shareholders today. It's a case of no good news, and they've worked through the implications of a recession to your bottom line.'

'But there is no recession.'

'Really? No signs at all?'

'Not as far as we can see. Look, I'm talking to Ray about this later. Let me see if we can create some good news.'

'Charlie, be careful. Let's talk before you release anything.'

'Of course, Hamish.'

'You've got some pretty pissed-off shareholders out there today.'

Mick Spring dropped Burrows, Sumner and Trevethan at the Savoy for the monthly gathering of the good, the great and the also-invited at the Media Business Club dinner. They checked their coats into the cloakroom and fanned out into the throng. Melvyn Davies watched his guest, Dennis Milligan, perform for a crowd of worshippers, clustering around him so they could drop into the conversation the next day that they'd had a chat with the man himself. For Milligan, three was a crowd. And a crowd was an audience. Burrows watched the Kodak smile fix itself on his features and knew that the friendly Irish gags would be turning into a routine – funny once or twice, but pretty dull ever after. By the bar were Ray Walker and Sarah Golanski, his guest, transformed from her navy business suit into a simple black gown. The two of them were engaged in the evening's business of working the room together.

Burrows pulled Sumner to the side of the crowd and said, 'Our Ms Golanski seems to be turning a few heads tonight.'

Sumner looked across to her. 'Very nice,' he said.

'So what do you think, Martin? Are we looking at Ray Walker's successor, you think?'

'One day, for sure,' said Sumner, 'but she's still got a way to go, don't you think?'

'She's bloody good, Martin. If we don't do something with her soon, she'll just get snaffled.'

'Yeah, but we still need a grown-up. She's certainly a little easier on the eye than Ray though, I'll grant you that.'

'Gentlemen, may I just interrupt for a second?'

The two turned abruptly as if caught in the act, to find the distinguished figure of Sir Malcolm Ryan, Chairman of Channel 6, standing behind them. Ryan was an impressive figure, well over six foot tall, with the tall man's stoop. Though well into his fifties, his hair was still dark grey and his face had the rugged features of the classic adventurer.

'Malcolm, hi,' said Burrows. 'You know Martin Sumner, don't you?'

'Yes, of course,' said Ryan, shaking his hand. He spoke slowly, deliberately, as if mentally checking each word to see whether it could be improved upon.

'I was going to search you out tonight, just to say how

terribly sorry I am about the events of last week,' said Burrows, penitently holding his wine glass with both hands and looking up at Ryan.

'Kind of you to say so, Charlie,' said Ryan. 'We lost a good man there.'

The two of them murmured agreement.

'How is his wife?' asked Burrows.

'Well, I suppose about as bad as could be expected. You know. There are two kids as well . . . not great at all.'

'Yes, I know,' they mumbled again.

'So let it be a lesson to you boys. Nik's work rate was off the scale. They think he just drove through a red light, you know. Nothing's worth that.'

'I know, I know.'

'And are you all right, Charlie? You got a little beaten up last week over it all.'

'Oh God, what can I say? I can't make it not happen. Bad timing, of course, but we were out of order.'

'Yes, it can get quite personal, can't it. Just keep telling yourself, "It's only television".'

Burrows had not been looking forward to this conversation. He was relieved that Ryan had chosen not to milk it.

Howell Snoddy, Her Majesty's Minister for Broadcasting, had disengaged himself from a group of radio people who were lobbying him intensively. Over the years he had perfected the learned nod and considered frown while thinking about something else altogether.

Ryan had started to ask how Henry Fleming was doing when Burrows felt a hand on his shoulder and turned to find the Minister, who greeted the group and said, 'Do you have a moment, Charlie?'

'Sure, Howell, what can I do for you?' Snoddy steered them to a quiet corner.

Howell Snoddy had a special relationship with his own vocabulary. He was a short and unattractive man, with thinning hair and a strangely convex face on which a pair of well-worn glasses sat awkwardly. He was expensively educated and loved an audience for whom he could showcase his verbal craftsmanship. A sixty-year-old locked in a former, finer time, he had nothing in common with Burrows; yet, because of his seat at the table where broadcasting policy was decided, Burrows nurtured the contact. He liked to pretend that his meetings with the Minister were torture, but he quite enjoyed Snoddy's convoluted style.

Snoddy was a career politician. He'd entered politics, charged with the fervour of public service, but the game had overtaken him. For sure, he still had all the language of the democrat and he'd grown better at deploying it. But the thrill of the chase, the staying in power, being in the newspapers, outmanoeuvring the opposition, these were the ambitions that now consumed him.

Burrows's ability to assist any of the political parties as much as they would like was constrained by the impartiality rules, which meant that none of them was ever happy with Acrobat's news coverage. Burrows reckoned that if the volume of whinging was equal he'd got the balance about right.

Snoddy was looking particularly dishevelled tonight, but Burrows knew that beneath the haphazard blend of twenty-year-old suits and shiny ties lay a political right hook which was not to be underestimated.

Snoddy organized himself so that his back was to the

room and began, his head raised, his eyes virtually closed. 'Charlie, in the fields of human endeavour, there are times when warring agendas meet.'

Burrows wondered whether Snoddy had delivered so many speeches from so many scripts that he'd lost the ability to speak in a normal fashion.

He was into his next sentence. 'As you're no doubt aware, the civil servants are applying the final jots and tittles to new media ownership legislation. I'm being asked to rule on whether we should relax things so that companies like Acrobat can expand by buying out their rivals.'

'Yes, we've sent you a few papers on that in our time.'

'For which I'm most grateful, Charlie. Very helpful indeed. But the issues of principle now give way to a question of trust. If I'm about to put more power in fewer pairs of hands, obviously I need to be satisfied that the beneficiaries of such a move will recognize the – shall we say – enhanced responsibility which would accompany their greater influence.'

Burrows wondered if he was going to own up to knowing about the secret programme monitoring scheme proposed by Nik Kruger.

'Sex and violence, Minister?'

Snoddy looked nonplussed. 'What about it?'

'Not enough for you?'

Snoddy snorted without amusement. 'Well, it's always bothersome, Charlie. We don't seem to be able to stop you playing to the masses.'

'That's what we're here to do, Howell.'

'No, you're there to serve the public, but back to my point . . .'

'Trust.'

'Indeed. In short, Charlie, I'm seeking reassurance that if I allow you to expand your company by acquisition, I am not cutting off my own nose.'

'Sorry, Howell, maybe I'm being very thick . . .' Burrows peered at Snoddy as if trying to read small print in his eyes.

Snoddy tried again. 'These days, Charlie, governments cannot afford to be indifferent to the attitudes of those who operate the media.'

'I'd have thought that wasn't a huge concern. We're all very law-abiding, Howell, we can't afford not to be.'

'Yes. I'm operating on a slightly more subtle level than the rulebook, though. Any move away from the current profusion of voices in the media is a risk for policy makers. After all, you are the people who control access to the hearts and minds of the electorate. We can't afford to find ourselves at loggerheads with you, can we now?' He tipped his face up towards Burrows, as if narrating a children's story.

'Riiiiight,' said Burrows, not wishing to put words in his mouth. 'So the reassurance you need is . . .'

'Well, come on, Charlie. I need to be able to reassure the Prime Minister that in allowing consolidation into fewer, larger media companies, I will not be arming the government's enemies against it.'

Burrows recoiled. 'You asking if we're friend or foe, right?'

'Alleluia, we got there. Give it some thought, Charlie. Let me know in the next couple of days if you can offer me any comfort in this regard.'

*

As soon as Burrows was steered away by Snoddy, Malcolm Ryan seized his moment. 'Look, Martin, hardly the ideal time or place to talk about this, but since we are now short of a Chief Executive, I wonder whether there's any sense in us having a small chat?'

Sumner swallowed too big a mouthful of Chablis, and tried to look cool. 'Um . . . what have you got in mind?' he asked, closing his eyes for a moment too long at the absurdity of his question.

'Well, I realize you are gainfully employed at Acrobat, and no doubt you've got a bristling set of restrictive covenants that would keep you in your garden for the rest of the decade, but would you perhaps be interested in a change of scenery?'

Sumner thought quickly. 'Malcolm, I'm very honoured, really. But I feel a certain loyalty to Charlie and Acrobat.'

'I understand,' said Ryan. 'I don't mean to catch you off guard. I thought I'd ask because you're going to want to play second fiddle for only so long, and obviously now is the moment when I can offer you the chance of a command . . . if that isn't too many metaphors.'

Sumner laughed.

'Look,' Ryan continued, pressing a business card into his hand, 'have a think about it and give me a call before the end of the week. Talk to you.' He dissolved into the crowd.

Charlie Burrows found his way across to Dennis Weaver, his investment banker. Weaver was a deal-doer, as much a good friend as an adviser. Pugnacious and direct, he always had several deals on the boil and spent his life in boardrooms and airport lounges.

'Charlie, Charlie, what have they been doing to you? You look like crap!'

Burrows pulled his thoughts away from Howell Snoddy. 'Yeah, thanks, Dennis. You can talk.'

Weaver feigned surprise. 'Well, thanks to you, too. You surviving, Charlie? Been in the papers a bit, haven't we? Know how much you love that.'

'The week from hell, Dennis.'

'Taken a bit of a walloping from the teenagers in the City. Little monsters.'

'I know. But fifteen per cent in two days. Apparently they're worried about some European advertising slow-down that Ray says isn't coming here. You get any whiff of it on your travels?'

'Authorized version: business as usual. Since I like you, unofficial version . . . yes, there are some signs of cold feet. But it's hard to know whether the market isn't just talking itself into it. Self-fulfilling prophecy, you know. That's why I always look so confident and cheerful.' He grinned cheesily.

'And knackered,' said Burrows. 'How many planes this week?'

Weaver was ready with the answer. 'Eight since a week last Sunday.'

'All Europe?'

'One New York, one Madrid, one Frankfurt, one Luxembourg.'

'Luxembourg – what d'you want to go there for?' queried Burrows.

'God knows.' Weaver took a generous gulp of his wine and grinned. 'And just to keep my air miles up, I'm off to Amsterdam tomorrow morning, six-thirty pick-up.'

'And you think *I* look knackered – have you looked in a mirror lately?'

'Not likely – ban them from the house.' Weaver caught sight of himself in the mirror behind Burrows's head. 'Aagh!' he recoiled in mock horror.

Burrows looked over his shoulder. 'Hey, look at that,' he said, 'a panda in a dinner jacket.'

'Ha bloody ha,' said the panda. 'So tell me, what did dear old Phyllis Grigson do wrong?'

'Not much at all, really,' mused Burrows. 'Got caught in the crossfire.'

'Poor old love. Still, it was a good innings . . .' Weaver's eyes flipped to the mirror again, expertly scanning the room for the next contact to be massaged. 'Look, why don't we see if we can't find ourselves on the banks of a little trout stream in Hampshire some time soon?'

'Sounds perfect,' said Burrows.

'I'll get my girl to give yours a call.'

'All right, mate, don't work too hard.'

'I'll follow your lead.'

Ray Walker had done this a thousand times. But tonight was a good night because Acrobat was in the news. Burrows watched distractedly as Walker hooked up with a group of his old drinking partners, to much shouting and uproarious laughter. 'What could possibly be that funny?' he asked himself while trying to concentrate on Hugo Trevethan's conversation.

Walker's friends, who arrived with noses already pink, were a society within a society. A community of businessmen in their fifties, all of whom had known each other for over twenty years and who looked out for one another.

Members were called 'mates' and at gatherings like this the credos of the society would be reinforced with statements like, 'I had to help him out – he's a mate . . . I couldn't take the deal away, could I – he's a mate.' The rulebook for mates eclipsed the flat-footed meritocracy of standard business practice.

Sarah Golanski was at the edge of a group of clients when Melvyn Davies made his way across to her. He put his hand on her back, pulling it away suddenly as it touched her skin.

She turned around. 'Oh, thank God it's you, Melv. I thought it was another dirty old man wanting to use client privileges for a grope.'

Davies smiled. 'They respect your mind, Sarah, you know that.'

'Some do.' She smiled and placed a hand on his forearm.

At that moment there was a crash as the gong sounded and the toastmaster launched into his anachronistic summons to dinner. The hubbub of conversation dropped, accompanied by a few titters from those who had been startled by the noise.

Burrows found himself sitting with Alastair Powell, editor of the *Daily Telegraph*, on his left side and a former radio company chairman on the other. He didn't know Powell well and introduced himself as they sat.

'Terrible doings last week,' grumbled Powell.

'I know,' said Burrows. 'None of us came out of it particularly well, did we.'

'None of you, but especially not Phyllis Grigson.'

Burrows looked to his right, wondering if he was going to be stuck with this all evening.

'I guess you could say that.'

'Good player, Phyllis Grigson,' Powell continued.

'Yes, she's still going to be doing some work for us.'

'So I gather. You'll be needing a steady hand to replace her. She's a tough act to follow, and you know how much we hacks love to dig around in the bins of a TV company.'

'Yes, why are we worth so much attention?'

'Come on, you love it. What else do you do it for?'

'Me? I do it because it's incredibly stimulating and has some small role in affecting our culture.'

'There you go then. If you're going to start affecting our culture, people are going to want to know what kind of person you are.'

'Come on, I'm just the bloke in the suit.'

'You'd like to be.'

'Sure. Why can't I just get on with my job and be judged on that?'

Powell was enjoying this now, and he turned in his chair to focus fully on Burrows. 'Because, my dear Charlie . . .' Powell's eyes darted to Burrows's name card to check he'd got it right '. . . if you wanted to do that, you should have got a job in IT or something. If you're going to set yourself up as the arbiter of what we shall and shall not watch, the public has a right to expect you to be someone with excellent judgement.'

'And you reckon that's why we're in the paper every time someone farts?'

'Sure.'

'So why does the *Telegraph* not do more with media news then?'

Powell shrugged. 'No good reason, really. Older age profile of readers, I suppose.'

'But if the media are so culturally relevant, shouldn't the *Telegraph* take more of an interest?'

'After the week you've just had, I'm amazed you'd want anyone to take more of an interest.' Powell laughed. 'No, you make a fair point; we should think about that. Young industry . . . all the thrills and spills . . . might appeal to younger readers.'

'Well, if you ever want a personal profile on anyone in the media, don't call me.'

Powell gradually engaged himself in the conversation next door. Burrows saw Dennis Milligan holding court with Melvyn Davies, his guardian and straight man. Sarah Golanski was enchanting a group of businessmen; he could hear her laughter rising above the clamour of talk and glasses and plates. Walker was describing something earnestly to another small group. He looked over his shoulder to see Martin Sumner looking relaxed, listening to an intense young man who appeared to have abandoned his dinner, his hands needed for the higher purpose of punctuating his points. Amid the clamour, Burrows retreated into the silence in his head.

And he felt proud. He'd created this team. It had its problems, for sure – name one that didn't. But these people were good. He expected too much of them most of the time. He knew their flaws too well. But to see them performing in this company, he was proud. Here, among the most elevated media personalities in London, they shone.

He looked around the room. A cauldron of ambition. So many intellects and so much energy devoted to corporate causes. Passion and adrenalin excited by the race. To be better than the guy in the next office, in the next firm. To be better than the year before. To deliver on expectations. To be the person respected by the market, by the customers, the colleagues . . . by themselves. Yet just folks. People keeping up the camouflage, playing the game within the boundaries. Concealing the one fear shared by them all: fear that if their humanity were exposed, they'd be somehow diminished by it.

Acrobat's closing share price 381p

Thursday, 11 March

Paula Conley brought in the post to Burrows's office, where he was reading the morning press cuts. 'Good night at the boys' brigade?' she asked, tenderly laying the opened letters in the tray.

'Not bad, not bad,' said Burrows, his eyes not moving from the sheaf of papers. 'You know, usual suspects.' Abruptly he looked up at her. 'Ah, but here's one that will irritate your anarchic leftie sensibilities, Pol. I had a most interesting chat with Her Majesty's Minister for Broadcasting, who clarified for me that in order for him to summon the political will to relax the ownership rules in our favour, he needs to know that we're not going to abuse our greater influence by doing anything irresponsible.' She nodded as he paused for effect. 'Like criticizing the government.'

She let her jaw drop open theatrically. 'He can't do that.'

Burrows grinned and shrugged. 'Appalling, isn't it.'

'Was there anyone with you?'

Burrows looked into the distance. 'No, he made sure we were alone.'

'So you said "No", obviously.'

'Not as such,' he said thoughtfully.

'Charlie, tell me you're not even thinking about this. It's a democracy – *free media*, remember?' She raised her voice as if trying to make contact with a halfwit.

Burrows looked unfazed. 'He's banking on the fact that it's easier for us just to agree than fuss about the principle. He's probably right.'

'That's obscene.'

'But clever. He knows we've got to grow, Paula. If the shareholders lose confidence in our ability to grow the value of their savings, they just shift their money into companies which are on the up; our share price falls and, before you know it, someone ghastly has bought the company at a knock-down price and we're all out on our ear.'

'But we *are* growing, aren't we?'

'Ah-ha! Good question. The City's got squiffy about it, and frankly the answer lies with our new Commercial Director, Mr Walker, who for some reason doesn't like me to have to worry my pretty little head about the numbers. Much easier for him to keep me in the dark, apparently. Could you fix me some time with him and Martin?'

'If the revenue's holding up, will you tell Snoddy to stick it?' said Paula.

He pursed his lips. 'I doubt it.'

Ray Walker was visibly uncomfortable. He had arrived with an armful of files – and Sarah Golanski for good measure.

Burrows began. 'Ray, if I can be completely open with you, we are in need of some good news here. I know you don't like getting our expectations up too high, but right now we have precisely the opposite problem.'

Walker opened one of his files. 'I understand the predicament, chaps, but I think you're on a hiding to nothing to raise your heads above the parapet at the current time.'

'We're on a hiding as it is,' said Sumner. 'Let's go from the top. What are you looking at as a revenue rise for the year?'

Walker lifted a meaty fist and pointed to Sarah Golanski. 'Go ahead, Sarah,' he said.

'It's early in the year to be overly definitive, but we're looking at about ten per cent revenue growth.'

'So that is a slowdown, then,' said Sumner.

'Nothing slow about that, mate,' bristled Walker, already aggressive.

'Well, that's just brilliant, isn't it?' Sumner marked the tempo with his water bottle. 'Two days after we tell the City we did a fifteen per cent increase and it's not going to slow, the revenue has hit the brakes. Ray, man, would it have been possible to have shared this piece of information with us maybe at the weekend?'

Walker closed his file, holding Sumner with a hostile stare. 'Do you have any idea how hard it is to generate double-digit revenue growth year after year after year? No reason why you should, of course.'

'You're missing the bloody point, man,' Sumner retorted. 'No one is criticizing you. I assume you're doing a great job of generating revenue. You're just doing a crap job of coming clean about what's really going on in the market.'

'Look, Charlie, if I could tell the future I wouldn't be sitting here now,' said Walker.

'Ray, watch my lips,' continued Sumner, his growing irritation made apparent by the increased tinge of Geordie. 'Here's how it is. Right now, our share price is going south. This is not good. The reason it is not good is that the government is about to change the ownership rules. At that moment, there will be a feeding frenzy in broadcasting; the strong will take out the weak. A good share price means we control our own destiny; a rubbish share price means someone else does. Sorry if I'm insulting your intelligence here, but it really is that simple. So we are going to reassure the market. OK?'

'I thought we weren't supposed to give market forecasts.' Walker brightened at the idea of a rule which might help him.

Burrows sighed. 'We're trying to help the market come to a consensus. At the moment the consensus they're getting to is that we're in the cack.'

'Hmph,' said Walker.

'Look,' said Golanski, lifting her eyes from her pad, 'how about something like this. "*Acrobat believes it will continue to outperform the market in the UK, meeting its own targets for double-digit revenue growth.*"' She looked up as the others mulled it over. 'It's upbeat, true, and it draws a line under their worst fears.'

Burrows pursed his lips and leaned over her pad. 'Ray?'

'Yes, I think that covers it. Good. Thank you, Sarah.'

'And thank *you*, Ray,' said Burrows with extravagant courtesy.

Abby Kelleher flicked her hair back and blew her breath out fast like an athlete as she was shown into Charlie Burrows's office. She had been interviewed by hundreds of people in her career and she knew the questions, knew the answers. She knew she could make him like her.

She was a little over five feet tall and wore precise dark

suits and too-high heels. Her hair was shoulder length and blonde. She thanked Paula as she slipped past her into Burrows's office and accepted a glass of still water.

Burrows had given Martin Sumner the task of bringing in a successor to Phyllis Grigson. The brief had blended the usual need for speed with the challenge to identify an individual with the personal characteristics of the Archangel Gabriel. Sumner had started briefing headhunters but he had heard that an English woman named Abby Kelleher, based in New York, had decided to return to London.

Abby Kelleher was undeniably a high-flyer and Sumner was impressed. Though still in her early thirties, she had taken her place alongside the CEOs of some distinguished American companies. Her appointment at Acrobat would itself make a major statement about the move to youth, and the calibre of her CV would help bury the memory of Phyllis Grigson.

Ninety minutes later Acrobat had a new Head of PR. Kelleher had lived up to her reputation, presenting them with the prospect of a new start in PR with an experienced and lively player.

'Very together, I thought,' Burrows said to Sumner, as Paula showed her to the lift. 'A bit of that American focus will do us no harm.'

'Weird accent,' Sumner interrupted.

'You can talk, you Geordie git,' said Burrows. 'Still, she had really done her homework. Very impressive. Never ceases to amaze me how few people bother. I interviewed a bloke once who kept getting the name of the company wrong.'

'Excellent! You give him a job?' asked Sumner.

'Yeah, Sales Director.' They sniggered together.

'So the Queen is dead, long live the Queen.'

'Looks like it. And of course the other nice thing about Miss Kelleher is that she can start next week. All helps.'

'As does the fact that she is fragrant and charming perhaps?'

'Fragrant, charming, and *on the payroll*,' stressed Burrows. Sumner had adopted a hopeful look. 'Don't even think about it, Sumner.'

'You don't want me to handle her induction to the company then?'

'I don't want you to handle her anything, thank you, Martin.'

Sumner turned away. 'Your mind is a sewer, man.'

Kate Davies put the phone down again. She had spoken to her husband's voicemail three times that day. She'd tried to be gentle, loving and accommodating, but she'd heard the undertone in her third message. She knew he'd been under pressure with the presentation to analysts and all. He hadn't said how it had gone. Not like him – but then, he was less and less like him. She still saw him, he still came home, he'd still talk. But he'd be exhausted, or distracted; his speech would be strewn with sighs. One way or the other, it was never the right time to tackle anything serious. So it all got left unsaid.

This was new territory for her. Communication which had once been instinctive now had to be modelled, practised, weighed. Knowing how he'd be was once a simple extraction from her own feelings. Not now. Robbed of spontaneity, she had to plan her responses. Should she rail? Fight for what they had? So many times the rage boiled up in her: reasonable, fair, righteous anger. But she knew it would drive him away. Her approval of who he was and what he did was one of the few remaining sinews.

So what options had she? Stuff it all down, play for a day in the future when he would return. Make sure he never lost the instinct that she would be a safe haven for the prodigal? Something in her spirit rose to the nobility of such a calling. Today, she resolved to make their shared times as good as they could be, see them through this valley. She'd do candles and music and his favourite dinner, with an expensive bottle of Italian red for tonight. She could do this. She called to tell him not to have a heavy lunch. But whatever manic-ness was taking place in the Acrobat Programme Department was more urgent.

Melvyn Davies took in the pandemonium around him in Studio I and caught sight of Sarah Golanski watching him from the other side of the floor. She waved subtly when he made eye contact. He walked over to her.

'How's it going?' she said. 'I'm just off now – I dropped into your office to see if you fancied a drink or something.'

'Thanks,' said Davies, 'but the first *MMOne* is on air in three and a half hours and . . .' he looked around at the chaotic studio '. . . we have rather a lot still to do.'

'I'll get out your way,' she said, picking up her bag.

'You're welcome to stay if you want to.' He sighed. '. . . long as you don't mind the sight of a grown man weeping.'

She laughed. 'I'll watch the fruits of your labours at

home. I've got this load of rubbish to get through tonight. See you tomorrow,' she laughed.

'If I still work here by then.'

'Break a leg, or whatever it is I'm supposed to say,' she called. He smiled until she disappeared around the heavy studio door.

Davies had been working nights on the revised *Midnight Minus One* show for that evening. He had endured a continuous barrage of phone calls and emails from Solveig Nilsen since standing her down with a promise of her return to her 9.30 show later in the year. 'Why do I ever believe a promise from you again?' After years of trying to stand out from an industry practised in dressing disingenuity as pragmatism, he was grazed by the injustice of being counted among the bad guys.

The young presenters he'd pulled in to replace Solveig were a couple of twenty-year-old kids whom he'd seen at the Edinburgh Fringe last year. They had worked hard on the new show. As Davies had said to the show's director, 'If they got ratings for their commitment, we'd have a blockbuster on our hands.' But they both knew it wasn't like that.

Davies was looking particularly dishevelled. Solveig's writers had stayed with her show, so, at a week's notice, availability outbid quality. As a political satire sketch show, it had to be topical, so the writers, all beards and cardigans, sat at a table in the production office with a television burbling Sky News *sotto voce* as they tried out gags on each other.

Davies looked around the door.

'How goes it in the creative department?' he said, pulling up a chair and sitting on it the wrong way round.

Two beards turned to face him.

'Progress progress,' said Beard1.

'We've got a lot of lines for a pantomime,' added Beard2.

'Yeah, something about us. We sit down to write sophisticated political satire, and out comes slapstick.'

'Oh no it doesn't,' sang Beard2.

'See what I mean?' Beard1 shrugged.

Davies gripped the chair back with both hands. 'Perhaps a bit less *Mother Goose* and a bit more *Spitting Image*,' he said.

At 10.30 p.m., the atmosphere in Studio 1 was thick with the narcotic cocktail of fear and expectancy that none of them could adequately describe, but which kept them at this crazy game. They had a script and a running order, the presenters were in make-up and, across the studio and in the gallery, order was being forced from the chaos of the day.

Ray Walker arrived with Geoff O'Brien, the man from Southern Foods. After a decent dinner, he was coming to see the first fruits of his sponsor money, completely unaware of the activities behind the scenes that had led up to tonight. There was no good purpose for his presence – indeed the exigencies of getting the show out rather overtook the niceties normally prepared for major advertising sponsors. Walker took care of his well-fed guest, describing the action in the studio with more authority than accuracy. Davies hurried over to shake his hand and received the best wishes of the diners, before retreating apologetically back to the set, where cameras were rehearsing their choreography.

'Top guy, Melvyn,' whispered Walker, now installed at the back of the production gallery. 'He'll be exec. producing the show tonight, so we can be confident everything will run to plan.'

'I never realized there'd be so many people involved,' confided the man from Southern Foods. 'And even now, at . . . five to eleven, there's still so much going on.'

The presenters were now on set, talking to the director in the gallery while a sound man arranged the earpieces for the director's instructions, plumbing the wire down their backs with pieces of gaffer tape. Someone was hammering down a piece of carpet on the steps of the set, which had been rebuilt in the last hour after Davies had declared them too narrow for presenters to walk down without watching their feet.

In the gallery, four or five people appeared to be talking simultaneously against the strident countdown of the production assistant.

'Three minutes, studio,' she called. 'We're into the break.'

Walker pointed to the bank of screens, identifying the Off Air screen as they watched the ads go out in advance of the new show. 'That's the one which shows exactly what's going out. It comes from the transmitter, so if there's any fault, we know first,' whispered Walker.

A woman pulled the director's attention away from the screens to show her a printout covered with pencilled arrows. Without emotion, she leaned forward to her studio mike and said, 'OK, people, we haven't got the footage of the Prime Minister's holiday yet, so he's going to the back and we'll do the Snoddy piece as item two.'

The presenters shuffled their pages in response to the

new running order, and the autocue operator obediently began cutting and pasting at her computer.

'If we don't have the PM at Butlins, we'll just do it with stills.'

The man from Southern Foods leaned over to Walker. 'This is ridiculous – *I'm* nervous. They keep changing it.'

'I know,' whispered Walker. 'The presenters never learn their scripts. It's all so last minute, they just read out what rolls in front of them on the autocue.'

Walker pointed excitedly to the Off Air screen as the *Night and Day* sponsor's ident appeared, and the second-by-second countdown from the gallery began. As the titles rolled, the director pressed down the button on her mike and said, 'Here we go, have a good show, everyone. Jeremy and Sue – enjoy!'

Twenty-five minutes later, after a constant barrage of countdowns and consultations, talking to the presenters even while they were on air, she leaned back in her chair, pushing back her hair, and thanked everyone in the gallery.

Walker seized his moment. 'Jo, this is Geoff from Southern Foods.'

'Ah, our glorious sponsors,' smiled the well-briefed director. She took his hand. 'Enjoy the show?' she asked.

'It was absolutely amazing,' nodded Geoff from Southern Foods, grinning broadly. 'I've never seen anything like it in my life. I'm exhausted – and I just sat here!'

'That's because there is nothing like it,' barked Jo. 'Live TV – miles better than sex.'

Walker seemed slightly perturbed by this turn of phrase, but Geoff O'Brien roared with laughter, causing several of the occupants of the gallery to stop and look at him. On cue, Walker joined in.

Davies arrived, looking even more dishevelled, if that were possible. 'Thanks, Jo,' he said. 'Good job, everyone.' He turned back to the director. 'Happy?'

'Never happy, Melvyn,' she snorted.

'Well, happy enough for a first outing?'

Davies turned to O'Brien.

'Happy, Geoff?'

'Never happy, Melvyn,' he mimicked.

'I can vouch for that,' shouted Walker, the two of them roaring with delighted laughter at the repartee.

Davies was profoundly tired. As he walked to the door, Walker grasped his forearm in a bear-like grip. 'I think we got away with that all right,' he whispered. His cheeks ballooned as he expelled a gasp of wind.

Davies recoiled from the stew of coffee, cigars, garlic on his breath. 'Yup,' he said. 'We'll decide that when we see the ratings in the morning.'

'Fancy a nightcap?' continued Walker. 'I'm taking Geoff to a little place I know.'

'Very kind,' said Davies without conviction. 'I'm going home, I think. We'll see in the morning if they loved us or hated us.'

He walked back across the studio floor, thanking and congratulating as he went.

As he passed through the heavy double doors and down to the basement car park, his wife was in their kitchen, trying to force the cork back into a bottle of Chianti. She blew out the candles and went to bed.

Acrobat's closing share price   380p

Friday, 12 March

At 7.30 a.m. on Friday morning, the announcement was released to the stock exchange.

'The Board of Acrobat has noted the cautious market sentiment surrounding the company with surprise. The directors believe that Acrobat's revenues will continue to outperform the market in the UK, meeting its own targets for double-digit growth.'

Melvyn Davies arrived late, drained from the night before. He turned on his computer before he had taken off his coat. He leaned over the machine, absently reading all the information it flashed up as it got its act together. He pulled the door closed behind him and hooked his chair with his foot, sitting to type in his password: ILYKATE.

He'd experienced the feeling many times before, the adrenalin excitement of bursting to find out how a show had performed. It would wake him up at night and he would play out little cameos of the following day. The resounding success. The calls to the talent, the press interest, the improved revenue possibilities. Or the failure. The other calls to the talent. The other press interest. The other revenue impact. In truth, there was no knowing. Everyone had their successes and their lemons. The show that had performed superbly in research, with the greatest presenters and the finest script, could be just rejected by the public on transmission. At that point the real work started. To press on or to pull it – every Programme Director's worst decision. The relationship with the talent was important – he had to be seen to be giving it a fair shout but, with the market as competitive as it was these days, no one could afford to keep a turkey alive for long. And then there were the shows that had been thrown together which somehow hit the public's nerve and became sensations.

Midnight Minus One Mark II had taken a massive amount of work to nurture into life against the clock. A show like that realistically needed months for the planning, even though the topicality of the subject matter did demand late writing of the scripts. But had he got the right team together? Would they work well together? The Beard Brothers were certainly odd, but there were probably enough laughs in the script to keep it alive. It wasn't as if it was up against anything particularly riveting on the other channels. Nevertheless, this was no way to prepare a new show. He'd have preferred to run some dummy shows to loosen them up as a team, maybe give himself a choice of writers over a longer period. A chill of doubt brushed past the fragile confidence he had mustered.

As he waited for the machine, he tried to guess what the show might do. To be comfortable he needed around 1.2 million viewers, with a decent share of younger and more upmarket people. These are the groups most sought after by the advertisers. Though older people buy as much toothpaste as anyone else, the shared assumption of the whole advertising industry is that when they hit forty-five, people fix their brand selections. And that better-off people are both more susceptible to making statements about themselves via the brands they choose and more able to afford them. But both the young and the well-off also use the television as a source of leisure less than the rest of the population, so advertisers have to work harder to reach them. They would, therefore, pay more per thousand for them.

Finally he got into his computer and clicked the overnight ratings icon, the data collated electronically by the research company from meters in several thousand homes. He scrolled slowly through the day, looking at the familiar shows, and as usual found no real surprises in their performance. It was delicious, this moment. He paused on the film to see – to his delight – that it had performed excellently, leaving a strong inheritance for his new baby. For all that viewers are quick to channel hop, it is still the case that the performance of a new show can be given a boost from the preceding programme, in this case the best film he could muster.

The movie had done well – a 15 per cent share would do very nicely, thank you. Davies scrolled the page down to see that 1.4 million people had stayed with it in order to find out what *Midnight Minus One* was about. Good number. The promotion for the show had been confined to on-air plugs, plus as much PR as they had been able to generate in the short time available, but it wasn't a lot.

Davies's eyes flicked over to the right of the screen, to find that the composition of younger and more well-off viewers was high. Because advertisers' appetite for these people was insatiable, Davies's task was to achieve the highest concentration of them within the largest audiences he could muster. The catch was that the two objectives pulled against each other. Younger viewers had television appetites that their parents didn't share, so a good haul of young viewers usually meant a small total audience. And whilst a mass-market game show could bring in many millions of viewers, such an audience would contain too many old and downmarket viewers, for which advertisers expected a discount. Three-dimensional chess.

Davies slipped his coat off, swirling it with one arm to miss the sofa and land in a mess on the floor behind it. He sat down and scrolled the screen downwards.

'Oh God,' he gulped.

By 23.20, the time of the first break, his audience had halved. He scrolled on. A creaking sound crept from his throat as he saw the very bad news. *MMOne* had bombed. By the end of the programme, only a quarter of the audience remained. The age profile was quite good, but on that scale of audience it was cold comfort. His hand swept through his hair and he slumped back into the chair. He stroked his chin and closed his eyes as he imagined the rest of the day.

Paula Conley took the call from the Duty Officer at midday. He had been on the phones all the previous night and called in as soon as he'd woken up.

'Obviously I've done all the normal paperwork, and I'm sorry if this was just the usual disturbed caller, but I didn't recognize his voice, and I do know most of 'em when I hear 'em.'

'Mmm hmm,' said Paula in a 'tell me more' tone.

'This one was asking for Mr Burrows's home number and I don't like that. You know, you get used to them ranting and raving, I mean, that's what you're there for. But he claimed Mr Burrows would know who he was and if I didn't hand over his home number I'd be out of a job.'

No, I can assure you that he's got that precisely the wrong way round,' declared Paula.

There was a moment's pause. 'Oh, so that was all right then.'

'Absolutely.'

'Did you get his name?' asked Paula.

'Oh yes, he made quite sure I got his name.'

Martin Sumner looked up when her phone went down and he leaned out of his office. 'Paula pet, what does Charlie's diary look like on Monday?'

'Usual traffic jam. He's going to see Henry in hospital first, so your morning prayers have been pushed back to ten o'clock. After that, he's back to back through till seven.'

'How long does he have for our Monday morning?'

'He's got an hour.'

'Any chance of ninety minutes?'

'Plus extra time?'

'May even go to penalties,' he said to himself as, for the hundredth time since the evening at the Media Business Club, he tried to imagine telling his friend about the opportunity at Channel 6. He had thought of little else since that evening. He wanted the challenge so badly, the chance to pull out of Charlie Burrows's slipstream and live or die by his own judgements. So when Sir Malcolm Ryan invited him to his home on Saturday, there was no doubt that he would go. Already he found himself consumed by strategies to build Channel 6.

'Well, Martin Sumner, if you're fantastically nice to me and buy me presents and flowers and ensure that I receive a massive pay rise this year, I could busy my little head with moving everything backwards for the whole *bleedin'* day.' She looked up and tilted her head coquettishly, 'If that is what Sir wants?'

'I'm sorry, Paula, it's just that I may have something for Monday's agenda that will be hard to resolve without the extra time.'

'*May* have, *may* have? You want me to piss off half of London for a *may have*?'

'*Will* have. Definitely.'

Paula pursed her lips and bent her fingers down to her keyboard, scattering her fingers over it incoherently, in a caricature of the typing pool girl.

'Be my pleasure, sir – I'll deal with it presently,' she trilled.

When Charlie Burrows had finished on his phone call, Paula took in the sheaf of post for the morning and laid it on top of the rest of the stuff in his in-tray.

'No,' he groaned. 'Mercy, Paula, no more post, please.'

'You know you love it,' she replied. 'However, I have something altogether more stimulating for you than anything in this little lot.'

'How do I know I don't want to hear about this?' He put down his pen and folded his arms.

'Well,' she began, as if telling a bedtime story, 'among the many millions of nutters who called last night to give us the benefit of their advice was one particular nutter who really did not like what he saw on *MMOne*.'

'Oh hell, I forgot to watch it. Was it any good – did you see it?'

'Well, I watched the beginning, but in order to be on tip-top form for you today, Charlie, I thought I'd better go and get some quality sleep.'

'And this particular nutter?'

'A Mr Howell Snoddy MP.'

Burrows closed his eyes. 'Oh no, did they have a whack at him last night?'

'Among others,' said Paula lightly. 'But that's their job isn't it? Take a bit of light-hearted stick.'

'Probably, yes, but I guess that in Snoddy's terms we just went from friend to foe.'

'Serves him right,' brooded Paula. 'Nasty little man.'

'The voice of purity. Would that it were that simple, Paula. Right and wrong are easy. Business is something else.'

'Something like expediency, perhaps?' She met his eye. Too intense. 'And talking of your favourite nutters, Ray would like a word. It's . . . guess what . . .'

'Very urgent?' He sighed. 'OK, let's talk to Ray.'

Burrows moved around behind his desk with heavy steps as she got hold of Walker on the phone.

'Good morning, Raymond. And how can I add value to your life this morning?' he began with forced gusto.

'No cause for levity this morning,' warned Walker. 'Seen the ratings?'

'No, not yet. What's happened?'

'*Midnight Minus One* died a death is what's happened.'

'OK, Ray,' Burrows's tone stiffened, 'what would you like me to do about it?'

'You're the Chief Executive – you should know we

will have a major problem with Southern Foods over this.'

'Well, manage it for God's sake, Ray. I'm the Chief Executive, you're the Sales . . . no, you are the Commercial Director. I come back to my earlier question . . . what precisely would you like me to do about it?'

'I'll deal with it,' muttered Walker and hung up.

'You're history, baby!' Burrows shouted at the dead phone, and to Paula, 'Can you believe the bastard hung up on me?'

Martin Sumner came into his office. Burrows was still ranting. 'Who the hell does that little shit think he is, calling me to complain about *MMOne*?'

'Did you see it?' asked Sumner.

'No. Any good?'

Sumner crumpled his nose and bobbed his head from side to side. 'Seen better, but first outing.'

'What did it do to Snoddy?'

'Oh, that bit was brilliant – glove-puppet thing, but you couldn't understand a word it was saying – just a torrent of long words strung together.'

Burrows smiled thinly. 'Sounds about right. But to hell with Snoddy. I'm going to kill Ray Walker.'

'Not in a moment of anger, Charles,' admonished Sumner.

'Come on, Martin. Hardly a knee-jerk reaction – we've been talking about this for ever.'

'Yes, and every time we talk about it we reach the point where we say Sarah's not ready to assume the throne yet.'

'Well, we just have to make that call,' said Burrows. 'OK, so she's going to need a bit of extra help. Why don't we make you Chairman of the Sales Division or something? That way we give her the support she needs . . .'

'And prove to the analysts that I do actually do something.' Sumner wasn't laughing.

Burrows caught his eye. 'Come on, Mart, they aren't the issue. We're not running the company on what they think. Listen, if we stick you in there as resident grown-up, the clients will relax, the staff will be fine about it, and the shareholders will recognize that we've addressed the concerns of the City. I like it a lot – and into the bargain, Ray bleedin' Walker need never darken our door again. Let's do it, Mart, let's do it.'

Sumner raised his eyebrows and got up from his chair. 'Why don't we think about it over the weekend – we'll put it on the agenda for our Monday session.'

'Not like you to be so sensible, Sumner. Give me a moment of joy in my sorry life – let me get the complacent fat bastard up here and nuke him.'

'Attractive as that proposition undoubtedly is, Charlie, Ray is probably the most litigious employee on the payroll. I suggest that at the very least you should have the lawyers look over his contract before you make a move.'

'No sense of fun,' lamented Burrows. 'Monday then. But you'd better have a good alternative if you don't like the Burrows plan. I think Sarah Golanski is a first-class executive. I'm not having her feel she's got to crawl off and find another job because we can't muster the energy to deal with Ray. Confucius say, "He who is afraid of taking big steps travels only short distances".'

'Right you are, Charlie,' said Sumner. 'I'll ponder those inspiring words over the weekend.'

*

Abby Kelleher was on the phone to her mother. Her newest suit hung on the wardrobe door, still in its dry cleaner's covers. Strewn around the sofa and the floor were Acrobat annual reports, old press releases, all her homework for her first day on Monday as Acrobat's Communications Director. On the battered laptop in the corner, a screen saver marched across the screen – *Abby's spin machine – keep out!!*

When her parents had divorced, Abby had opted to go to America with her father but never had a day when she didn't miss her mum. For the twelve years she'd been in New York, they'd spoken on the phone several times a week and seen each other three or four times a year. Now it was lovely to be back again.

She'd had some complicated relationships with the wrong sort of men, almost always men she'd met through work who fell for her success, her reputation or even her accent. She told her mother it was as if she wore a badge saying, *Hi, I'm Abby, why not abuse me?* So she threw herself all the more diligently into her job and loved it like a husband. Meanwhile Mum was constant, loving and reliable, and she owed her everything, even her fascination for the lucrative world of PR.

'So, Mom, any final words of advice from the old hand?' The American accent was quite pronounced, inlaid into her English diction, but not quite replacing it.

'Just be yourself, get established, you'll be in the swing of it in no time.'

'You know what?' She hunched her shoulders. 'I'm actually nervous.'

'Course you are, love. But there are some nice people there. Some to be careful about too, but I guess that's true anywhere. You know what you have to do.'

'Can I give you a call tomorrow?'

'Can you?' She raised her voice in mock outrage. 'I'll be very upset with you indeed, young lady, if I don't get at least *a* call tomorrow. I'll be in all day, so if you need moral support, you have my number.'

'I love you, Mom, I won't let you down.'

'I love you too, darling girl. I know you won't.'

Phyllis Grigson sighed deeply as she put the phone down. It was great to have Abby back in London.

When the baby went down for his lunchtime nap, Kate Davies stuck on a Miles Davis CD and pulled out the Chianti she had opened the night before. She poured herself half a tumbler and sat down with a sandwich. He'd gone in late that morning, but the conversation over their coffee had been hard work. Once again she wondered if someone else was siphoning off the *joie de vivre* that should have been hers.

As Miles's trumpet wept though *Blue in Green*, Kate closed her eyes and held her tumbler to her breast with both hands. Only yesterday she'd been able to clamber on top of all this pain, all this injustice, and do the decent thing. Sad he hadn't been there to see it. Suddenly there was a rush of emotion. What kind of idiot was she? What kind of stupidity to believe he was coming back? Just get over the next little hump in the road, then it would all be fine and dandy again. Come on, Kate.

But the very thought of leaving was too huge to embrace. For all the hurt of it, this was familiar, reliable, it was her life, for goodness sake. And the boys had their dad. Kind of.

167

Her mind played each side of the argument as the music thrummed on, and gradually she felt sleep coming. No solution, but a blessing right now.

Ray Walker sighed deeply as he picked up the phone to Geoff O'Brien at Southern Foods. As he was put through, he went into his patter, cheery tone, airily confident . . . 'Geoff, hi, it's Ray.'

'Ray, hi, thanks for last night – I can still feel it this morning but it was a great night . . . How did we do?'

'Well, not a vintage first outing, I have to say, but with a new idea like that, you have to allow people time to get it.'

'How many, Ray?'

'Well, the show averaged around six hundred thousand . . .' Walker tailed off.

'Oh dear. What about the profile?'

'The profile is good, though, as you'd expect, we lost some audience during the course of the show, so that's where we're concentrating next week. But if there's any carping in the press, I just wanted you to know we're across it and everything's going to be fine.'

'What are you telling me, Ray?'

'I'm telling you that some of the best shows in the world start a bit light on ratings, but we're on the case. Melvyn has a ton of ideas.' He cleared his throat. 'What I'm saying here, Geoff, is that there are two kinds of sponsors in the world. The good guys work in partnership with the company. Together we get it right and give you a property that will last you for years. The other guys are short-term ratings buyers and nothing more.'

The line went quiet for a moment.

'And you're asking yourself whether you're dealing with a good guy or a bad guy.'

'Geoff, I know you're as accountable for this as we are. All I can say to you is that if the ratings for the show don't improve, we will pay back the difference in free airtime, or we'll give you another sponsorship. Basically the relationship with Southern Foods is very important to us, so I'm saying that we won't leave you out of pocket on the deal. Look, why don't we meet up early next week with Melvyn? He can tell you how he plans to adapt the show, and you can take a view.'

O'Brien tapped the phone with his ring. 'I'll see how it goes in the press. I can't afford to get lumbered with a turkey, but we don't want to fall out again, do we.'

'Absolutely, Geoff. We'll make sure that doesn't happen.'

Phyllis Grigson smiled maternally as Carrie McGann came into the wine bar. She had got there early in order to find a quiet table, and she selected one at the back of the bar under a bricked-up chimney breast. She struggled to stand in the constricted space to give her a hug and kiss her on the cheek.

In unison they said, 'How are you?' and laughed.

'You first,' said McGann. 'How is freedom?'

'Unremunerated but has its compensations,' she said. 'Like wonderful lunches with old friends. As you can see, I've started before you.' She clanked a chilled bottle from the bucket by her side. 'May I tempt you, Miss McGann?'

'Always,' she said. 'But seriously, how are you, Phyllis?'

'Just getting used to a new life at the moment,' she said, a semitone less confidently.

McGann frowned. 'Early days, I suppose.'

'Well, I won't pretend. So far, it's quite hard. I'm already sick of the sound of my own knife and fork.' She looked up sheepishly. 'So much of me was tangled up in that job that without it I'm not sure what I'm for.'

McGann reached over and squeezed her hand. 'But, Phyllis, listen to you. You're you, you're fantastic. Everyone is still talking about you all the time.'

Grigson stretched a grateful smile. 'And next week it'll be Phyllis Who.'

McGann's manner steeled. 'Phyllis, no. Come on. You're not going to lie down and let them roll over you?'

'What do you suggest I do? I signed away the chance of any further redress when I accepted my settlement.'

'So that's it?' McGann looked shocked. 'After seventeen years, that's it – it's just over?'

'Well, I think that was the point. I'm too old, apparently.'

'That's bollocks, Phyllis, and you know it. Everyone knows what you put into that place.'

'I suppose I'd be lying if I said I wasn't hurt.'

'Of course you are. He screws up, you leave? Where's the justice in that?'

'Carrie, Carrie, you're more upset than I am. I'm dealing with this in my own way.'

'Man, if it was me, I'd be out for blood.'

Grigson smiled thinly. 'Well, my dear, they say revenge is a dish best served cold and, right now, it's all still a bit too hot to touch.'

'I think you're being amazing.' McGann took a gulp of wine. 'Well, no I don't, I think you're in denial.'

Grigson did not rise to the fervour of the young

woman. 'Look, it's just the transition. I've got enough money, loads of friends and time to see them all at last. Think of me next Monday morning when your alarm goes off.'

Half a smile broke through McGann's indignation. 'Anyway, Phyllis, I was wondering if I could ask your advice.'

'You have but to name it,' she said with a flourish that made them both laugh. 'What can I do for you?'

'What do you think of Alastair Powell?'

'Alastair Powell? Editor of the *Telegraph*. Feisty, decent, self-made, bit of an old fart. Why?'

'Because I had a call from feisty, decent Alastair Powell yesterday, and I'm seeing him about a job tonight.'

'Really? What's the job?' Grigson leaned forward. 'How could you not tell me straight away?'

Carrie McGann smiled. 'Because we were talking about you, which is much more important.'

'Yes yes . . . what, what?'

'Media Editor?'

Grigson beamed. 'Reeaally. Finally the old goat is taking the media seriously.'

'What do you think?'

'Great move, Carrie. Great move. Allows you to build on your success at *The Times*, broaden your skills . . .' Grigson was genuinely pleased.

'Do you think I'm up to it?'

'Oh, you're a great little writer, you'll take to it like a duck to water.' She smiled broadly. 'But just one piece of advice. Let him persuade you he's serious about this. I've been at him for years to do this, and I'm not alone. Make him come to you. Make him explain what has changed his mind. Is he committed to it? Don't look desperate to get the job is all I'm saying.'

'Even though I am.'

'Even though you are.'

Ray Walker swaggered into the Programme Department, his shirt and loosely knotted tie out of place among the jeans and trainers. He saw that Davies had Monica, his PA, with him, but he opened the door and stood with his eyebrows raised until she stopped what she was saying.

'A word about *Midnight Minus One*, Melvyn?'

Davies looked flustered, his eyes bouncing from Monica to Walker. 'Um . . . yes, of course, Ray.' He looked at Monica. 'Could you give us a few minutes, Mon?'

Monica glared at Walker, who either didn't see or didn't care. Pointedly, he waited in silence until the door had closed behind her.

'Right, I've spoken to the client, and the long and the short of it is that I've convinced him to stay with us. Not a happy camper. Not a happy camper at all.'

Davies leaned forward on to his elbows. 'Well done, Ray, that's what you do, isn't it?'

Walker bridled. 'It is indeed what I do, and I've done it. Unless I'm much mistaken, your bit is to come up with shows that keep the audience glued to their seats.'

'. . . at seven days' notice,' said Davies.

'Look, we can't all work in perfect conditions all the time.'

'Ray, this show was a disaster waiting to happen. The big mistake I made with it wasn't on air. It was allowing you to bamboozle Charlie into forcing me to make it.'

'Unless or until you want a job at the BBC, you're in

a commercial world where you don't just pull a show with a sponsor's name attached to it and shove it into the summer.'

'And you think that the position we're in now is a lot better than that, do you?' fumed Davies.

'Look. I've bought us some time, against the odds, from a client who was ready to tear up our deal and go back to the cold war I just got us out of.'

'Yes, with the usual expedient short-term patch. What did you promise him this time?'

Walker stopped short and took a deep breath. When he spoke it was in an altogether more agreeable tone of voice. 'You leave the customers to me. I had to concede a meeting with you next week as the price of him not pulling out immediately.'

'For God's sake, Ray, I'm not having a meeting with your bloody client. What are you thinking about? When have we ever done that before?'

'Needs must.'

'Bollocks. It's a show that goes out at eleven o'clock at night. It's experimental. And as you and I both know all too well, it was thrown together at the last minute. Is that what you want me to tell your precious client?'

The more irate Davies became, the more inappropriate was Walker's calm, but he maintained it nevertheless.

'Let's go and see the guy so he can tell his boss he's had a crisis meeting with the TV company and given us what-for. We'll listen to his worries. Make the right noises. I told him you have a string of great ideas as to how to put it right . . .'

'Well, I don't. I haven't got a fucking clue how to put it right. In fact, it's so wrong I should have pulled it on

Thursday. And you know what? You know whose name it's got at the end of it? Whose reputation it's got attached to it? Let's think now – is it Ray Walker's name? Oh no, it's Melvy –'

'Southern Foods,' said Walker, as he smacked the desk between them for emphasis. He held Davies's eye as he got up and left.

Charlie Burrows took the final call of the day from Hamish Perrin at the brokers.

'Some signs of life, Charlie.'

'Where did we get to?'

'Up to four fifteen.'

'Oh. So they didn't really believe us.'

'Well, remember that they're getting trading information from other sources too. ITV is being pretty low-key. They've just had results for some of the big Europeans, and their markets aren't that thrilling. Basically, they're short on TV marketplace reassurance at the moment. They're not going to believe you can buck a trend that's killing everyone else.'

'And the management stuff?'

'I think it's fair to say they're waiting and seeing. At the end of the long day, this is a management team that hasn't gone far wrong for them. They know you well. I think your firm defence of Martin's role was well received. Walker and Davies were impressive and have good track records. If there's anything, it would be good to get some really high-profile non-execs with no shareholder affiliation on the board. But we've talked about that.'

'Not the Activa way, I'm afraid. Anyway, we've taken a step in the right direction?'

'Sure, I guess I'm saying it's going to need some more good news to keep it up there. People aren't ready to believe that Acrobat is able to buck a European revenue turndown, if that's what we're about to get.'

'Don't talk us into it, Hamish.'

Acrobat's closing share price   415p

The Weekend, 13–14 March

Kate Davies had decided. At 9 a.m., while her husband was still sleeping off the week, a friend picked up the kids. She was immediately nervous, busying herself with unimportant household chores, distractedly primping up cushions on the sofa. At 10.30 she made a cafetière of strong coffee and carried it, with a couple of mugs, up to their bedroom. As an afterthought, she put the tray down at the bottom of the stairs and cut a fresh rose from the garden, placing it between the mugs.

'Morning, you,' she whispered as she entered the frowsty room. A harumph came from under the bedclothes.

She opened the curtains and sat on her side of the bed, looking at herself in the wardrobe mirror. She suddenly realized that she held it in her hands to make this the biggest day of both their lives . . . or just another Saturday. The man in the bed had no idea, one way or the other. She contemplated her image again, this time seeing a power that had not been there before. The woman who looked back at her was not a victim – not condemned to a sentence of hoping helplessly for change.

They had had a bad run these last weeks. The prospect of this day had arisen before, but on previous occasions the build-up of pressure had been dissipated by a look, a comment, a moment in which their spirits connected. That was all it took. A second – less than a second –

when that inner crackle of connection would detonate all the accumulated hurt.

But her capacity for love and pain seemed to be located in the same place. And as she hunched her emotions to protect herself from more hurt, the moments of connection seemed to stop. Once, she had admired him for what he'd achieved, but now the achievement was the addiction that was driving them apart just as surely as if it were cocaine. Except everyone thought he was marvellous. Success, the socially acceptable house-breaker.

She looked back at the tousled hair of the man in the bed. Naked, vulnerable, not an aggressor. The world saw self-assurance, poise, achievement. She had helped him wrestle down the shades of self-doubt which tugged constantly at his composure. She had tried to share his suffering, but the pain she had assumed didn't seem to diminish his load.

For long minutes she looked at the man, who had apparently fallen back into a deep sleep. What to think of him? Her mind was in paralysis. She didn't hate him, she hated this. She hated what he had done to them. But he hadn't set out to hurt her. He'd just been doing his job. God, those words.

Yet she'd worked in television. She knew the whole business existed in a state of panic. And her husband had risen through the company to win what he always called the best job in the world. This scruffy boy who had wanted to pull himself together to provide for her and their kids.

He hadn't changed. In her heart she needed a culprit. She needed to blame the man for what he had done to them. For driving her to the point where she would become a single parent. Where her beautiful boys would be deprived of the most important man in their lives, except for sticky weekends, as they grew apart. He didn't deserve that. He was surely just shipwrecked and thrashing too hard to see the lifeline. A victim too.

What had her boys ever done to deserve such a terrible punishment? It wasn't their fault. That everything they had built together should be sacrificed . . . to what?

Kate looked at herself in the mirror and watched a tear slip down her cheek. She picked up the rose and stroked its stem, her fingers tempting the thorn, touching its shape. She looked at the man – the boy, the silly foolish boy who had got himself into this stupid life and didn't know when to stop. He'd got caught in the machinery – an industrial accident had made him become someone else. He still looked the same, his mannerisms were all the same. Outwardly he was the man she had married. But inside, he'd gone somewhere else.

Tears now fell down both cheeks and she thought she was going to sob deeply. She put the tray on the floor, holding her breath, and tiptoed to the bathroom, leaning on the basin, looking at the woman she'd become and pitying her. 'Building for our future' was what they'd said. And here they were. The future had arrived, and the man couldn't remember her name. All those years, waiting for tomorrow, building the house that had blown down.

Could she become the aggressor? Could she seize control and tell him to go? Take control of her life. Would it stop the pain? It would share it, certainly. Would that make it more bearable?

She splashed some water on her face and tied her hair

up in what he called a 'paintbrush' – a short ponytail. She went back into the bedroom, scooped yesterday's clothes from the chair and got dressed in the bathroom.

Downstairs she scrawled a note – *Morning Sleepy. Taken the lads out. Call me when you're awake. Kx*. She read it and screwed it into a ball. How easily her resolve faded. She pulled out the notepad and sat with her pen poised over it for a long time. As she framed new words, a tear splotched the blank page. She tore it off and, stifling a scream, wrote: *M – Gone away for a bit. See you. K.*

It was a shabby little epitaph to their years together. But the big and beautiful fanfare that might have been there in any decent adieu had been crowded out by the distance in his eyes. By the emptiness of the man whose energy for life – the very magnetism that had drawn her to him – had been neutralized by the time he reached their home each night.

She went back upstairs and stood in the doorway, looking at the heap of bedclothes. She couldn't see him in the tussle. At that moment the misery of her choices tumbled on to her, like opening a cupboard full of objects crammed in long ago. Her eyes were flooded with tears. She raised a hand to her lips and, before turning to go, bent her fingers just once in a stifled wave. Her voice was the merest whisper, 'Bye.'

Monday, 15 March

Charlie Burrows crept reverentially into the ward where Henry Fleming was under observation. He hated hospitals because he never knew how to behave in them. It was a strange hierarchy, with its own by-laws. Though never expressed, he was expected to observe a rule book which dictated how loud he could talk, where he could go and when. He announced himself in a whisper to the ward sister, who directed him to Henry Fleming's room in a pointedly loud, sing-song voice. Burrows edged around the door and, to his relief, Fleming was propped up in bed reading *The Economist*.

'Charlie!' He seemed to start when he saw Burrows appear.

'Henry. I know you want a decent single malt, but they told me grapes and flowers were still top of the pops in these places.'

Fleming was smoothing his hair down and adjusting his dressing gown. 'How kind of you to come and see me. How's it all going?'

'Oh, you know – usual old bollocks. Not the same without you, et cetera et cetera. OK if I sit down?'

'Of course, of course.'

Fleming flustered around as if making a move to shift papers and magazines from his bedside chair, but he was tethered by his attachments and managed only a little futile arm-waving.

'So tell me all,' he said, coming alive. 'What's happening?'

Burrows mused for a moment on how much to tell him. 'You'll have seen our outstandingly crap share price and no doubt read about probably the crappest analysts' meeting I've ever done.'

'Yes, I saw,' said Fleming, as if responding to news of a death in the family. 'How's the revenue?'

'Easy, Henry – I thought the point of you being in here was to stop you worrying about all of that.'

'Yes, Maggie's made them promise not to give me a phone. She caught me talking to George Salzman.' Nothing in Fleming's manner intimated that he could see the funny side of being caught out by his wife.

Burrows laughed anyway. 'I think I'd choose the analysts' meeting ahead of the wrath of Mags. Still, we struggle on. Kind of running a slide rule over Charisma TV for when the government finally gets round to freeing up the ownership rules.'

Fleming nodded. 'You've always wanted Charisma, haven't you?'

'In every possible way,' laughed Burrows. He looked up to see a feeble smile on Fleming's face.

'Anyway, Charlie, there is one urgent thing I have got to talk to you about.'

'Come on, Henry – can't it wait?'

'No, it's already waited too long, actually.'

'Tell me how you are before you start worrying about work.'

Fleming recounted the points as if from a clipboard. 'I'm fine. On the mend. Worry too much. Not fit enough. Plenty of New Year's resolutions to be going on with.'

'Except you're not going to wait till New Year, right?'

'Apparently I'm not. But look, there was one thing that is really bothering me.'

'Don't tell me – the movie.'

'How did you know?'

'Because I lie awake at night worrying about it too. Ray is looking after it while you're away, which I confess doesn't grant me much solace.'

'Well, he *isn't* looking after it or he'd have discovered what I'm about to tell you. And if he *has* discovered it and isn't telling you . . . I don't know what kind of game he's playing.'

Burrows felt a stab behind his stomach. 'Go on,' he said.

'The night before I . . . keeled over . . .' Burrows realized that he hadn't thought through how to describe what had happened to him. 'I had a call from George Salzman. The Germans are out of the deal. They've got financing problems – in fact, the bottom is falling out of their world. I had to make an instant judgement call, which I really needed to talk to you about, but you know how these things seem to go in Hollywood.' Fleming paused for breath and took a huge sigh.

Burrows could see sweat glistening on his brow. The dagger in his stomach flicked him again.

Fleming continued. 'In order to stay with the project I had to increase our exposure. I didn't want them to think we were, you know, bureaucratic, not able to play the game at their level, lose Scarlett Johansson, so I made the call.'

'How much?' whispered Burrows.

'Twenty-two,' Fleming gulped, his face straining to

interpret Burrows's response. 'Ten million more. I figured we could probably find an accounting mechanism to protect this year's earnings.'

Burrows was impassive. 'When was this, Henry?'

'It would have been a couple of weekends ago.'

'Before the results announcement.'

'Yes.'

Burrows swallowed the somersault in his gut. 'I told them twelve.'

'I know, Charlie – that was the right number till the Germans pulled out of the deal.'

'Did you sign anything?'

Fleming winced visibly. 'Yes.'

Burrows looked at the figure of his FD and tried to dismiss a sense of pity. He'd lost a stone and a half – mainly from his face, by the look of it – and his complexion, usually a little florid, had a wash of grey about it. He made his decision.

'Look, Henry – you concentrate on getting better. Don't spend time going over this – you were hardly in much of a state to put in a call to me really, were you?'

'Well, no but . . .'

'Don't worry about it. If we've raised our stake in the movie, we make more money when it becomes a crashing success, don't we?'

'Oh God, Charlie, if only the City would see it like that.'

'Leave the City to me – just you get back on your feet again.'

In the car Mick asked all the right questions, but he could tell that this was a time for silence as his boss brooded in the seat next to him. The City had been at best permissive about the Hollywood plan. What the company had embarked upon as a way of breaking the mould, they had only ever seen as a black hole waiting to gobble their cash. He'd toted Henry Fleming as the reason to believe it was all buttoned down, but even Henry had been bludgeoned or seduced into buying out the German co-financiers. Ironic. They were right. What was it about Hollywood that made perfectly sober men and women lose their grip?

Burrows found himself looking forward to seeing Martin Sumner. Martin would have some taciturn comment that would keep them sane. Burrows's mind turned to the events about to unfold. He'd deal with Walker this morning. Martin would have to take on the movie project as part of relieving Walker of his duties. Burrows knew that the Walker process was going to be horrible. He'd be on to the lawyers – he called them his 'attorneys' – in a heartbeat. Walker would lash out at anyone and everyone, but especially at his Chief Executive. Oh well, it would end. It would be ghastly for as long as it took to settle it, and then it would end. Everything always did. You geared yourself up for it, you lost some sleep over it, it felt as if it was going to last for ever, but it would always end. Burrows liked to pick a day in the future, look at it in his diary and know that the pain would be over by then.

Walker's departure would end the long-running mis-match between his scratchy solo approach and Burrows's aspiration for the team culture of his company. At every single staff presentation the leaden figure of Ray Walker in his ill-fitting designer clothes had clumped across his vision of shared corporate values.

Walker was from a different generation. Burrows didn't know much about his early years – he never shared anything about his private life. But he imagined a day when some old-style mentor had sat young Raymond down and told him, 'Always look after number one. Never trust anyone you don't control.' Walker was a hugely effective executive and, though he had tried the new language introduced by Burrows to the company, he wore it as unconvincingly as his Armani suits. He could put it on when it was needed to pass as a team player, but deep down he believed that any concession to anyone else was giving away something that was rightfully his. The great Brazilian striker who could put away the goals most men would miss, but never made one for anyone else.

Melvyn would surely be pleased. He never made much fuss, but he'd been hurt by the Walker machinations. No love lost there. And, of course, Sarah was the underlying reason why he could move Walker on, in fact why he had to. Though there was still a significant experience gap, Sarah Golanski was a team player, and she was good. If he meant all that stuff he said about opportunity culture, she had to get her chance. Who knows how good she would be if you took the lid off her?

Burrows gazed out of the side window of the car, idly watching as a parked car was clamped by two jumpy-looking officials. Mick Spring saw him looking.

'Bastards,' he offered under his breath.

Burrows looked at him. 'Just doing their job, Mick.' Burrows sighed hard.

'You OK there?' said Spring, looking over at him.

He laughed wryly to himself. 'Same old stuff, Mick,'

said Burrows. 'I wish I had a quid for every minute I've spent dreaming up plans to get rid of bloody Ray Walker.'

'Old school,' said Spring, returning to his driving.

Was he being harsh on Ray Walker? Was he trying to create a team of people just like himself? Surely Ray's skills should be accommodated. Didn't every team need a genius striker? Was he putting camaraderie ahead of shareholder value? What would the shareholders think about the demise of Walker? He couldn't afford to risk a further blow to their confidence. Maybe this *was* the wrong time.

Or was it a new era?

Abby Kelleher arrived at 9.30 a.m., to be met by Martin Sumner. He apologized for Burrows's absence, walked her to her new office, and stood aside in the doorway for her.

'Welcome, Abby – this is the nerve centre – the site of many future glories, I trust.'

'Thank you, I hope so,' she smiled, and dumped her case in the corner.

'You're going to do just fine. Bear in mind that Charlie wasn't exactly easy with the press before his recent glitch. He's going to be even more cautious now.'

'Yes, I thought about that,' she said. 'I'm a believer that fences can always be mended. In the end they can't afford not to have a relationship with Charlie Burrows. We just have to re-establish that relationship on our terms.'

'Well, good luck – just bear in mind that our man is scarred by this.'

'Leave him to Auntie Abby – I'll sort him out.'

*

Sumner was waiting for him when Burrows arrived at the office. 'Ready for me, oh great one?' he said.

Burrows looked over at his friend. 'Only if you've got your nettle-grasping gloves with you.'

'Naturally,' said Sumner. 'Never go out without them.'

Paula appeared with coffee as Burrows reeled off the items they had to cover. 'I see we have the full ninety minutes today, Pol.'

'Special request of Mr Sumner,' she responded.

'Thought we'd need some additional grasping time,' said Sumner.

'Excellent. Let's get on with it.'

Burrows liked stuff like this. Any decent manager could make the judgement calls demanded of him most days. The momentum of the organization kept it moving and, to be fair, it was his job title that opened doors and got him heard. But every now and then, the opportunity arose to make a real difference to the company he ran. Times like this demanded his management, his leadership, his decisiveness. These were the moments that kept him interested. So he felt energized by the opportunity – keen to work through the details with his friend and confidant, assess the risks, package them, deal with them, write the announcements, the staff briefing, the press. This would be a good one for Abby Kelleher to get her pearly white teeth into.

'OK, Mr Sumner. Today's dish of the day is Walker and his glorious future – in somebody else's company. I seem to recall you wimping out of this when we last talked about it. Have you returned from your weekend refreshed and ready for a scrap?'

'Not actually all that refreshed, Charlie.'

Something in Sumner's tone alerted Burrows to a shift

in the mood. He sat down at his table. 'Something up, Mart?'

'Bit of a big one, Charlie. I saw Malcolm Ryan on Saturday.'

Burrows had nothing to say. In a second, the adrenalin to deal with Ray Walker bled away. He tried to compose his face.

Sumner continued, haltingly, as if he would stop at a signal from Burrows that it was too much. 'I went to his house. You been there?'

Burrows managed to shake his head.

'Amazing place – we're in the wrong business, mate. Anyway, the bottom line is that he wants me to go to Channel 6.'

Burrows was fighting with the controls to bring himself around to this development. He straightened the papers in front of him. 'And you? What do *you* want?'

Sumner sighed hard, pulling a face as if only now, with the compliance of his friend, was he able to ask himself that question. 'I'm tempted.'

'Tempted – not like you to sit on the fence, pal.' He heard the strained bonhomie in his own voice. Pal?

'Sure I'm tempted, but you're my friend first and I didn't want to come here and present you with a *fait accompli.*'

'Thanks.' Burrows was entirely thrown by the conflicting messages. Friends, rivals, faith, trust, treachery. He said, 'You've got to do what you think is the right thing for you, Mart.'

He nodded. 'I've been over this in my head a lot now. Can we separate business from pleasure, Charlie? That's the question.'

Burrows knew the right answer. 'Yeah, of course we can. What do you think I am?'

'I don't think anything, Charlie. But let's not minimize this. If I go, I'm not just leaving Acrobat, I'm joining Channel 6.'

'Look, you and I were friends before we started this, we'll be friends after it too. But before we get into that, are there any buttons I can press that will get you to tell Ryan to piss off?'

'Like I say, I didn't want to just hit you with it.'

'But you want to do it. We wouldn't be having this conversation if you didn't want to do it.'

'Well what do *you* think, Charlie? Am I going to be number two for ever? That wasn't a vintage moment for me at the results meeting, you know, the analysts wondering what the hell I do here.'

'Oh, come on, Mart, that's just ignorant prodding.'

'No, of course. But I like winning, Charlie. You know that. And I need to know if I can do it on my own.'

Burrows knew that this was not a discussion about 'whether' but 'how'. In a few minutes the flow he had planned for the day, the week, even the next phase of Acrobat had been diverted. Sumner was key to the Walker plan. He got up and strode around, his glasses pushed on top of his head. He paused at the old juke-box, looking into the machine at the ranks of 45s awaiting their orders.

'When do you want to go?' he said without turning round.

'Up to you, I think. I've left it very open with Malcolm.'

The mention of 'Malcolm' stung Burrows. 'So have you told him you're going?'

'I told him that, subject to this conversation with you, I wanted the challenge, yes.'

'So "Yes" then.'

'Yes, Charlie. I'm going.'

Burrows felt cuckolded. Sumner talked of friendship, though he'd spent the weekend in this liaison with another. This aggressor. He gazed at the juke-box, unable to think clearly. At the front of his mind was a fog of betrayal.

'Sooo, when do you want to start?'

'Me? As soon as is decent, I guess.'

'Oh bugger this, Mart — we were going to deal with Ray. And I'm going to have to garden leave you the moment this is announced . . . which is today in theory.'

'I haven't resigned. You have to announce it when I resign, but let's give ourselves a few days to think things through before we do that. We don't want to do it today.'

Burrows felt a twinge of relief. 'No, not today,' he managed.

'Look, Charlie. You *can* still trust me.'

Burrows looked up from his scrutiny of the Wurlitzer. The defector talked of trust. His voice was measured, kind even. 'Trust you to do what — trust you not to try and take our audience, or our revenues? That'll be your *job*, Martin.'

'Trust me not to make any use of information that belongs to Acrobat.'

'I don't see how you can help it.'

'Just trust me, that's all.'

Henry Fleming and the twenty-two-million-dollar movie deal sprang to his mind. He couldn't tell Sumner now, could he. At a stroke he felt incredibly alone.

'Look,' said Burrows, 'just tell me there is nothing I could say that would make you stay.'

Sumner became very still and looked Burrows in the eye. Quietly he placed his pad on the desk in front of him as if to punctuate the moment. 'You could say that, if I go, that's the end of our friendship.'

Burrows paused, buying a second, knowing what he had to say. 'Well, that would be untrue. Our friendship is what is important. All the rest of this stuff is just what pays the mortgage.'

'Do you really think that, Charlie?'

Burrows fumbled with his pen, opening and closing it between his finger and thumb. 'When all's said and done, yes, that is what I think. I fight very hard for this place, Martin, you know that as well as anyone. And if I go over the top now and then, I'm sorry. Maybe I care too much. But when it comes to it, my family and friends are where it's at for me. Non-negotiable.'

Sumner watched him with fascination. They never talked this directly, describing their feelings about one another. He held Burrows's eye. 'I want you to know that that is the one thing you could say that would make me reconsider. Because I consider your friendship a bigger and more valuable prize than a bus load of Channel Sixes.'

Burrows wanted to hug him. Instead he said, 'All right, mate. I know you've got to do this, and – you know what? I hope it goes bloody well for you . . . within reason.'

The two men laughed together, holding each other's eyes. Burrows knew this was the moment of parting. They'd say goodbyes and there'd be speeches and gifts and presentations, but this was the moment.

*

Melvyn Davies had spent the weekend pursuing Kate on the phone but failing to speak to her. Work was a relief after that, though there was little about this week to excite him. He had a meeting with the *Midnight Minus One* production team at 10.30. They would be looking for the kind of long-term guarantees he couldn't possibly give them. Yet he knew that a creative team could not function with a sword of Damocles hanging over it. They were usually too scared to be completely direct, which helped him fudge his way through the unvoiced questions and send them out, ready to pull together for this week's effort. But he knew they were sailing into the wind. He'd commissioned some 'fast and dirty' research into the show over the weekend, but they'd largely be on their instincts about what had worked and what had not.

He knew there'd be pressure from Walker, that Solveig Nilsen would be nervous that the format was a poor man's version of her own postponed show. She was booked to see him on Tuesday – that wouldn't be much fun either.

But his head was full of Kate. That note. He'd tracked her down to her parents' home in Cornwall. Her mother had told him to give her some space. He looked at his diary to see when he could go down there or something. It wasn't easy. The injustice hurt him like lemon juice in a cut. He was only getting on with what they'd started together, wasn't he? She of all people knew the score in a TV company. But even as these thoughts crowded into his head again, he knew there was more to it than that. He knew his hours spent on his career were no longer for the benefit of Kate and the boys, but for a more personal appetite.

At some point, when he hadn't been looking, he'd started to get his self-worth at the office and only guilt from his home. Kate was just hurt by the whole thing. He couldn't talk to her about it like they had done in the old days. It just sat there between them like a lumpen creature. They'd got so used to its presence that they just lived with it, like the scribble on the wallpaper in the hall. For some minutes he sat gazing at the table in his office, as if trying to memorize the pile of junk there as in a child's game.

And then there was Sarah. He'd try to see her tonight. He imagined their conversation – 'My wife doesn't understand me.' He opened his email and typed her name.

Four floors up, Charlie Burrows shook hands with Howell Snoddy and showed him to a chair at the table. Snoddy was focused, refusing to rise to any of the light-hearted nonsenses with which most meetings began. Once he got to his point it was immediately clear that Snoddy was in search of reparations more than reassurances. He had come to deliver his lines and he wasn't going to be wooed.

'I offered you a gentlemen's agreement. I've handed you the tools to assure your ability to expand in the way you've been whining about since God knows when. But no. You inaugurate a programme which sets out not only to vilify me, but which is clearly targeted against this government. If there were a more provocative route, I'm sure I don't know what it is.'

'Howell, one of the delights of my job is that I am responsible for a twenty-four-hour station, a fraction of whose output I view in advance.'

'Then how can you be responsible for it? How do you avoid the kind of recklessness we are discussing?'

'I have a great team.' As he said it, he thought it might have been nice if Melvyn had bothered to forewarn him they were going to have a whack at the Broadcasting Minister of all people.

'Well, it clearly doesn't work,' barked Snoddy, impatience evident in all his movements. 'However, the issue of my personal treatment is the lesser of your problems. The other is a bigger and more serious issue.'

Burrows considered expressing doubt that anything could be more important to the Minister but decided this wasn't the moment.

'There are consequences in making an enemy of this government.' Snoddy paused for effect. 'This nasty little show has drawn Acrobat to the attention of the PM and half the cabinet.'

'The Prime Minister? Hasn't he got bigger things to worry about?'

'He is very media-aware, you know that. I had to suffer the ignominy of procuring a tape for him to see for himself. Having done so, he is not a happy man.'

'Are you offering me a deal here, Howell?'

'No, I am not. I tried that once, and it was ineffective. But you seem to expect the government to keep these things in different compartments. You people want us to work hard to help you get rich, while sitting nice and still so you can take potshots at us.'

'But, Howell, they *are* in different compartments.'

'For you, perhaps. Not for the government. You want me to go in to bat for you on ownership regulations with a cabinet that is hostile to you. I'm here to tell you that it just doesn't work that way. This vindictive little programme has got to go.'

Burrows had imagined that this would be a ritual fencing match before they went their separate ways. Now he looked aghast as Snoddy finally made the point he'd been sent to make.

'Let me get this clear. You're saying that this government's position is that unless I pull this show, you will frustrate our plans to expand our business. Plans shared by the whole industry to drive out wastage and become more efficient.'

'Spare me the lobbying. I really have heard it all before. As I said, I'm not offering you a deal here.'

'It sounds a lot like it.'

'Good grief, no. I am merely trying to share a few home truths with you. All I'm suggesting is that it is in your hands to create the circumstances in which the government is likely to look favourably on some of your more commercial requests.'

'Well, Howell, I'm stunned. I'm stunned that this government doesn't feel it can cope with a programme with a small audience at eleven o'clock at night.'

'I would have thought those were exactly the reasons why it will not cost you a great deal to cancel the show. It hardly had a triumphant start.'

'Neither did *Monty Python*.'

'Well, of course, the decision is entirely for you. But it would be a great help if I were able to pass on to the cabinet today that this programme was, shall we say, a nettle in the hedgerow, rather than a continuing thorn in our side. The timing couldn't be more perfect; the Secretary of State is discussing the issue of ownership regulations with her officials this afternoon.'

Burrows realized there was no coincidence about the

timing of Snoddy's mission. The response could not be to fend the Minister off with assurances, or even buy time. Burrows had to take the offer, not send him back empty-handed. The show was a late-night event. Out of the spotlight. It wasn't as if this was a peak-time show that had launched on the back of huge publicity. He had no alternative but to make the call. He knew he would have a tough time with Melvyn and Ray, but he also knew that Acrobat's faltering share price desperately needed the kind of shot in the arm that a relaxation in the ownership regulations would give it. In that context it was a no-brainer.

'So, I kill the show, you relax the rules.'

Snoddy looked at him through lizard lids. 'I think I have made it clear that this is not a transaction. I am merely pointing out to you that a conciliatory step today would be very timely.'

'OK, Howell, I guess I understand what you're saying. You have my word that the show will not continue.'

Snoddy's beam belied the smugness of his victory. He immediately tried to lighten the moment by reverting to a different tone.

'Thank you, Charlie. I appreciate your understanding and I hope we can put this episode behind us.' He stood.

'I'm counting on it,' said Burrows.

As Paula showed Snoddy out, Charlie Burrows wondered which of the ghastly tasks facing him he should knock off first. The most urgent was to get a fix on the *Marilyn* project, and now he had to deal with Walker on the *Night and Day* sponsorship. And Melvyn. He should talk to someone about Sumner's decision. But who? Martin Sumner was his confidant at moments like these.

If ever there were a day he needed his friend at his side, this was turning into it. He put his head in his hands as if, by holding it steady, he could still the clamour of ideas jangling inside.

As Howell Snoddy was settling awkwardly into his chair in Charlie Burrows's office, Melvyn Davies arrived at his meeting with the *Midnight Minus One* production team. He had asked them all to attend, as much to send a message about the seriousness of their plight as to get all hands on deck to resolve it. He had thought hard about this show. It was new in style and the great British public always took time to embrace the unfamiliar. It was on the back foot, the hand-to-mouth scriptwriting was a major problem. They needed a stock of material to work with, more time to nurture it to life. Ideally, he should pull it off for a month to allow it to breathe a bit, but Walker had impatiently squashed that idea because he needed the sponsorship revenue to make budget this month. So his options were both ugly sisters.

'OK, people,' he said, calling the unruly group in his office to order.

The Beard brothers had been there first and occupied one of the sofas, and as the others had arrived they had taken up position in places of decreasing comfort around the office. As the hubbub subsided, he continued.

'Everyone knows we had a tough job to do last Thursday. We did it to the best of our ability, and the audience figures were challenging. Let me give you the good news to start with. We are still on air this Thursday . . .' a desultory cheer went up from the group and the atmosphere lightened noticeably. 'But we are not out of the woods yet. We did well with younger viewers, but we didn't do enough to stop them turning off and going to bed.'

One of the Beards spoke up. 'It's just too late, isn't it? I mean, everybody's going to be thinking about going to bed, come eleven fifteen, aren't they? Really.' He looked around the room for support.

'Sorry, Nigel. Can't accept that. There are plenty of shows that keep people awake because they can't bear to miss them. They just didn't like it enough.'

Beard1 looked abashed but kept quiet.

'I've got some research into what worked and what didn't, so we'll refocus the show this week around the popular stuff. We'll record a sketch or two in advance of the show and use them as promotions. That sound acceptable?'

It was a rhetorical question, but that didn't stop Beard1 from answering.

'Sorry to be difficult, Melvyn, but I thought the whole point of the show was to do it at the last minute in order to be absolutely *au point* with the news.'

'No, Nige, the whole point of the show is to get a frigging audience.' Nervous laughter. 'What this show needs is not a different slot, or different competition, or more promotion. It has to be able to be great under any and all circumstances. What this show needs is word of mouth. If there's evidence that it's starting to attract a following of devotees, I promise you it is in the schedule for the rest of the season. To achieve that I want to see this group working as a team. It's not for Nigel and Justin just to write the gags and Jeremy and Sue to deliver them. I want this whole group to cancel everything, and rebuild me a show that we're going to be proud of.'

Davies sensed that the team was rising to their challenge. He worked them with his words, to believe in themselves and the chance of plucking greatness from the embers.

'Right. I'll leave this research with you. Have a look at it – it's not gospel, it's a steer, that's all. I want to see a show that has some real balls: punchy, funny, pointed, edgy . . . It's eleven o'clock at night, so I don't need *Jackanory*. And what the people are telling us is they like the rude bits.' He put on a poor Hollywood accent. 'Let's do this together people.'

They laughed as they filed out of his office. Davies watched them go and granted himself a moment of pride at his ability to rebuild their spirit.

Burrows would have given a lot of money not to have lunch with Ray Walker at a time like this. Hours before, blissfully, this guy had been in the departure lounge. Now he was vital to Burrows's crew. So far, this day had been a contender for the worst in his career. But cancelling the meeting would only have generated more pain.

Walker was guarded but cheerful as he entered Burrows's domain. He saw the sushi waiting for Burrows and recoiled. 'Don't know how you can eat that muck,' he said.

'That muck happens to be my lunch, thank you very much.'

'You're welcome to it.'

'Thanks.'

Walker watched with a look of deep distaste as

Burrows made theatre of splitting his chopsticks, loading up a lump of sushi and dunking it in the little plastic pot of soy sauce. 'How's your ham sandwich?' he said, his mouth too full of food to speak clearly.

Walker pulled at the packaging. 'I'll tell you in a minute.'

'Now, Ray, where are you on picking *Marilyn* up from Henry?'

'Right, *Marilyn*, yes. I'm waiting for the green light from you to get on a plane to meet the partners.'

'In the meantime, what have you found out?'

'Well, it's early days. Still in the scripting stage, but attracting a lot of the right sort of interest, I can tell you.'

'Ray, I have reason to believe that this project needs some urgent hands-on management.'

Walker stopped chewing. 'What do you know that I don't?'

'Nothing you couldn't have learned by talking to Henry Fleming.'

Walker spoke with childish petulance. 'I'm trying to give him some peace.'

'And meanwhile the project is rudderless. Come on, Ray, get a grip. See Henry, for God's sake, will you? Form a point of view on what is happening and let's meet to discuss it. Like tomorrow.'

'Oh, tomorrow – I've got a client day, which I obviously can't miss.'

'You're the Commercial Director now. Doesn't that help?'

'Of course not. I'm still the most senior seller. Got to be there. Why don't I jump on a plane to the States, meet and greet, and we'll talk a week today?'

'Too late by a mile. I need you to be up to speed on this straight away.'

'Look, it's all about perception out there. If I phone up and start trying to catch up on what the story is, they're going to think I'm an idiot.'

'What about the Germans?'

'Again, I want to get a full briefing before entering the ring with any Germans.'

'So what you're telling me is that essentially this project has been unmanaged for two weeks.'

'No, of course not. Rishi is across it, and, as far as I'm aware, they are keeping Henry in the loop as far as possible. And in case you weren't watching, the Sales Department has been falling over itself writing a re-forecast for you in the last few days. What do you think, we're all sitting with our feet up on the desk reading magazines?'

Burrows laid down his pen with exaggerated care and looked up at Walker. 'The Germans are out, Ray. Our commitment to this project just grew by ten million dollars.'

Walker did not pause. 'Why wasn't I told? Am I supposed to be some sort of detective here?'

'You're supposed to be in charge.'

'Which I am. This is clearly a communication issue, you're trying to make something out of it, but these things happen on a baton change.'

'I'm not trying to make anything out of it, Ray. We can't function if I cannot be confident that my managers are managing.'

'Meaning what?'

'You wanted the Commercial Director role and I gave

it to you in good faith, despite the fact that you leveraged a very difficult set of circumstances to get it.'

Burrows realized that he didn't usually speak to Walker in this way. No one spoke to Walker in this way. He wondered why. Walker seemed wrong-footed by the directness of his approach, and Burrows's confidence grew. If he was now going to have to make it work with Walker, he had to establish some new terms of engagement. He pressed on.

'And let's face it, Ray. It's not that unusual for you to use whatever you need to manipulate advantage for yourself. In order to enjoy the benefit of your undeniable sales skills, I seem to have to put up with all kinds of behaviour which is entirely inconsistent with the team values that I ask of you.'

Walker regrouped. 'I think you'll find that the team values in the Sales Department are stronger than anywhere else in this company, certainly than that ragbag of a Programme Department.'

'That's quite possibly true, Ray, but I don't want a team within a team. The sales team is great at bonding with itself but, with precious few exceptions, it is exceptionally poor at relating to the rest of the organization.'

'Look, if you're not happy with the quality of my work, I can arrange a conversation with my attorneys. I'm sure a settlement can be agreed.'

Burrows had been here before. When the arguments ran out, Walker became playground bully, getting his way by being prepared to contemplate a greater scale of violence than anyone else.

'Oh stop resigning, Ray. It's pathetic, and one of these days I'm going to accept.'

Walker blustered. 'I assure you, I'm perfectly serious. And I'm not resigning.'

'Well, I'm not firing you, so you can forget your bloody attorneys. As Chief Executive of this company I insist on my right to define its culture. If you're not respecting that culture, I reserve the right to talk to you about it without eliciting your resignation.'

Walker realized that he had been holding a ham sandwich in front of his face for the duration of the dialogue. He put it down, speaking more quietly now. 'All I will say is that it is not your *culture* that pays the bills. While you're sitting here, hoping everyone will be friends, I'm out there taking the decisions that will get us the money in. You may think you could do it a lot better. Maybe you're right, in which case I invite you to try. And I reserve the right to defend myself when attacked.'

Burrows considered the man in front of him. There weren't many people he really despised in business. Over the years he had met plenty of people with whom he wouldn't have chosen to share his Sunday lunch, but by and large they were just folks doing their job in their own particular way. Walker had chosen to punctuate the end of his speech by snapping at his ham sandwich with aggression. Burrows realized that he was stuck with this man who lived in another age and spoke another language. With a deep breath he pressed on.

'Right, Ray – having established that I'm not going to take over from you as Sales Director, we're agreed that you are going to move fast to get a grip on the movie project. We should meet on Wednesday if you're off playing golf tomorrow.'

'That's fine,' said Walker, beginning to tidy his place

and wiping his jowls with a slurping noise. 'And it's Commercial Director.'

'I have another item on my agenda.'

'Right.'

'*Midnight Minus One*. I'm pulling it.'

Walker sat up straight. 'You're joking.'

'No, I'm not joking, Ray. I'm afraid that right now we have bigger fish to fry with the government than pressing on with a show that has died on its first outing.'

'No, it's not possible, I'm afraid. I've spoken to the client and got him to see Melvyn later this week.'

'Then you're going to have to unspeak to him, Ray. I'm sorry, this is one occasion where I didn't have the chance to talk to everyone in advance. I haven't spoken to Melvyn yet.'

Walker looked to be deep in thought.

'Come on, Ray – you can manage this. It's not the first time we've had to deal with a turkey.'

'Yeah, except this is Southern Foods.'

'Ray, I know all the arguments. Just deal with it, will you?'

'You know, I wonder why I bother. One step forward, two steps back.'

'Thanks, Ray. I know you can sort it.' Burrows went over to the fridge to get himself a bottle of water. 'Want a drink?'

'No, thank you. I'll go and get on the phone.' He gathered up the remains of his sandwich and his papers and stalked towards the door.

'Hope the client day goes well,' called Burrows. 'Talk to you Wednesday.'

Walker said something muffled and Burrows found himself rejoicing that his Commercial Director would be out of the office the following day. 'This is ridiculous,' he told himself.

Rather than go back to his own office, Ray Walker took the rest of his lunch to the Programme Department, where he informed Melvyn Davies that in light of its poor quality, *Midnight Minus One* had been summarily cancelled.

'How's it going love?'

'Hi, Mom.' Abby Kelleher smiled as she heard the reassuring voice on the phone.

'Everything OK?'

'Well, I've had a bit of a sticky start with Charlie.'

'Reeaally!' she drawled. 'Tell me, tell me.'

'I'm worried about it, actually. I'm not going to get anywhere here if he's suspicious of me from day one.'

'Give him time, Abby. Our Mr Burrows is not at ease with the press. I've been the pair of old slippers, and he's probably missing me a bit.'

'I do hope so.'

'Just take it a step at a time. Prove to him that he can trust you. In the end he's got to have absolute confidence in you if this is going to work.'

'I know – bad start.'

'Keep your nose down. Work hard. Send him emails late at night – he notices that sort of thing; he'll come around. If all else fails, you can always charm him.'

'Ha, ha,' she said humourlessly.

'In that case, better stick to Plan A.'

'OK, thanks, Mom.'

'That's my girl.'

*

At 7.30 p.m., Melvyn Davies was in Vinopolis, the cathedral to wine reclaimed from the arches on the south bank of the Thames. It was inconvenient for both of them, but that imbued it with a sense of immunity from discovery.

When Sarah arrived, he didn't know whether to kiss her. Had she been a producer or someone, any woman from another company, then he would of course have sprung to his feet and given her the standard Oscar winner's kiss on both cheeks.

She too was uncertain. The story in her head, fed by too many airport novels, ran with an ease and pace that reality had not matched. In her plot, the sound of lush strings should have been rising in the background, everything around them turning hazy, as they wrapped themselves into each other's spirits. But Melvyn was in a different scene.

He stood and put his hand on her shoulder as she slipped her jacket off. He caught it and arranged it over a spare chair. She was wearing a simple white shirt, almost mannish, yet perfectly offsetting the fall of her hair to her shoulders and the gentleness of her features. He ordered a bottle of Montagny, pleased at her complicity that the evening would last longer than a single glass each.

'So,' she said with a brief sigh, 'had a good one?'

'Totally crap,' he said, the images of his day wafting across his mind. 'You?'

'Oh, you know, the usual.'

As the waiter poured his wine he said, 'I had the privilege of telling an entire production team that Acrobat is not the kind of company that pulls shows after one outing, so we would work hard together on the next episode of *Midnight Minus One*, only to be informed, by bloody Ray Walker of all people, that the show has been cancelled by our Chief Executive.'

'Yes, Ray told me about that. He was livid too.'

'I'm sure,' he said, unconvinced. He took a long draught of the wine, as if it were beer.

'We're going to have to give away some free airtime to buy them back from this.'

'That's easy enough, isn't it?' said Davies. 'I mean, if you don't sell it today, it isn't worth anything tomorrow. Like airline seats, isn't it?'

'Kind of. Except by giving them free spots we bring the price of their advertising down, and it's very hard to get it up again.'

Davies snuffed out the candle with his re-moulding. It didn't seem much of a hardship to him. He slumped back in his chair, throwing an arm over the back of it. 'Sarah, Sarah, why do we do this to ourselves?'

She shrugged. 'Career, purpose, fulfilment, success?'

'Ah, the "S" word. Whatever it means.'

'What does it mean to you?' She settled in her chair, glad to have moved beyond the quicksand.

With no hesitation he said, 'Distinctiveness.'

She pulled back from the table as if to get a better perspective on him. 'Famous?'

He weighed this a moment. 'No, not necessarily famous. But significant. My big fear is that I get to the end of all this and I might as well have not been here.'

'Well, there's no fear of that, Melv.'

He shook his head. 'Of course there is. We're in the hands of bean counters. Who cares if we do something outstanding, daring and brilliant? Long as it gets the ratings up.' He shook his head. 'So the people I love get put on hold while I do battle with your man from the soap powder company.'

The mention of love caused Sarah to pause at the boundary of new territory. She decided to take the risk of going in, at least to see if he would follow.

'But at least Kate understands. She's seen the challenges inside a TV company with her own eyes.'

He did not look up. 'Kate's gone.' He drained his glass and watched it all the way back to the table.

She smothered her planned rejoinder, embarrassed.

'Saturday.'

Now unsure of her role, Sarah looked at him intently. His openness marked a step towards increasing intimacy, and that much was thrilling. Yet this vulnerability was too fragile to be a foundation for anything new.

'On the bedside table were two cups of coffee on a tray. And a rose.'

'Oh,' she said quietly.

'Beautiful. She'd cut it from the garden. God knows how long it had been there. The coffee was cold and the rose was wilting.'

'A picture,' she said, closing her eyes at her response. He didn't see.

'Acrobat gave me my wife. And then it took her away again.' He looked shrunken, defeated. He shrugged and tried a smile. 'Probably for the best.'

Sarah wrestled with her conflict of interest as they sat in silence. When she had waited long enough for him to continue, she said, 'Is it really over between you?'

He spoke in disjointed sentences. 'I don't know. If we

passed the point of no return, it happened when I wasn't looking. Which is all too likely.' Another shrug.

'Maybe time will help,' she persisted.

'Maybe,' he said, 'though there's a lot of hurt now. She doesn't approve any more. She doesn't like who I've become or what I do . . . and you know what? She's right.'

'That's wrong, Melvyn. Acrobat makes a difference to people's lives. Just think if it had all been for a widget manufacturer?'

'Ha – or a furniture maker. It's all the same, isn't it? Work is work. It has no right to my whole life.'

She nodded. 'I know what you mean.'

'Of course you do, Sarah. You joined the same club.' He affected a ringmaster's sing-song: 'Welcome to The Club, Ladies and Gentlemen. Here we offer you everything you will ever need to lose yourself in the company of like-minded adults. Club members can expect to earn more, be more famous, get tables in all the right restaurants; so come with us, run with us on our journey to this wondrous place.' He faced Sarah. 'So we did. What else would we do? Surely worth making a few sacrifices for success; no one wants to be a failure, do they? And we made it. We became respected members of The Club. Great. We gave everything to join. And now I see it. I've been paying my membership dues in the currency I could least afford. Trust.'

Golanski shifted uneasily. Now he had torn the cover off these wounds, the flow was unrelenting. 'But I like my work,' she said.

'But don't you see, it's a drug. You don't *like* it. You can't do without it. We're all in it together, Sarah. This is our tribe. It's where we belong now. It's where we get all our significance, all our self-worth. Without our work, what do we stand for, what do we mean? Who are we?'

'Don't be absurd, Melvyn.'

'No, I'm not. Listen – I've never seen it so clearly. Who are you?'

'What?'

'Seriously – I've never met you before. Introduce yourself to me.'

'Oh come on, Melvyn.'

'Come on, do it, please.'

'I'm Sarah Golanski. Happy now?'

'Sarah Golanski who?'

She sighed and put on a 'do I have to' face. 'I work for Acrobat.'

'Ah, doesn't that feel better. Now I see how you fit. You're the Deputy Sales Director of Acrobat. You are a proper person. I conform, you conform, we conform. You're in the club, so I'm safe with you. We know we both play the same damn-fool game as each other, and because we're all doing it together it's all all right.' She shook her head. 'Well, it's not all right, Sarah. It's bloody not all right.'

He fell quiet, his passion suddenly doused. She was transfixed by him. She did not speak. Searching his face, she wondered at the options coursing through his mind. For a part of a second she thought she saw a new composure return to him. He met her gaze again.

'I'm sorry,' he said.

She smiled and let go a little giggle of relief, placing her hand on his again. 'I'm honoured that you could share your heart with me.'

'No, I'm sorry. That was over the top. You don't deserve that. It's just . . . well, you know.'

'Yes, I do know.'

The anger of moments before had capitulated to quietness. 'You've become very important to me, Sarah.'

She felt her insides collapse on themselves. 'You too,' she breathed.

They sat in silence for some minutes.

'Ready for a new start?' she said.

'Something like that,' meeting her eyes with a conspiratorial smile.

She tilted her head, asking for more.

'I've spent forty years trying to do the right thing . . . not lose people's approval. And look at me.'

She started to remonstrate, but he wasn't listening. A seam of confidence had returned to his features.

Finally he said, 'So. Goodbye to all that.'

She sat watching him until the silence became unbearable. 'What next then?'

He flashed his collaborator smile again. 'It starts with dinner for two.'

He'd made his decision. She had an instant to make hers. Knowing it may be the wrong one, but knowing it was the only one, 'Why not?' she said with a flick of her hair.

Acrobat's closing share price   420p

Tuesday, 16 March

'So, Piers, you have had some success finally.'

Piers Carrick looked at the clock on his bedside table. 7.04 a.m.

'Arnaud, how nice to hear from you. How was your holiday?'

'Oh, you know, good. But you have been busy, I see, with our good friends at Acrobat. Until yesterday's announcement, the share price is down twenty-five per cent in two weeks in fact.'

'So it was,' said Carrick, pulling himself on to one elbow and combing a hand through his hair.

'This announcement is obviously desperation. You keep up your good work, and perhaps in another fortnight we act. Do you agree?'

Carrick got out of bed and stood absurdly in his pyjamas as if that would make him sound more convincing. 'It's certainly starting to move in our direction, no doubt about that.'

'And you have some plans to keep it moving downwards, no?'

'Absolutely, absolutely, Arnaud.'

'Good. I see you next Tuesday as normal?'

'Fine for me, Arnaud.'

'OK.' And he was gone.

Carrick's wife Charlotte had surfaced. 'It's seven

o'clock in the morning. Do I take it de Vigny is back from the Caribbean?'

'He certainly is,' said Carrick, slipping on a silk dressing gown.

'Is he upset with you, as per?'

'Funnily enough, no. He's rather pleased with me, as it happens.'

Roger Collier exuded calm. He had made a lot of money out of Acrobat, and he still owned 3 per cent of the company. He had stayed on the board despite occasional desultory efforts by various shareholder advisory groups to remove him on grounds of longevity or non-independence.

Burrows liked Collier. When the heat was on, Collier could be relied upon to keep a steady hand. And, unlike Sharma and Carrick, he had no agendas other than what he perceived to be best for the company. He was a popular figure around the offices, taking time to stop and chat with the staff, waving at people on phones in offices as he made his way around the building.

Furnished with his coffee, Collier came quickly to the point. 'Right then, Charlie, how can I help?'

'Well, to be frank, I'm absolutely beleaguered. Wherever I turn there is another pile of crap. The revenue's going south with the ratings and, whatever I do, the share price falls. Sorry. Normally I guess I'd be having this conversation with Martin, but he's going off to run Channel 6.'

'Oh no,' sighed Collier, bowing his head as if there had been a death in the family. He stroked his beard as he weighed up the impact of the news.

'Oh yes, I'm afraid,' said Burrows. 'So I'm down a COO and an FD in the most competitive times we've ever faced, an aggressive government about to relax the ownership rules . . . and the share price is in the tank.'

Collier snapped out of his mourning and pulled a pad from his briefcase. 'Got it,' he said, organizing two pens alongside his pad. 'Let's get to work on this. This could be a real opportunity.'

'No, really, Roger. Losing Martin is a real problem.'

Collier pressed on, undimmed. 'We can't change Martin's decision, can we?'

Burrows shook his head.

'No. So it's "Thanks for all you've done, Martin"; we move on. No whingeing over what we can't change. Does he have a successor?'

Burrows grimaced.

Collier looked up from the diagram he was sketching. 'Ray?'

'Ray would certainly think so.'

'Yes, but Ray is not the Chief Executive. So, with the greatest respect to Ray, we don't really want to know about what he thinks just now. We'll come back to it later, no doubt. Do you need a COO?'

'I've really enjoyed having Martin there. He is great at all the stuff I'm bad at, and I think it has, you know, worked well for us to have someone in that role.'

'And to provide reinforcements to help deal with Ray from time to time, perhaps?'

Burrows laughed knowingly.

'Which leads on to an obvious question.'

'I know. Martin and I were going to deal with it yesterday. I realize why he's been stalling me now.'

'What was the plan?'

'We were going to move Ray out, put Mart at the head of the sales function, with Sarah Golanski reporting to him.'

'Very elegant. Can it work without Martin?'

'Roger, everything in me wants to go for it. But it's a hell of a step for Sarah and, with the share price vulnerable, I don't think I've got a lot of brownie points with the market right now. Not the time for taking such a big risk, with rumours of recession as well.'

'But if I hear you right, your management style is consultative. You need a partner in crime, someone to weigh your ideas with. Someone who just gets it. Melvyn?'

Burrows shrugged and tipped his head from side to side as if to evaluate the thought. 'Melvyn's great, but I don't really want his head anywhere than in the shows. You know, I think he's a genius at what he does. Moving him off it would be like buying the best striker in the country and sticking him in goal.'

'Is that how he sees it?' persisted Collier evenly.

'Right now, I think old Merlin is having a few problems – nothing that we haven't all had to deal with at one time or another. I'll keep an eye on him, but now is certainly not the time to distract him from the ratings.'

'How about Sarah Golanski?'

Burrows's mind returned to the Media Business Club, which now felt like a month before. He'd been proud of Sarah, watching her dealing with customers and industry players with charm and poise. She was good. Her approach to creating a revenue statement had been just right. And she was young. If he was going to be able to hire the best people in the market, he had to send a clear message about opportunity, and there was only one way to do that.

The effect of Sarah Golanski on his emotions was exactly the opposite of Ray Walker. He felt supported, liked, even forgiven by this young woman with so much potential.

'She's brilliant,' he said, warming to the solution.

'Can you elevate her without putting Ray's nose out of joint?'

Burrows considered this for a moment. 'Not possible I'm afraid.'

'He got his Commercial Director role?'

'Yes, but this is a man who phones his lawyers if someone's in his car park space. He'll be looking for constructive dismissal or anything that can give him something in the bank for a future negotiation.'

'Which is why he has to go when we're ready. Good, now how well do you think Sarah understands the rest of the business?'

Burrows was enjoying this, watching the balding head bob up and down from his pad, tracking down a solution. 'Actually, of anyone in sales, she understands it best. She's liked everywhere in the organization, because she has time for people. I think they'd go out of their way to make this work for her.'

'Maybe send her off to school for a bit to broaden her beyond the sales speciality? Looks like it might be an appointment that would go down well internally, and with the clients. Not with Ray, but we understand that and we just have to manage it. Feels like a good result to me.'

Burrows was on his feet, his mind racing over the next steps as Collier packed his papers away, taking another glimpse as the pad disappeared into his bag and nodding his approval at it.

'Roger, thanks. What can I say? Thanks.'

Collier could not have been more content. 'Call me and let me know how you're getting on. Are you going to tell the Chairman?'

'I'll give him a call.'

Collier placed a hand on his arm. 'You don't need me to tell you this, but just work through the steps before you embark on this. There are a lot of people who have to get the right messages in the right order.'

'Sure will – I'll give you a call. Thanks again.'

Melvyn Davies picked up the phone again. On his desk lay his attempts to script what he had to say to her: corners of documents, the back of the audience research book, each abandoned in favour of the next attempt to get it right. This time he dialled the number and waited, his heart beating the seconds. Her mother answered the phone in her polite and quizzical style.

'Mum, it's Melv. Please don't hang up.'

Her voice changed, clearly making the announcement to whoever was with her. 'Oh. Hello, Melvyn.'

'I just wondered if I could have a couple of secs to talk to Kate.' He heard a door slam, followed by some whispered dialogue.

She came back on the phone. 'Sorry, Melvyn, I don't think that's a good idea.'

'Is she there?'

'Um, no.'

'Could you ask her to ring me when she can.'

'I can ask her.'

'Thanks.'

'Goodbye, Melvyn.' The clatter as the phone went down.

Phyllis Grigson picked herself up from a sofa full of newspapers and walked to the window. When her husband had left, they'd sold the rambling old house in Haslemere that held too many memories for them. Grigson missed the joy of greenness. She loved the horses, loved their smell, and she loved the sound of them at night, tramping around the paddock next to the old house, snickering softly to each other. The night sounds of Holland Park were very different.

The sounds in her head were different now, too. In two weeks she had changed, she knew it. The colic of injustice would not leave her alone. Over and over she returned to the place of her humiliation, re-working the events, drawing the same senseless conclusion.

When Abby had moved to the States, Grigson had poured her life into her job, adopting the younger members of staff as surrogate family, regularly staying late to listen to them air their anxieties about life, love, work. But now that she had no job to consume her, Abby was everything. She knew it and the fact that she would play her part in her mother's healing was never in doubt.

But for now, above all, she felt the buzz of resentment at becoming the sad, lonely old fool with plenty of money, no partner, friends too busy for her. She determined to fix some lunches, see some people, and stay in the loop. For the hundredth time she told herself not to get embittered but to channel this poison in a way that might just dispel it. Her thoughts were pierced by the phone.

'Hi, Mom, it's me, got a minute?'

Grigson smiled at her daughter's voice, her accent still unsure whether it lived in Britain or the States. 'Hello, love. Always.'

'It's just there are a few things.'

'What have you got?'

'I've been through the transcript of the analysts' meeting last week and been checking out some of the stories. You know what? There are some real inconsistencies between what the directors said and what is actually going on.'

'Really, how big? I mean, there are always little exaggerations here and there.'

'Well, take this investment in Hollywood. Charlie Burrows told the City that the company's exposure to Hollywood was twelve million dollars.'

'Yes,' she said. 'I recognize that number.'

'It's the wrong number. I went and talked to Rishi Kapur about how it all worked, and it turns out we're in for twenty-two million.'

'*Twenty-two?*'

'Bit of a big difference, isn't it.'

Grigson's tone changed. 'Look, Abby, before you do anything with this, you have to check your facts. When was the investment made? Has it always been twenty-two? And the key question is, was it twenty-two at the time of the announcement? Find out what he said about the level of investment – I bet the analysts were putting pressure on him to limit it.'

'I've got it here,' she said, '. . . "our exposure will not exceed twelve million dollars".'

Grigson was quiet for a moment. 'Do the homework,

Abby. This could be big. Charlie Burrows could be in a lot of trouble.'

Henry Fleming ambled in his garden, wrapped up against the chill. It was a day begging for a bonfire, crisp and swirling. His head was crackling with the urgency of getting back. The pressure was building with every day, the same thoughts visiting him over and again, beckoning him back: 'Got to get back. Underachieving. So much to do. Sort this Hollywood thing, get the City lined up for a revenue slowdown, steady the boat for a bid when the rules change . . .' On and on.

Suddenly, and without warning, a different voice cut through the hectoring: 'Why?' He sat down on a damp seat among the trees.

After a pause the first voice chirped up again. 'They need you. You're a very good Finance Director, Henry.'

'What kind of reason is that?' said the newcomer. It sounded composed. Fleming listened carefully.

'Come on, Henry. Don't go throwing the baby out with the bath water; it's been very rewarding, bought you and Maggie a nice lifestyle.'

'At a price.'

'Oh really, what's come over you? Come on. It's time to get back; the welcome, the familiarity, re-occupying your place in life. You don't belong here, shuffling around like an old man.'

But the new voice persisted. 'You've been given a chance to think new thoughts, make a new life. Don't miss it.'

There was a freshness to this new extremist thing which pleased him. He needed to live with it longer . . . to continue to pace around it, get to know these thoughts, see if he trusted them.

He got to his feet again and shuffled through the damp spring grass. It would need cutting again soon and the cycle would begin again. He stooped at one of the flowerbeds, looking over the soil, wondering at its inhabitants. He let himself down gingerly to his knees and picked up a brown-treacle lump of earth, pressed it between his fingers, rubbing the loam into his fingerprints. It felt natural, honest, to have mud under his fingers. He kneaded the soil for a while and wiped his hands on the bark of a young birch tree they had planted when they bought this house. His fingers left a trail down the silvery bark. He wondered what changes would pass during the life of this young tree, growing up to give its shade to the next generation and the one after. Long after I'm gone, he thought, catching himself as he realized the significance of the last few weeks. Something in my life that is not transient, not temporary. Just one enduring achievement. Earth's shadows fly. But something lives on.

Acrobat's closing share price   420p

Wednesday, 17 March

Ray Walker was concealing his excitement exceptionally badly. Burrows's words had itched away at him throughout yesterday's client golf day. How dare the CEO accuse him of failing to manage the movie? He would give him no possible reason to repeat that charge. He called Sylvia and had her book his trip straight away. Checking to see that no one was watching through the window of his office, he opened the top drawer of his desk and, without bringing out the pack, parted the folds once again to read his ticket: *London Heathrow to Los Angeles. First Class*.

He'd always aimed higher than sales, something the new 'Commercial Director' title had promised but had yet to deliver. He knew he could do the sales bit, and the respect accorded to him for his skills in that area was gratifying in its way. But after a lifetime selling TV spots, the challenge no longer moved him. From time to time he would think back on the boy who left school with a handful of CSEs and found his way into selling. Neither he nor any of his classmates could have envisaged this: the second home in Tuscany, the Armani suits, the Gucci ties, the first-class travel. Such ambitions would have been discounted by them all as mere daydreams, at best, forgivable escapes from the every day.

Having achieved it, Ray Walker dared to ask for more. He knew that his brand of business was much better suited to Hollywood than anyone else's in the company.

Now he would show them. Fleming was scared shitless of the snappy American street fighters with their slick, easy talk. If they had a rule book at all, it contained only one word. Win. They would always see Fleming as just another European with a big chequebook, feeling his way into their domain, biding his time till he had worked out how to play a game he was always going to lose.

At three this afternoon he'd be sipping champagne in the first-class cabin of the BA flight, choosing his movie, his wine, his canapés. He had briefed Sarah Golanski on what might come up before his return and had had Sylvia book the Bel Air, snuggled in its trees at the heart of Beverly Hills. He smiled as he anticipated the stretch limo Sylvia had arranged for his use while in town. He suppressed a chuckle as he pictured Fleming picking his way around town in beaten-up old cabs. No wonder they saw him coming.

He called in Sylvia and dictated a memo to Charlie Burrows.

Following our discussion on Monday I have concluded that the only way to get a grip on the situation in Hollywood is for me to be present in person. This project has been beset by enough communication problems. The only way to avoid further complication is for me to deal face to face with our partners.

Accordingly, I have fixed with George Salzman that I will have dinner with him in LA on Thursday and he has arranged meetings with the other players on Friday and over the weekend. I will return to the office fully apprised on Monday morning.

Sarah Golanski is of course briefed on Sales Department matters and my office has my contact details for the few days I will be in California.

I have asked Sylvia to fix us some time together to discuss my findings on my return.
Ray

He signed it with the illegible flourish he had nurtured and asked her to deliver it personally when he'd gone. Then he emailed Melvyn Davies.

Melvyn

As you know, Charlie has asked me to take control of the Marilyn project. This entails me going to visit with our partners in LA at short notice. It is of paramount importance that the meeting with Geoff O'Brien of Southern Foods is not cancelled. The main thrust of the meeting is for you and he to talk. I'd be grateful if the meeting were to go ahead without me. Sarah can join you or supply any briefing materials you require.

Ray

Burrows got Walker's memo as he was about to leave for lunch with Sarah. Immediately, he saw that his carefully plotted agenda was going to be wrecked. He needed Walker there to manage his response to Sarah's promotion – and anyway, didn't they have a meeting planned for today?

'Pol, can you get Ray, please?'

He squeezed the memo into a tight ball and hurled it across the room, missing the bin by several feet. Why did this guy have to do this? Why couldn't he . . . what . . . obey? Burrows didn't want a regime like that. But Ray Walker took the freedoms upon which such a consensual approach depended, and he hijacked them to achieve dividends exclusively for his own account. Burrows looked at his watch.

'Ray's left for the airport,' called Paula. 'Mobile?'

Sarah would be down at the car by now. 'OK, give him a try.'

Moments later, she called again. 'Mobile's switched off.' The frustration boiled in him.

The exasperation was soothed at once by the sight of Sarah Golanski, looking up from a copy of the *FT* as he arrived in a swirl of apologies.

'No problem, just watching my net worth decline,' she smiled.

'Oh, you too,' said Burrows. In the car she told him how sorry she was about Martin's move and they chatted easily about the challenges he faced at Channel 6 until they arrived at Cecconi's. It was Burrows's favourite place for big announcements. Like the Connaught for big deals, he liked the significance of these places, which gave him a sense of playing at home. An army of Italians busied themselves around Sarah. Cecconi's was the perfect fusty Italian; he'd been told off for taking his jacket off in there once. The other diners appeared to be Mediterranean royalty, aristocrats, only rarely any nasty newmoney media types.

They shared the fabulous egg tagliolini to start. Sarah was trying to avoid two courses, but he regaled her with stories of how fantastic it was until she relented. After their main courses were delivered, he moved towards the goal of their meeting, enjoying a frisson of excitement as he did. For all the crap that fell to him as Chief Executive, this was one of the real perks: a conversation that would make someone's day, and might even change their life.

'Sarah, I wanted to tell you about some thoughts I've been having regarding changing the shape of the management structure.'

She looked up from her plate, immediately interested, guileless. 'Great.'

'I want to bring some more youth into the frame and start to build a more convincing succession plan. Every challenge is an opportunity and all that.'

'Yes, I read that book too; doesn't always feel that way, does it. Mmm, this is lovely.'

The moment had come. He could barely suppress a silly grin. 'I'd like you to consider taking Martin's job.'

She could not have looked more astounded if at that moment he had fired her. For a moment she was silent, composing some words. He saw a flush creep over the top of her simple black linen dress.

In the end she managed, 'Me?'

Burrows smiled broadly, thrilled by the goodness of giving. 'You' he said.

'Oh my God.' She put her fork down. 'Me?'

'Take some time to think about it. I don't want an immediate answer. Any time before coffee would be fine.'

Her jaw dropped again.

'Joke, Sarah. Joke.'

'Sorry.' She laughed at herself. 'Wow, I'm just . . . you know.'

'I very much hope you'll like the idea. I'm personally very excited by it.'

'Yes, it's brilliant. Why me? I mean, I leave sales?'

After the initial wham, her thoughts were all coming at once.

Burrows finished his chicken, noticing with enchantment that her lunch had finished at the moment of the news.

'Right. So would I be taking on Martin's role intact?'

'That would be the clear intention. We'll send you off to business school for a couple of months, probably over the summer when things are a bit easier; give you time to play yourself in, work more closely with me, Henry Fleming, Ray and Melvyn, your fellow board directors.'

'The board? I'd be on the board?'

'Pretty odd COO that's not.'

'Oh my goodness. I never thought. Wow, the timing of this . . . wow.'

He tilted his head. 'The timing?'

'Gosh yes.' She gazed at him, fighting to order her thoughts. Another one hit her. 'What did Ray say?'

'Ray doesn't know.' She looked confused. He continued. 'At this level, Sarah, I don't go asking Ray's permission to release you. If you say yes, he'll be my first call.'

'Oh no, wouldn't *I* talk to him? He's been very good to me.'

'We'd organize ourselves so that the moment I put the phone down you would call him. He's in LA.'

'I know . . . we're talking about doing this before he's back?'

'Got to. I can't sit on the news of Martin's resignation over the weekend, and I need to announce your appointment – if you accept – at the same time. Smooth management succession etc.'

'I see.'

This was clearly as big an issue for her as whether she

would do the job or not: talk to Ray on the phone. They both knew how he would hate that.

She collected herself. 'Thank you. I really don't know what to say. I'm honoured. I'd like to think about it a bit, if I could.' The thrill of achieving a lifetime's ambition was checked by her expectations of the different conversations she'd have to have with two men. Ray and Melvyn.

Carrie McGann, surrounded by the cacophony of the newsroom at the *Daily Telegraph*, picked up her phone at five o'clock. It was a first for her – the anonymous caller.

'I will not reveal my identity, but I have some information that may be of use to you.'

Her scepticism lost a short battle against her curiosity. 'Fire away,' she said.

'Martin Sumner is going to Channel 6 as Chief Executive.'

'What?' she said. 'How do you know this?'

'That's it,' said the voice, and hung up. McGann replayed the words, trying to identify the intonation. Whoever it was had been deliberately muffling their words.

She slumped back in her chair, her thoughts buzzing. Highly plausible, now she thought about it. She rated Sumner. Why not? When you think about it, he's the obvious person: a man with something to prove, whose hiring would also damage their main competitor. Of course. She pulled together her phone numbers – Martin Sumner, Charlie Burrows, Abby Kelleher, Malcolm Ryan. Looking at her list, she decided to go for Burrows. She'd enjoy the effect of her call.

'Hi, Charlie, it's Carrie.'

Burrows was still enjoying the afterglow of his lunch with Sarah Golanski. He had worked through his list of people, and it had gone well. The Walker conversation would be the tricky one.

'Good afternoon, Carrie, are we OK?'

'All things are possible,' she said.

'What can I do for you?'

'I'm following up a story that Martin Sumner is leaving.'

Without a stumble, Burrows said, 'As you know, Carrie, we never comment on market rumours.'

'Oh, come on, Charlie, this is a bit of a big one to fob me off with a "no comment on market rumours".'

'Carrie, you know and I know that Acrobat attracts more than its fair share of speculation and rubbish.'

'So this is speculation and rubbish?'

'If we responded to every kooky idea that someone puts into the head of a journalist, we'd never get anything done.'

'Charlie, is this a kooky idea?'

'There you go again. I said, we're not going to start commenting on every rumour that goes around Groucho's.'

'You're not denying it then.'

'I am neither confirming nor denying it. I'm not dignifying it with a comment.'

McGann tried another tack. 'So if I ran a story saying Martin Sumner is leaving Acrobat to become Chief Executive of Channel 6, I'd be making a fool of myself. Right?'

'Carrie, that's for you to decide. I can't do your job for you.'

She realized he would stonewall her for the rest of the

day if he had to. 'Well, thanks, I suppose. Can I run another question past you?'

Burrows was relieved to get off the hook. Obviously she wasn't sure enough of her source to nail him. But he knew she'd be on the phone, working her contacts till she found something. It meant that he didn't have till the end of the week to get the announcement out. And he certainly had to get in touch with Ray Walker the moment he landed in LA.

Carrie McGann was on to her next question. 'I also heard that Hugo Trevethan will stand down at next year's AGM.'

'Have you now? Well, you're miles ahead of me. And I think I'd probably know, don't you?'

'So I've got that wrong.'

'Come on, Carrie, it's complete bullshit. Where do you get this stuff from?'

'Sorry, just have to follow these things up.'

'I understand. Have you made contact with my new PR supremo, Abby, yet?'

'Yes, she seems fine.'

'Always happy to take your calls, Carrie, but do feel free to call her too, won't you.'

'Sorry to waste your time, Charlie. See you soon.'

She laid the phone gently on its cradle and punched the air. 'Yesss.' He'd fallen for it. Refuse to comment on market rumours only when they're true.

Burrows called in to see Sylvia himself. As usual, he ran into her discomfort at having to deal with him directly.

'Sylvia, I have to talk to Ray the moment he gets to his hotel in LA. When will that be?'

She blinked an artificial eyelash, choked with mascara. 'Mr Walker will be landing at 18.05, which will be 2.05 a.m. our time.'

'Oh hell. Please will you get him a message to call me at my hotel as soon as he gets there.'

Sylvia repeated the words as she copied out the message. He watched the long red nails and wondered how on earth she could function with those talons glued to her hands.

To fill the silence he explained, 'It's the Broadcast Awards tonight and I've got an early start. I'm at the Hempel. Paula's got the number.'

Back in his office, he called Abby Kelleher to tell her about his conversation with Carrie McGann.

'I don't think she knows whether either of her stories is correct.'

'Right, I'll give her a call,' said Kelleher.

'I don't think so, do you? Don't want her to think we're panicking. I suggested she call you directly in future.'

'Did you "no comment" her?'

'Yes. Well, I "no commented" the Martin thing and just laughed at the other one.'

'Oh.'

'Anyhow, how are you doing with my releases?'

'I've got a couple of drafts here for you when you want them. An internal announcement, a Stock Exchange one-liner and a press release.'

'That was quick. Sure, bung them up to me on the email. I'll try not to frustrate you as much as I did Phyllis with all my changes.'

She laughed. 'That's all right. That's what a draft is for. It only gets annoying when it's been slaughtered by a committee. When you're happy, we'll give them to Martin Sumner to take a look, if you agree?'

'Fine. Talk to you later.' Maybe she was going to be fine after all.

He called Sumner to tell him of the leak.

Sarah Golanski looked at her watch again. She had started worrying she was in the wrong place, as she always did when someone arrived late. At 7.40 she watched as a cab pulled up outside and a large bunch of flowers walked in with a breathless Melvyn Davies behind them. She laughed, her voice piercing the buzz of private conversations. The front-of-house girl offered to take the flowers and put them in water.

'Congratulations, Chief Operationg Officer,' he said, flopping into the chair opposite her. For a moment she thought he might kiss her. So did he, but somehow he was installed behind the table too soon.

He poured himself a glass of white wine from the bottle in the bucket and held it up for a toast.

'To you,' he said.

She lifted her glass to his and bent her wrist around it so their hands touched. 'Are you sure you're OK about it? I haven't said "Yes" yet.'

'Me? Sure. It's brilliant news, and well deserved.' He pulled the bottle out of its bucket to read the label. 'This is nice. I see you've upgraded your wine budget already.'

'Cheeky bugger,' she said.

'Well, it's my treat tonight anyway. Might as well start currying favour right away.'

She snorted at him. 'Now don't start, Melv. It won't change anything between us.'

'We *might* get to work a little closer.' He bounced his eyebrows absurdly. Again, that jingling laugh. He filled their glasses. 'Anyway, one thing I insist tonight,' he said. She cocked her head. 'No serious talk. Honestly, you were so intense last time!'

She biffed his arm and pulled what passed for a fierce face. She knew that tonight was a next step, the thrill of each other enhanced by the recklessness of the venue. Zilli's is a small but exuberant Italian in Soho, certainly on the repertoire of many in the television business. And it was obvious that this was no business meeting between colleagues.

The waiter had to return three times for their order, such was the tumble of their conversation. They both played the ritual instinctively, their hands marking the evolution from apparently accidental brushing of accentuated points or jokes shared to deliberate touches. Finally, as if choreographed, they interlocked their fingers across the table, lightly adjusting them from time to time to renew the feeling of each other. Davies sensed where this evening was heading. This talented, beautiful woman was making all the pace, and what could he do about it?

Once you've been to one TV awards night, you've had the whole experience. Too many people at tables packed together so close that, by the end of the first course, everyone is already fed up with the attempts of sweaty waiters to deliver the salmon or lamb through the mêlée. Always salmon or lamb. Burrows usually pretended to be vegetarian; it's harder to knacker an aubergine.

He was placed at the top table, along with the Director General of the BBC and the Chief Executives of Channel

4 and Five, as well as the Chairman of the judges. As usual, Georgia was seated next to the big shots, while he got to talk to their partners. It was a deal he liked. As the categories wore on into the evening, he drank too much, though this didn't distinguish him greatly from the majority of the crowd. Burrows always knew he'd had enough when he craved a cigar. The cigar made him want a brandy, and so the spiral would begin.

As his brandy arrived, he was accosted by a diminutive man from the Broadcasting Standards Commission; he had clearly made the journey from the other side of the banqueting hall for the express purpose of interrogating Burrows about *Midnight Minus One*. There was no escape. Georgia excused herself and edged through the crowd to engage with some less demanding company. Burrows stood to take his punishment, going through the motions of a dialogue with the standards man while his eyes roamed the room behind his head. He briefly wondered where Melvyn Davies was, but suddenly he caught sight of Martin Sumner, sitting at the Channel 6 table, laughing as he chinked his glass with the young, good-looking group there.

He felt a punch in his stomach, as if he'd caught his wife with another man. The standards man was chopping at the air, his head down, apparently trying to prove some point or other by sheer physical effort. Burrows looked down at the animated balding head. It didn't entirely seem to matter whether he was there or not, as the man hadn't yet paused to allow him to speak. He wondered if he could just creep away. He interrupted the other's flow with a banal comment about the risks of being at the cutting edge and excused himself awkwardly, saying there was someone he had to catch. The man's little face laid bare his disappointment. Burrows left him standing there, gawping, among the great and the good and stalked towards the Channel 6 group.

He had no idea what he wanted to say . . . just to embarrass Sumner. Surely the guy knew it was too soon to be hobnobbing with them in public like this, flirting with the girls, ha-ha-ha-ing at their nothing observations? He swirled the brandy in his glass, taking a messy slurp as he milled through the throng, avoiding picking up the greetings offered by people as he passed.

As he approached the table, he averted his gaze so he could appear to run into them by mistake.

When he was level with the table, Sumner called to him. 'Hey, Charlie, over here.'

He turned his gaze from the nothing he'd been looking at and started, greeting Sumner as his eyes travelled around the table. The conversation had stopped, and people nodded to him as his eyes swept across them.

'So, Mart, this is your new family.'

They laughed tentatively, all except Sumner. He knew Burrows too well to find his choice of words light-hearted. He got up and put his arm round Burrows, steering him away from the group so they could get talking again.

'You cool, Charlie?' he said quietly.

'No, Martin, I am not *cool*,' he sneered, too loud.

Sumner led him further from the table, towards the edges of the hall. 'What's up, mate?'

'I'll tell you what's up, mate.' He turned to confront Sumner. 'What's up, mate, is you, mate, two bloody days after you drop me in it, parading yourself in front of the whole industry like some stop-me-and-buy-one corporate tart.'

Sumner's Geordie timbre returned. 'Get used to it, Charlie. I'm going. It's happening.'

Burrows wrestled himself free of Sumner's arm which was still sitting on his shoulder.

'Don't patronize me, Martin. I know you're going, but unless you've forgotten, you are still under contract to Acrobat and we've made no announcement.'

'Meaning?'

'Meaning it's too bloody soon to be kissy-kissing with your new mates.'

'I'm just saying "Hello", Charlie, for God's sake. Look, man, it's not a personal slight.'

'You don't think it's personal? You think this is just business?'

'In the end, yes, I do. You are going to have to get over it some time. Why not start now?'

Burrows paused and looked at his friend. 'And to hell with the last seven years, right?'

Sumner shook his head in frustration. 'No, Charlie, not *to hell with* the last seven years; move on from it, build on it . . . brand new day.'

Burrows could see that this was going nowhere. He had to get out of it before it just became a slanging match, though a part of him was up for that too.

'I guess it must have meant more to me than to you.' He turned to walk away with the last word.

Over his shoulder he heard Sumner say, 'That's bollocks, Charlie, and you know it.'

Burrows knew it all right.

*

In the hotel room, Sarah Golanski allowed him to feel her full weight on him as she pressed him against the door. Without releasing him, she reached out and dimmed the lights. Her face was so familiar but so unbelievably thrilling in this crazy new context. Had her eyes always been this dark or this persuasive? He buried his face in her hair, and her hand ran down his head to the vulnerable skin of his neck. She placed both hands on his face, lifting herself away from him. She touched a finger to his lips when he tried to speak, his face registering confusion at her restraint. She crept across the room, seeing the boy in the man looking back at her.

'Why don't you order us a bottle of champagne?' she breathed, tiptoeing into the bathroom and slipping the lock.

The shower was heavy, the soap aromatic and delicious on her skin which tingled at the intimacy of her fingers. She reached up and turned gently under the torrent, massaging the oily suds over her body. As each moment passed, the ecstasy of anticipation wound its cords around her until she could bear it no longer.

Slowly, deliberately, she smoothed the thick white towel over her skin as she watched her shape in the mirror, opaque with steam. She heard the knock and the slam of the door as the champagne arrived. She finished quickly now, slipping on the towel robe from the back of the door and sweeping the sleeve across the mirror to check her reflection. She raised her eyebrows at the confident woman who looked back and whispered, 'You look gorgeous, sweetie.'

The moment she re-entered the bedroom, she knew something had happened. It felt different. He had gone.

*

Burrows was panicking. He could feel the emotion rising. Where the hell was Georgia? Going looking for her would mean another fifty pointless conversations with industry people. He stifled a nauseous wash of fury as he pushed his way through the throng away from the Channel 6 table – anywhere. He made his way to the toilets, locking himself into ten square feet of sanctuary.

He blocked out the braying of the young men, echoing in the room, his head dizzy with injustice. Everything about Channel 6 was hostile to Acrobat. It occupied a unique position of mistrust in his head. They wanted his audience, his revenue, his best people (obviously) and his headlines. And now his closest friend was occupying that same space – mistrust, conflict, dispute. His best intention to be real competitors and real friends with Martin Sumner had failed its first test. Business and pleasure. Burrows knew he had no idea where the dividing line fell.

He had to get out. From his pocket he pulled out a pen and a business card and scrawled: '*G. Can't find you. Feel like crap. Gone back to hotel. See you there. C.*' He found Abby Kelleher talking to a journalist and signalled behind the woman's back. Abby detached herself.

'Everything all right, Charlie?'

'Actually, I feel terrible. I need to get myself to bed, but I can't find my bloody wife. Do you mind telling her I've had to go – I've written it on a piece of paper here.'

Kelleher read the back of the card. 'Oh, poor old you. Sure, leave it with me.'

The Hempel, his favourite hotel in London. Suite 110, the bed in a gallery suspended from the ceiling by a hundred slender rods, a single plush mattress on its

238

wooden floor, always worth the excuse to stay in town despite the £800 price tag. He took the lift to the first floor and rolled along the featureless white corridor to the door at the end. He leaned his back against the door as it made its satisfying clunk to close out the world. He shrugged off his coat, tugging off his bow tie as he rounded the short flight of stairs up to the bathroom. He supported himself heavily on the sink and tried to avoid the eye of the drunk in the mirror. He wrenched at his clothes, leaving them where they fell.

He glanced at the naked figure before him. Someone had said that the secret of business was staying an inch ahead of the hounds of discovery. When it looked like they were on to you, it was time to move on. He looked himself in the eye. The features were drawn, shadowed. 'Time to go, Charlie?' he asked the man.

Immediately he knew the answer. Why did it drive him so hard? Throughout his career, he'd always aspired to the next step upwards, perhaps in order to wrest a little more control over his life from the manager above him. Being number one was just the logical consequence of that plan. But it had been a tease. He'd got there now and, if anything, he was more constrained than at any previous stage of his career. Now, most of the time he had to bottle up what he really thought, because being the number one meant everything had particular resonance for someone. People would dissect what he said to find its 'true' meaning, because he was number one. He'd had to learn a whole new language of defence in order to prevent the market running away with price-sensitive ideas. He couldn't buy or sell shares in the company when he wanted to without it being in the press.

His income and all the terms of his employment were public knowledge. The wide-open spaces for which he had done battle had turned out to be a box.

Oh sure, he'd enjoyed the winning. But maybe the race was now more important to him than the goal. Did he still have a goal? What was he trying to prove now? And to whom? Now that he occupied the number one spot, winning meant something new. It was a more public goal, being seen to succeed. Building his reputation. When you boiled it down, was that what was left: what people thought of him?

He splashed cold water on his face. He'd faced down moments like this before. Moments when it seemed that the real skills in the company belonged to the others, like Walker and Davies. Despite the blear in his head, he recognized this as another such onslaught. It was only confidence that kept you ahead of the hounds, he knew it. All the best people suffered these moments, because being the best demanded the catechism of self-review. It wasn't easy to open the fire of one's self-assurance to gusts of doubt. And the aftermath of tonight's clumsy tirade at Martin Sumner had blown at the flames till they were cold and blue.

Again he remembered Ray Walker's call. Wonderful. He looked at his watch – 1.15 a.m. Probably a couple of hours yet. His mind ploughed relentlessly on: now irritated by the thought of Georgia, butterflying around the ballroom at the Royal Lancaster; now returning to his status, his future; dabbling with incomplete ideas; writing headlines in his head. Was this a maudlin end-of-evening depression, or a terrible glimpse of truth?

He flopped on to the bed, considering the cage formed

around him by the bars, and tried to marshal his thoughts. He flicked through some TV channels, starting with his own, found his share price on Teletext, grumbled at the further 5p slippage, and fell heavily into a sleep shared with the insistent, shapeless spectres of Sumner, Walker, Marilyn Monroe, de Vigny and Sharma.

He didn't stir when Georgia arrived at 2.25 a.m.

Acrobat's closing share price 415p

Thursday, 18 March

Burrows's head was thick, but he started the day with a curse at Walker for not phoning last night. His wife groaned heavily as he crawled out of bed. He pretended not to hear, but she didn't wake anyway. He picked up the papers as he left his room; the torments of the night belonged to yesterday. The day ahead was full. Much too much to do, for him to fret about the meaning of life. Get on with it.

Blinking back the fug of last night's brandies, he went to check out at the desk in the vast, minimalist cavern of the Hempel's reception area. He turned on his mobile, which rang immediately with a voicemail message from Martin Sumner.

'Charlie, it's me. Why haven't you got this bloody thing on? Have you seen today's *Telegraph* yet? They've gone to town on us. Look, I'm going to stay at home till I hear from you. I'll try and get hold of Abby now. Call me when you get this.'

Burrows dropped his overnight bag, scrabbling through the *Telegraph* to the media pages. It was unmissable:

Acrobat Hit by New Defection

CARRIE MCGANN

He swallowed an expletive.

Acrobat, the faltering television group, was this morning waking up to news of a second major defection in a fortnight as Martin Sumner, the group's popular and effective COO, has accepted the role of Chief Executive of Channel 6, Acrobat's arch-rival.

Martin Sumner has been at Acrobat for five years and is widely considered to be the architect of the group's successful growth strategy. His departure will come as a grave loss to the beleaguered group, whose share price has been depressed by a succession of surprises to the market.

Acrobat Chief Executive Charlie Burrows refused to comment on Sumner's departure, though at last week's results presentation, he said of his colleague, 'For the record, Martin Sumner is an invaluable member of this management team, without whom you would expect this group to add considerably less value for shareholders.' This morning, shareholders will be waiting with particular interest for a statement from the company.

There is no news yet of a successor, though observers believe that the obvious choice is Commercial Director Ray Walker, who would bring a strong and experienced hand to assist Burrows at a time when doubt exists over the future of Henry Fleming. The group's Finance Director has been in hospital for three weeks following a major heart attack.

Two weeks ago, Phyllis Grigson, Director of Communications, resigned suddenly in mysterious circumstances after aggressive remarks about the late Nik Kruger were attributed to sources at the company.

Burrows was frozen in the lobby of the hotel. He finished reading the piece, breathed, 'You little bitch,' and rushed outside to find Mick Spring. He grabbed the car phone and fixed up to meet with Abby Kelleher as soon as they both arrived, left a voicemail for the lawyers on Sumner's notice period and garden leave options, and called Sumner, who now felt like the enemy.

He spent the first part of the morning with Abby Kelleher, who impressed him with her command of the situation. She did not appear in any way thrown by the leak, and worked through their options, volunteering to return in a few hours with some draft releases. She told him he had a lovely wife – they'd had fun together last night. He agreed.

At eleven, Melvyn Davies appeared for his routine meeting. This was booked weekly in both their diaries for the year ahead but regularly gave way to other, more urgent items – usually in Burrows's agenda. Burrows was in half a mind to cancel it today, but Davies was excited about some new programme. What with the Kate thing, Burrows thought he ought to hear him out at least.

'Consumerism is the current affairs of today, Charlie. Look at the ratings of any of the classic current affairs programmes: *Panorama* shuffled around the fringes of the schedule; *World in Action* dead, apart from a few specials. The mass audience isn't interested in what's happening in obscure republics. It wants to know what Richard Branson's going to do about his railways and how to get your money back off some crappy tour operator. We know the customer is king, but how many of us feel that's how we're treated on the high street? Listen to people in the pub. That's what really gets them animated. Tales of woe at the hands of some bank or other, because we've all been there. But this isn't like any other show. We do it live. Real time. Scary. Edgy. Move it on from the orderly pre-packaging of *Watchdog*.

Burrows listened with growing fascination. Davies had a knack of finding the pulse of the times. He talked of being in front of the wave. Said the top of the wave was fine for its few moments, but it would always pass under you and leave you in its wake. As he watched his colleague describe his ideas with such animation, Burrows acknow-ledged to himself that Davies had swallowed some tough decisions with exceptional grace over the past few weeks. It was good to see him back on form.

He'd found himself unsure of how to act towards his colleague in the context of his separation from Kate. He couldn't say anything about the personal stuff, best not to get into that. Davies would have said something if he'd wanted him involved. But the least he could do was to get behind Davies's instincts. At the same time he could reassure his Programme Director that he didn't have to behave like Ray Walker to get his voice heard. It was good to see a burst of the old 'Merlin' magic. And for sure, it was good to be thinking about shows and audiences as opposed to politics and the bloody share price.

It was midday. Paula interrupted the meeting to say Ray Walker was on the phone from LA. Burrows looked at his watch and sighed deeply, mainly for Davies's benefit.

'OK, don't go away, Melv. I'll take it in Mart's office.'

Walker sounded untroubled by the fact that the clock on his bedside would read 4 a.m.

'I've seen the *Telegraph* piece,' was his opening gambit.

Burrows was momentarily thrown. He had planned to chew Walker off for disappearing off to LA without a by-your-leave.

'Sylvia faxed it.'

'Oh. Good.' Burrows recovered.

'I suppose it was inevitable at some point,' continued Walker, apparently not noticing Burrows's incoherence. 'I mean, he's young, he's got a certain amount of experience. Not surprising that a guy like that would think he can run something himself.'

Burrows attempted to regroup. The weight of last night's excess was beginning to hang on his shoulders. He couldn't carry it as well as he used to.

'Ray, what the hell are you doing there?' he blurted out.

'Nice to be missed,' said Walker without missing a beat. 'If you like, I can find out the time of the first plane out today – be back at your side by Friday your time.'

Burrows wondered if he was serious.

'No, don't. That would be daft. But I thought we were meeting today.'

Burrows waited for the familiar bluster that always accompanied such dialogues with Ray Walker.

'I merely thought it was time to get on with it, you know. I mean, if you'd prefer we sat and had meetings about the problem, that's fine with me, but I thought you wanted something done.'

Its predictability didn't diminish Burrows's irritation.

'The last time we spoke, we agreed to meet today. You told me you couldn't call anyone in advance for fear that they'd think you were some sort of boy scout.'

'Look, if you think I've come out here for the sake of my health . . .'

Walker stopped, expecting Burrows to interrupt. He didn't.

'With Henry Fleming on the bench, I took the view that it was important to get a move on.'

'Did you talk to Henry?'

'Henry Fleming? No, I didn't. I tried his home number but his wife said he wasn't to talk to anyone, so I thought I'd not waste any more time. If that's wrong, then I apologize.'

'It's not wrong; it's not what we agreed. And you know it.'

'Then I apologize. I'm not here to do my Christmas shopping, you know.'

'I know that, Ray.'

'Well then,' Walker huffed as if he had successfully trumped all of Burrows's cards.

'Look, OK, you're there. Let's make the most of it. You can fix this *Marilyn* thing. We don't want twenty-two million bucks of exposure here, Ray. We went in for twelve, the market thinks it's twelve. Even the bloody board thinks it's twelve. If you can get on the plane with us back at twelve, that will be worth your trip. And if they don't like that, offer them nothing.'

'Pull out altogether?'

'Absolutely.'

Walker sighed theatrically. 'Well, what was the point of going into it then? Have we changed our minds about movies all of a sudden?'

'No, we haven't, but we have told the market that our involvement is capped at twelve million dollars, so right now we're ten million out of line.'

'So what are you saying?'

'I'm saying the market isn't going to forgive us a discrepancy like that – or, rather, it isn't going to forgive *me.*'

The line went quiet for a moment too long.

'You really think that?'

'Yes, I do,' said Burrows.

Another pause. 'I see.'

'All of which adds up to the need to get this thing back to where it should be. And if that's not doable, I'd rather tell the City that we've pulled out altogether than that we've bet twenty-two million dollars of their money.'

Walker regrouped. 'I'm not making any promises here. I'll ask some questions and take a view.'

'OK. Keep me in the loop though, Ray, right?'

'If there's anything significant I'll be in touch.'

'Thanks,' said Burrows, and turned his head to the main item on his agenda. 'Ray, I need to make a strong response to this news about Martin Sumner. The shares have fallen again.'

'Fifteen p,' said Walker, proving just how astute he could be at 4 a.m. on the other side of the world.

'Something like that. So what we need is a solid statement that indicates we have the management strength in depth to ride this out.'

'Right,' said Walker. 'As you know, my commitment to the company is beyond doubt. I seem to have upset you somehow by getting on with the job in hand and travelling out here to deal with the pressing issues presenting themselves, but that's because I care.'

Once again Burrows wondered whether he had just got this guy wrong. Was he what he said he was? Dedicated in his own way? He was still talking.

'So if you feel the time is right, I believe I can bring the right combination of experience and determination to the senior management team . . . I think that was what the newspaper was getting at.'

Burrows's moment of clemency for Walker came to an abrupt end as he saw that, once again, he was going to have to confront him.

'Ray, Martin's absence undoubtedly adds a cutting edge to your new role, but I don't want to make another change in your title so soon after announcing your promotion to Commercial Director. And I want you still to be solidly focused on sales. You're the best there is, and I'm not going to squander your talents on an administrative role.'

'I wouldn't see COO as administrative, more an acknowledgement of the number two slot.'

'I don't see it that way at all, Ray. I see it as being my *alter ego*, capable of stepping in for me at meetings I can't attend –'

'So, obviously then, party to all your policy discussions.' Walker's tone had an edge to it now.

'I'd expect you to be closely involved in all of that too, Ray,' he said as a whisper in his head reminded him that this was the last thing he wanted. Still, now wasn't the time to tell Walker the whole truth and nothing but the truth. Only last weekend he'd been plotting his departure. He dived in. 'I'd like you to think about who you will appoint as your deputy.'

Walker was confused. 'Sarah's not going anywhere.'

'I've asked her to consider becoming COO in Martin's place.'

It was almost as if Walker was expecting it. He didn't miss a beat. As if he had taken the time to write himself a short script. 'You know that would be completely un-acceptable to me.'

'That's why I wish you were here,' Burrows said as a rejoinder. 'I've had to make some big decisions in a short space of time, and your absence could not have been worse timed.'

'Well, that's as may be.'

'I've decided that the time has come to bring on the next generation. I think our senior management team should feature a woman, and I believe that Sarah is up to the challenge.'

'What did the board say?' enquired Walker.

'Ray, what do you care what the board said? You spend your life denigrating the board for being out of touch. Why this sudden interest in their point of view?'

'Because, frankly, I'm staggered. How does this affect my reporting line?'

'You would continue to report to me.'

'And Melvyn?'

'Melvyn too.'

'Well, that's something. Look, I've made a decision here; I think I should be there. I'm going to get on the first convenient flight out of here today. This is no time to be on the other side of the world.'

'It's fine, Ray. You're there, the project is out of control. I need you to fix it for me.'

'You see, that's where I don't understand this. You need me to fix the biggest problem you've got, and yet now I find I've been passed over as your number two.'

'I don't see it that way. You are Commercial Director, which is a title that you can make your own, Ray. And

I'm prepared to add more weight to it as we go along if it's working out.'

'But you saw the article. People are expecting the job to be mine.'

'I don't recall appointing Carrie McGann as head of HR. I need you to –'

'Look, I'm forced to consider my position on this.'

Burrows recalled that the last time Walker had said those words, he'd made himself promise to accept. That wasn't possible any more. In the absence of Martin Sumner he had little choice but to bring Walker back on side, even as he promoted his deputy to COO. For God's sake, it was easy if the man would just go with it.

'It doesn't affect your position, Ray. You remain the highest-paid director after myself, reporting to me on the most important aspect of our operations.'

'I think I need to take advice on that. I'll call you later.' And he was gone.

Once again, Walker had stolen the conversation, dictating its pace and length, hanging up with so much only half communicated. Burrows's mind scattered through a few useless options before turning to the figure of Melvyn Davies, still hunched over his papers, fine-tuning them as he waited for the meeting to continue. What a contrast! He would go and green-light Melvyn's new show. God knows, he deserved something to go right.

'Sorry about that, Melv. Got a name for this masterpiece then?' he asked.

'Working title only at this point: *Mind Our Own Business*.'

Burrows laughed. 'OK, why don't you go ahead and make it.'

Davies smiled confidently and shook Burrows's hand.

'Good call, boss. This one's going to be big. Remember this moment for your memoirs.'

Burrows laughed. He was right to keep Merlin focused on the programmes. He was outstanding. It was good to be in a position to make his day.

Ray Walker looked at his watch, pulled his Bel Air bathrobe around him and slodged to the fridge in his hotel slippers. He pulled out a bottle of mineral water and swigged from the bottle as he rummaged in his brief-case for his 'black book' of all the phone numbers he would ever need, diligently maintained by Sylvia. He riffled through the pages to find 'G'.

Abby Kelleher appeared with her laptop a few minutes later.

'Ready for me, Charlie?' she said, hovering at the door.

'Sure,' said Burrows, who had spent the intervening moments window-shopping his options, but with no real intent to buy just yet.

Kelleher laid out three documents. 'These reflect the changes you made yesterday, and I've tweaked them again to take account of the fact that it leaked, and I've got Martin's points in here.'

'Where the hell did this leak from?' Burrows grumbled as he sifted the papers.

'People moves are always the most difficult things to keep quiet. It's such big news that anyone who knows tells just one friend, you know, "on the quiet".'

'You should have seen him at the awards last night, hardly the master of discretion.' Burrows felt a twinge of guilt as he recalled his own impetuous behaviour.

'Someone told the paper yesterday,' she said with surprising confidence. 'They'd have gone to press by last night.'

Burrows relaxed. 'Then that means one of you, me, Ray or Melv. Or Mart.'

'Or Channel 6.'

'Oh. Do you think?'

'Sure. They've got the most to gain: strong statement of intent, reassurance to people internally, and the sooner they get the process of extrication going, the sooner they get their man.'

'I suppose so,' said Burrows. Something in Abby Kelleher's confident perkiness wound him up. Everything about her was pert and unruffled, nicely turned out, from her folio of papers to the absurdly small mobile phone that was permanently attached to her. If it was that obvious that it was going to leak, why the hell hadn't she said something? A wispy conspiracy theory crossed his mind.

Her phone began its ring. She interrogated its face and said, 'Oh hell, Charlie, it's the *Telegraph* again. I think I'd better take it, don't you?'

'Sure,' he said, relieved to have time to investigate his theory. She strode out of his office – rather manfully, he thought – gesticulating while explaining something to the journalist.

Then she was back, composed. 'They're planning to run a story tomorrow morning that Martin Sumner's replacement is to be Sarah Golanski.'

Burrows's insides did a backflip. 'That woman has open season on us,' he said.

'I told her she's really barking up the wrong tree this time, right?'

'No, Abby, wrong.'

'What?'

It went quiet. Burrows got up and walked to his window, as if the purposeful bustle of the traffic could offer solutions to the perpetual balancing act he had to perform.

'I'm stunned, actually. I can't believe you didn't tell me. I denied it outright, because I trusted that, after our little false start, you wouldn't leave me out of the loop again. How could you let me write all those announcements without telling me the other half of the story?'

Burrows didn't like having to defend himself against this woman who had imported her New York rule book into the company he ran. 'I'm sorry you're upset,' he said, slowly and deliberately. 'Obviously I wasn't in a position to discuss the identity of Martin's successor until she had accepted the job.'

Kelleher persisted. 'I'm not trying to get a special inside track for any reason other than to do my job. It seems to me that Acrobat is a very leaky place indeed. If you want me to play plumber, I have to know a few facts.' She pulled her hair back off her face, sighing, 'God.' Her tone moderated a little. 'I can help you here, Charlie, really.'

Burrows decided to accept her moderation. 'OK. Look, I'll try and do this better. I know we've got leaks – and, if anything, it's getting worse. I guess I was just working on the principle that the more people who are in the know, the more likely it is to leak.'

'I guess all I'd say is, it's *who* is in the know. If I'm in the loop, I can defend you much more effectively if anything does seep out.'

Burrows recalled his relationship with Phyllis Grigson; it would have been unthinkable not to have discussed all this in advance with her. He knew it was a fair point – but again, that wispy suspicion.

'OK, I'm sure we'll get there, Abby.'

'It's early days, I know. But you *can* trust me. And if you want me to take a look at these leaks, I will.'

'Good idea. Look, I'll call Sarah now, and let you know as soon as we can say something.'

Golanski was on the phone when he called but, after some negotiation in her office, she came on the line.

'Good morning, Charlie,' she sang.

Burrows felt his spirits rise. This was going to be good. 'Good morning, Ms Golanski,' he said, 'or may I call you Chief Operating Officer?'

She laughed lightly. 'Yes, you may.'

Burrows leaned back in his seat, lifting his face to heaven and closing his eyes as if in some ritual of thanksgiving. 'Oh, Sarah, I'm absolutely delighted. We're going to have some fun together.'

'Um,' she began, arresting his celebration, 'I talked to Ray.'

'Ah yes,' he said, 'so did I. How was he?'

'He was quite nice, actually. He said you'd phoned and there were some things you and he still had to talk about, but he congratulated me and said it was a "fillip" for the sales team.'

'But you got the impression that Ray was going to be OK?'

'Well, he didn't let me in on your discussion – adults only, you know.'

'Is he staying in LA?'

'Apparently, yes. He has his meetings set up today, starting with breakfast with George Salzman, but he's coming back at the weekend.'

'Oh good. When I spoke to him, he was talking about coming straight back.'

'I suppose he feels he should have been here for an announcement like this.'

'He would have been if he hadn't taken a unilateral decision to go to LA.'

'Unilateral?'

'Sure. I try not to dictate what people do at Ray's level – but you know Ray.'

'Yes, I do,' she said. 'He can be strong-willed, but it's only because he cares so much about the company.'

Burrows realized he was going to have to tread carefully here. 'Actually, I hope that one of the fruits of your appointment will be a better working relationship with Ray. He's great at what he does, but we don't really seem to be pulling together.'

'I know, he's a complex character. He needs to know that he is top dog right now.'

'Well, he isn't, Sarah. He's a very senior member of a team that includes you and Melvyn and Henry.'

'Oh, yes. How was Melvyn about it?' she asked tentatively.

Burrows rifled through his memory. He found that these days he mainly had a capacity to remember bad news.

'Melvyn was great,' he said. 'You two get on well, don't you?'

'Oh yes, fine, most of the time.' She tried to model a standard working relationship. She was not at all ready for anyone to imagine that there was anything else. Well, there wasn't now, was there?

'OK, well the fragrant Carrie McGann appears to have the story already, so we're going to have to fast forward the process of internal announcement and get a press release out today.'

'Carrie? How on earth does she know already?'

'We have too many people who ought to be able to keep their traps shut and can't. Anyway, congratulations, COO.'

'Thanks, Charlie. I'm going to need your help, but I'll give it my absolute utmost.'

'I know you will, Sarah.'

He put the phone into its cradle. He felt good about Sarah Golanski's appointment. This was going to be fine.

He got hold of Martin Sumner at home that afternoon. Sumner sounded guarded.

Burrows seized the moment. 'I just want to apologize about last night.'

'It's all right, Charlie. I guess we'd both had a bit too much sherbet.'

'I suppose.' Burrows paused before picking up his tone. 'Anyway, I've just called to let you know before you read it anywhere that I have appointed a successor to you as my deputy.'

'Sarah Golanski.'

Burrows was crestfallen. 'How the hell did you know that?'

'I had a call earlier from a certain Phyllis Grigson, offering me her services. She told me.'

'Phyllis Grigson? That's ridiculous. I'm chasing this

piece of information all over town. How did she know?'

'Oh the usual "reliable sources", all that.'

With an effort Burrows tried to hold his equanimity. 'So what do you think?'

'Bold move, Charlie. What did Ray say?'

'Ray is breathing threats from his hot tub in LA.'

'LA?'

'He's taken over the *Marilyn* project, remember?'

'Oh, right. He's happy for his young protégée, is he?'

'He's told *her* he is. He's told me he's considering his position.'

'Hah! Imagine my surprise.'

'Don't need a new Sales Director down there at Channel 6, do you, Mart? One careful owner?'

Sumner laughed, relieved by Burrows's levity. Reluctantly he changed the tone. 'Charlie, dare I ask, have you talked to the lawyers about my start date?'

'No, sorry, haven't had a minute; but they're working on it.'

'It's just that we've got some big issues looming, and Malcolm is really pushing me to give them a date.'

Burrows found the mention of 'Malcolm' an affront. Jilted for *Malcolm*. He wasn't at all sympathetic to *Malcolm's* problems. He sighed heavily. 'OK, Mart, I'll get on it.'

'You *can* trust me, you know. I won't embarrass you. Effectively I'm gone from Acrobat. I won't announce a start date, and I'll go in informally – have a kind of soft launch. That work for you?'

'Not much I can say, is there?'

'I'm trying to help, man.'

'Sure you are.'

*

Ray Walker was enjoying this a lot. By the time the concierge had called him back with times of the planes home, he had decided that a few days with a stretch limo in LA were not to be missed. He'd made his point. Burrows could stew on it over the weekend, and he could pick it up on Monday when he'd heard back from his attorney.

He had breakfasted that morning with George Salzman at the Bel Air. In light of his commitments for lunch and dinner that day, as well as the possibility opened by Salzman of cocktails with their director, he had reluctantly stuck with mixed berries and a bagel, much though he loved the way the Americans did breakfast: fruit, bacon, pastries, syrup on the same plate.

The two of them were cloned around the room. The tables, located at discreet distances from each other, were all occupied by earnest groups in smart suits. Walker realized he was the only one wearing a tie and resolved to remove it after breakfast. He had felt reassured after an hour with Salzman, who was rude about the Germans for pulling out, complimentary to excess about Acrobat for picking up their share, and name-dropped the biggest stars in the world.

Together they had ridden in the stretch Lincoln to meet with their partners, all of whom Walker found charming and excited by the prospect of working with their new British friends.

As they drove to lunch he turned to Salzman. 'I'm getting a good feeing about this, George.'

'So you should,' said Salzman, patting him generously on the shoulder. 'Fortune favours the brave, Ray. While your rivals are fighting each other for the best of the rest,

Acrobat will not only have first pick, you'll also have a share of the upside – which could be very nice indeed.'

Walker relaxed into the soft leather, snapping open a Diet Coke from the trough of ice in the side of the car. Burrows had no understanding of this world.

'Tell me more about this director of ours,' he breathed.

Melvyn Davies opened his email. Still no response. Once again he typed, 'Please call me. I need you back.'

Acrobat's closing share price   400p

Friday, 19 March

In his office Charlie Burrows grabbed the press cuts on Sarah's appointment and breathed a deep sigh.

'So far so good,' he said to no one as he put down the final article. They had been merciful to her and, if anything, he thought he detected a layer of congratulation that he had moved quickly to fill Sumner's gap and been bold enough to take a risk on the next generation of leaders. Carrie McGann commented that Ray Walker had been unavailable for comment, which left a clear scent of disquiet over the appointment, but Abby Kelleher had obviously got to the others to head off that kind of speculation.

Burrows had an email from Marcus Newman, king of the analysts. He explained that his team were planning a note to investors about Acrobat. He wondered if he could have some of Charlie's time today and put a few questions to Ray and Melvyn.

Burrows trotted out a friendly reply, muttering, 'More than my life's worth not to, Marcus, my dear.'

Recollecting his dressing-down at the hands of Abby Kelleher, he sent her a note telling her of his impending dialogue with Newman and invited her to sit in.

Melvyn Davies was not used to being dressed in a shirt and tie. He sat in the reception of Southern Foods' grumpy-looking building in Marylebone Road, looking around at the workmanlike decor. The furniture looked as if it had been delivered in flatpacks and the reception-ists were from Central Casting. A mouse-like matron in her mid-fifties appeared to be in charge, her neighbour an overweight woman with a seep of sweat clotting her armpits. Neither looked up when Davies arrived. He stood silently while they fussed with pieces of paper. It occurred to Davies that if they were actresses he'd have to fire them for being so bad at looking busy. In the end, the mouse found a moment's pause in her activities and looked up at him.

'Morning, Geoff O'Brien, please.'

The other one looked up and the manner of both changed to an efficient pleasantness. Just at the mention of a name. O'Brien's secretary appeared in a few moments and led him, tottering along on five-inch stilettos, down a labyrinth of depressing, faded corridors to a vending machine, where she paused to ask if he'd like a coffee. Davies would have loved a coffee but somehow couldn't face standing there while she programmed his choice into the machine.

'I'm fine, thanks.'

'You sure?' she squeaked, clacking off down the corridor again.

O'Brien was a big, warm man. He proffered a bear-like hand and gripped Davies's shoulder with the other. He seemed genuinely pleased to see him. 'Hi, Melvyn, come in, sit down. Great to see you. Thanks for coming. Appreciate it. You been asked about coffee?'

'Yes, he has,' said the secretary person.

'I'll have a black with, please, Tina. You sure, Melvyn?'

'White without, please,' conceded Davies. 'You got the

message that it was just me this morning?' he began.

'Very brave of you to come out without the minder,' guffawed O'Brien. 'Let me get straight to the point. We are not the kind of here-today-gone-tomorrow sponsor you may fear.'

Davies wasn't sure how best to react. He nodded. Then he shook his head in the hope that that covered it.

'Our relationship with Acrobat is important to us. All the more so, having had a bit of a falling out over the last couple of years. Obviously these are sensitive first steps. I've committed twenty-five million pounds to this relationship, so I need to be able to demonstrate to my board that we've done the right thing by throwing our lot in with you guys again.'

Davies was impressed. This guy had set out very clearly in a few sentences that the ball was in his court to fix this lucrative relationship. He'd done it so nicely too.

'Geoff, I know I speak for Ray when I say that the relationship with Southern is critical to us too. In fact, he mentioned it at our results presentation last week.'

This seemed to be the right approach. O'Brien appeared to be impressed. Davies took courage.

'So when something goes wrong, like it did on *Midnight Minus One*, we do realize that this affects you as much as us. I understand your frustration at the first episode. I shared it, but that's the wonder of telly. No matter how long you spend perfecting it,' he wondered what O'Brien would think if he knew how long he had actually spent on this show, 'you never know till it goes out whether you're going to be a prince or a prat.'

O'Brien laughed. 'It's the same when you launch a new brand of coffee, like *Night and Day*. All the research in the world is no substitute for real people in real kitchens. *That's* when you find out.'

Davies relaxed. This guy was not going to bawl him out; he really did understand. They talked for some time about programmes and brands they had both launched which had been spectacular successes or terrible dogs. Davies realized he was still being appraised and made sure that his dogs were only modest flops, and well worth the attempt.

O'Brien concluded, 'So you see, we really do understand about satisfying the fickle tastes of the great British public, and that's the point I made to my board earlier this week. There, but for the grace of God, and all that. I have the backing of the board to stick with *Midnight Minus One*, and I've amended our press ads so they now promote the programme.'

As he continued, Davies was confused. It appeared that he had been brought here to listen to a speech about the company's loyalty to a show that had been pulled. O'Brien was still talking.

'So how did we get on last night?'

'What?' said Davies.

'Last night's show. I had to be out at a dinner. I thought you'd know the results by now.'

Davies's head spun. The bastard had taken himself off to LA without telling his client that the show had been cancelled.

His options coursed towards him. One appealed much more than the others. 'I'm surprised Ray didn't tell you . . .' O'Brien's face looked as if he didn't like surprises. 'We wanted to give ourselves a chance to get it really right, so we skipped last night's episode. We'll be back next week and we'll add one to the end of the run.'

O'Brien paused for a moment. 'I'm amazed that Ray didn't say anything, but it seems eminently sensible,' he concluded. 'What thoughts do you have for the rest of the series?'

Davies busked his way through another twenty minutes of discussion before they stood to shake hands and Tina the secretary tottered in to lead him wordlessly back through the labyrinth. He said a polite goodbye to the two harridans in the melamine reception area. As he walked to his car, he felt a frisson of freedom, churned with fear at the consequences of his choice in there. Still, it was Ray's job to talk to the bloody clients, wasn't it? What the hell did he think he was playing at?

Charlie Burrows took the call from Marcus Newman before lunch. Newman was very good at what he did and was respected among the chief executives whose share prices he could influence with a stroke of his pen. Burrows briefed Kelleher on the importance of this conversation. If he was going to lift the heads of his people, get his company off the sick list – even think about becoming a predator when the ownership rules were lifted – he needed a strong share price and a very much improved impression of Acrobat and its management. He and Abby Kelleher were hunched around the speakerphone in his office.

Newman ranged around the company's affairs in his languid way. The revenues, the ratings, the *Marilyn* project, management succession. Burrows was upbeat and confident on them all.

After thirty minutes' grilling, Newman adopted a concluding tone. 'So essentially you're saying that the conditions exist for Acrobat to outperform the market this year.'

'We're looking good, Marcus.'

'Good news, good news,' said Newman. 'So a big result is still on the cards and you're feeling good about life.'

'Yes, I am really . . . apart from the bloody share price. Not to put too fine a point on it, I'm amazed at the market's attitude to us at the moment. We're doing brilliantly, and all we get is murmurings. Any excuse to downgrade us.'

'It's twitchy across the whole media sector. And you know how the market is; in the absence of a constant stream of good news, it panics about every little doubt that creeps into its mind. Actually, Charlie, got to be off now, got a call coming in from Gutersloh. I'll call Melvyn later.'

'I'll tell him to expect you.'

After his meeting at Southern Foods, Melvyn Davies went straight to Wardour Street in Soho, where he spent a couple of hours with Alicat, the production company responsible for *Mind Our Own Business*. Originally they had developed the show for Channel 4, but the broadcaster had got cold feet about a live consumerist programme, so they were ahead of the game with their research. Davies told them he was going ahead with the show for the week after next, and was obliged to stay for a lunch of ham sandwiches and champagne. Together they had agreed on the shortlist of stories to be developed for the following week's transmission, and

Davies was able to review their research so far. He liked what he saw.

By the time Davies got back to Lancaster Gate it was three thirty.

He dumped his briefcase and went straight to Charlie Burrows's office. 'Charlie – there's just something I need to tell you.'

'Uh-oh, it's Friday afternoon and there's something you need to tell me. I think I've had enough of these for one week, Melv.'

'No, no, not that!'

Burrows shuddered. 'OK, then carry on – I can deal with anything but that.'

'I went to see Geoff O'Brien today.'

'Right. How did Mr O'Brien take the news of the demise of his show?'

'Mr O'Brien didn't know.'

'What?' Burrows whipped off his reading glasses. 'How can he not know? It should have gone out last night.'

'He was out last night. He thinks he missed it.'

'But he'll want to know the ratings today from his people, won't he?'

'I told him it didn't go out.'

Burrows winced. 'Tough call, Melv. How was he about it?'

'He was fine. I didn't tell him it was cancelled. He thinks we've given ourselves an extra week to get it right.'

'Oh shit, Melv, why did you tell him that?'

'To allow Walker to bloody-well do his own dirty work. He's the only one who can fix this; he knows what he can do for compensation. The way I've left it, he can tell O'Brien that we took a decision next week. I've kept him alive.'

'Well, I guess you're right. So when *are* we going to tell Southern Foods that their new show has bitten the dust?'

'Look, I'm sorry, Charlie, I really thought we could have made something of that show. *You* cancelled it, and that's your prerogative. But I created it, nurtured it and stood behind it when the cast were all panicking. So, for pity's sake, don't have a go at me for not playing messenger boy to its death as well. I do shows; Ray does clients.'

Burrows relented. 'Sure, Melv. Sorry. And how are the shows?'

Davies became animated immediately. 'I stopped off at Alicat on the way back. *Mind Our Own Business* is looking good. I've got John Garrett directing, which is a real coup. I've shuffled the schedule for the week after next; I've given it a Tuesday nine thirty slot and got the new schedule billed to the programme listings magazines and newspapers today.'

'Can you get it up and running so quickly?'

'Yeah – the production company are pretty much ready to go.'

'Great – looking forward to it.'

'Er, one more thing?'

Burrows sneaked a look at his watch. 'Sure.'

'I spoke to Ray last night.'

'Lucky you. What news from Tinseltown?'

'I'll tell you – he asked me not to, but he called me to try and wind me up about Sarah's appointment. I think he was sounding me out for a palace revolt or something.'

A stab in the stomach. 'After the week I've had, he's welcome. What did you say?'

'Nothing much, really – I just let him talk. But I got the very clear impression that he was leading to a point where he could accept Sarah as COO as long as he was Deputy Chief Executive.'

'For pity's sake. Deputy Chief Executive. What the hell does that mean?'

'To Ray? Everything. It's about how it looks, isn't it. Designer suits and a big title – never mind that the suits don't fit and the title means nothing.'

Burrows laughed out loud.

'He drives me mad too, Charlie. But at least that's not fake. He's a completely authentic bastard.'

Burrows threw his head back and laughed hard. Davies watched, pleased to share the moment.

'Melv, relax. It's unthinkable, OK?'

Davies smiled his understanding. 'Look,' he said, 'I know you've had a crap week. If there's ever a time when you want to . . . you know . . . just talk, you know where I am.' He finished in a rush, as if relieved to have got to the end of his speech.

Burrows knew this guy was going through his own private nightmare. The PA telegraph had featured Davies's split from his wife for the last week. Yet here he was, ready to take on someone else's pain. He felt a swell of gratitude and affection for Davies that he knew he couldn't express to him.

'Thanks, Melv. You're a great guy. I appreciate it,' he managed.

Their eyes met. 'You too.'

Acrobat's closing share price   402p

The Weekend, 20–21 March

Maggie Fleming crept around the door and, seeing him awake, butted the door open with her hip, introducing a tray with two mugs, a small teapot and a pile of pills. 'Good morning, and how is my number one patient this afternoon?'

'Hi, Mags.' He patted the bed, moving his legs over to make room for her to sit.

'How are you feeling?'

'Well, obviously I'm exhausted because it's been so hectic since I came home; reading, sleeping, going to the bathroom, that sort of thing.'

'Give yourself time, Henry. Honestly, your body has been through the biggest trauma –'

'I'm joking, Mags. Really.'

'Are you now?' She bustled unnecessarily, plumping his pillows, rearranging books on the bedside table, pouring the tea.

'Actually, I just realized something,' he said. She sat on the bed and took his hand. 'I'm not worrying about work.'

She cocked an eyebrow and gave him a mock schoolma'am look. 'Is this the latest wheeze to get me to plug in the phone again?'

'No, honestly. Standing back for a bit, the whole perspective on my work is different.'

She was wary. 'Henry, we've had these talks before –

usually just before we come back from holiday . . . after you've phoned the office every day.'

'Just proving I was vital, I suppose. But this is different,' he continued, not wanting to lose the progression of his thoughts. 'Really different. It's like, being out for these three weeks, I've had to hand things over, you know, *really* let go in a way that I've never done before.'

'Henry, where has this all come from?'

'I don't know – maybe it's those drugs you're force-feeding me.'

She wrapped both hands around her mug of tea. 'Go on,' she said.

'Well, I'm not sure there's much more to go on to. It's like . . .' He circled his new discovery, developing a description from a new angle. 'It's like I needed to create this swirl of momentum to get everything done. Now the momentum's gone, I've realized that it wasn't a means to an end at all. It had become the end. I was actually scared of losing it, because it was all I knew. It was what got me promoted and bonussed and all that. But after three weeks' sleep and these mind-altering drugs, the momentum has gone, and I don't think I need it back.'

She didn't turn to face him, instead pretended to fuss with the teapot. She pressed her lips together and tilted her head back to make the tears stop. 'That's *good*, darling.'

He sensed something in her voice and reached out to her. She turned around slowly and he met her eyes. 'Mags, I'm not going back.'

She closed her eyes and the tears welled over.

He tugged her hand. 'What was that poem you were reading when we were in the Coronary Unit?'

'That was Shelley,' she said fondly, '*Adonais*.'

'Can you remember it? Something about "earth's shadows".'

She steadied her emotion, closing her eyes again. The tear trails were still on her cheeks as she spoke.

'The One remains, the many change and pass;
Heaven's light forever shines, earth's shadows fly;
Life, like a dome of many-coloured glass,
Stains the white radiance of Eternity . . .'

Her voice cracked as she started the last line.

He slipped his hand into hers, and they sat together in silence for a time.

'Life's too short,' he said.

'Of course it is.'

'That's what your Shelley meant with his "earth's shadows fly". Life's too short.'

'Too short,' she said, as if not daring to waylay this direction with a word out of place.

'Mags, I realized a terrible thing.' She looked at him, her face concerned. 'I don't care about the company,' he said. 'Isn't that awful? I don't care whether it succeeds or fails.'

'Really? You don't care?'

'No. Not one bit. Oh, I like the people, but all the stress, all that bother for something that is just going to pass.'

She didn't want to argue, but she did want to test this new bravery. 'But you're brilliant at it.'

'Exactly, Mags. That was the reason I was doing it – because I was good at it. What kind of reason is that?'

'You work too hard, but don't throw the baby out with the bathwater.'

'I *have* to throw it all away, Mags. Don't you see, I'm

addicted to it. If I grant it any value at all, I'll go back, I know I will.'

She watched him for a few moments, recognizing the certainty in his manner.

'What will you do?'

'I don't know, Mags. Will you still love me if I'm an unemployed bum?'

'I married you when you were on two thousand a year. If you finish up earning five, I've had a result.'

He laughed and knew it was going to be fine. He'd taken her for granted.

'I don't know what I'd do without you, Mags.'

'Well, you're never going to have to find out, are you? Now give me that mug and don't start getting worried about things. It's all going to be fine.'

'Too much excitement for one day, Matron?'

'Much too much. I'm going to get something for your dinner. We'll have a chat then.'

As she shut the door, a voice from under the bedclothes said, 'And how about a bottle of Bordeaux?'

Around the waste-paper bin in Melvyn Davies's study lay ten crumpled balls of paper. For an hour he had tried to pen the right note, but it was as if even the words didn't believe him and refused to collaborate.

He tore off the final sheet and switched on the kettle, looking at his watch again. He phoned Kate's parents again, once more hearing the voicemail tape whirring, three hundred miles away. This time he didn't leave a message.

On an impulse, he walked upstairs and hesitantly peered around the door into his sons' bedroom. At once a cramp settled on his heart. All their little things. The spaceman wallpaper Kate and he had found when they knew they were having a boy. He flicked the mobile above the baby's cot and twisted the knob on his music box. It sprang into life, playing its only silly tune, so reminiscent of that wonderful moment when the boys had finally given up their hold on the evening. He sat on the bed, picking up a much-loved toy giraffe that had been overlooked on that morning, sitting it on his lap.

He leaned down and smelled the pillow, and the loneliness tore at his soul. Carefully he tucked the giraffe into bed, then closed the door firmly. He walked down the stairs and into his study. He thought for a moment before picking up the phone. Her number was engaged. And again.

The third time, it rang, and his insides leapt in unreadiness.

'Hello?'

'Hi, Sarah, it's me, Melvyn.'

Her tone immediately betrayed her defensiveness. 'Oh. Hello, Melvyn.'

'I thought we should talk.'

'Is there much point?' Her voice was metallic, unyielding.

'Well, if it's up to me, the answer's "Yes". I realize it takes two to tango, though.'

She snorted at his words. 'It certainly does, Melvyn, as I found out on Wednesday night.'

'Yes. Look, I'm sorry.'

'Not a great moment for a girl, Melvyn.'

'I know. I'm sorry.' She could hear his breathing, heavy and deliberate. She waited for his next word. And waited.

He sighed. 'Life, eh?'

'No, Melv. I need better than that.'

'I know you do. You deserve better than that, Sarah. You really do.'

'But?'

'No buts. I'm just disorientated right now. I'm trying to take one step at a time. I guess all of a sudden we were about to take a lot of steps at a time. When things, er, stopped for a moment, I realized that.'

'Don't you think it might have been nice to have stayed around to share that with me? Or am I so terrifying?'

'Of course it would have been better. I seem to be doing a better job of destroying things than building them right now. I wasn't sure if I was . . . if we were, you know . . . ready. I panicked.' His efforts to articulate his thoughts finished in a heap.

What was it about this man? She realized she was having to work at staying offhand with him.

'Did you get the champagne?' he said foolishly.

'Yes, I did. And I drank most of it.'

'I'm sorry. Really.'

She heard the meaning in his tone. It was abject, desperate. Melvyn was complex, bruised, but he really seemed to want her. It can't have been easy for him to call. She knew she could forgive Wednesday.

'So where do we go from here?' she said, deliberately lightening her tone.

There was a pause as he decided whether he dared say it. 'Don't we have some unfinished business with a bottle of Moët?'

Monday, 22 March

Marcus Newman had done them proud. As Charlie Burrows sat in his office reading the report, the old confidence coursed back through him. Before he finished the small print, he called Melvyn Davies.

'Well, my dear Merlin, I don't know what it was you said to Mr Newman, but it did the trick.'

Davies warmed to Burrows's approval. 'Really?'

'Listen to this, this is the executive summary:

'Acrobat has been punished after a poor shareholders' meeting, but we believe the reaction has been overdone. The company has moved quickly to restore the management team after a senior defection, proving strength in depth, and admitting new talent to a team that is long on expertise. The underlying business is good, costs are well under control and the company will benefit this year from a restoration of good relations with Southern Foods, following the absence of this large-scale advertiser from the client list last year. Management is not seeing the slowdown in revenues rumoured elsewhere, and is still predicting double-digit revenue and profit growth for the year. This would make Acrobat a significant outperformer to the rest of the sector. It seems now inevitable that new ownership legislation will be published by the government this week. The changes will finally allow Acrobat to grow by acquisition, applying its proven sales and programming skills to under-performing rivals. We have upgraded the stock to a BUY, with a target price of 600p.'

Burrows paused to allow the splendour of the moment to engulf them both.

Davies managed, 'Wow – all I did was promise him some tickets to the Clapton concert.'

Burrows laughed, as much from relief as at the suggestion that Newman was susceptible to any such cajolery. It had been some time since he had not been firefighting for the company's image.

'Takes you back a bit, doesn't it, Melv? Remember when all our reports were like this? They love you when it's bowling forward, but, man, can they turn when it gets sticky! Says something about their view of management, doesn't it? When it goes well, it's the market, and when it goes wrong, it's incompetence.'

Burrows was on a roll. Even at the end of a phone line Davies could tell his head was somewhere else.

'You know what, Melv?' Burrows continued. 'A report like this, and a six hundred p share price target, puts our little world in a whole new light.'

'Right,' said Davies, trying to move his enthusiasm up to match Burrows's. 'Happy days are here again, then, is it?'

'Absolutely. Big "Thank you" to Marcus. Now, if Ray can pull in the numbers and we can find a way around this *Marilyn* nightmare, we're laughing.'

'*Marilyn* nightmare?'

'Long story,' said Burrows. 'Catch you later, Melv.'

*

Phyllis Grigson had been through the newspapers again. She read them as a professional, identifying the pieces that had just been copied from the press releases, seeking out the articles written by her mates. Now she was bored. Like yesterday and the day before, she had been spinning out an inadequate number of unimportant tasks in order to occupy the maximum possible time. She tried not to dwell on the contrast between the impatience of the tasks that used to fill her day and the ocean of fiddle-faddle that now stretched drably before her each morning. She decided it was time to check in with Ray Walker, and she swept up her phone.

Grigson was a woman accustomed to trading her time and energy for a countable result. She never agonized about the point of it all – just got on with it. But no job, no point, no life. The injustice scalded her.

'Walker.'

'Ray – answering your own phone! – what's this? Cost cutting at the old firm?'

'Hello, Phyllis – no, Sylvia's gone off to the chemist to get me some headache pills.'

'When did you get back?'

'Came in yesterday at three o'clock. They say day two is the worst.'

'How was it – rest of the trip good?'

'Oh, really, you should see it out there. It's all so much more professional than what we've got going here.'

'Really?'

'Oh, for sure. Henry shouldn't be running this, but he made absolutely the right call. This is a winner. We've got a great director and you should see the names who

278

are biting at this one. It's like a table plan at the Oscars.'

Grigson laughed to hear her friend use an expression he'd clearly picked up in the last few days.

Walker was still talking. 'Burrows is wittering on about bringing it back to twelve million or even getting out altogether, but honestly, if we rat on our partners now, that's it, we can forget any future involvement in North America for Acrobat. And thinking long term, I believe that's the last thing we want.'

'So you're still in for twenty-two?'

'Yup,' said Walker as if it was the only conceivable outcome. 'If a company like this can't afford a sensible risk investment in a key source of programming, we might as well all pack up and go home.'

'Twenty-two million?'

'Phyllis, you don't know the half of it. That's nothing compared with what these boys put up on the projects they believe in. Time we joined the bigtime, that's what Charlie Burrows wants, isn't it?'

'Does he know yet?'

'I'm seeing him later.'

'Good luck.'

Grigson smiled to herself as she looked over the page of shorthand she'd written in her reporter's notebook. Once a hack, always a hack.

Abby Kelleher and Charlie Burrows sat opposite each other on the sofas in his office. The coffee table between them was invisible beneath drafts and re-drafts of the internal note designed to waft his new confidence around the building as fast as possible. Words successively spurned, hostages to fortune despatched until the precise flavour was achieved, whole paragraphs relocated around the page with the sweep of an arrow.

The door opened suddenly, Paula was framed in the doorway with a single sheet of paper. 'I'm really sorry, Charlie,' she said, every feature dejected. 'I've got a fax from Ofcom. It's a press release. I thought you'd want to see it straight away.'

Kelleher picked up her mood. 'Want me to wait outside, Charlie?'

'Oh God, now what?' Burrows reached for the paper. 'No, stay here, Abby. Safety in numbers.' He ran a heavy hand through his hair and set to read the sheet.

In a moment he threw himself back on the sofa.

'You total bastard, Paula, I don't know why I put up with you.'

Paula had retreated to the doorway, where she was sniggering uncontrollably.

'Dare I ask what it is?' Kelleher asked hesitantly.

'I'll tell you what it is,' said Burrows, glowering at his PA, 'it is the turning point. It's the announcement that they are relaxing the ownership rules. It's fifteen per cent on the share price is what this is.'

Burrows read the release again. It was everything he'd been lobbying for, arguing for and, in the end, making deals for. Finally. After all the misery of the last few weeks, Burrows felt renewed.

'Ladies, you are witness to the rebirth of Acrobat. After weeks of wading through relentless crap, today, finally, is the day it all changes. Thank you, Marcus, thank you, Howell. This is it, baby. We're coming back.' He sprang to his feet, clapped his hands and said, 'OK, Pol, let's get on with this crapshoot. Could you fix me some time with Mr Holidaymaker Walker today? Tell Melv we're off to the races if you would, and Henry – any sign of Henry this week?'

'No, we're not expecting him back yet.'

'OK, perhaps you could put Rishi on alert, and ask him to let Henry know at least. He'll be grateful for something to worry about. Abby, we need to rewrite this note. It just got a lot more convincing.'

'OK,' said Paula, mirroring the new mood of efficiency. 'Like to involve the new COO?'

'Ooh, shit – don't tell anyone I forgot, will you?'

Abby mimed fixing a padlock to her lips.

'Only if you're very nice to me,' said Paula.

'Deal.'

'Nice cuppa char to toast the new era?'

'Perfect,' he said and roared back to his desk. He clapped his hands again, rubbing them together and letting out a whoop of celebration. 'Yeah, baby. Here we go.'

Ray Walker wasn't looking terrific. Not that the designer suits ever helped much, but he had significantly overdone it with the first-class hospitality on the return flight. He'd particularly enjoyed being able to pick his own movie and had caught up on the work of some of the potential stars for the Acrobat version of *Marilyn*. In the end he'd only managed a couple of hours' sleep. So when he had to get up for a day at work, his body was insisting it was 11 p.m.

Above his greyish pallor he sported a few beads of sweat on his upper lip. He was aware of his condition and dabbed at his head with a 'Mr Happy' handkerchief throughout their meeting.

What a bizarre guy this is, thought Burrows, mesmerized by the silly handkerchief. *Obviously a dearly loved grandad for some kid*. However, his quiet interlude with the family side of Ray Walker was short-lived as Acrobat's Commercial Director set about winning his case.

'Right, how are things?' he said as he laid out his papers in front of him in his normal fashion.

Burrows couldn't resist trying to read them upside down, the pencilled stage directions that Walker had drafted for his scene.

'Things are actually going pretty well for a change. We've stopped mucking about with internal issues and we're making some progress. Did you see the Newman report on us?'

'Yes, I had a brief look – it seemed encouraging.'

Burrows was momentarily nonplussed by the moderation of Walker's review.

'Well, yes, *very* encouraging, I'd say. With a decent share price, and new ownership legislation, we could be on for Charisma TV.'

Walker looked sceptical. 'Is it doable?'

'We need some fancy legal footwork, but yes, it is.'

Walker was distracted. He hadn't come to talk about acquisitions. He had nothing prepared.

'OK,' he said, 'the next item on my agenda . . .' he looked up at Burrows '. . . had we finished on that?'

Burrows smiled pragmatically. 'Sure, whatever.'

Walker lifted a corner of each of his pieces of paper and scrutinized them as if asking who wanted to go first. He plumped for one of them. 'We'll come to the Sarah thing in a minute. Let's knock off this *Marilyn* . . .'

'OK, where do we stand?'

'We're in for twenty-two and that's it.'

'What do you mean – that's it? I told you to come back with twelve or zero.'

'Sorry, no. My understanding is that you asked me to go out there as a senior executive to investigate the situation and make an informed decision.'

Once again the man offered up this half-baked logic in the place of loyalty, this invariable dissent in place of the allegiance Burrows needed from his team. Enough. No more. In a moment, a shaft of pure clarity illuminated the gloom of this guy's intransigence. Removing Walker was doable if he could pull off the Charisma TV deal. Their Sales Director was good: young, dynamic, and relevant to the kind of culture he wanted to lead. It would be a sublime move. Keep Ray till the deal was done to reassure the City, then despatch the bastard with full commercial honours. It would send a great message to the Charisma people that they were being embraced, not swamped. His euphoria rose. This day was turning out to be a classic. Funny how great moments come in threes.

Burrows steadied his exhilaration as if it were an excitable horse that might at any minute escape his control. His Charisma deal was still a long way off. But there was a real plan in there. He returned to the present. Walker was waiting, belligerent.

His anger rose again. 'Number one, I specifically asked you *not* to go out there. Yeah, but good old Ray knew a lot better. Hell, you're Ray Walker. No one tells *you* what to do, do they, Ray? No no no. So you just take yourself off to LA – and then guess what? You're all offended that you weren't here to talk to me about Sarah Golanski.'

'We'll come to that in a minute,' Walker blustered, keeping his agenda intact.

'Yes, Ray, we bloody will. In the meantime, there are one or two business disciplines that make this whole bloody theme park work. Like, while I am Chief Executive, if I ask you to deliver a particular result, no matter how senior you are, you do it. Unless or until you're running your own company, Ray, that's how it is. Are we clear?'

Walker blinked at him. He spoke very quietly. 'So you want to take all the decisions, is that it?'

Burrows heard perfectly well, but this technique of Walker's irritated him. 'I can't hear you when you whisper, Ray.'

Walker turned the volume up too high. 'I am merely saying that you might as well have sent the post boy then.'

'Look, Ray, brilliant and exceptional though you are, you do not know everything that is going on. This whole baby is balanced on a knife-edge right now. The City is worried about the movie, but they'll live with it up to a point. I've told them that our expenditure is capped at twelve million, so it is capped at twelve million. End of story.'

'I think you should hear me out before you close your mind,' whispered Walker. 'Or, of course, we could just put this in the hands of the lawyers and hope for the best?'

'What are you saying?'

Walker savoured the moment. 'What I mean is that I have spoken to our attorneys in LA. We cannot renege on the deal Henry Fleming took us into. Put simply, it isn't an option. We haven't a contractual leg to stand on.'

He shrugged. 'I mean, go ahead if you think you know better, but we'll never be able to do business there again.'

Burrows couldn't distinguish his aversion to the news from his distaste for the messenger. Nice choice to present to the City: gross mismanagement or blatant defiance of the wishes of the shareholders. He said, 'So we're stuck with this, then.'

'No, not stuck with it. This is going to add significant numbers to the bottom line. You want my opinion? We have nowhere near enough money in movies.'

'Indulge me for a while till I find a way out of this hole, would you, Ray? No more movie money, OK?'

He glowered at Walker, who affected a look of pure innocence.

'At some point I think it would be good if you would talk to our partners in the States. They like to feel that the top man is behind it.'

Burrows nearly choked. 'Not now, Ray.'

'Obviously not now, you're much too busy. But when you have time.'

'Right, yeah. When I've got time. Now, you wanted to talk about Sarah's promotion.'

Walker shuffled his papers and traced his finger along point one. 'The first concern here is obviously the timing. Why this had to occur when I am out of the country obviously rings alarm bells.'

'We've dealt with that, Ray.'

'I mean, it's the question people are asking.'

'Which people, Ray?'

'Internally, externally; unlike some, I make a point of keeping my ear to the ground.'

'Unlike who, Ray?'

'Well, not mentioning names, but the point is that the sloppy way in which this announcement was handled was very damaging for me.'

Once again the clarity of his vision was being fogged by Walker and his gonzo logic. Yet something new was happening. He could feel it coming and, like a birth, he knew there was nothing he could do to stop it, to make it happen sooner or later than its moment. He was calm. Not wanting to miss what was building, almost nervous that Walker might back down, apologize, do something to abort the climax. All the frustrations, the tolerances and indulgences of this man's belligerence that he had bundled away unresolved were coming out for the moment, like a pub crowd gathering for a rumble, standing on tiptoe to see what was going to happen. Still his demeanour was calm, his only anxiety that this idiot would somehow fail to hang himself on the rope he was paying out to him. He wondered if Walker could feel it too, but the man showed no sign of departing from his script.

Walker raised his eyes and removed his reading glasses theatrically. 'So, under these circumstances, once again I find myself having to seriously consider my position . . .'

'Resign, Ray.'

Walker's flow stopped, his lips were thin. Burrows hated him.

'I beg your pardon,' he said: the bully, accustomed to facing down opposition with the threat of greater violence than his rival.

'You heard me.'

Silence.

Burrows knew this was it. He didn't want to force it or give Walker any way out. This was the showdown. He allowed the silence to continue until Walker was about to speak.

'If you're considering your position, what conclusion did you come to?'

'Eh?'

'Presumably you've come here with a resolution in mind.' Everything in him wanted to go on, to release the stuffed-down resentments, but he knew that he must respect the natural rhythm of the process.

Walker tried to retreat. 'I am merely making the point that by this action you have put me in an impossible position.'

'So your only possible response is . . .' Too far too far.

'Listen, mate, if you're trying to muscle me out –'

'Is that what you want? Do you want out?'

Walker brought his hand down hard on the table. 'Of course it's not what I want. Do you think I get myself on a plane and go halfway round the world because I want out? Do you think I bust my arse creating the best sales team in the country because I want out? I put the best part of my working life into this company, before you got here. You passed me over before because you wanted to give your friend a job, and now you have an opportunity to recognize the contribution I make, and you go and appoint someone . . . don't get me wrong, she's very good . . . one of the best people I ever hired . . . but you want someone who is young enough to be my daughter as COO of the company.'

Burrows clasped his hands in front of his face. 'That's right, Ray.'

'So what are you going to say to me?'

'That's my final decision. Like the *Marilyn* decision. Like the *Midnight Minus One* decision. It's final and *you* will work constructively with it.' He paused on '*you*'.

'Or what?'

Burrows shrugged as if he really hadn't thought that far. 'To use your words, consider your position.'

They sat in silence.

Walker stirred himself, his tone faintly reasonable. 'This is not a solution.'

Burrows pulled his glasses off his nose and, sticking one side-piece in his mouth, cocked his head to invite more. His mind raced. Dare he lose Ray in the run-up to a Charisma deal? Ray would go with as much noise as he could muster. It would spook the market and perhaps crater his deal anyway. It was a risk too far right now, but the sight of Walker in retreat was delicious. He knew he couldn't win this in the short term, but he could savour the moment for a while. He pushed his chair back and put his feet on the desk. Breezy.

'There's only one way you stay.'

'What's that?' said Walker quickly.

'It's a whole new deal, Ray. I've had it with the old way.'

Walker started to say something, but Burrows just raised his voice until the challenge had stopped.

'I've had it with you dressing up your naked ambition as sacrificial company service; masquerading as my trusted ally while you tell your drinking buddies I've lost the plot; learning the language of teamwork just to cover the meanness of your single-mindedness. Taking every opportunity you can to try and marginalize your board colleagues. It's pathetic, and I can't tell you how totally sick of it I am. I agree with you – the sales force is probably the best in the country. But if the price of that is this: you swaggering around the place, threatening me or anyone else who confronts you . . . consulting your *attorneys* every five minutes, I'm not interested any more. That's it – you can go. We'll put on a nice show for you and everyone can say "good old Ray, got out when the going was good".'

Burrows paused; he couldn't tell what effect his words were having on Ray Walker. The adrenalin was rushing him.

'That's it, Ray. You choose. But know this: if you choose to stay, you choose to join a team, with me at the head of it. And when nip comes to tuck, we do it my way. OK?'

Walker looked at his papers, turning them as if in search of an answer.

Finally he looked at Burrows. 'So it's you or me, is it?'

Burrows pulled a face of exaggerated puzzlement. 'No – it's much more simple than that. Your continuance as a senior director of this company is contingent on your preparedness to accept that I am its Chief Executive. Your agenda and mine will be indistinguishable. If you don't like that, there's no point in keeping this pretence up; we bring it to a conclusion right now. Your call.'

Walker got to his feet, grabbing his papers into a messy bundle. Burrows had outplayed him this time. Obviously this was no time to resign. He needed a big punchy exit-line. He leaned over the desk and said, 'Like I said, it's you or me.'

Acrobat's closing share price   520p

Tuesday, 23 March

Geoff O'Brien was having a good day. He was looking out over Marylebone Road, half reading the research results on a new flavoured drink they had launched earlier in the year. It was going well, another runner from the Southern Foods stable successfully into the race.

His PA buzzed him to say that he had a call from Mel Park at the agency. Mel was responsible for buying the commercial airtime on *Night and Day*.

'Hi, Mel, any problems?'

'Everything running pretty smoothly on all the standard campaigns,' she said. 'I just wondered where you got to with the Acrobat guy last week on *Midnight Minus One*?'

'Um.' O'Brien sent his memory in search of the meeting. 'We . . . agreed . . . that . . .' He got it. 'Ah yes, we agreed that I was going to be a good guy and give them a chance to get it right. I've done a note to the board explaining what we're doing and, as far as I can tell you, it will be with us again this Thursday.'

'That's what I thought,' Park mused. 'I've just been checking the listings for this week, and it's not there.'

O'Brien's mood changed abruptly. 'What? What's there instead?'

'It's some late-night movie.'

'Their programme guy told me it had a breather last week so they could fluff it up, but it would be back this week.'

'Well, maybe it's stayed in the fluffers for another week, because it certainly isn't going out on Thursday.'

O'Brien was annoyed. 'What the hell are they doing? You'd suppose that, after last year, they'd be treating us like royalty . . . In fact, the programme guy said as much when he came to see me last week. I'll call Ray; thanks for letting me know. I don't think we can allow ourselves to be seen to be buggered about in the market, do you?'

'Absolutely not. Look, if you want to pull off Acrobat again, I'll tumble the numbers overnight, see how I can buy back the impacts elsewhere – be a big day for Channel 6! I'll give you a ring in the morning.'

When Sarah Golanski arrived at her desk, it was dominated by a very large bunch of red roses. Suppressing a grin, she rummaged in the folds of tissue to find the envelope. It said, '*There is nothing like desire for preventing the thing one says from bearing any resemblance to what one has in mind.* – Proust'.

At the window of a chintzy dining room in a château south of Paris, Piers Carrick was phoning his office every fifteen minutes to check the share price. The government's announcement of easier ownership rules had been well received and throughout the morning the share price continued its rise, pausing for breath at 525p, slipping five pence and then pressing on upwards. With every rise, he felt more sick. He knew the man with whom he would be having lunch would be totally *au fait* with the latest number.

The door swung open and the sun-kissed figure of

Arnaud de Vigny bustled in. He did not greet his visitor.

'What the hell is happening?' he said.

'The ownership rules are changing, Arnaud. And they've had a very good analyst's report.'

'Surely you covered the analysts? What is the point of convincing the rest of the world that management is unstable if this Newman comes out and says everything is just fine actually? Totally ridiculous.' De Vigny muttered something to himself in French which Carrick couldn't – and didn't want to – translate. He felt a trickle of sweat on his back and a sense of surprise that he had allowed himself to be rattled like this.

'I don't think you fully understand, Arnaud . . .'

The response was swift and predictable. 'Listen, Piers. All the time you tell me I do not understand these rules and systems of your market. OK. Fine. I do not understand, and that is why I have you. But I tell you what I *do* understand. I do understand that my intentions in UK will not be arrested by your incompetence. I will not have Mrs Celia Sharma laughing at me.'

'Now then, Arnaud. I'm sure she's not,' Carrick attempted, before de Vigny continued.

'Piers, I do not know what you have been doing and I do not want to know. But I tell you now, unless you deliver this strategy, perhaps the authorities in the City of London might start to wonder at the strange movements in the Acrobat share price. Perhaps they may even ask themselves what is Piers Carrick's role in this. What do you think? This is possible, no?'

A jolt of adrenalin spasmed through Carrick's body. He was not accustomed to threats as naked as this. His mind sifted his responses. Threaten de Vigny that any such betrayal would expose him too? No, de Vigny would have taken care of that. Teflon clean. He looked at the Frenchman, squat, guzzling away at the remains of his plate of food. He knew de Vigny could out-intimidate him. This kind of showdown was his way of life. Little thug.

De Vigny finished his meal and swept a white napkin around his lips. As he raised himself from the table, he said, 'You have one week.'

Monica had cleared a small space on Melvyn Davies's desk just big enough to stack his post. On top was the usual sheet of paper with the list of people he had to call. The names at the bottom of the page had been there for weeks. Davies would often get so bored with seeing them that he'd just cross them off and tell the ever-vigilant Monica that he'd dealt with them. He scanned the list of recent additions, looking for interesting calls, and was surprised to see 'Phyllis Grigson 7177 8533' among them. It was odd, seeing this unfamiliar number next to Grigson's name, he was so used to 'Phyllis Grigson – extension 2006'. Apparently she wanted lunch; that would be nice.

By the end of the day, Burrows knew he had fixed Acrobat's ambitions in the minds of the journalists working for the morning papers. It was good to be back. He called Georgia and asked her to pull a bottle of something decent out of the cupboard for later.

As they drove home, he chatted idly with Mick about his fickle world, where one day he was 'Burrows the beleaguered' and the next 'Burrows the hero'.

'So you're going to buy another TV company, right? I'm sorry, I can't help hearing. But I don't talk to anyone. You know that,' said Spring.

'No, of course. That's the plan, but there's a very long way to go yet.'

'Oh, right. What happens next, then?'

'It all still hangs on the share price. If the market gets cold feet again, we're stuffed. I need a rising share price to convince the Charisma TV shareholders that they're on to a good thing. If the share price falls, the value of the offer falls, making it easier for Charisma's shareholders to say "No" to us.'

'It's going up though now, right?'

'It is indeed. We were up to five forty-five by close today. It's fantastic, but the market's very jumpy still. We've got to move quick and we can't afford any more screw-ups.'

Spring nodded quietly.

Ray Walker stayed in his office late that night, entertaining fantasies as treacherous as in any Shakespearean plot. He jotted his options down on a yellow legal pad, in search of a comeback from the dialogue with Burrows that did not require the grovelling apology he was not prepared to make. 'You or me.' Not a very smart thing to blurt out, but he'd been losing the argument and needed an exit.

He knew he had some cards left to play. Burrows's strategy to restore his reputation depended on the acquisition of Charisma. It would be near impossible to pull off if he lost another experienced person. A warm thought grew on him. Maybe Burrows would have to do the grovelling.

Despite the bounce in the share price, he'd never known a time when Burrows's reputation had been so low. Burrows was desperately vulnerable on the *Marilyn* thing but, as Walker's pen described and deleted his options, he knew it had been handed over to him from Henry Fleming so publicly that any explosion which did for the Chief Executive would as surely maim his Commercial Director. Just following orders? No. Couldn't possibly make it stick. He'd bragged about his $22 million intransigence too widely for that.

Burrows's foolish revenue promise was an obvious underbelly. If the revenue died and Burrows had to make a profits warning, that would be the end of it for the share price, any plan for a bid, and Burrows would be back on the defensive. The sales reports that Walker had seen that day had not been so encouraging. But again, would the building collapse on the chief sales-man too?

His mind dawdled on down this route, wondering if he had the credibility externally, and with the board, to accede to the throne. It would be a great finish to his career. Would Sarah Golanski be his Sales Director, now Burrows had turned her head with this COO nonsense? Where did Melvyn Davies stand? He was too significant a figure in Acrobat's success, both internally and exter-nally. But he was flawed, a man driven by his emotions. Walker had no great warmth for him, but he could always be seduced back with a few grand. Henry Fleming? Just the accountant – be fine, probably. Bring back Phyllis; justice for a good mate.

So with Sumner gone, who was his competition? Walker lifted his jacket off the back of his large leather chair. He'd entertained these pipe dreams many times. But maybe this was looking better than before. Just in time.

Acrobat's closing share price 545p

Wednesday, 24 March

The new ownership rules were the main story on all the business pages. Acrobat was well represented, after Burrows and Kelleher's efforts on the phones. Ken Hathaway, the Chairman of Charisma TV, was quoted, saying that his company was determined to stay independent. But Burrows was wired, fielding calls from the advisers, undaunted in his new plan to pursue Charisma TV, make a hostile bid if they wouldn't come quietly, fiddling with the numbers, excited that the share price now made it all a possibility.

Henry Fleming sat at the table, his breakfast going cold, while he re-read the *FT*'s story about the changes. He scarcely breathed as his eyes careened through the piece.

'What's that, love?' said Maggie, leaning on the back of his chair and munching a piece of toast.

'Hang on,' he said without tearing his eyes from the print.

At the end, he turned to look at Maggie, who was reading the story over his shoulder.

'That doesn't affect anything, does it?' she said, sweeping the breakfast things from the table.

'Well, yes, it does,' he breathed.

She didn't look over her shoulder, busying herself with some dishes.

'But it doesn't affect *us*.'

Fleming got up and moved across to her. He put his hand on the nape of her neck and felt the tension there.

'No, you're right, love. Long term, it doesn't affect a thing.'

She turned inside the frame of his arms and looked into his face. Her eyes spoke her fear. 'What do you mean, "long term"?'

'I mean, I'll just have to postpone it for a bit. I can't do it to him. He's going to go after Charisma TV, which will go hostile. And he's got a big hole in his accounts, which I put there. I don't think I can honourably resign right now.'

'Why not?' Her eyes filled with tears which did not flow.

'Because it would play into the Charisma TV people's hands. It gets rough in a hostile bid. Both sides seize on anything they can to diminish the credibility of the other side. It's a war.'

Now the reservoir overflowed – first one cheek then the other.

'Honey, honey, don't cry. It'll be fine. I'm not going back for good. This'll be over in a few weeks and we'll pick up where we left off . . . planning some wonderful times together.'

'But we agreed this was *our* time – no more Acrobat, Henry. You said it. You decided.'

'I know, but I'm still FD. I can't leave him in the lurch, love.'

'But Henry, they didn't even tell you about the bid. You found out from the newspaper. That's how much they care about *you*. They've forgotten you exist. Why can't we forget *they* exist?'

Fleming was becoming less placatory as the conversation continued. 'It's a question of doing the right thing, Mags.'

She looked at him as if she didn't recognize him. Still the tears flowed.

'The right thing,' she said quietly.

'Look, I'll go and see Charlie this week and tell him I'm out as soon as I've resolved the Hollywood thing and the Charisma deal is done. I'll get Rishi to do all the work. It'll be great training for him.'

She steadied her voice. 'Henry, if you go back in there, you won't come out. You said as much yourself.'

Fleming looked dazed for a moment. Then he regained himself. 'I will. We decided this together. I'm just saying I need a couple of weeks to see this through and then I can stop with an easy heart.'

She laughed morbidly. 'That's just the point, Henry. If you go back in there, you won't stop with an easy heart. You'll stop with a stopped heart.'

She didn't say things like that for effect. He watched her for some time. She held his gaze.

'I'm fine and I'm *going* to be fine, Mags.'

She shook her head and wriggled away from his effort to embrace her. A tear landed on his forearm as she pulled herself away.

Left on his own, he dropped back into the chair, scrutinizing the single tear, watched it run through the hairs on his arm and drop to the floor. He had made his decision.

Sarah Golanski had agreed to have a quick lunch locally with Davies today, because he had an evening session with some American game-show producers. Maybe she'd just frightened him. Moved too quick to crystallize that shadow of sexual possibility which had lingered on the sidelines of every encounter. With each liaison it had edged closer, like a child trying to be caught. Until that night.

But she knew she had been touched. She didn't know if healing was possible, but when she looked into her emotions, expecting to taste the bile of her rejection, she found instead a willingness to forgive, if that was what it took to unlock a future with him. This was working. He had made himself vulnerable to her. This was real. This man had given her access to his soul.

He was halfway down a pint of bitter and reading a wodge of press cuttings when she arrived.

'Monsieur Proust, I believe,' she said, extending her hand.

He jumped to his feet, affecting a sitcom French accent. 'Beautiful lady. I am honoured to share your *compagnie*. Do you care for the pint?'

She chuckled loudly, her laughter filling the pub.

Davies continued. 'Perhaps a *sandwich exceptionnel*. We 'ave both kinds – *fromage* and 'am.'

'Sit down, you embarrassing man.' She tugged him on to the bench next to her.

He landed close to her. Their faces were very close. The kiss was inevitable.

'I'm sorry,' he said. 'You know, about last week.'

There was a moment's silence, then she kissed him again. 'Let's forget it,' she said.

A silence sat between them. They both wrestled with it. Eventually he said, '"Thank you" seems the wrong word.'

She laughed again. 'Why don't you shut up and get me a drink?'

He went to the bar, blubbering his apologies.

When he returned with her wine, he attempted a return to what he could recall of normal conversation. 'So, anyway, how's the new job going?'

She was relieved to get into a flow. 'Oh, fine, I think. Charlie's gradually managing to find time to brief me on things, in among the chaos.' She turned to face him. 'But I'm really worried about Charlie and Ray.'

'He nodded. 'Your old mentor can be a bit difficult for the rest of humanity, you know.'

'He's his own worst enemy, isn't he. I think Charlie was hoping my appointment would help. If anything, I think it's made things worse, so far,' she sighed.

'Come on, Sarah. It's not your fault, is it? They've always bickered.'

'I know, but it's never been this bad before. This *Marilyn* thing has really put the cat among the pigeons.'

'Ah, the *Marilyn* nightmare, I presume,' he said diffidently. 'I have no idea what that's about.'

She looked at him, surprised, and took him through the story.

'So Charlie tells the City it's twelve max, and sends Ray to LA to get it down and Ray refuses. Thinks it's a brilliant investment.'

Davies shook his head. 'That guy doesn't get it, does he?'

She breathed in, as if about to launch the case for the defence. And breathed out again. 'I suppose not.'

'Anyways,' he concluded, 'I haven't brought you to this lovely public house to talk about Ray and Charlie's latest spat. They'll get over it, and then there'll be another one along in a minute.'

She placed a conciliatory smile on her face. 'No, sorry. Very boring.'

When Burrows emerged from his lunch meeting with the bankers on Charisma TV, Paula told him she had taken a call from Henry Fleming.

'The boy Fleming – is he OK? Time for the grand re-entrance? Couldn't be better.'

'He didn't say, but he's having breakfast with you tomorrow at eight.'

'Brilliant.' Burrows was back in his office, skimming through the pile of mail.

He grabbed his briefcase and made for the door. 'It'll be a late one at the bank, Pol – could you ring Georgia and let her know. And I don't want any calls while I'm there, thanks. I shouted at the bloody cast of thousands for leaving their mobiles on during our meetings, so, leading by example and all that.'

So when Carrie McGann called to seek a comment on her latest tip, Paula Conley suggested she call Abby Kelleher. McGann decided not to bother.

Acrobat's closing share price   548p

Thursday, 25 March

As he set off for his breakfast with Burrows, Henry Fleming discovered he was nervous. It had been nearly a month since his coronary and he was still weak; sitting in the back of the cab to the station, he was glad of the familiarity of the route. Maggie had sent all his business suits to the cleaners and the unwrapping of the cellophane wrapper had been like a reunion with an old friend.

He tried to concentrate on his newspaper but found that his eyes were skating through the lines, unconnected to his brain. He gave up and watched the scene rush past the window, rehearsing his lines for his meeting with Burrows. He'd managed to find 'the decent thing' in many former campaigns and, after wrestling down the emotiveness of Maggie's confrontation, he had made what he knew was the right choice for this situation.

He had travelled so far in three and a half weeks that he toiled to re-navigate his mental passage to explain it for Burrows.

It was 7.45 when he reached the hotel where Burrows would arrive late for their breakfast. He walked past the entrance to the end of the road to look at the Acrobat building, seeing it with eyes undimmed by repetition like last time. To think it was just twenty-five days ago.

In that time, normal life at the building had continued. People had come and gone up and down those steps. Programmes had been transmitted, spots bought and sold. Earnest memos constructed by earnest people. Four weeks ago it had been the driving force of his life. He found it hard to recall. How would those people ever understand what he had gone through while they had pressed on with the day-to-day stuff of day-to-day business? It would be hard to be back.

At 8.10 Charlie Burrows bounced into the breakfast room of the hotel. He was well known there and always took the same table behind a pillar and by the window. It was his interview table, so he knew exactly where to find Fleming.

'Henry, you old bugger. Good to see you.' He shook his hand warmly.

'Morning, Charlie.' Fleming felt like one of Burrows's interviewees.

'Blimey, Henry you've lost weight – you're looking great. How're you feeling?' Burrows chattered, studiously friendly.

'I'm fine, thanks, Charlie. How are you?'

They ordered their breakfast and Burrows enthusiastically recounted the events of the past few weeks. Fleming listened with fascination at the ephemera which had commanded Burrows's total absorption while he had brushed shoulders with eternity.

'It'll be great to have you back, Henry. When are they going to tear up your sick note?'

Fleming had prepared himself for this moment. He had worked out his speech but, in the moment, the words were not to be found. His head filled with images from the last month: the coronary care ward, his wife reading to him, that tear. The woman at his side for so many years, waiting for the moment when he would finally have time for her. A month ago the thuggish coronary had threatened to steal her life savings.

'I'm not coming back, Charlie.'

Burrows just looked at him, weighing up the moment. Wanting to negotiate but knowing also that his normal tools of persuasion might just be too blunt for this.

'Have they told you "That's it", mate?'

Fleming considered the neatness of this escape. In a second he rejected it. 'No, Charlie. I've made my decision.'

'Not now, Henry. Surely?'

Fleming was again presented with the opportunity to adapt his choice. 'Well, actually . . . yes, now.'

'But we're going after Charisma TV,' said Burrows. 'It's going to go hostile.'

'I know,' admitted Fleming.

'Come on, Henry. You know what they'll do to me if you go off in the middle of this.'

'I know. When I called you yesterday, it was the press report of the bid that made me pick up the phone. I was going to come back just long enough to help you do it, then make a planned exit, successor in place and all that.'

'I can live with that.'

'Yes, but I can't.'

Burrows looked shocked. 'What, literally?'

'I just don't know, Charlie. I suppose there's a risk, yes. A hostile bid isn't the most relaxing of occupations for a guy with a dodgy heart. But it's not what I meant. I meant I can't do it to Mags.'

'She's been through a lot,' said Burrows, opening a new gambit.

'Yes, she has, and I'm not going to put her through any more. If I can't do this for myself, I'm going to do it for her. It's like I've read my own epitaph, Charlie. You ever done that? Ever wondered what they'd write about you if you keeled over tomorrow?' Burrows looked non-committal. 'Maybe not, but I have,' Fleming continued. '"Here lies Henry Fleming, a good accountant."'

'Oh come on, Henry, you love your work, and you're brilliant at it.'

'Thanks,' said Fleming. 'But I've realized that being good at something is not a good enough reason to do it.'

'It helps,' said Burrows, knowing he was losing the argument.

Fleming continued. 'For years I've been saying that Mags is the most important person in the world to me. But if you'd followed me around for a couple of weeks . . . if Melvyn had done one of his beloved "fly on the wall" documentaries on me, you would never have guessed.'

'Maggie understands, though, surely – you've got a good job, a lot of responsibility, she knows it's demanding, same as Georgia. We're blessed with wonderful wives.'

'I agree. But for me, now is the time for the actions to speak as loud as the words.'

'Shit, Henry, you couldn't have chosen a worse time to grow a conscience. I'm counting on you.'

'So's Maggie. And you know what, Charlie, *I'm* counting on me to make a big decision for once. This is the narrow path, you know, and I nearly missed it. But the past twenty-five days have given me time to pause and consider. This is the route I have to take now. I'm sorry about the timing, I really am, but it's another bid on another day. You'll be fine.'

'It's hostile,' said Burrows lamely.

'Sorry, Charlie,' concluded Fleming.

Burrows pulled one last weapon from the bottom of the bag. 'So, what notice are you on?'

'I'm on three months, but I want you to let me go with immediate effect.' He held Burrows's gaze.

Burrows groaned and slumped back in his chair, a gesture Fleming took as submission. He pulled an envelope from his top pocket and placed it on the table between them. Burrows looked at it with distaste.

'I think, the moment I hand this to you, you have to announce. The last thing you need is a lame duck Finance Director in a hostile bid.'

Burrows peeled his eyes from the envelope, back to Fleming. 'And you're handing it to me right now, are you, Henry?'

'I am.'

DAILY TELEGRAPH Business News

Charlie Goes to Hollywood. Exclusive

CARRIE MCGANN

Two weeks ago Charlie Burrows, Chief Executive of Acrobat, assured analysts that the youth television group's controversial investment in movies would be capped at $12 million. Yet in that time he has seized the opportunity to double the group's exposure in what has been called 'the greatest casino in business' to nearly $25 million. SuperKino, the German partner, withdrew from the precarious deal, leaving the way clear for Burrows to snap up their stake.

Investors are dismayed by this apparent snub to their concerns. One analyst said, 'If this is true, frankly, I'm stunned that he should choose this route. Film is a high-risk business, so naturally investors are cautious. There is no evidence that it's a business Acrobat understands, so the management were left in no doubt that the $12 million was as much as the market would bear.'

Burrows himself was unavailable for comment but sources at the company said that Ray Walker, the highly experienced Commercial Director of the group, had recently taken over responsibility for this deal and visited Los Angeles. An executive, who refused to be named, said, 'The decision to increase our investment was taken before Ray got involved. When he found out, he immediately went to LA against Burrows's wishes to try to resolve the situation.'

The article wound up with a summary of recent events at Acrobat, including the 'abrupt departure' of Phyllis Grigson; readers were referred to a commentary piece laden with Enron undertones.

Burrows thought his heart would stop as he read the piece. He had known that the news would have to emerge, but in the run of events of the last few days there had hardly been an appropriate moment. At least he could have wrapped it with some good news. He could certainly have sugar-coated the conclusion of the piece, that the decision to defy the market was conceived by him as a deliberately provocative act.

Abby Kelleher arrived to find him gazing into space, the newspaper article in front of him.

'Charlie,' she said, waiting for him to turn his head. 'This is not just another leak. This is all deliberate. Someone is trying to kill us,' she added, her voice low.

He looked at her, expecting more.

'There's always the odd leak here and there. But this isn't that. This is a concerted campaign against us. Someone is out to bring the company to its knees.'

Burrows looked back at the paper. 'Or me,' he said. He was still too stunned to be angry. 'What perfect timing, Abby. One day out of the crap, share price at an all-time high, and we have some Judas playing politics. Silly me, I was almost enjoying myself for a day or so there. Who would do this?' He looked at her coldly. 'Eh?'

'There are some obvious front-runners,' she said.

Burrows's gaze held her firmly. 'Ray on your list?' he said.

'I don't know him all that well, but . . .'

Burrows raised the page again, deciding he had no choice but to trust her. 'What you don't know, Abby, is that Ray Walker and I have had a row. I sent him to LA to get us out of this bloody deal, and we seem if anything, to be further in. He has totally defied me, not for the first time, because he thinks he knows much better than me how to run this business.'

'But would he go out of his way to damage you like this?'

'Just read it, for pity's sake. "Ray Walker, the highly experienced Commercial Director . . ." He could have written that himself.'

'Are his press contacts that good, then?' she asked.

'They're OK. He mainly used to use Phyllis to do his dirty work, but he's been around a long time. Everyone knows Ray.'

'If you're right, we have to starve him of information. If he's set on a course of . . .'

'. . . killing me,' said Burrows. Him or me. The words crystallized the threat and provoked a surge of indignation towards his adversary.

'Well, OK, killing you, we have to make sure that he has no new information. We're going to have to run this bid without him.'

'We're going to have to run this bid without Henry Fleming too,' said Burrows, pulling the envelope out of his inside pocket. 'He's resigned.'

'Oh, blimey,' said Kelleher. 'What notice is he on?'

'I've let him go.'

'Can you do that without board approval?'

'No idea, but I have. There's no point in holding him to it; his heart's not in it . . . if you get my drift.'

He noticed a half-smile forming on Kelleher's face. She was waving her pencil as an idea formed in her head.

'What?' he said.

'The *Marilyn* overspend is Henry's fault, isn't it?'

'Yes, he made the original decision, but it's a bit tough to say the heart attack was his fault.'

Kelleher was shading the margin of her pad. 'And today he resigned. Are you thinking what I'm thinking?' she said.

Burrows caught it. 'We couldn't do that to him . . . could we?'

She smiled coquettishly. 'We don't have too many options here, Charlie. And we need to get you off the hook – and fast.'

Burrows tutted. 'I hate myself for even thinking about it,' he said. 'Tell you what, we both think about it and we decide before lunch.'

'We have a very vicious mole here, Charlie, and if you're

going to beat it, you're going to have to leave your manners at home.'

Hamish Perrin was every inch the traditional, unruffled stockbroker. Today his normally languid tone had a twist of tension in it.

'Morning, Charles. Undesirable developments.'

'Yes, Hamish, very succinctly put. Looks like we have a mole in the house.'

Perrin considered this. 'Right, well, I think we should have spoken earlier about this, Charlie.'

Burrows pushed a hand through his hair. 'I'm sure you're right, Hamish. But if I rang you with all my problems, neither of us would get anything done.'

'Of course. But this one was probably a little bigger. Anyway, the share price has fallen twenty-five to five fifteen, but I'm afraid you have to brace yourself for worse. I think the market is trying to make up its mind what it thinks about the Hollywood thing. It doesn't quite know how to spreadsheet it. It would be very helpful if Henry's deputy, what's his . . . ?'

'Rishi?'

'Yes, Rishi, if Rishi would do a conference call this morning to explain how it might affect future earnings.'

Burrows laughed emptily. 'He's an accountant, not Mystic Meg.'

'I think he's going to have to find a crystal ball, then.'

'Are we bollocksed for the bid now, do you think, Hamish?'

'Too soon to say that. Hold on and we'll see whether the market is still factoring in the Newman report. In the meantime, Charlie, if I may say so, I think this has come out in a way which is not good for you personally.'

'No, I was just talking about that when you rang.'

'Well, it's obviously your call, but I think the market needs to hear from you on this. You were pretty clear at the analysts' meeting.'

'I'm on the case. And just for your further joy, Henry Fleming has resigned.'

'Oh my word! Are you announcing first thing tomorrow?'

'Yes, I suppose so.'

'Right. Golly. No relationship between the two events, is there?'

'Interesting question, Hamish. We'll talk later.'

Abby Kelleher's plan was looking increasingly attractive.

Kelleher returned before lunch with a sheaf of alternative announcements. She arrived, looking composed and organized, with her trademark folio of papers and mobile phone.

'This is easier than I thought,' she said. 'We don't have to drop Henry in it. He's done all the work for us.'

Burrows grimaced. 'What do you mean?' he said, making sure his tone suggested distaste.

'Well, look, the market is waiting for an announcement from us about the *Marilyn* money, and what it's going to get is an announcement about Henry Fleming leaving the company. Don't you see? We don't have to make the connection. They'll piece it together in a flash. And if they really don't get it, I can brief, off the record, that one of Henry's responsibilities was the film project, blah blah blah. The vultures have their lunch. And it's not you.'

Burrows watched her as she folded her arms with that QED look of hers. The notion of Henry Fleming as culprit was a very foreign one. Fleming was cautious, decent and honourable, the classic FD. His sin had not been to increase the investment, but to fail to communicate the fact. And he'd failed to do that because he was concentrating on staying alive. Burrows still thought it was too long a hard luck story to cut any ice with the market, but what harm would it do to let Fleming take a bullet for his Chief Executive? Sure, Burrows knew he was responsible. He was responsible for it all. But Henry was retiring anyway. He didn't need his reputation any more.

'Come on, Charlie, you've got to fight back,' she was saying, her movements pugnacious. 'We can win this, and you can come through it with a bigger group under your control and a bigger reputation.'

That word again. As he modelled the future possibilities for himself, he came back to it again and again. When you boil it down, he was a brand in a market. He traded on his reputation, nothing else. His credibility to sustain this job or get another was held proud by this single sinew which he spent his career building and strengthening, but which could be snapped through weakness, through negligence, through the deliberate machinations of another. The thought arrested him. Kelleher was talking again, but he had to deal with this thought. *Fight back against whom? Is someone trying to finish me?*

Ray Walker had the information, Phyllis Grigson had the contacts. '*You or me.*' It added up. He interrupted her.

'OK, Abby, let's do it.'

'OK?'

'Yep. Sorry, Henry, but you'll enjoy your retirement anyway. We're going to war here and we can't afford to fight bile with charm.'

She laid on a thick Texan accent. 'All right,' she said, and he cocked his head in response to her cheerleading, egging him on to defy his nature in pursuit of . . . victory seemed the wrong word . . . survival? Sorry, Henry. Needs must.

Ray Walker sat with his fingers stuffed into the handle of his mug of coffee, his features grim as he surveyed the newspaper. He wondered what would happen next. He had not been consulted by Burrows on the aftermath to Carrie McGann's piece. Had he already been classified as the enemy? He wasn't happy with an all-or-nothing bet. Not his style.

He needed allies, especially if Burrows fell. Impulsively then, he set off to see Melvyn Davies and found him in his office, the press cuts left open at the article.

He walked in and closed the door behind himself. 'A word if I may?'

Davies looked up and pushed his papers away.

'The reason I came to see you was that I know you and I have had our moments. Nothing we can't deal with. But we both have a vested interest in coming out of this intact.'

Davies was silent for a moment, preparing his response.

'You mean this, Ray?'

'Too right I mean it.'

'So what was all that Southern Foods thing about? The one where I found myself doing your dirty work?'

'No,' Walker protested. 'I felt the *Marilyn* project was running away from us. If it went pear-shaped, it would have had my name on it.'

'And Southern Foods? Might have been nice to warn me.'

Walker smiled his best winning smile, ignoring the invitation to argue. 'Sounds like you did a good job. I'm seeing him tomorrow. I'll tell him we had irrevocable problems with the show and we had to write it off. He won't know. Got anything else coming up that I can give him?'

Davies sighed. This guy really was impossible. 'Nothing springs to mind,' he said. 'How was Hollywood then?'

Walker came alive. 'You got to come with me next time. It's fantastic. It's real television, and we're real players; we're really in there.'

'Which is why Henry upped the ante?'

'I tell you, in my opinion, if he hadn't taken that deal he wouldn't have been doing his job.'

'Really?' said Davies, inviting more.

'The film is a cracker. Our partners are all in for more than us, and *they* do this every day of the week. We'd be mad to turn down an opportunity like this, especially when the revenue's so weak.'

'Is it?'

Walker nodded his head melodramatically. 'Oh yes. I'm still working on the detail, but, apart from Southern Foods, it's a lot worse than any of us thought.'

'Really?'

'Yes. But don't say anything to Charlie yet. I need to get a firm grip on it all before I make my report to him.'

'How bad?'

'Could be twenty million short.'

Davies winced. 'Shit, what does that do to the profits?'

'No idea, matey. Strictly top line, me. The rest of it is Burrows's problem.'

Davies whistled.

'You see my point. That's why we need this film income. If all goes well, we'll see some of it next year, and then the bonanza will come in the years after that. If we're into an advertising recession by then, it's a must. You mark my words, this is going to be our lifeline. And the sooner we get behind it and play it like we mean it, the better it will be for our long-term position over there.'

'What about the problem with the City?'

'Charlie's just got to get a grip on that. That's what he's supposed to do, isn't it? I get the revenue in, you get the viewers, he does the shareholders.'

'He's got a hill to climb now, though.' Davies nodded towards the newspaper.

'Look, *they* don't manage us. It's a question of trust. But he's got to show some leadership. They don't believe in it because it's so bloody obvious *he* doesn't.' Walker pursed his lips, his analysis complete. 'Likewise, if Charlie doesn't trust me to make a ten-million-dollar judgement call for a billion-dollar company, he should get a new Commercial Director.'

'Maybe if he knew the revenue situation he might see it differently.'

'Well, leave that one with me if you would. Seriously, I haven't told anyone. Since Sarah's thoughts are on higher things these days, it falls exclusively to yours truly to pick this up.'

*

By the time he arrived home, Henry Fleming was convinced he'd done the right thing. The journey and the meeting had drained him completely. Maggie was at work; he had four or five hours before she arrived back. He would take a nap and recover some energy for her. He opened his briefcase and pulled out a single orchid and the card he had bought. Inside he wrote, *'I'm all yours now. Let's have an adventure. Love you, Henry xx.'*

Abby Kelleher arrived to present Burrows with her suggestion of two separate press releases.

HENRY FLEMING TO LEAVE ACROBAT

Henry Fleming, Finance Director of Acrobat for the last twelve years, today announced his retirement from the company following a period of ill health. Charlie Burrows, Chief Executive, said,

'We fully accept Henry's reasons for choosing to leave the company at this time and we wish him well.'

Fleming will leave immediately and Acrobat will begin a search for a new Finance Director. Fleming's responsibility for the US film project will pass to Ray Walker. Ends

'That it?' he said to her.
'Tells you everything you need to know,' she said.
'Seems a bit terse.'
She looked at him evenly. 'It is.'
'All right, and this one . . .'
'This one buys you some time, and if you send it out

at the same time as the other, I think you have a pretty clear message.'

ACROBAT REVIEWS US OPPORTUNITIES

Acrobat Group confirms that it was invited to increase its investment behind its US film initiative. Charlie Burrows, Chief Executive, said:

'Success in the direct sourcing of movies from Hollywood would substantially improve Acrobat's competitiveness in this critical area of our programme schedule, as well as broadening our sources of income. The board of Acrobat recognizes the vicissitudes of this kind of investment; accordingly we have chosen partners with proven success records. Precise details of the group's investment will be released when negotiations have been completed. In the meantime, responsibility for this project has passed to Ray Walker from Henry Fleming, whose resignation was announced this morning.
Ends

Burrows looked up at her. 'Very neat,' he said.

'Does the job, I think,' she said with obvious pleasure.

Burrows silenced the complaint inside. A lifeline is a lifeline.

Melvyn Davies appeared for the last meeting of Burrows's day.

'Bad day, Mr Chief Executive?'

Burrows managed a battle-weary grin. 'Probably the worst in a very lousy run. But we're still alive. You get my email earlier?'

Davies looked blank.

'About Henry. He's going.'

'Oh no. What is it – his heart?'

'Don't know really. I think he's kind of mentally checked out. Too much thinking time, Maggie's worn him down, given him a whole new passion for mowing the lawn.'

'Shame, he's one of the good guys.'

'Well, he is, yes, but when you look at it, the *Marilyn* nightmare was down to him. I don't know how long he's been planning his exit, but this business is just too tough if your head is somewhere else.'

'Charlie, I spoke to Ray.'

'Oh yes, what's going on in Ray's head?'

'It was a long discussion, but the essence of it is that he thinks Hollywood is the bigtime, and you haven't got the bottle for it.'

Burrows exploded. 'What?'

Davies raised his hands. 'Sorry, that came out wrong. It's more he thinks it needs selling to the market, and you haven't even taken the time to understand it.'

Burrows was unconsoled by Davies's second attempt. 'The little shit. I tell you, Melv, he's poison.'

Sarah Golanski's face appeared at the window. Burrows looked up and waved her in.

'Hi, am I interrupting?'

'No, come in, Sarah,' said Burrows. 'We're just exchanging conspiracy theories. I thought this was just a patch of bad luck, but at the very least it looks like we've got someone leaking like a sieve, and, at worst, someone trying to bring me down. In either case, my thoughts naturally swing to your old friend, the Commercial Director.'

Sarah Golanski bridled. 'Charlie, I know he's a bit of an old bugger, but I know Ray and I don't buy that he would suddenly turn on you after all these years.'

Burrows was unconvinced. 'So who would then, Sarah?'

'Phyllis,' she said, sitting back in her chair with a satisfied look. She raised her eyebrows and shrugged.

'Go on,' said Burrows.

'Well, with Phyllis you have motive and means. Ray says she's very low and she's still very popular with all her press buddies.'

Burrows paced to the window. 'Yeah, but Phyllis has been out for weeks now. She wouldn't have known the Hollywood numbers.'

Davies said, 'Actually, Charlie, now I come to think about it, I had a call from Phyllis this week, trying to fix lunch.'

Burrows didn't turn round. 'Is that unusual?'

'Well, yes, I haven't heard from her since she left. We get on fine, but I couldn't tell you the last time we had lunch together.'

'Fishing trip, do you think?' said Golanski.

Burrows was clear. He stalked to the window. 'Sorry, don't buy it. Phyllis may have motive and means, but she doesn't have menace. She's just too nice to dream this up on her own, no matter how low she is.'

Davies lifted his feet up on the coffee table. 'But Ray has enough menace for two.'

Burrows swung around from the window. 'The old boys' society bites back – Ray and Phyllis, each with their own little grievance, trying to get even.'

They both looked at him.

Golanski said, 'No, not Ray.'

'I know this isn't easy for you, Sarah. But I don't think you've seen all there is to see of Ray Walker. Ray has said enough to my face and behind my back . . . he's behind this, I'm telling you.'

She shifted in her chair as the varnish on Burrows's new theory hardened.

When he returned to the desk, Burrows had a new resolve about him. 'Right, look, let's just keep this between us, can we? I'll talk to Abby, who is OK, I think.'

Before he left he emailed his theory to Abby Kelleher.

Henry Fleming awoke at dusk. The day had tired him more than he'd thought. He shuffled to the bathroom in the half-light, pulling on his dressing gown. He splashed some water on his face and set off back to the bedroom, suddenly startled by the silhouetted figure sitting motionless in the armchair. He took a step or two forward.

'Mags?' he ventured.

He saw that the silhouette was holding his orchid, and he made out the card, open on her lap.

She rose to greet him. 'Hi,' she said simply, reaching up to kiss him. As her face approached his, he made out the course of the tears, blue on her cheeks in the twilight.

'You did it,' she whispered, not daring to make it a question.

'I did it,' he whispered back. 'Ready for that adventure?'

Before he finished, her face was on his cheek again,

the warmth of her tears squeezed into him. At that moment, Henry Fleming felt an unfamiliar sensation. He was proud of himself.

Acrobat's closing share price   510p

Friday, 26 March

Mornings for Abby Kelleher followed a routine. She maintained that it was the only way she could get herself out of bed and functioning. When she arrived at the office, she was still on autopilot. Coat on door. PC on. Empty briefcase of last night's reading. *Grande latte*. Mobile on charge. Open email. Press cuttings . . .

The familiarity was interrupted by an email from Charlie Burrows whose subject was '*Walker and Grigson*'. She swallowed too big a mouthful of coffee as if it was impeding her concentration, and leaned forward, suddenly fully awake and functioning.

She read the email a couple of times and sat with her coffee to her lips, pondering her next steps. Grabbing her phone and papers, she moved purposefully into action.

Ray Walker went through the same protocols as Melvyn Davies to gain entry to the Southern Foods headquarters. He was just more used to it. He followed the unspeaking secretary through the labyrinth to get to Geoff O'Brien's office.

O'Brien was there with Mel Park. They didn't get up when he entered and he wasn't offered a plastic mug of coffee. Walker had been here before. He knew he was in trouble and that he had to seize the advantage. His tone was business-like.

'Morning, Geoff, morning, Mel.'

'Morning, Ray. Thanks for coming in,' said O'Brien. Park affected a close interest in her papers.

Walker dived straight in. 'Thanks for your time this morning. My agenda is just *Midnight Minus One* and general housekeeping.'

'Right, well, Ray, our agenda is somewhat bigger than that.'

Walker stopped his bustling and looked up. He noticed that Park was still not meeting his eye.

'We spoke about the show. I thought we'd dealt with that.'

'I haven't got you here to moan about the performance of *Midnight Minus One*, Ray,' said O'Brien.

'Right, well, over to you then.' Reluctantly Walker conceded the initiative.

'I had a good meeting with Melvyn last week . . .'

'Oh, yes, sorry about that, I was out of the country and . . .'

'I know, Ray. We had what I thought was a very helpful discussion about the show and what could be done to sort it out. Good guy. Knows his stuff.'

'Excellent guy,' Walker nodded enthusiastically, keen to make the most of their moments of agreement.

'To get straight to the point, I thought it had been a very good use of my time, until I discover this week that by the time the meeting took place, Acrobat had, without reference to us, already cancelled the show.'

Walker's composure stayed intact. He'd been in enough hot spots not to panic. 'Cancel it before the meeting? No. They wouldn't have done that without my knowledge.'

'You're wrong there,' said O'Brien. 'Mel's got the

listings for next week, which you have to supply when?'

'I'm not sure of the actual final date.'

'Let's just agree then that it was before last Friday.'

'Geoff, that's a big assumption,' Walker parried.

'Ray, stop arguing.' O'Brien became more terse. 'I know, right? I know that you lot are jerking me around. For whatever reason, you've pulled the plug on this show. Now, you once asked me whether we were good guys or bad guys. Let me tell you what I did after we had that conversation. I got all our print advertising adapted to promote *Midnight Minus One*. It all now mentions Acrobat, the time, the day. *Good* guy, I'd say, wouldn't you? So what are *you*, Ray? Good guy or bad guy?' He waved down Walker's effort to answer. 'Let's look. You piss off out of the country when you should be managing this situation. You send along your nice Programme Director who thought I knew the show had been cancelled. You should have seen the look on his face when I raised it. He defends himself by pretending the show is still going on, and you're coming in here today to tell me sad news, "Sorry, Geoff, we've just decided the best thing is to cancel the show."'

Again Walker tried to intervene, raising a hand, opening his mouth – anything to stop the crescendo of O'Brien's wrath. O'Brien knew what he was trying to do.

'No, shut up, Ray, will you, I haven't finished. You are making me look like a tosser. And I don't like that, Ray. I have gone to the board of this company and informed them that, as a result of a newly rebuilt relationship with your organization, we are returning to advertising with you. Our plan this year shows a total of twenty-five million pounds, which I guess must make us your biggest client, doesn't it? No matter. As a gesture of good guy-ness I spend *additional* money to do my bit for the cause, adapting the print ads, paying late copy surcharges with the bloody magazines – and now all those ads will refer to a programme that doesn't exist.'

Walker tried again.

'No, still not finished, Ray. I invest a very large amount in my sponsorship idents for the show – keep them interesting, as requested – and those are now useless after one week.'

'We can deal with that,' Walker managed to say, speaking quickly.

'Shut up, Ray, please. I know you can deal with it – and believe me, you will. So the nett of this is that I have invested a considerable amount of this company's advertising budget in a new relationship with you and Acrobat, and I am left with the strongest of impressions that you don't give a shit.'

He raised his voice to drown out Walker's cry of complaint.

'What I am very close to doing, Ray, is to cut the lot.'

Walker looked horrified.

O'Brien held the silence until Walker was about to speak again. 'But what I *am* going to do, is to give you a chance to repair our relationship.'

Walker cleared his throat. 'Well, first, thank you, Geoff. I realize this hasn't been handled well. We've had some staffing issues. Um, I was, as you know, out of the country and Sarah, well, Sarah has been promoted to COO, so she's broadening her base, which is obviously good for her. I'm afraid I have no idea how the decision to cancel *Midnight Minus One* wasn't communicated to you, indeed, taken with you. But right now, I am here to do whatever needs to be done to get us on the right track again; you have my word on that.'

'Reinstate the programme then,' said O'Brien, not taking his eyes off Walker.

'What?' said Walker, buying time.

'You heard,' said O'Brien. 'Won't cost you much and we'll work with you. I've already demonstrated that. And that will save me the job of going to tell my Chief Executive that I've wasted several hundred thousand pounds of his money. Believe me, Ray, if that is a conversation you make me have, twenty-five million pounds goes to Channel 6. Am I clear?'

'Forgive me, Geoff. This is obviously not a decision I'm able to take off my own bat.'

'We understand that, Ray. Shall we say Monday?'

Maggie Fleming had been out to buy the full crop of newspapers, and together she and her husband leafed through them, drinking tea and reading out passages to each other.

She was shocked. The clear implication was that Henry had been summarily fired for increasing the company's investment in Hollywood. They barely touched on his health, which was registered as an afterthought, Fleming thought, to make him look like a wimp as well as a law unto himself.

Maggie was furious. 'How dare they print this stuff?' she fumed.

'They're just doing their job, Mags.'

'How can you be so relaxed about it? Their job is to print the facts, isn't it?'

'Their job is to sell newspapers. Not always exactly the same thing.'

She wasn't placated. 'Well, in the end it is. If they print lies, people stop buying the paper don't they?'

'What would you rather read: something worthy and factually perfect, or a rattling good yarn with heroes and villains?'

'The truth.'

'Then you're very unusual, Mags.'

'Can't we get them to put it right?'

He shrugged. 'No, it's not going to happen, is it? Only you, me and Charlie know the true story. He's not saying anything – this gets him off the hook, so why would he? And no one's going to ask us. That was our moment, honey. We're yesterday's news now.'

'It's sordid . . . after all you've done for that man . . .'

'The people who need to know do know. As for this . . .' he brandished a copy of the *Daily Mail*, 'let's line the cat-box with it.'

Abby Kelleher tapped on the window of Melvyn Davies's office. He leaped up, lifting a pile of scripts from his sofa and urging her to find a place and sorry about the mess. She arranged herself cautiously on the sofa, propping her pad on her knee while trying to save her papers and pieces from sliding down behind the cushions.

'Thanks for your time, Melvyn,' she said as she tried to find the position in which everything balanced. 'I hoped we'd get to do this earlier. It just seems to have been a scrum since I started, and all my good intentions to have nice, orderly, introductory chats with everyone have been totally overwhelmed by emergencies.'

Davies laughed good-naturedly. 'Welcome to Acrobat,' he said.

'I just wanted to spend a half-hour together, have you talk to me about the company, the good points as you see them, any PR black holes that you think I ought to be aware of, that sort of thing.'

'Phew,' said Davies. 'Where to begin?'

They talked for nearly an hour about Davies's perceptions, his hopes and dreams, his fears for the future; and he briefed her in detail on *Mind Our Own Business*. She promised him a ton of coverage in the press for the launch.

As she was gathering up her things, she said, 'Oh, Melvyn, can I ask you one more thing?'

He'd enjoyed the dialogue; it had been a long time since someone had shown so much interest in his point of view. 'Sure,' he said.

'Off the record, can I ask you your point of view on something?'

He nodded.

'I've stumbled across something I think might be a bit of a landmine if we don't handle it well. I should have taken it up with Charlie, but we kind of ran out of time. Apparently the long-term executive scheme kicks in when the share price hits six pounds.'

'That's right.'

'Did you know that if there's a takeover of the company, Charlie has a kicker on his deal that gives him a three-million-pound lump sum? Is that common knowledge?'

'Jammy bugger. Why don't we all get one of those?'

'Apparently because it was thought that in that event, his job would be most in jeopardy. You know, they'll need a Programme Director and a Sales Director, but not necessarily a Chief Executive.'

'Wow. For three mill they can bring in their own Programme Director. Not very fair, is it?'

'You see what I mean about landmines. I'll try and find out some more about it. Anyway, it's as well for me to know this kind of thing in advance so I can manage them if it leaks out at the wrong time.'

'If you find out it's true, let me know.' He laughed. 'I could be seeking a revision to my contract.'

'I will, but in the meantime, mum's the word.'

Monica came in and said, 'Sorry, Abby, I've got your PA on the phone. Says she's got the *Sunday Times* on hold and it can't possibly wait.'

Kelleher raised her eyebrows and tried to pull herself up off the sofa. In her attempt to pick herself out of its depths she placed a hand next to one of the piles of Davies's papers which had been shoved up to make room for her. It toppled into the place where she had been sitting.

'Aaah. Oh no, I'm so sorry, Melvyn,' she said, shepherding her own papers into her grasp.

'Don't worry about that,' laughed Davies, 'Monica's a bit behind with the filing.'

Monica's jaw dropped in mock outrage.

Charlie Burrows read the press cuttings of Fleming's resignation. He sat back after he'd raced through the deck. The company wasn't off the hook, various fund managers saying they would be seeking a fuller explanation of the Hollywood thing. But the mob had its villain. Henry Fleming had been caught squarely in the cross hairs, the press pack tutting about when good guys go bad. He didn't feel so great about that, but Henry had what he wanted. He snatched up his phone.

'Well done, Ms Kelleher,' he said.

'I think we did a good job there,' she said with considerable satisfaction.

'Thank you, Abby; I appreciate it. That was my number one nightmare and we've come through relatively unscathed. Look, I just wanted to say "Sorry" for not telling you about some of that early stuff.'

'Oh, that's all right,' she said. 'I do realize I needed to earn your trust.'

'Well, you have,' he said.

When he had hung up, she closed the door of her office and phoned her mother.

Burrows was scheduling a meeting with Rishi Kapur in order to get his head around the damage *Marilyn* would do to his profits when Paula arrived in his doorway.

'Charlie, I just had Ray on the phone. He's on his way back from Southern Foods and he's desperate to see you.'

'Probably thought up some good rejoinders,' muttered Burrows. 'OK. Wheel him in when he gets back. He didn't say what it was about?'

'A matter of the utmost sensitivity and importance, apparently. He's not going to tell *me*, is he? I am but the oily rag.'

'Utmost sensitivity. Aren't they all? OK, maybe give me another meeting, twenty minutes after Ray's starts, and interrupt me.'

Paula was familiar with the technique.

'Let's have a word with our favourite stockbroker in the meantime, shall we?'

*

Perrin told him the market had been unhappy about Henry Fleming's departure, seeing him as a grown-up on the board. It was having trouble digesting that Fleming had been the author of the *Marilyn* overspend. The share price was off again, but only by fourteen pence.

'Henry won't be very pleased with that,' mused Burrows. 'He'd be hoping for at least thirty p.'

Melvyn Davies was awaiting the arrival of the production team from Alicat, the independent production company making *Mind Our Own Business*. Monica was tidying up his office – or at least making new orderly piles next to other orderly piles. She berated him affectionately about his mess as she went.

He laughed. 'Look, this is just the way my mind works, isn't it. I know exactly where everything is.'

'Melvyn, don't lie to yourself. The only reason you ever find anything is because I make copies of it before it vanishes in this hellhole.'

As they carried on their banter, Monica tried to plump some life into the cushions on his sofa.

After ten minutes of activity, Davies's office was looking quite neat. He gazed around and clutched his throat in mock horror, affecting an operatic Italian voice. 'My beautiful office, what have you done to it? You've destroyed years of work, you crazy woman.'

Monica merely smiled at his performance. 'There's a mobile down here,' she said, rummaging down the back of the sofa. 'Probably one of the many lost children from the Melvyn Davies phone family.' She pulled it out and passed it to him.

Davies examined it suspiciously. 'No, it's not one of

mine. Mine's . . .' he waved an arm at the desk . . . 'over there somewhere.'

'I rest my case,' she said with a look. 'I wonder whose this is, then?'

'Have a look at the phone memory – you can tell by the names in the address book.'

She handed it over to him and set about relocating some of the mess outside his office.

Davies went into the address book and tried 'ME'. No number. He scrolled down one and found 'MOM'. He frowned for a moment and carried on through the names.

'Got it, Mon. These are all journalists on here. Eureka! This phone belongs to Abby Kelleher. I thank you.' He bowed to silent applause. 'I'll give it to her later.'

'Want me to tell her PA it's here? You know what Abby is like without her phone.'

'Sure. Nifty little thing, this. Why can't I have a groovy phone, Mon?'

'You have to make do with cheap ones till you can prove you're grown up enough to look after a nice one.'

He continued to scroll through the names in the address book, idly enjoying the feel of the handset. There was something about that first entry. He returned to it: MOM – 0207 177 8533. Absently he jotted it down on the front cover of his pad.

'Can I come in, please, this is urgent.' Ray Walker bustled into Burrows's office, still wearing his coat and whisking a bead of sweat from his face.

Sarah Golanski got up to go, but Walker said, 'I would have thought it was better if Sarah stayed, if that's all right with you?' He looked at Burrows.

'Fine by me. She is the COO after all,' he muttered into his briefcase as he pulled out his papers.

Burrows caught Golanski's eye.

'Right,' Walker began as if addressing a large audience. 'We have a crisis at Southern Foods. It appears that on his visit to the company last week, Melvyn not only failed to tell Geoff about the cancellation of *Midnight Minus One*, he actually implied it was coming back.'

'He told me,' said Burrows.

'Wonderful!' Walker shook his head. 'I, of course, was in LA, but basically the fact that he lied to them has now been found out and they've invested additional money in a magazine campaign supporting the show. In short, we have no alternative but to reinstate the show.'

'We're not doing that, Ray,' said Burrows.

'Then you can wave bye-bye to twenty-five million.' Burrows thought he saw a trace of triumph on Walker's face. He pushed down the heave of anger with difficulty. 'What are you saying?'

'I don't know what's unclear about that, but unless we reinstate *Midnight Minus One*, that's it, they pull the lot.'

Golanski whistled under her breath. 'They would too.'

Walker warmed to Golanski's involvement, raising a stumpy finger to punctuate his words. 'You're right, Sarah, they would. You remember last year, don't you?'

She looked at Burrows. 'I handled the negotiations last year. They're a very proud company. Last year it was the price. They were just trying to make a point. They pull off one channel pretty much every year just to keep the fear up.'

'Have they pulled off anyone this year?' asked Burrows.

Walker and Golanski exchanged a glance.

'No,' said Golanski. 'But the price deal has been done. This is about market power now. "We're the customers, you do it our way or we take away our toys and play with someone else."'

Burrows looked at Walker. 'I have no problem with inventing a new show called *Midnight Minus One* and transmitting it with a *Night and Day* sponsorship. But the political satire show is dead and buried.'

Walker sighed. 'They're not going to buy that.'

'What's it to them?' said Burrows. 'They can have the same presenters, the same writers, they can have the same bloody camera crew if they want.'

'You're not grasping the problem at all,' said Walker. 'If I could have switched their sponsorship to a different show, I would have done it.'

'It's not a different show.'

'Of course it is.'

Golanski stepped in again as the temperature rose. 'Charlie, they are very difficult people. If Geoff O'Brien has decided that this is what he wants, this is what he wants. Trust me. I suppose if I was spending two hundred and forty million a year on TV, I'd be pretty choosy too.'

'But if we can get him the same type of audience at the same time of night, with a show that people like . . . surely . . .'

'Geoff likes *Midnight Minus One*,' said Walker.

'And the Prime Minister doesn't.'

Walker snorted in derision. 'So we have the government telling us what we can broadcast now, do we?'

'No one tells us what we broadcast, including Geoff O'Brien. But I did a deal with the government and we got the ownership rules changed.'

'God, if that ever came out, the shit would fly,' said Walker.

Burrows's heart turned to ice. With difficulty he pulled himself back to the issue. 'Shall I go and see Geoff O'Brien?' he said.

'If it makes you feel better,' said Walker. 'I have been dealing with him since he was a brand manager fifteen years ago. But if you think you can do better . . .'

'I'm certain I can't do better than you, Ray. But there are times when a visit from the Chief Executive makes the right statement.'

'Honestly, Charlie,' said Golanski, 'these guys aren't interested in statements. If you get involved, you'll never get out of it. Every tiny thing that goes wrong, he'll pick up the phone to you.'

Burrows looked at Walker again. 'So your recommendation is that I put the programme back and tell the government "Too bad".'

'What are they going to do? They've changed the rules now. They're not going to tell the world you had a deal, are they?'

'It's the principle,' said Burrows inadequately.

'Well, here's your chance to decide how much your principle is worth to you – this one has been valued at approximately twenty-five million pounds.'

At 5.15 p.m., Abby Kelleher was sitting in Ray Walker's office.

'I really appreciate this time, Ray. I know this is a very tense time for everyone. I should have done this before. I just wanted to touch base, say "Hi", see if there are any things you want me to be aware of, messages you'd like to get out, that sort of thing.'

They talked about Walker's issues: the pressures, the triumphs and the track record of the sales team at Acrobat. A confident smile played around his lips as he described their exploits and she began to formulate a new perspective on Ray Walker. He was old school for sure, an inveterate name-dropper, but she had seen none of the witless aggression he appeared to be famous for. He told her about his trip to LA, the chance to work with new companies with new disciplines and different styles, to broaden their horizons and make some money too. He sounded to her like a schoolboy visitor to Disney-world. He told her he wanted to work closely with her and she was to ask anything any time. A classic Ray Walker charm offensive.

As the meeting headed towards its close, she said, 'Ray, can I ask you something pretty sensitive, just between us?'

'Fire away.'

'It's just that, reading through some of the small print in my mountains of homework, I've discovered that if we get taken over in a hostile bid, Charlie Burrows gets to pocket five million quid. Is that something you were aware of?'

Walker laughed, his manner giving nothing away. 'That says it all, don't you think, Abby? This is the guy who accuses me of feathering my own nest. Five million.' He shook his head despairingly.

The sharing of this indiscretion at Burrows's expense appeared to seal his respect for her. He jotted it down on his pad.

'Well, strictly between us now,' Kelleher warned, wagging a teasing finger at him.

He didn't laugh. 'Of course,' he said.

Later that evening, Abby Kelleher had a drink with Sarah Golanski. They chatted about their careers and compared views on the Acrobat people. Before long they got on to the subject of the leaks, dimming their voices lest anyone hear them.

'Charlie is convinced it's Ray and Phyllis,' said Golanski.

'Do you agree?' asked Kelleher.

Golanski didn't hesitate. 'No, absolutely not. I know Ray better than anyone here. I know he can be a bit curmudgeonly . . .' Together they reacted to her choice of word . . . 'Pig obstinate, but he's diamond-centred, is Ray.'

'Well, obviously I don't know him so well, but he does throw his weight about, doesn't he.'

'No,' said Golanski decisively. 'Charlie's got this wrong. Ray's whole . . .' She struggled for the word. 'His whole *being* is wrapped up in the success of the company.'

'Not in the success of Ray Walker?'

'No. If he's got an agenda, it's no more than proving that he's as good as any of the college boys. He doesn't like being told what to do, that's all.'

Kelleher took a deep breath. 'What about Phyllis Grigson?'

'Phyllis, yes, do you know her?'

'Everyone knows Phyllis.'

'Phyllis is lovely,' said Golanski, and Kelleher relaxed imperceptibly.

'Not the mouthpiece for Ray Walker then?' Kelleher checked.

'Oh God, no. Phyllis was badly treated over the Nik Kruger thing. But she's a lovely person. And she put a lot into building this company. I could see her being pissed off, but I can't see her trying to wreck the place.'

Kelleher relaxed again. 'I was a bit worried about all that Nik Kruger thing when I started, but Charlie seems to be on the side of the angels . . . most of the time.'

'Oh, I think he's just missing Martin. I'd say he's in mourning for the loss of his partner in crime.'

'He's really going for it on Charisma TV, isn't he?'

'I think he sees it as a way of restoring some credibility, you know, getting over some of that awful stuff.'

'The Hollywood numbers . . .'

'Yes, and the last results presentation was pretty ghastly, apparently. I think he sees pulling off the Charisma deal as his way back into their good books.'

'I feel a bit sorry for him sometimes,' said Kelleher, with a question in her voice.

Golanski laughed. 'Lonely at the top and all that?'

'But well remunerated.'

'Absolutely.'

'Especially if we get taken over, I see.'

'What?'

'I noticed in the small print of the last report and accounts that, if we get taken over, Charlie gets a million quid for his troubles.'

'Really? Well, whatever. Quite sad, to be reading the small print, Abby.'

She laughed. 'That's where you find all the sexy stuff.'

Charlie Burrows had his final meeting of the day with Rishi Kapur to look at the numbers. Kapur was small, neat and earnest. He had done a brilliant job of taking over from Henry Fleming.

'Charlie, the current forecast for this year has a nice bottom line of sixty million pounds, on revenues of three hundred and eighty million.'

'Great, that's the theory. What happens when you factor in the current revenue projections?'

'We're doing an awful lot better than the other guys,' said Kapur cautiously.

'All right, don't spare me. How's it looking?'

'We're about twenty million behind forecast on revenues . . .'

Burrows closed his eyes. 'I wonder when the Commercial Director was planning to tell me.' Kapur looked nervous. 'And what does a twenty-million-pound revenue hole do to the bottom line?'

'Twenty million less ad revenue would translate to a full year profit of about forty-four million pounds.' Kapur clattered away on his calculator. 'That would still be a modest uplift on last year, which would be not bad at all in times like these. But it would of course not be a double-digit increase. And we've been telling the market we would . . . do . . .' Kapur trailed off.

Burrows looked at the tidy, bespectacled figure, trying to make it all come out right, and he smiled. 'OK. Let's stop dreaming. What happens when you factor in this Hollywood nightmare?'

'Well, obviously it takes a lot out of the cash flow. It depends how you want to account for it. We tend to be pretty conservative, which the City likes. That would imply we take the whole charge this year, although it would not be very tax efficient.'

'And that would mean . . .'

He bent over the calculator again. 'We'd finish with a profit of about thirty-eight million pounds.'

'Yuk – less than last year.'

Kapur looked crestfallen for a few moments. 'There may be something we can do to lose some of it in the accounting, though. Want me to chat to the auditors?'

'Oh, I think so. I see the gentle twitch of a lifeline before me.'

As Kapur left, Burrows flipped his TV to Teletext to see that the shares had dipped back below the 500p mark.

He sat gazing at the rows of figures the neat little man had drawn for him. The budget column with its 'nice' 60 million of profit was absurdly comforting. He looked to the column on the right, in which Kapur had modelled the downward drift in revenues, and he shrugged. He'd have to make a profit warning. No way around it.

And what if he dug in his heels on *Midnight Minus One* and Southern Foods pulled out their £25 million? On the right hand of the page was a column showing the lower revenues and the full cost of the Hollywood movie invest-ment. Kapur had underlined '38' in the profit column with two neat lines. Taking his pencil, he crossed it out and replaced it with '13'.

'Ugh, *very* unlucky number,' he muttered. 'Well, Prime Minister, looks like the money or my life. You win, Geoff.'

Acrobat's closing share price   496p

The Weekend, 27–28 March

Abby Kelleher phoned Burrows early on Sunday morning.

'Sorry, Charlie, did I wake you?'

'Umm, no, I was . . . just dozing.'

'Right, when are your newspapers delivered?'

'I expect they're here.'

'Look, we've been done again. The *Sunday Times* has a story from "*inside sources*"' – she pronounced it with distaste – 'saying that our revenue projections for this year are miles short of budget.'

Burrows was wide awake. 'Oh shit, what's it say?'

'OK, I'll give you the main bits.'

'Information received by this newspaper suggests that Acrobat, the high profile television group which is rumoured to be preparing an aggressive bid for Charisma Television, has very significant revenue problems.

'Analysts are in the process of revising their full-year profit estimates for the group, which last week admitted that it had massively overspent its agreement with shareholders on film financing.

'The news that it is not just spiralling costs but also declining revenue will concern analysts, who have watched in dismay as the Acrobat share price has yo-yoed up and down over the past few weeks.'

'They might have called me,' she said. 'Thought I might destroy a good story, I suppose.'

'Ken Hathaway, Chairman of Charisma TV Broadcasting, the unwilling object of Acrobat's predatory affections, said, "I'm afraid this is what has worried us all along about Acrobat. They talk a good game but when you dig a bit beneath the surface, there are quite significant holes in the reality."'

'Bastard,' said Burrows.

'Only two weeks ago, the company tried to shore up its flagging share price by taking the unusual step of announcing its confidence in a double-digit revenue increase, despite the apparent slowdown in advertising revenues. The company's rapprochement with Southern Foods, which last year did not spend with Acrobat, is the backbone of this revenue story, but sources close to the company say that the relationship with this key client is also highly problematic.

'The combination of a revenue shortfall, together with the increase in costs implied by last week's revelations about the group's commitments in America, will make for a fundamental reappraisal by analysts when they reach their desks on Monday morning.'

'That's it.'

'Shit,' was all the Chief Executive could manage.

'Do you want to meet up today?' said Kelleher.

Burrows was cold. 'This is going pear-shaped, isn't it, Abby?'

'I've put down a few rat-traps. I'm hoping someone will nibble on the bait in the next few days. But right now, how much of it can we deny? If we can say it's all bullshit, it's just another aggressive press article. But we've got to be able to put that together today so that the analysts have some antidote before the market opens tomorrow.'

'Well, they've got the revenue story right. I think Southern Foods will be all right, but all that that means is we have a revenue crisis as distinct from an apocalypse. And I think there's an accounting thing we can do with *Marilyn*, but . . .' Suddenly his temperature shot up. 'Do you know what? Ray frigging Walker hasn't even mentioned the revenue problem to me yet. I'm bailing out the boat while he's hacking away at it with a pickaxe. Him and his charming assistant, Phyllis.'

'But . . .'

'I'll explain later. The main thing is, we have got to find something to say for tomorrow's paper, otherwise this bid is dead . . . and so am I, most likely.'

'I'll draft some stuff and see you in the office later . . . say eleven?'

'Look, thanks, Abby – you've been brilliant. See you there.'

Melvyn Davies spent the weekend reviewing tapes in his home, work in progress from shows he had commissioned, audition tapes for new characters for the soap. Since Kate had gone, he had managed to turn the living room into a replica of his office. Papers and VHS tapes had begun their incursion and were now well established in this new territory. Coffee cups and fast food packaging lay abandoned in their midst.

Davies swept a hand through his hair and finished his notes on the first cut of a new drama planned for the autumn. He closed the pad and lolled his head back. Once again the flow of his thoughts coursed back to Kate. His ability to dam them up behind the wall of work was deteriorating as each day passed. It had been two weeks now, and she hadn't returned a single call. He swung his feet up on the sofa; perhaps sleep would succeed where a relentless attention to work had failed. He moved the pad to the coffee table, balancing it on a tea-stained mug. As he shuffled some cushions behind his head, he noticed the number he had scrawled on the front of the pad. MOM – 020 7177 8533.

'Ah yes, Mom. 7177 8533. I know where I've seen you.' He flapped a hand down beside the sofa till it encountered his briefcase, which he hoisted over to his lap. In the front section was a transparent folder with the list of calls awaiting his attention, studiously updated by Monica. It ran to a second page, where he discovered what he was looking for:

'Phyllis Grigson wants to buy you lunch. Call her on 020 7177 8533.'

Monday, 29 March

The press could not have been worse. The fruit of Burrows's Sunday with Abby Kelleher had been dismissed as defensive chaff, nowhere as good a story as the follow-up to the *Sunday Times*'s revelations. Acrobat had been moved down a notch from 'beleaguered' to 'crisis-ridden' in the commentators' reports. The news of the revenue shortfall ignited apocalyptic stories of meltdown at Acrobat as the journalists speculated about how bad it could be.

But there was now a new undertone about Charlie Burrows. Tentatively, clearly under the watch of the news-papers' lawyers, there were the beginnings of suggestions that the flow of information had not been as frank as it should have been. Institutions that had bought the shares at over £5 were in a state of high anxiety concerning the level of disclosure of the revenue problems. They complained bitterly and publicly about the upbeat trad-ing statement which was a mere two weeks old, and Newman's report which had been issued just one week earlier.

Newman himself was quoted by almost all the news-papers, defending a research paper which had contributed to a 30 per cent increase in the share price. He referred to conversations with Charlie Burrows, just ten days earlier, in which Burrows had stressed his confidence in the quality of his projections. As ever, Newman was buttoned down, able to quote from the notes he took at the time of the meeting.

Burrows sat at his desk, his insides jangling: the share price had fallen to 357p; the Charisma TV bid was dead. He considered running. Just walk out of the office, catch a train home, pack some things, get in the car with Georgia and be discovered running a fish restaurant in Suffolk in two years' time. He visualized it for a moment, prodded back to the real world by the pitiless tug on his insides.

He made a note of all the people he would have to speak to today, and another note of what he would say. First on his list was to secure the Southern Foods money, but he had yet to decide how to confront Ray Walker. For now, get the stuff done. He called Sarah Golanski in and told her his decision on *MMOne*, asking her for a complete re-forecast of revenue in the current year by lunchtime.

Golanski spoke in hushed tones as if someone had died. She seemed keen to get away quickly.

He called Melvyn Davies and asked him when he could realistically reinstate *Midnight Minus One*. Davies said he could get it back on air the following week, and they compared thoughts about the press coverage.

'I suppose I should have been prepared for this, Melv.'

'What do you mean?'

'Ray doesn't take prisoners, does he. He said it was him or me, and now he's out to destroy me.'

'You reckon this is all deliberate?'

'Come on, Melv. Look at it. There's nothing accidental about the timing or the content of these leaks. They are designed to present me as out of control of the company and deliberately misleading investors. But it's such a clumsy campaign. If it wasn't for Ray, I would have known about the revenue problems. We would be out of bloody Hollywood altogether. Who else knew about the revenue catastrophe? That story about him going straight to LA to sort it all out. He's not even bothering to cover his tracks.'

'He's got to go, hasn't he?'

'If anyone went now, they'd expect it to be me, not him. No, we're stuck with him for now. I was hoping to get the Charisma TV deal under our belt, and then kick Ray into touch. But the share price was off twenty-eight per cent already when I looked.'

'Twenty-eight per cent?' Davies howled.

Burrows raised his hands. 'I know. It's a massive over-reaction, but this isn't about reason and logic. And at that price, our raid on Charisma is a dead duck.'

'So we're stuck with Ray?'

'For now I don't think we have any alternative. The market is strangely reassured by his presence. So that's the end of that brilliant plan.'

'Shit.' Davies sounded winded. 'So what happens next?'

'Well, unless we can convince them we're not in the crap, the share price is going to stay in the tank. Our bid for Charisma TV will wither away and the questions over me are going to get louder.'

'So, fifteen-love to Ray?'

Burrows snorted humourlessly. 'Game-and-set, Melv. You've got to hand it to him, he's played a blinder.'

'Shit, What the hell can we do?'

'Until we get this Southern Foods money locked in, not very much. I still owe the analysts something on *Marilyn*, but Rishi is seeing if he can find me an accounting treatment that will stop it annihilating this year's profits. I kinda think it might be a bit late for accounting treatments.' He sighed deeply.

'You all right, Charlie?' Davies asked.

Burrows sighed again. 'Yeah, I'll be all right.' He snorted. 'Old Henry got out at the right time, didn't he?'

'Look, I'm around all day today. If you need anything, just call. There's nothing I can't drop – I'm just putting the final touches to the show.'

'Your consumer fight-back show? You got a name for it yet?'

'Oh yeah. "Don't Get Mad, Get Even".'

'Words to live by, Melv.'

Sarah Golanski found Ray Walker surrounded by a mess of press cuttings and reports from his sales team. He was flicking an expensive ballpoint against the big coffee cup. He hadn't seen her.

'Got a moment for an old team-member?' she said.

He looked up and made a tired smile. 'Hello, Sarah. Always got time for you. Come in.'

'I bring glad tidings of great joy,' she said.

'Could do with a bit of that round here,' he grumped.

'We're OK to reinstate *Midnight Minus One*.'

Walker laid on the sarcasm. 'Oh, well done, Charlie. Probably not the hardest management decision he's ever had to make. I'll get on to Geoff.'

'Are you all right, Ray?'

He looked surprised. 'Me? Yeah, sure, why wouldn't I be? We're a few points down on target. Stock market's gone stupid, as usual. Up to Charlie to sort that out. Everything down here's perfectly under control.'

'He reckons the Charisma TV deal has had it.'

'Oh has it? Oh well. It'll come back, I expect.'

She narrowed her eyes to peer into his conscience, but saw no further than the practised veneer of a life of client reassurances.

'Ray?'

He looked at her with raised eyebrows, his manner light.

'What's going on?' she said.

'What's going on? We are witnessing our Chief Executive screwing up the company. Running scared, when he should be out there, leading from the front.'

'I hate it – you two not talking.'

'Look, I've got nothing against Charlie Burrows. You and I both know his strengths and weaknesses, Sarah. He and I have fallen out because he accused me of something I didn't do, and I'm not letting that stay on the record. But if he apologizes to me, I'm quite prepared to let bygones be bygones. I've never held a grudge against any man. But I am not being muscled out of this company on some trumped-up charge, like Phyllis. What he did to her was a disgrace. I can't forgive that.'

She looked at him hopelessly. Until a couple of weeks earlier, this man had been her patron. She had trusted him with her future and he had never betrayed her confidence. Now that he stood accused of treachery on the highest scale, could she too raise her hand against him?

As if he saw her thoughts, Walker said, 'You see what kind of a place he's turning this into? Never mind opportunity culture. It's a paranoia culture if you ask me.'

'Charlie thinks you would leak the kind of stuff that would force him out,' she persisted.

'He's doing a good enough job without my help.'

'But, Ray. He told me you said, "It's you or me" or something.'

'I did.'

She shrugged. 'Well . . .'

'Did he tell you *he* asked for *my* resignation?'

'No?' She slumped back in her chair. 'This is so complicated,' she said. 'I don't know what to believe.'

He looked at her hard. 'Yes you do,' he said.

The silence was long and uncomfortable. Walker broke it.

'Anyway the solution is staring him in the face.'

'Is it?'

'Sure.' Walker was on stage, confident, smug, playing out his story for maximum impact. 'This isn't about Charlie's job. He's blinded by his own self-importance, but this is bigger than him.'

Sarah Golanski fought to clear her mind.

He beckoned with his hand, nodding his head in time, the coach. 'Come on, who has the most to gain from a low share price?'

'Well, no one involved in the company. All our interests rely on a strong share price. Someone from outside?' She shook her head. A knowing smile hung around Walker's face. 'But all the leaks rely on inside information, Ray. It can't be someone from outside.'

'It's not external,' said Walker.

'Who then, Ray?' she said, her frustration rising through this performance.

'Who wants the share price low? A buyer.'

'Who?'

'De Vigny. Come on, he's made no secret that he's desperate to buy the company, and he's been a minority holder for too long. He's fed up with Sharma. You know him. He plays to win. And Piers has access to all the management information.'

Golanski pursed her lips. 'How do you know this, Ray?'

He smirked, slopping tea into his mouth from the ever-present mug. 'Me? I keep my ear a little closer to the ground than most.'

'Yes, but quite a lot of the leaks have happened with information the board didn't know.'

Walker was unfazed. 'Perhaps if Henry Fleming was here, he'd have smelt a rat, but dear old Rishi wouldn't know that it's not OK for board members to ring him up and fish around for information.'

'You think it was Piers?'

'Sure. Adds up, doesn't it? He's driving the price down to buy the company at a bargain basement price,' he ended with the satisfaction of the compelling explanation – finally. 'Meanwhile Charlie Burrows runs around, blaming people for the dysfunctional management relations he's created out of his own obsessions.'

She slumped in her chair as the full force of Ray Walker's hypothesis grew on her. It made sense and it played to her instinct that Walker was innocent.

She was excited, almost breathless with relief. 'Ray, you've got to talk to Charlie.'

Walker sat back coyly. 'I haven't done anything. I'm not going to start running around trying to clear my name.'

'Then let me talk to him.'

'No. If Charlie Burrows and I are ever going to be able to work together again, he's got to trust me. Not because you talk him into it. This time he has to come to me. No shortcuts.'

'But, Ray . . .'

'It's how it has to be, I'm afraid. It may take a little longer but it will make for a better resolve. Trust me.'

Miserably, Sarah Golanski agreed not to say anything.

'And no go-betweens, Sarah. This stays between us, right?' Walker was relaxed, smiling. 'Trust me. We'll come through this in better shape than we went into it.'

All over the Acrobat building, clandestine transistor radios were brought out for the Gerry Duffy media business programme on Radio 4. People were clustered around them like wartime families, anxious for news from the front. In the offices, the more senior people kept their own counsel, preferring not to have to react in front of their staff.

Duffy chronicled the story in tortuous detail:

'When Charlie Burrows told analysts that the departure of Martin Sumner would result in the loss of significant value for shareholders, no one imagined how right he would be.

'The deft touch that saw Burrows and Sumner build Acrobat to a seven-hundred-million-pound television empire appears to have departed with the popular Geordie COO, as he leaves to join Channel 6.

'Sumner's exit was accompanied by that of Phyllis Grigson, the respected Communications Director of the group – someone whose depth of experience would not have gone amiss recently. And in the last week, Henry Fleming, the experienced Finance Director, has resigned following a massive heart attack. Where he has replaced these three seasoned executives, Burrows has chosen relative newcomers, significantly down-weighting his senior management team.

'*The pressure is beginning to tell on those who are left. Reports from the company tell of serious friction between Burrows and his two most senior deputies, Ray Walker and Melvyn Davies.*

'*In a statement yesterday, Burrows tried to put investors' minds at rest, claiming that the revenue shortfall was only a few percentage points short of the company's target, but he was not able to confirm that the much-trumpeted double-digit revenue increase promised to the market could still be delivered.*

'*Analysts were far more concerned about the profit projections for the group, unconvinced by plans to write away an unprecedented twenty-two-million-pound investment in the high-risk business of movie production. Marcus Newman, responsible for a very upbeat report on which Acrobat's bid for Charisma TV was founded, was particularly scathing in his criticism of the company tonight. The normally circum-spect leader of the media analyst pack said, "In the last couple of weeks, information from the company has been either misleading or non-existent." He declined to say what he thought should be done about the situation. Today, Acrobat's share price lies in ruins alongside its planned bid for Charisma TV.*

'*Tonight, the shares have fallen to two hundred and ninety-five p, fifty-six per cent down in just one week, inviting speculation that the once acquisitive Acrobat group may itself now be vulnerable to bids. But in an interesting twist today, this programme has learned that, should that happen, Charlie Burrows will be rewarded for his efforts with a massive three-million-pound payout.*'

Alone in her office, Abby Kelleher's heart skipped a beat. 'Gotcha,' she said.

*

At midnight, Henry Fleming listened to the rise and fall of his wife's breathing as he lay in the dark. The twinge of pride still flickered in his soul. But he had left something behind in Acrobat. The cost of making the right decision had been far greater than the salary he had left behind. There, he had been Henry Fleming, board director of a company everyone had heard of. People were impressed by who he knew, the celebrity stories, the influence. Some kind of fame. Now he was what? Henry No-label. Someone who used to be something.

He'd told her he was addicted to it and, as he lay there waiting for the choices he had made to catch up with his will, he wondered how long the cold turkey would last. He reached across to his bedside table, feeling the stone she had given him, etched with the words, '*Carpe Diem*'. He traced the letters with his finger. 'One diem at a time,' he told himself.

Acrobat's closing share price   321p

Tuesday, 30 March

Charlie Burrows unlocked his office door with a sense of foreboding. As he pushed it open, a folded piece of paper scraped along the carpet. His mind said, 'What now?' but it turned out to be from Melvyn Davies: *Have a good day. I'm here if you need me. MD*

Dear old Melv. He looked around his office with a sense of history. This was it. This was the big day. By tonight it would all be clear – one way or the other. He knew what he had to do to wrest his company back from Ray Walker and, as usual, he pulled out another piece of paper to plot his campaign: the people he would need to talk to, the steps he would need to take. This was no longer about Charisma TV, keeping the share price up, or keeping the team settled. This was about survival.

Ray Walker had demonstrated that he cared about none of those things – just winning. He couldn't beat an adversary who was more single-minded than he. Today was about two things: taking control and destroying Ray Walker.

Abby Kelleher didn't sleep well. The springing of her trap and the weight of its implications lay on her all night like a late meal; Burrows must have been on the phone till midnight, as far as she could tell.

At 6.15 a.m. she decided to do something useful about the torrent of thoughts racing around her head and sat down in front of her laptop in her nightdress, crafting press releases. First, she undid the damage she had done with the story of Burrows's payout. She wrote a vehement denial of the story, challenging Duffy to come forward with any evidence for his charge. As she wrote, it occurred to her that for such an experienced journalist as Duffy to have run with the story, he must have been very confident in his source. A trust built over time? After a succession of good steers?

By 8.15 she was in the office. She went in search of Burrows, only to discover that he already had a roomful of advisers. Stifling an expletive, she made a detour via the Programme Department. Davies's door was open, his coat flung over the back of the sofa and the computer blinking and bleeping its way into life. No sign of him, however. She hung around for a few minutes, then with a mixture of frustration and relief she returned to her office, where the press calls began, and didn't stop.

An hour later, Sarah Golanski walked into the Communications Department. She caught Abby's eye and put a finger in the air, mouthing 'One minute'. Abby beckoned her in, finishing one call and carrying on without catching her breath into the mobile. As Golanski sat down, she raised her eyes to the sky and repeated her 'one minute' gesture.

Kelleher finished her call and slumped into her chair.

'You're wearing the carpet out, girl,' said Golanski with a grin.

'I can't think when my bottom is stationary,' replied Kelleher.

Golanski said, 'You want to be careful who you say that to.'

Kelleher laughed distractedly. 'I need to talk to you, Sarah.'

'Oh. I just popped in to see how you are.'

'Well,' said Kelleher, her brow deeply furrowed, 'I think we may make it.' She nodded.

'Really?' Golanski sounded genuinely excited.

'Yes. I think there's enough of a sense out there that it's all been rather overdone. The underlying business can't possibly be less than half as good as it was last week.'

'What about Charlie? Is he getting better reviews after this morning's bloodbath?'

She bobbed her head from side to side, pulling a face. 'The trouble for Charlie is that people think he's been too frugal with the facts. The general sense is that he has to take some punishment for that.'

'Punishment? Like what?'

'You know, he's going to take a lot of flak. But if he can ride this out and hold his nerve, I think he'll live.'

'Well, that's brilliant,' said Golanski, a note of enquiry in her voice.

'I agree,' Abby Kelleher declared. 'I wouldn't be here if he hadn't backed me.'

'You and me both.'

Kelleher took a deep breath. 'Sarah, can I ask you something; just between the two of us?'

'Sure,' said Golanski.

'How well do you know Melvyn?'

Golanski did everything she knew to appear collected. She shrugged her shoulders and pursed her lips, anything.

'Pretty well, I guess. Why?'

'What's he like?'

'Good guy. Works too hard. Some would say a genius

at what he does. Charlie and Martin used to call him Merlin . . .'

Kelleher smiled. 'But what about his . . . you know . . . loyalty?'

Golanski pulled her head back as if to seek a different perspective on this proposal. 'Melv? You can't think it's him?'

'I have my reasons,' said Kelleher.

Golanski closed her eyes and shook her head. 'I don't think so. Doesn't add up.'

When Golanski left, Kelleher followed her to the stairs and then walked into the Programme Department for the second time that day. She saw him from across the floor, sitting on the back of his sofa, watching a tape. She tapped on the window, feeling her nerves jangle.

'Hi, Abby, come in, how are you?'

'Fine, thanks – you got a minute?'

'Sure.' He swept his coat off the back of the sofa and moved a pile of papers for her. 'Like a coffee or something?'

'Had one, thanks. Melv, it's about the leaks.'

'Yes, I have a theory,' he said evenly.

She stopped, her prepared narrative suddenly waylaid. 'You do?' she managed.

'Want to hear it?'

'Sure,' she said weakly.

'Sorry, how rude of me. You go first.' He smiled expectantly.

Her momentum had been lost. 'Melvyn . . .'

'Abby,' he mimicked, still smiling broadly.

Did he know what she had deduced? 'Are you going to tell me it's Ray Walker too?' she asked.

'You first,' he said, bouncing forward in his chair, a puppy-like fascination on his face.

'Well . . .' she started tentatively, waiting for him to try and divert her again. He didn't. Just sat there with his butter-wouldn't-melt look.

'I've been a little devious,' she began.

'I know you have,' he said, his face still full of fun.

She opted to continue. 'I laid a little trap last week, to see if I could catch the mole, and I fed you some information . . .'

'Oh and *I* thought you were going to own up to your *other* devious little plan.'

She pulled her face back, frowning her incomprehension.

He held the moment for a tantalizing second. 'You're Phyllis Grigson's daughter, aren't you?'

Her mouth fell open. She looked at him imploringly.

'Strange thing to keep secret, Abby?'

'How the hell did you know that?' she blustered, suddenly furious to be thrown so sharply back against the ropes.

'Oh, you know . . .' He stayed calm and light.

'It's got nothing to do with whether I can do this job or not,' she started, hating him for stirring this apology in her.

'Nothing to do with it? A series of damaging leaks starts after Phyllis gets bundled out the door. By all accounts she's bitter and twisted. What could be neater than to get her little girl in to sow some havoc? Feed her some lines, wow Burrows and Sumner with her grasp of the company's issues. Get Charlie's confidence when he's down, and then shaft him for treating *Mom* like that.'

She flushed. 'Is that what you think?'

He shrugged. 'I can't imagine there's any other explanation. Anyway, let's hear your theory.'

She bounced herself on to her feet from the sofa. 'It'll wait,' she said as she swept out through the door.

When Sylvia brought in his coffee, she found Ray Walker had been joined by Sarah Golanski.

'Oh, excuse me. Coffee, Sarah?'

'I'm good, thanks.' She'd had Sylvia's coffee before. As the door closed behind her, both of them tried to resume the dialogue simultaneously. Walker won.

'We talked about this yesterday. He hasn't even had the courtesy to telephone me.'

'Ray!' she shouted. 'Courtesy isn't the most important thing right now, is it?'

'I'm sorry, Sarah. I've worked my fingers to the bone for this company. I think that counts for something. Why should anyone think that after seventeen years I wake up one morning and decide to undo everything I've delivered in that time? No thank you, Sarah. I'm not getting myself sucked into his paranoia.'

She turned down her tone. 'Ray, I'm agreeing with you. But look, Charlie's not even thinking about de Vigny. He thinks you want his job. And if I didn't know you as well as I do, I'd have to say I see his point.'

Walker was visibly wounded. 'You would?'

'Yes, Ray, I would – if I didn't know better. Until you factor in Piers Carrick, he's working on the theory that only four people know the revenue numbers. You, me, him and Rishi. In his mind, out of that group you have a much better motive for stirring up trouble than anyone else.'

'Five people.'

She was confused for a moment. 'Five? Who's the other one?'

'Melvyn knew about the revenue. I told him.'

'Melvyn?' she said, and her insides drained into her legs. 'What did Melvyn know?'

'He knew the revenue problem.'

'Did he?'

'Yeah, but where does that lead us? Melvyn trying to bring the company to its knees. That's as stupid as trying to pin it on me.'

'Right,' she said meekly. She gathered herself. 'All I'm saying, Ray, is: talk to Charlie. Please. For me.'

'I'll think about it,' he said crustily.

She knew he wouldn't. As she stood up, she said, 'Did you talk to Geoff O'Brien?'

He smiled a broad, triumphant smile, raising his arms parallel with his shoulders as if acknowledging the applause of thousands. 'His master's touch,' he swanked, bowing slightly.

She grinned. 'All of it?'

'Twenty-five big ones, Miss Golanski.'

It was a look she had seen many times before while she was learning her trade from this man. Winning deals was his oxygen.

'You're a genius, Ray.'

As she left his office, that look of childlike joy told her all she needed to know. It wasn't him.

Back on the fifth floor, Golanski found Burrows sitting on his PA's desk reading the morning newspaper cuttings, an escapee from the room full of advisers. Failing to suppress a grin of jubilation, she told him the Southern Foods money was safe. He was pathetically grateful to her, thanking her repeatedly.

'Not me,' she said. 'Ray's your man.' She paused for a moment, dabbling with the thought of playing intermediary. Was this what her new role demanded?

She returned to her office and wrestled with her loyalties. If she ignored Ray's instructions, she reckoned she would be able to reconcile him and Charlie; but Walker had always demanded absolute loyalty, especially from her. She knew Ray. She'd never win his trust back again. Obstinate bugger. She sighed heavily, suddenly becoming aware of someone in the room. She looked up with a start.

'Oh, Melv. You frightened the life out of me!'

'Just thought I'd see how life is, up at the top,' he grinned, his manner immediately relaxing her.

'We have some good news this morning. I'm delighted to tell you, Mr Davies, Southern Foods are back on.'

'So I'm making *Midnight Minus One* again, right?'

'Oh yes, of course. Double good news.'

'I expect someone would have told me in due course,' he said, his bonhomie fading a little.

'Sorry, Melv.'

'Ah, the lot of the creative.' He rallied, draping the back of his hand on his brow theatrically. 'Anyway, all that stuff about caring how the company's doing was a front. I wondered whether you might make a humble Programme Director's day by agreeing to have an early dinner with him tonight?'

Her heart skipped a beat. In the thick of this quagmire of loyalties, there was still the delicious evolution of this relationship with Melvyn. Finally the path seemed to be breaking clean of the tangle of complications which had torn at them like gorse. Just when Acrobat was becoming impossible.

She smiled her foxy smile. 'How could I resist?'

'The bad news is that I do have to pop back here in time for 9.30 to watch my new baby programme's first outing, but until that moment I am entirely yours.'

'Are you now,' laughed Golanski, and she realized that they had never been this uninhibited together in front of their work colleagues. She regained her professional composure, as he, with his back to the rest of the office, made his eyebrows dance up and down with a stupid grin on his face.

He put on an actor's formal office voice. 'Right you are then, Miss Golanski. I will ask my staff to email you with a venue for that meeting.'

She tried to remember what normal sounded like. 'Most excellent,' she said, wobbling her head for effect. 'See you then, Mr Davies.'

Davies turned to see a sombre line of dark-suited advisers filing out of Burrows's office with Rishi Kapur. He caught Paula's eye.

'Been there since eight,' she whispered. 'Fun-looking group.'

They watched the procession together and he poked his head into Burrows's office. 'Everything all right on the bridge?' he asked.

Burrows looked up. 'Under fire but undefeated,' he said. 'So far.'

'Look, Charlie, have you got a minute, there's something I think you should know.'

'More good news?'

Davies closed the door behind him. 'I've been doing a bit of digging,' he began. 'You know, on this mole thing.'

Burrows put down his pen and peeled his glasses off, straight into his mouth. 'Mm hmm.'

'I know you think it's Ray and, fair enough, you've every reason to. But I have another theory for you. If you're looking for motives, Phyllis Grigson has got to be right up there, correct?'

'Yes, I think she's working with Ray.'

'She's got to be working with someone well placed on the inside, hasn't she?'

'Sure.'

Davies paused for a beat, causing Charlie Burrows to look up at him. 'Well, would you be surprised to know that her daughter works here?'

'Her daughter? We don't have any Grigsons, do we?' Burrows grabbed the phone list.

'No. No Grigson, but someone following in her mother's footsteps . . .'

'Abby Kelleher? You're kidding me.'

'I'm not. I found out by accident. I confronted her this morning, and I'm sorry, Charlie, she owned up.'

'Abby Kelleher and Phyllis Grigson. Oh my God.' For several seconds he was silent. 'I had an inkling about her, you know. But I thought I was just being paranoid. Shit, I've been feeding her all the lines she's used to choke me.'

'I know. Killer, isn't it,' said Davies.

Burrows threw his head back, breathing deeply. Davies thought he heard a catch in his throat. 'Melv, what are your movements today?'

'Whatever you want them to be, really. I'm working

with the guys on the final running order of *Don't Get Mad* this afternoon; I've got one change I need them to make. I've got a dinner engagement I could cancel, and I'm back here at 9.30 to watch the show go out.'

'Man, you work too hard,' said Burrows. 'OK, I'll get Abby in here and suspend her, I think. I've been a total idiot. I've told her everything. Shit. Abby Kelleher, who'd have thought it?'

Abby Kelleher approached Burrows's office at a defiant pace, but her eyes bore the weight of her anxiety.

'Charlie, I need to talk to you urgently, please.'

'You certainly do, Abby. Mind if Sarah joins us?'

She looked terrified. 'I'd rather it was alone if you don't mind.'

Burrows persisted. 'She won't bite. I'd like her to join us.'

Kelleher glanced at Golanski, who made a sort of reassuring face back as the three of them went into his office.

'Right, Abby.'

'I know how this looks, but I've come to tell you I know who has been leaking . . . you know.'

Burrows looked confidently at her over his glasses. 'Go on.'

'It's Melvyn, I'm afraid.'

Burrows didn't wait. 'Nice try, Abby. I think there's a much more likely solution though, don't you?'

She sighed a ratcheted sigh. 'I owe you an explanation, I know. I wanted to get on in this business because of what I can do, not because my mother has one of the most famous names in PR. So when I applied for my first job, I became Abby Kelleher. It was my mother's maiden name. She was furious with me. But you've got to realize how hard it is to be the kid of a successful parent, especially if you follow the same line of work.' She wiped her hair from her face. 'I've never taken any leads she's given me. My career is all my own work.'

'Till you came here,' said Burrows, unwilling to release the theory that had brought him the morphine of a solution.

'No, you're wrong. I did all the work for my interview, and I've never called on my mother for help. Do you think she wanted me to come here? You're not exactly her favourite person, Charlie. She did everything she could to persuade me not to go for the job. But it was the right next step for me. Believe me, if she could have stopped me, she would.'

She looked from Burrows to Golanski and back, seeking some sign that she had placed a doubt in their minds.

'I know how it looks,' she said. 'But I promise you the leaks have nothing to do with my mother, and nothing to do with me. I've done a bloody good job for you, Charlie. It's been two weeks of total hell. But can you honestly say I've let you down in that time?'

Burrows was silent. She waited.

'It was me who told you we had a mole. It was me who got you off the hook on the *Marilyn* money. Would I have done that if I was trying to undermine you?'

Golanski looked at Burrows, who stayed silent. She was aching to speak. When the silent duel had lasted for ten seconds she butted in. 'Why are you so sure it's Melvyn?'

Kelleher spoke cautiously, monitoring their responses.

'I laid a trap for you all. You know the Burrows three-million-pound poison pill story?'

'Was that you?' said Burrows.

'I'm sorry. I had to feed you all something Duffy would gobble up without checking. And since it was open season on you, I knew he'd love a nice little fat cat story. I don't know anyone here very well, so I guess I didn't start with any preconceptions about who it might or might not be. I let it come out in conversation with a number of different people. But I told everybody different numbers. When I heard three million pounds on Gerry Duffy's show, I knew it was Melvyn.'

'One million pounds,' Golanski whispered.

'So you *were* responsible for the leaks, then.'

'I *was* responsible for *that* leak,' she offered without animosity.

Burrows shot back, 'Can we believe *a single bloody thing* you're telling us? Nothing like this happened till you joined the company. But here you are, trying to finger one of the best guys who's ever worked here.' Her eyes filled with tears again.

Burrows was well into his speech. 'What you don't know, Abby, is how much Melvyn Davies has helped me these past few weeks. He's busted his arse for this place. For God's sake, his wife left him because of the hours he puts in here. I'm not saying that's right, but you can hardly question the guy's loyalty. He adores that woman.'

Sarah Golanski turned abruptly to face him. 'He does?' she said, the words torn out of her.

'Of course he does.' Burrows was in full flight. 'She's fantastic. She used to work here, you know. She was his best friend, his lover, mother to his kids . . . God, he loves those boys, soulmate, you name it. Their split is a disaster, and it's all because he put this company first.'

Golanski felt the hole open up inside her. 'I see,' she said, suddenly aware that Abby Kelleher was watching her intently.

Burrows felt it too, but he blundered on. 'Anyway, the point is that here is a guy who has given everything for this place. I think we owe his sacrifice some respect, don't you? Rather than playing tricks on him and trying to catch him out. And telling lies about me to the newspapers.' He looked at the crumpled form of Abby Kelleher. She had nothing left to say. 'I suggest you get out of here, Abby. You're suspended till further notice.'

Since she had received Davies's call to present *Don't Get Mad . . .* Solveig Nilsen had been fired up by the chance to grow in front of a broader audience. Davies had been clear that the path to the bigtime lay through the mainstream. He'd explained that this was his chance to make it up to her over the *MMOne* mess with a new, mass-market, prime-time documentary. He still loved her style and wanted all the old rebel that had propelled her to notoriety to be in evidence in this show. He told her this would really make people sit up and take notice of a new star.

'This one is different consumerism from *Watchdog* and *We Can Work It Out*,' he said. 'It's live, for a start, which makes it edgier; it really puts the customer in the driving seat. This isn't going to be the usual litany of whinges, followed by something cobbled up by the company's PR people to tell us how misunderstood they are and how Mrs Whatnot is just a confused old bat. We'll be calling them up live, which is why we've kept our stories secret, even from you, Solveig. I want real reactions from you. No rehearsed outrage. This will be real investigative journalism into the rich corporations that jerk their customers around.'

Solveig Nilsen loved it. The secrecy added to the sense of event about the programme, and the atmosphere in Studio I was as charged as anything she had ever experienced.

Davies had been around most of the day, bringing a presence and focus to the final preparations. Alicat, the production company, had shot a number of packages, and researchers were, even at 6.30, pulling together information and data, constantly amending the script which Solveig would present, live, from the autocue. She knew she was great at that, and relished the opportunity to perform to her strengths.

At seven o'clock, Melvyn Davies made his apologies. Some dinner, apparently. Been in his diary for ages and couldn't possibly be moved. He told them he'd be back by nine, to ring him on the mobile if they needed him, and he strode off with a single backward glance, taking in the hubbub of the studio.

La Poule au Pot sits in its own little square on the way down from Victoria to Chelsea Bridge; it is the corner of some foreign field that is forever France. Inside, it is like an ancient French farmhouse whose occupants are much too busy churning the butter or tending the vines to bother about the accumulation of pots and the sheaves of dried flowers hanging in the gloom overhead, picked out by the light of candles on each of the tables.

Davies reckoned they hand-picked the waiters specifically for their ability to massacre the English language. As he arrived, he was greeted by two or three Gallic shouts of welcome from within the restaurant, and one young man in jeans and a polo shirt stepped forward to compare his name with the large black book by the phone.

'Oh yes, Monsieur Daveez, your lovely lady is 'ere already. I 'ave a beautiful table for you over 'ere. You will be a bit squeezy, but that is not a *problème* tonight, I think?'

Sarah looked stunning in the candlelight. She kept doing this to him. In the evening she would be reborn from her workday self, subtly painted and hauntingly lovely. She wore a simple powder-blue blouse with a black sweater around her shoulders, her hair deeply black, harbouring brilliant sylphs called out by the candlelight.

He leaned over and kissed her, lifting her face to his and cradling the fine lines of her cheek in his hand for a moment too long. 'You look beautiful,' he said.

She was genuinely taken aback. After the dialogue in Charlie Burrows's office today, she had been ready for a Melvyn Davies distracted by his love for his missing wife. She had prepared a speech of sorts about the boundaries of their relationship, hauling it back from the fullness of the other night to something that would not demand too much of her.

Then there were the suspicions at work. Despite everything, she found she could not fully share Burrows's conviction that the case against Melvyn was misplaced. For Sarah, the charge still lay out there, a landmine.

Davies sat down, not releasing her hand. Sarah shoved her misgivings down. The landmine would have to be dealt with, but for now it could stay buried. Not lose this.

'So do you,' she said, laughing out loud at her cheesy response.

The waiter returned with a bottle of Chassagne Montrachet, and he caught her eye.

'My treat,' she said.

He picked up the glass. 'A toast.'

She followed suit, extricating her glass from beneath the dish of crudités crowded on to the tiny table.

'To the future,' he said, and turned his full attention to her. There was a new look in his eye.

She thought, *Typical, just as I decide to jam on the brakes* . . .

Together they enjoyed the performance of the waiter, who recited the list of specials with no notes, their eyes meeting to acknowledge particular howlers of pronunciation. She started to relax. Whatever her misgivings, only Melvyn could make her feel this way. As they ate, there was a confidence in him that she hadn't seen for some time. He was funny, assured, teasing her one minute, testing her the next. She felt fantastic.

They ordered coffee and he told the waiter he had to leave at 8.45.

The young man made a preposterously French shrug, half turning his back on Sarah and nodding his head in her direction. 'Oh, but *monsieur* . . . ?' He appeared to be too lost for words to continue.

'I know,' said Davies, joining the charade. 'Ridiculous sense of priorities.' He pointed at his own head. 'Very stupid.'

'You said it, *monsieur*!' said the waiter and shrugged one more time as if he'd perfected the movement, so he might as well show it off.

Davies waited till the waiter had swept away and then he turned back to Sarah, picking up her hand as if it were an ornament on the table. He placed it gently in his and considered it carefully. 'Sarah.'

Something inside her said, 'What's coming now?' but the warmth of his company had anaesthetized her to the warning.

'Yeess,' she mimicked his tone.

He didn't take his eyes from her hand. 'Do you remember when we had that conversation about work?'

'And which of the many conversations about work would that be?'

'It was the first time we went out together.'

'I remember,' she said. It was when he had talked about Kate so much, but she shut that out lest its pungency overwhelm the new fragrance of this evening. 'The Club – being distinctive, all that.'

'Yes,' he said. His eyes swooped up to meet hers. 'And now I think the time has come for me to leave.'

'What?' she said, instinctively withdrawing her hand, her head suddenly ablaze with the consequences, the gentle swing of the dinner immediately lost.

'I wanted to tell you first.'

'Melv, why? Oh no, that would be awful. Where to?'

'Oh nowhere else.' She was relieved for a second, but he continued, still holding her eyes, still confident. 'It's not Acrobat. It's the whole system.'

'What do you mean? What are you saying?' The swarm of possibilities still fogged her ability to work through this systematically.

'That night was when I saw it first. The club we join because we think it's the way to success, and we stay because everyone else does. Highest honours to the ones who sacrifice everything they hold dear.'

He paused to take a sip of wine. She knew not to speak.

'I guess that was one of the most significant evenings of my life. That thought – I couldn't get it out of my head. I knew I'd have to go, and I thought of just leaving there and then. But what would that have achieved? We pity the people who just quietly creep away, don't we. Stick 'em in the "can't hack it" box. Look at Henry Fleming. Just made the best decision of his life, and we talk about him in hushed voices – "Poor old Henry, he's not well, you know." So The Club moves safely on and the members are vindicated. We couldn't possibly admit that Henry just made the best decision of his life, because what would that say about us? Only the weak leave.'

'What are you saying?' Her whole being was quiet, focused on the moment.

'Well, I don't aspire to the pity of my peers, that's for sure. If I'm going out, I'm going out strong. Distinctively.' He smiled.

The waiter appeared at his shoulder. 'Mr Daveez, there is a cab for you.'

He looked at his watch. 'Right.'

She didn't get it. 'What are you saying, Melvyn?'

'I'm saying goodbye.'

He picked up her hand and kissed it, his eyes not leaving hers. She thought she would choke on the pain of this moment. So sudden. So totally unexpected. Too much left to say.

'Where are you going?'

'I'm going back to the studio to finish the show, but

things will move quite quickly after that. I just wanted us to have these moments together, so you'd have time to understand.'

Before she could answer, he eased himself out of the small space and walked to the door. He didn't look back until he was outside, raising a hand to her through the rain-crazed window of the restaurant and disappearing into his taxi.

She was too stunned to cry. She ordered another coffee and an Armagnac to steady her soul. Then she set out to interpret what had happened. Her first thought was the steadiness of his attitude. Over these few weeks she had come to know Melvyn Davies as a febrile, restive creature, a man of trigger-happy emotions. Yet tonight he had been calm, strong. He had come here to terminate whatever it was that was going on between them and he had done it with an ease that was impossible to reconcile with the turbulent spirit which had entwined itself with hers.

But goodbye? Now it was happening too fast for her to catch it. An overflow of tears rushed down her cheeks and she turned to the wall, affecting some business with the handbag under her chair.

Restored to presentability, she warmed her Armagnac in the cup of her hands, realizing they were deathly cold. She swapped the glass for her coffee cup as her mind tried to clear a path through the dense jungle of what had happened.

Had she got him so wrong, this instinctive hothead? He was going, but not quietly creeping away. 'Going out strong'? This wasn't a spontaneous eruption of passion.

Abby Kelleher came to mind, her face earnest as she quizzed her: 'How well do you know Melvyn?' She sniggered ironically to herself. Well, the answer was 'No', wasn't it. She had certainly never met tonight's brave-heart.

She picked over that conversation. Charlie simply wouldn't accept that Abby's litmus test was for real. Fair point. Melvyn *had* given everything for Acrobat. Why would he hurt it?

Suddenly she felt sick, as if she had been thumped hard in the stomach. He had given her all the pieces of this puzzle and she had refused to slot them together. She put the coffee cup down and signalled the waiter for the bill. He *had* given everything for the company. 'Acrobat gave me my wife. But then it took her away again.' All that talk about 'The Club'. Her thoughts came faster now, the conclusion her obsession had censored, now forming with undeniable clarity. 'Not just creep away like Henry'? *'Don't Get Mad, Get Even'*? Out loud she said, 'Oh my God.' She looked at her watch. 9.08. There was still time. She grabbed at her mobile and stabbed out Charlie Burrows's home number from the memory.

Melvyn Davies strode back through the swing doors, brandishing his pass with a flourish at the security desk.

'Working late again, Mr Davies.'

'Just one thing to finish off, then I'll be away,' he replied.

There was an audible sigh of relief from the studio floor as he swept in.

'Everyone ready?' he called. 'Where's Solveig?'

Solveig joined Davies, John Garrett the director and

three of the production team in the office at the corner of Studio 1.

He pulled his running order out of his pocket. 'Right, we're going with the item on unscrupulous food companies first. OK, Solveig? It'll all be on the autocue. It's a great package. Slave labour in the supply chain. The film is devastating, so I want pathos, passion, deep caring for this one, OK?'

Solveig Nilsen nodded her agreement, wired on the adrenalin of this process.

'Next item, Airwaves Mobile Communications. A business, built on the pocket money of our kids, that can't do its sums. A great piece of film here. Plenty of crying kids and livid parents brandishing bills at the camera. Solveig, I want you to give this one all you've got. Make like these are your mates, your brothers and sisters who are being ripped off by these bastards, right?'

Nilsen nodded again.

'After the break, we have this dodgy car dealer welding together write-offs. Did we get that woman whose husband was killed?'

'Yes, we did,' said the producer. 'She only agreed tonight, so it's a bit lashed together.'

'Good, I'd like to see that when we finish this meeting. Does it work?'

'Oh yes, it's good stuff.'

'Excellent,' said Davies, 'and then we close on the health club with dead things in the kitchens.'

'Every kitchen's got dead things in it,' said Solveig Nilsen to laughter all round.

'Not these dead things, Solveig. I'm not telling you any more. I want you to react to the package as you see it. OK?'

'Just don't throw up on air,' said Garrett in his heavy Scots accent.

'Right, good, we've got twenty minutes.' Davies pushed the momentum again. 'You all right, Solveig?'

Solveig couldn't have been better. 'Ready to rumble,' she said.

Melvyn Davies loved this. The deadpan voices in the production gallery belied the tension they all felt. The lighting was set in the studio. Solveig Nilsen was rehearsing her opening lines to the camera.

He slipped out of the gallery and down the corridor to Master Control, from where the show was sent up the line to the BT Tower and from there to transmission masts around the country. On duty were one engineer and the continuity announcer, forever in her soundproof booth to handle unforeseen eventualities, bad feeds, transmission problems with her reassuring voice: 'In the meantime, here is a little music.'

The engineer looked up when Davies typed in the security code and entered the windowless room.

'Hello, Melvyn, didn't know you were in tonight.'

'Hi, Ajay. Yup, just making sure the new show goes with a bang.'

The engineer looked back to his screens. Solveig was on a screen marked Studio 1.

'She's great, that Solveig Nilsen, isn't she?'

'*I* think so, yes,' he said, as Solveig made her choreographed turn to face Camera 2. They listened to her run through her opening lines again.

'Interesting stuff,' said Ajay.

'Yeah,' agreed Davies as if it hadn't really occurred to him. 'Actually, Ajay, now you mention it, this show has been a bit controversial in the making. We've had a couple of threats from people who have a lot to gain by keeping things secret. Obviously, if anyone gets through to you . . .'

'Don't worry, Melv. I know what you mean. I'll let you know if I get any bother. The show must go on.' He looked at Davies for approval.

'Indeed it must,' he replied.

'Charlie? It's Sarah.'

'Hi, Sarah.' Burrows picked up on her alarm immediately. 'What's up?'

'Charlie, it's Melvyn. It *is* him. It's not Abby or Ray or Phyllis. It's him!'

Burrows clearly couldn't relate the words to her panic. 'What? Who?'

'Charlie, listen. Abby was not lying. All the leaks came from Melvyn.' Burrows tried to interrupt. 'Charlie, no. This is not about a few leaks. He's trying to kill us. He's going to bring down the company!'

Burrows was riveted by her panic, trying to catch her momentum, but he still didn't get it. 'Why? Melvyn? What's happened?'

'I can't talk right now, I'm going back to the studios. You've got to pull *Don't Get Mad*.'

'But Sarah, it's on air in fifteen minutes.'

'Please trust me. Just pull it. Get on to them, tell them who you are and tell them to stick in a movie, anything. A blank screen would be better than letting it go out.'

'Give me one minute on why, Sarah. Of course I trust you, but help me out a bit here.'

She sighed. 'Look, I just had dinner with Melvyn.'

'You did? Just the two of you?'

The fury rose in her. She was out of the restaurant by now, walking fast down to Sloane Avenue to pick up a cab. He could hear the breathlessness creep into her voice as she spoke.

'Charlie, just listen, dammit!! He said "Goodbye" to me. Told me he was leaving Acrobat.'

'Leaving? Melvyn? Why?'

'Charlie, shut up!' She composed herself. He could hear her breathing hard now. 'Yes, leaving, but he said he wasn't going to go quietly. Oh, there's too much to explain. He said things would start to move very quickly now, and then he left to do his show. Don't you see, Charlie? *Don't Get Mad, Get Even* is what he's going to do. He doesn't care any more. He thinks the system stinks and it's taken everything from him. Calls it "The Club". Charlie, this show is his payback.'

'Did he tell you that?'

'Not all of it. But it adds up. It's obvious. Seriously. You've got to stop it going out.'

Finally Burrows agreed. 'All right, I'll try, but no one's going to take instructions from me over the phone. I'm coming in. Tell them you're acting on my authority.'

It was 9.18. The rain was coming down harder now as Sarah Golanski reached the corner of Lower Sloane Street. She gazed through the weather to the lights of Chelsea Bridge. No yellow taxi lights in sight. She looked past the Royal Hospital. Nothing. A cab was waiting at the lights with a businessman in the back. She ran to it and tapped on the window with her ring. Slowly, oh so slowly, the electric window ran down.

'All right, love?' said the cheeky cockney face, half lit by the lights of his instruments.

'No. It's an emergency. Please will you take me to Acrobat Television in Lancaster Gate. Right now. I'll pay you a hundred pounds.' She foraged in her bag.

The businessman had surfaced from his slumber as the cabbie flicked his eyes into the driving mirror. She saw the light on his face turn orange, and then to green.

'All right with you, mate?' he said to his passenger, but she was already in, making her apologies as the taxi made a U-turn and set off back towards Sloane Square.

Davies moved around the studio floor, exchanging a look with Solveig, laying a hand on a cameraman's shoulder, encouraging, reassuring his team. With two minutes to go, his fingers closed on the floppy disk in his pocket and he made his way around the back of the set to find a young woman waiting in the gloom, her face lit only by the light of the autocue screen. On her monitor were Solveig's first words of the show, in her hand the control device to ensure that the words rolled at the right speed for the presenter.

'Sorry, Estelle,' he said. 'Last-minute change if you would.' He held out the disk for her. Without drama, she glanced at the clock.

'No problem, Melvyn,' she said.

In the foyer of the Acrobat building, the security guard flipped a page in his book. The only light was from a reading lamp on his desk and a television burbling away by the guest chairs, its noise echoing unnaturally in the marbled lobby. He was supposed to leave it turned to Acrobat, but tonight there was football on ITV and he had half an eye on the match. The 'On Air' light over the door of Studio 1 came on and changed the tint of the darkness to red.

Davies was on the studio floor, standing behind the cameras in the darkness where he would not distract the presenter. He wore a headset and microphone to listen to the dialogue the viewers would never hear.

As the long countdown reached ten, he heard John Garrett's Glaswegian growl in his ear. 'OK, Solveig. Ready to go. Plenty of passion.'

She squared up to the camera.

'5–4–3 – and, Solveig, go.'

'Every day you and I spend money. We have an enormous range of choices. This programme is designed to help you make better choices about the things you buy and the services you use, by giving you *all* the facts about the companies that provide them.'

She made her turn to Camera 2.

'We begin tonight's programme with a report into a company which is prepared to spend more than most on its image. Perhaps it has to.'

John Garrett's assistant noticed it immediately. '"Perhaps it has to"? Where did that come from?'

She grabbed the script, tearing open the bundle to the first page. Garrett was watching the autocue monitor.

'Southern Foods is not a name you will know. But you will have heard of its brands. The company spends a quarter of a billion pounds a year to make sure that we think only good thoughts about its products. And it has been a highly effective deception. Until tonight.'

The production assistant froze with the pages open in

front of her. 'Southern Foods? "Highly efficient deception"? My God, what's she doing? She's making it up as she goes along!'

Garrett's eyes had stayed on the autocue screen. 'No, she's reading what she's seeing. This is a new script. This was supposed to be tough, not libellous. What the hell . . . ?'

'Want me to talk to Estelle?' said the assistant, leaning towards the mike switch.

Garrett pulled back her hand. 'Not while we're on air, you lummox,' he groaned, propping his chin on his elbow to watch this new show unfold. 'Find Melvyn.'

The camera cut in close to Solveig Nilsen as she continued to read the charges against Southern Foods. She raised her eyebrows imperceptibly, the only hint of surprise at the devastating words parading in front of her.

'Behind a rather drab façade in Central London is the Headquarters of Southern Foods, occupied by the people who last year returned profits of over three hundred million pounds to their shareholders. This programme has learned that in the quest for earnings on that scale, there's not much Southern Foods will not do.

'Just three weeks ago, Southern Foods launched a new brand of coffee, *Night and Day*. You may wonder why we need another coffee, but companies like Southern Foods thrive on our desire to try something new. However, they make absolutely sure that no one else thrives in the process.'

The picture turned to an exhausted young woman, a baby swaddled on her back, at work in a Kenyan coffee plantation.

*

Burrows was driving as if his life depended on it. He used the kerb to get the big Mercedes around cars at traffic lights, creeping out into the flow to get through on red. At home, Georgia held the phone up to the television so he could hear every word of Solveig Nilsen's steady unravelling of his company over the speakerphone. Georgia could hear him crying out at the report from the phone and cursing other road users for their pace. He was in Kensington High Street, mired in a tangle of buses and taxis.

Ray Walker was alternately trying to call Burrows's home and his mobile phone. Marooned in Beaconsfield, he could only watch as the blows fell on his carefully husbanded relationships.

Sarah Golanski jumped from the cab, shouting thanks and leaving the money on the seat for the bemused businessman to deal with.

The security guard looked up abruptly as she crashed into the foyer. 'Quick, let me through.'

The man was stuck. His orders were plain. Whatever anyone says and whoever they may be, they do not go through a door with an 'On Air' sign on.

'I'm sorry, lady, I don't know who you are, and you can't go in there.'

'I am Sarah Golanski, the Chief Operating Officer of this company. Believe me. You *have* to let me through. There's a crisis.'

She turned to indicate the TV, only to see Desmond Lynam discussing the final score in the studio.

'Shit,' she breathed, her mind racing. 'Look, would you

recognize Charlie Burrows's voice if I got him on the phone?'

'Charlie Burrows? I suppose so,' he said.

She grabbed one of the phones on the reception desk, barking at him to switch the TV to Acrobat and turn the sound up. She waited an eternity for the call to go through while the security man walked around the desk with his remote control. She looked at her watch. Nearly 9.40. They'd be coming into the break soon. Solveig Nilsen was on the screen with, behind her, a picture of children clustered round a mobile phone. As Burrows's voicemail message started up in her ear, she saw the logo of Airwaves Mobile Communications replace the picture. A £5 million client. The simultaneous events made her scream her frustration.

'Listen, you. Open this fucking door. Now!'

It was the wrong approach. The security man folded his arms and, with a slight toss of his head, said, 'There's no need to be like that. No one goes through these doors when we're on air. I'm only doing my job.'

Melvyn Davies watched Solveig do her link into the mobile phone piece. He turned off the feed from the studio and made a call from the phone in the production office. Five minutes later, he unlocked the door and picked up his coat.

At 9.45, Burrows's Mercedes slid to a halt in front of the building. He jumped the steps into the building, to find Sarah Golanski watching the commercial break in the foyer.

'Quick!' he called as he came through the door. 'Let us in.'

The man jumped to his feet, a look of panic crossing his face. 'Just show me your pass,' he said.

'What?' they chorused.

'It may be a silly job to you, but it's the only job I've got. Just let me do it.'

Burrows slapped his pass on the counter. Without a word, the guard pressed the button which opened the door from the foyer into the studio. Sarah narrowed her eyes at him as they ran through, leaving him alone and bemused as the introductory sequence for Part Two began.

'Master Control,' Burrows shouted. They ran down the corridor and stopped, mesmerized by the keypad which faced them.

'What the hell's the combination?' he said.

'Shit, I've got no idea.' He pummelled on the door, which just absorbed his blows into its acoustic depths.

She turned and ran back into reception, reappearing moments later with a reluctant guard.

'Please,' shouted Burrows. 'Get me in here.'

The man pursed his lips and dibbed at the numbers.

The door flew open and Burrows took control. 'Hi. I'm Charlie Burrows,' he said absurdly as Ajay looked round.

'Blimey,' he said. 'Yes, I know you are. Everyone's out tonight, aren't they?'

'I want you to stop the transmission of this show now, please,' said Burrows evenly.

Sarah Golanski opened the door to the continuity booth. 'This programme is going off the air,' she said. 'Would you get ready?'

Ajay remained motionless, weighing the Programme

Director's warning against the presence of the Chief Executive and his deputy.

'Want me to tell 'em in the gallery?' he said.

'No, just do it now, please.' Burrows's voice gathered urgency. The Off Air screen in front of them showed images of a woman crying, a female interviewer prodding her along with insistent questions.

Ajay moved a fader and the Acrobat logo came up on the Off Air screen. Sarah nodded to the continuity woman.

In the production gallery, they saw it straight away. John Garrett said, 'Shite. We're off air.'

Everyone in the box looked up. Garrett spoke into his studio mike. 'Melvyn, where the hell are you? We're off the air – in the middle of the fucking show. Melvyn. Are you hearing me?'

At the back of the studio, behind the lights, a headset was hanging over the corner of some scenery, Garrett's voice tinny in the headphones. 'Melvyn? Melvyn?'

The production assistant flipped a switch. 'Master control, what's happened?'

A voice they weren't expecting came from the speakers in front of them.

'This is Charlie Burrows. I am the Chief Executive of Acrobat. I have taken this programme off air.'

There was an instant's silence, followed by chaos as everyone spoke at once.

Garrett swore again, kicked his chair back and marched to the door. The car dealer piece was still running, telling its vindictive story to no one. 'Tell Solveig to stand by, will you?' he called over his shoulder.

But Solveig knew. She tore her earpiece out and hurled it to the floor.

The director was not a young man, but he punched open the studio doors and squared up to Burrows outside Master Control. 'Who the hell are you?' he snarled.

'I am Charles Burrows and I'm responsible for what is transmitted by this station.'

'You can't take a show down in mid-transmission.'

'If I'd got here sooner, believe me, sunshine, it wouldn't have gone out at all.'

The director was still far too emotional for a dialogue. Burrows thought that, in his frustration, Garrett was going to hit him. Burrows saw his eyes move to the door of Master Control behind him.

'And you can forget going in there. This show is dead.' He took a pace to his left so that he completely obscured the door.

The director persisted. 'Listen, pal, I don't care who you are. But if you don't move from there, I'm calling the police.'

'Do it,' said Burrows.

Garrett turned on his heels and stalked to the door.

Burrows called after him, 'You might just check with the security man out there before you do.'

'Bollocks,' shouted Garrett.

Burrows slipped back into Master Control to see that they had put in a 'short' – flim-flam films of various lengths that were kept for unplanned gaps before the next programme. Burrows was relieved to see a windmill revolving gently to some Jean-Michel Jarre music on the Off Air screen.

Sarah Golanski was standing behind the engineer like a hijacker. 'Did you find Melv?' she asked.

'No, I got set upon by a screaming Scot. I've been playing sentry outside here.

The large illuminated clock read 21:56:48.

'What time's the break due?' he said to Ajay the engineer, who was wondering whether anyone would believe him in the morning.

Ajay looked at his computer monitor. '21.58.20.'

'When does this windmill thing finish?' He waved a disdainful hand at the screen.

'Whenever I fade it out.'

'OK, so we're back on track in a couple of minutes, are we?'

'We certainly are.'

'Thanks, Ajay, you've been great.'

Golanski clapped him on the shoulder, and the two of them marched out of the little control room.

'We've got to find Melvyn,' said Burrows.

'OK, you look in the offices, I'll check the studio,' she said, believing that she had the better chance of finding him.

The door to the studio was ajar now. As she slipped in, Burrows leaned back into reception. 'Do you know Melvyn Davies? Has he come through here?'

The guard pointed at the small screen in front of him, on which images of various doorways flashed up in succession. 'Not through here, Mr Burrows, but I saw him drive out the car park about . . .' he consulted his watch '. . . ooh about ten, fifteen minutes ago. I saw him after I let you into MC. Didn't seem in a rush particularly.'

Burrows slumped down into one of the guest chairs in reception. Above the cacophony of possibilities crashing in his head, two words rang louder than the rest. 'It's over.'

*

The driver accelerated on down the M3, blinking away the assault of headlights in his eyes. He drove faster now. His actions still fizzed in his mind. It had certainly turned out to be distinctive. Hadn't it, Dad?

He glanced at the small toy giraffe safely tucked into its seat belt next to him. He had played the reunion scene in his head a thousand times, modelling the moves.

Kate had been non-committal on the phone. Suspicious of why he should set off to see her at this time of night. Not surprising, though she didn't yet know everything about the man who would arrive. Didn't know of the massive exorcism he'd put himself through to redress the balance. Wash away the sins.

Had he really done it all for her? In part. Well, no. It was redemption by vengeance, pure and simple. The only possible payback to the impregnability of The Club.

The sacrifice would surely give her something to trust. All the defeated promises would surely now be forgotten. What he had done in these last weeks was his down payment on a future which he could build as heroically as she had. But did he deserve another chance? As the journey passed and he crossed the Tamar into Cornwall, his confidence ebbed. What if she refused to have him back? The lose–lose. Man, what a bet.

A few minutes after 2 a.m. he pulled off the B road and down the lane leading to Kate's parents' house. They'd been here so many times together. He loved the grass growing down the middle of the road, the signature of a totally different pace that had convinced him he was on holiday many times before.

He pulled the car into the driveway, the tyres scrunching on the sparse gravel. In there were his boys and Kate.

He sat for a moment. There was no light. He didn't want to knock. He had run this scene so many times. But now he felt more a spectator than a participant.

Davies got out of the car, touched immediately by the silk of the wind and the Cornwall smells. Looking up at the house for a sign of recognition from within, he crept around the back. An outhouse door squeaked with every gust of the wind as if trying to attract his attention. He completed his tour of the house, his spirits falling. He looked back at the car. There she was. Composed, beautiful, but reserved.

He picked up his pace, not concerned about the noise of his footsteps any more, but her manner told him to approach her slowly. He laid a hand on her arm. 'Thanks,' he said.

She gazed at his face, a silent interrogation. Then she took his arm and led him to the house.

'Can I see the boys?' he said as they disappeared behind the stained-glass panes of the front door.

Burrows dropped Sarah Golanski at her home after midnight, and fretted his way home, his head full of tomorrow. Georgia was sitting up in bed, waiting for him. She was stunned. She told him Ray had been phoning all evening, incredulous that Burrows hadn't returned his calls. Her voice was empty, just passing on the information. 'And you had a call from Phyllis,' she said.

'Phyllis?' He was slumped on his side of the bed, half undressed. 'What did she want?'

'She wanted you to know that Abby makes her own life and that she had nothing . . .'

'I know,' said Burrows.

Georgia continued. 'She said if there's anything she can do tomorrow, she realized it would be a busy day and she'd be happy to come in and man some phones for you with Abby.'

Burrows felt a sting of tears, then slumped his head back with a snort. 'God,' he said, 'I got her wrong, didn't I?'

Acrobat's closing share price   315p

Wednesday, 31 March

In the morning he chose his clothes deliberately, knowing that today he would be stared at. Georgia told him to keep her in the loop; she said she would be at home all day and please call her.

Something made him walk up to his office via the Programme Department. It was 7.05 a.m. He looked through the window into Davies's empty office. Amazing the guy could even think in this mess. He tried the door. Unlocked. For a few moments he just stood there, gazing around like a pilgrim at a shrine, wondering at the choices which had been made in there and their terrible consequences. He walked inside, into the workshop of the man who had destroyed his company. He searched in his heart for the resentment that must surely be there. His gaze moved around the familiar disarray to the shelves above the desk. The Bafta face on its side at the back, split away from its stand. The photograph of Kate and the boys. All the little icons of a life.

On the desk, propped against the phone, was an envelope. On the front it said **'Private and confidential. Charlie Burrows.'** He snorted a humourless laugh, sat down and reached for the envelope, turning it in his hand before pulling out a single sheet of paper with a hand-written message.

Charlie

>*This was not about you.*

>*It wasn't even about Acrobat.*

>*I took a mistress, Charlie. I didn't love her and she didn't love me. But she enthralled me. I thought I was in control but of course I was not.*

>*My wife discovered the affair. She gave me chance after chance to make the right decision and I knew that in time I would. But I was infatuated. So I made her promises, I made her wait; I made her the enemy.*

>*I should have seen it sooner but when I looked around at you and the other fools I saw myself. I took courage from you who had all taken the same mistress. Brilliant people reinforcing each other's lousy choices because they cannot imagine not being part of the Club.*

>*Now, when I am ready to do the right thing, I find that the words I need have been emptied of all meaning by my vain repetition. Why should she accept anything I say? She has to know that this time it's bigger than a promise.*

>*I have no idea whether this will be enough. I guess by the time you read this I'll know. I hope things work out for you.*

>*Melvyn*

Burrows turned over the page. He ran his eyes over the script again. Quietly he sighed. 'Fucking hell, Melv.' Then he picked himself out of the chair and flipped on the shredding machine by Monica's desk. Without emotion he watched the machine devour Melvyn Davies's confession.

Melvyn and Kate stayed up all night, talking at the table by the Aga, drinking tea till the yellowy dawn. He told her everything: his remorse when she left and what had happened with Sarah Golanski; that evening with his mother and the end of his father's life investment; the sense of total powerlessness. And his answer to it all.

She had kept her distance.

'What happens next?' she asked, as the hens began to fidget outside.

He pushed his chair back across the flagstones. 'That depends on you,' he said.

'No,' she said, playing with her cup. She fell silent.

He waited for her verdict as more of the animals began their day. He looked out of the window, revelling in the familiar view but wondering if he would be back in his car before breakfast.

Again, the magnitude of his bet returned to him. When he turned back to her, she was watching him; her face had changed. She rose from her side of the old kitchen table. 'No, Melvyn. It depends on us.'

He took her hand as she placed it on his shoulder. 'It *is* going to be different,' he said.

She smiled – for the first time. 'Yeah, yeah. Show, not tell. What are we going to do for money?'

After a moment he turned to look up at her. He smiled stupidly. 'I wondered about making furniture.'

A little before 7.15 a.m. a tousled, barefoot little boy appeared in the doorway, carrying his blanket and a bear. Kate turned to see him. Melvyn Davies bit down hard to stop the tears. Without a word, the boy pattered over the worn flagstones and hitched himself on to his father's lap. Wriggled into a safe place, in his sleepy voice, snug and contented, he said just, 'Daddy.' Davies could hold back no longer and the pain began to unwind from deep within his spirit.

When Burrows plodded into the fifth-floor office suite, Paula got up and walked to meet him.

'Pol, what are you doing here at this time?'

She spoke quietly, respectful at the accident scene. 'I saw it last night. Thought you might like some moral support.'

His eyes stung. He squeezed her elbow.

'There's quite a list of people who want to talk to you already. Guess what, Phyllis is in Abby's office with her; they're working the phones together.' He snorted and shook his head to clear his eyes. 'And Ray's in your office.'

'Of course he is,' said Burrows, stopping for a moment.

He raised his head to the ceiling and sighed hard.

'OK then, here we go,' he said, squaring his shoulders and entering his office.

Ray Walker rose to his feet.

'Morning, Ray.'

'Er, morning. Did you get the message that I called last night?' Walker was gentle, deliberately courteous.

'Yes, but I was here till gone midnight.'

Walker nodded. 'We've had it.' For a rare and brief second, his eyes met Burrows's.'

'No, Ray. *I've* had it.'

Walker appeared unsure. 'No, I mean, we've lost the Southern Foods money.'

'And the rest, I expect.'

'Yes, very probably.'

Silence.

'What do you want me to do?' said Walker.

Burrows stifled a laugh, not because it was funny, not because he was embarrassed, but at the absurdity of this whole scene. A laugh at the irony that at this moment of perfect weakness, the only ally at his side was this man, the constant antagonist, finally offering his help.

Again he met Walker's eyes. 'Just keep me informed as the day unfolds, and maybe give some thought to your acceptance speech.'

It clearly wasn't a new thought to him. 'You think?'

'I don't know, Ray. Stranger things have happened.' Burrows felt a wash of total isolation.

Walker clambered to his feet and, with considered formality, stuck out a hand for him to shake. 'You know where to find me if you need me.'

Burrows took his hand, empty of feeling. Walker's pace faltered as he reached the door and he turned into Sarah Golanski's office, closing the door behind him.

Throughout the day, Walker dutifully kept the news coming. First the call from Geoff O'Brien, then the mobile phone people. They took out their five million too. The car dealer withdrew another half-million. By mid-morning it was clear that they had to make a profits warning, and a *sotto voce* Hamish Perrin steered them through it.

Rishi Kapur estimated that the full-year profits would be a third of the forecasts, before the effect of any lawsuits. It emerged that there was no chance of making the payments into the *Marilyn* movie. Burrows was on autopilot now. He braced himself for Walker's reaction, but it never came. Walker was sanguine, philosophical, his new agenda already granting him a bigger perspective.

One of Kate Davies's old office friends still had her mother's phone number in Cornwall. Paula got hold of it for Burrows, and he sat and looked at it for minutes, before shoving the paper into his pocket. No idea what to say.

Burrows watched the share price on Ceefax on the television in his office. It started the day at a lowly 315p, but after the profits warning it sank to 144p. He fretted for each fifteen-minute update, watching the protracted detonation of the powder trail laid by his trusted colleague.

His phone rang. It was Martin Sumner. The Geordie burr prompted an instinctive relaxation, but Sumner's voice was purposeful. 'You OK, Charlie?' he said.

Burrows laughed. 'Did you see it?'

'Last night? Oh yes, I saw it.'

'Then you know how I am.'

'What the hell was Melv doing?'

'Making a point, apparently. Merlin's final spell.'

'Nightmare.' He paused. 'What are you going to do?'

'Oh, I've gone, Martin. The guillotine is falling. I'm just waiting for the dull thud.'

Sumner was genuine. 'There but for the grace of God.'

'Funny really,' said Burrows, 'I've done everything I could think of to put as much distance between myself and this moment for twenty-five years. And now it's here, I need it like Novocain.'

'Look, I'm sorry, man.'

'It's only a job, Martin. More to life than work, isn't there? We work to live, not live to work.' He paused. 'Had to think about that.'

Sumner laughed tepidly.

Burrows rallied. 'Seen the share price?' he said.

'Sure. Look, that's why I was ringing.' Sumner cleared his throat. 'I don't know how you're going to feel about this, but Channel 6 has made an offer to buy out Acrobat.'

Obvious, really, but it was the last thing he expected. He couldn't think of anything. He didn't know how he felt about it.

'How much?'

'I'm sorry, Charlie, I'm not allowed to talk to you about detail. I insisted that you find out from me, though.'

'Very kind,' said Burrows. 'Friendship before everything.' He tried to sound light.

Sumner's voice was studiously grave but unmistakably veined with excitement. 'Malcolm Ryan is talking to Hugo now, and de Vigny is involved. He's going to put in some new money so he'll finish up with a majority stake in the new group. Collier has agreed, and the major institutions, so we're well over fifty per cent.'

'Oh good,' said Burrows quietly. 'So it's a done deal then.'

Burrows heard the rustle of paper. Sumner cleared his throat again, changing his pace. 'It is, Charlie. Obviously your contract will be honoured in full, but it falls to me to inform you that . . .'

Burrows took the phone away from his ear. He looked at it for a moment and heard Martin Sumner's voice recede, scripted formalities. Without another word he replaced it in its rest. He picked up his jacket, cast an eye around his office, running his hand along the front of his beloved Wurlitzer. Paula was on another phone call. He walked around her desk and kissed her on the forehead. And out of the building.

As he turned the corner into Craven Terrace, he didn't see the large car pull up outside his office, or Ray Walker trotting down the steps to meet de Vigny and Carrick as they emerged from it.

His head was a clutter of incompatible emotions. Euphoria that it was over. Fear that it was over. Excitement at what would happen next. Anxiety at tomorrow's press. Already the self-examination – where did he go wrong? A plea for clemency, for sympathy, that he knew would be ignored in all the many breathless lunchtime conversations which would begin today. The streams of column inches, the hindsight geniuses. The injustice heaved in his spirit.

He walked until he reached Paddington station. In Praed Street he stopped by a flower-seller. Roses for Georgia. This was the moment they'd looked forward to, wasn't it? Time to grow old together. A little earlier and certainly more sudden than they'd imagined, but . . . He turned away to look at the world. Having thrived on his public success, how would she cope with his total public failure? A road-sweeper clumped lethargically past, his barrow grazing the road as he stopped to gather dust. Burrows inhaled deeply, his breath catching like a sob.

He pulled out his mobile phone and pressed the direct dial for his wife's mobile phone. He cleared his throat, waiting for the familiar message.

'Hi, it's me. Look, everything's gone wrong here.' He waited, wondering what would come next. 'Georgia, I'm sorry; I tried but . . .' Again he stopped. 'I'm just going to . . . go away for a bit, get some things clearer. I guess it'll all be in the paper tomorrow.' He paused for a long time. 'Look, we'll talk soon, OK? I'm sorry, love.'

He turned the mobile phone over in his hand, looking at it without affection. As he disappeared into the station he dropped it into a waste bin.